Also by Paul Salsini

Fiction:

The Ghosts of the Garfagnana: Seven Strange Stories of Haunted Tuscany

The Fearless Flag Thrower of Lucca: Nine Stories of 1990s Tuscany

A Piazza for Sant'Antonio: Five Novellas of 1980s Tuscany

The Temptation of Father Lorenzo: Ten Stories of 1970s Tuscany

Dino's Story: A Novel of 1960s Tuscany

Sparrow's Revenge: A Novel of Postwar Tuscany

The Cielo: A Novel of Wartime Tuscany

Nonfiction:

Second Start

For Children:

Stefano and the Tuscan Piazza

Stefano and the Christmas Miracles

A TUSCAN TREASURY

Stories from Italy's Most Captivating Region

Cover Photo by Ivano Stefani. The church in Piazza al Serchio in the Garfagnana

PAUL SALSINI

Award-winning Author of "A Tuscan Series"

A TUSCAN TREASURY
STORIES FROM ITALY'S MOST CAPTIVATING REGION

Different versions of "Also Under the Tuscan Sun," "Elion" and "Anna and the Television Priest" were published in "The Fearless Flag Thrower of Lucca" (2019).

The author found the following books most helpful: "A House in the Mountains" by Caroline Moorehead; "Partisan Diary" by Ada Gobettti; "A Soldier on the Southern Front" by Emilio Lussu, and "The White War" by Mark Thompson.

iUniverse books may be ordered through booksellers or by contacting:

iUniverse
1663 Liberty Drive
Bloomington, IN 47403
www.iuniverse.com
844-349-9409

ISBN: 978-1-6632-2551-1 (sc)
ISBN: 978-1-6632-2552-8 (e)

Library of Congress Control Number: 2021914408

Print information available on the last page.

iUniverse rev. date: 07/15/2021

For Barbara,
Jim, Laura and Jack

And for my beloved cousin Fosca,
the inspiration for "Rosa" in "A Tuscan Series"

AUTHOR'S NOTE

I THOUGHT it would be fun, both for me and for readers, to explore the captivating land of my roots with a wide-ranging collection of stories from Tuscany. A few deal with tragic events, but most, I think, will leave you smiling. The stories are not arranged chronologically. The oldest ("Letters from the Front") is set during World War I and the newest ("Nonna's House") during the COVID-19 pandemic. And other stories are set at any time in between—I thought readers might like to discover a new time frame with each story. A couple of the stories might be classified as historical fiction: the stories set during both world wars, the frantic arrival in Bari of the refugees from Albania, for example. Three stories are set in Florence, but others range from Cortona to Pisa to Pienza to tiny Monteriggioni and many places elsewhere in Tuscany.

CONTENTS

ALSO UNDER A TUSCAN SUN

I wondered what impact Frances Mayes' best-selling "Under the Tuscan Sun" would have on Cortona, the site of her famous Bramasole.

YEARS LATER, Bruno Pezzino would still remember the exact time and place when he first heard about something that eventually would change his life and that of his beloved Cortona. It was Saturday, March 24, 1990, and he and his three old friends were at their usual table outside Bar Sport facing Piazza Signorelli.

It had been another rough week. Again, Bruno had no customers for Pezzino Tours and he was worried. How long could he support his growing family if no tourists came and the business dried up? How long could the family afford to live in their sprawling apartment in the center of the city?

The Italian economy was bad enough, but tourists to Tuscany hadn't yet "discovered" Cortona. Close to the border of Umbria, it was off the beaten track, with only Arezzo as the nearest city.

Tourists always made Florence their base, exploring the treasures of the Renaissance and shopping in the expensive shops and markets. Then they might go to Pisa to have their photos taken with the Leaning Tower. Or to Lucca to walk on the walls that circled the city. Then to San Gemignano to see the medieval towers. Or to Montepulciano to buy wine. And to the Chianti country to drink wine.

And that was only Tuscany. There were still so many other places to visit in Italy: Rome and Venice and Milan and Assisi and Naples and Capri and Sicily and on and on.

If they'd heard of it at all, and few tourists had, the medieval city of Cortona was a place "maybe we'll find time to see some other time."

Perhaps, Bruno thought, spending time with his friends would help him forget his worries. Although it was still March on that Saturday, temperatures were already climbing as the four friends sipped their espressos and broke open their brioches while watching farmers sell vegetables in the market under the arches of the nineteenth-century theater across the way.

There was Tino Armenti, the oldest at eighty-five. Tino always seemed angry. If someone wished him a *"buongiorno"* he'd say: "What the hell is good about it?" If someone said the weather was warm, for Tino it was cold. If someone thought the tomato crop was coming in early, he complained that it was late. And on and on.

Tino's wife didn't want him around and loudly suggested that he get out of the house. He suggested that she mind her own business. She told him not to get angry. This made him even more angry and so he lowered himself into his wheelchair and bumped down the cobblestone street to Piazza Signorelli.

Sometimes Bruno lost his patience with Tino, too, but then he wondered how he himself would feel if he had lost his right foot, his right arm and his right eye to a hidden bomb during World War II. Tino had fought with the partisans in the battle for Monte Battaglia but, like other war veterans, he never talked about it.

Cesare La Rosa was seventy-six. He had farmed north of Cortona for many years but when his wife died three years ago his son and daughter-in-law insisted that he live with them. He resisted. He was perfectly fine living alone, and farming was the only thing he knew. But Francesco, the son, warned that if something happened to him, no one would know about it.

"What's going to happen to me?" Cesare asked.

"You never know," Francesco replied.

So Cesare moved into the apartment near the church of Santa Maria delle Grazie al Calcinaio. It was a mistake. His daughter-in-law, Luisa, kept nagging him to straighten his room, clean up after he ate, dress better. Then there was the problem with the three children, all under ten, who seemed to run rampant and scream all day long. Cesare was glad to get away, even if only for a little while on a Saturday morning.

The fourth member of the group was Giuseppe Scotti. Unlike the others, who wore work clothes and heavy shoes, Giuseppe invariably had on a white shirt and a dark tie with a coat draped over his shoulders, even on hot summer days. When he took off his cap he revealed a bald head with a fringe of white hair. His blue eyes always seemed sad.

Giuseppe had been a schoolteacher for many years and had never married. He lived alone in a single room near San Benedetto and took his meals at a *trattoria* a block away. Every morning, he was the first to arrive at the church for Mass and the last to leave. After that, Giuseppe walked to the outskirts of Cortona, slowly treading a mile and a half to a small shrine at the side of the road. He had built the shrine himself some fifty years ago. It held a white Virgin Mary against a blue background, reminiscent of a Della Robbia. Before arriving, he picked a spray of flowers, oleander perhaps, or Queen Anne's lace or fennel, and tied them with a weed. He placed these at the bottom of the shrine, paused for a moment, wiped his eyes with a white handkerchief, and walked back to town.

Every day for fifty years. Except for once, in the late 1960s, when he was hospitalized for three days after falling and breaking his left arm. He walked a little slower after that.

Bruno, Tino and Cesare knew all about the shrine and his daily walks, but they never—ever—talked about it. Giuseppe never talked much about his walks either. But then, he didn't speak much, just listened and occasionally smiled. Often, he looked off in the distance, his mind even farther away.

The conversation that Saturday morning, as it had for months, involved the World Cup championships that would be held in Italy from June 8 to July 8.

"I just heard they might not have the new stadium at Torino ready," Bruno said.

"Of course they won't have it ready!" Tino shouted. "Has there ever been anything in Italy built on time? *Boh!*"

"Well, they'll probably finish it," Bruno said.

"And what about that other new one in…where is it again?" Cesare asked.

"Bari," Bruno said.

"They won't finish it in time," Tino said. "It'll be a cold day in hell."

"Well, it will be worth it," Cesare said.

"At the way they're spending money?" Tino said. "They're already way over budget for all the ten stadiums. Who's going to pay for it?"

Cesare said he hoped he could watch the games on television but that the grandchildren made so much noise it would be difficult. Bruno wondered if Stefano Tacconi would be the goalie for Italy. Tino disagreed at length, giving fourteen reasons why someone else should be chosen, until finally Bruno decided it was time to go home.

As they were clearing their cups and paper napkins, Giuseppe spoke for the first time that morning.

"Oh, on my walk yesterday, I saw a sign that Bramasole was for sale."

"What's Bramasole?" Cesare asked.

"It's an old villa outside of Cortona," Bruno said.

"It's a heap!" Tino shouted. "Who would want to live there? Anybody would be crazy to buy that place. *Stupido!*"

IF CESARE WAS IGNORANT about the matter, most people in Cortona knew about Bramasole. Of all the old villas in and around the city, it was one of the largest. With a name combining *bramare* (to long for) and *sole* (sun), it stood three stories high at the end of a narrow street off a great walking boulevard south of the city. It was tall and square, the color of apricots, with a tile roof, faded green shutters and an iron balcony on the second level. Because it had been vacant for thirty years, the grounds were overgrown with blackberries and vines.

With so much else on his mind, Bruno thought only briefly about the sale of the villa that Saturday. He wondered, though, why anyone would want to buy a two-hundred-year-old building that certainly would need a great deal of work.

"Someone very rich," he thought. "But I hope they don't tear it down. It must have been beautiful once."

Bruno's wife, Veronica, was making his lunch, the usual Tuscan soup and a panini, when he returned home. She always tried not to bring up their financial worries, but a problem with the refrigerator could not be ignored any longer.

"The thermostat just won't work anymore, Bruno. We'll have to call someone."

"OK, OK, I'll do it Monday."

"We'll have enough to pay him, won't we?"

"If he doesn't charge too much."

"And we really should have that broken window in the living room repaired. There's such a draft."

"I think I know a carpenter who wouldn't charge much."

"Maybe he could do some plastering in the living room, too."

"We'll see."

Veronica went back to making rice balls for dinner on Sunday. She'd already made fennel seed *foccacio,* six loaves of bread, *bracioli* from sliced veal, and a couple of desserts. The rest could wait until after Mass on Sunday.

No matter what their financial hardships were, one thing the Pezzinos would not scrimp on was the Sunday dinner they had for their family. In 1990, the family spanned four generations. Veronica's father, Luigi, blind and bedridden, and her mother, Maria Elena, occupied a large room in the center of the apartment. Frequently in tears, Maria Elena rarely came out except to get meals for her husband.

The oldest son, Rudolfo, his wife, Roberta, and their two-year-old son, Sergio, somehow fit into the next room. If they had another child, Rudolfo said, they would have to move, but Bruno and Victoria insisted that they could always make room.

The twins, Massimo and Michele, were now nineteen years old, out of school and working, but still sharing the same room they'd had since they were infants. Massimo sorted artifacts in the Etruscan Academy Museum, and Michele worked for a real estate agent, Anselmo Martini, in an office on Via Sacco e Vanzetti in the lower part of the city. Michele helped fix up properties when they were on the market. Massimo and Michele each had a girlfriend, both of whom, fortunately, were able to entertain the boys in their homes. It would have been awkward otherwise.

The youngest daughter, Luciana, was now ten, and her brother, Silvio, was nine. Both were demanding their own rooms, but there weren't any to spare.

Meanwhile, the oldest daughter, Analisa, and her husband, Pippino, had moved their own family into a big apartment right across the hall. Their three older children, Lorenzo, Luca and Franca, were joined last year by Carlo and Clarissa, another set of twins. The doors between the two apartments were always open so it didn't matter who ate where, or for that matter, who slept where.

Everyone always—always—sat down for Sunday dinner, even Maria Elena after she was certain that her husband was sleeping. Sometimes the group even expanded. Pippino's parents and younger brother often arrived bearing freshly made apple pies. Roberta's sister, a manicurist, was a frequent guest and often took care of female fingers afterward. Bruno's nephew, Piero, who lived in Florence, was a monthly visitor, entertaining the family with Florentine gossip.

On this Sunday, with everyone talking at once, the din was overwhelming, and Veronica interrupted the conversation by placing two more platters of *bracioli* on the table.

"Mangia! Mangia!," she said. "All right, let's do our turns."

As always, everyone went around the table reporting on what had happened in the last week, their new purchases, the newly acquired skills of their precious children, the adventures that Massimo and Michele recently had. The twins were still excited about their jobs.

"It's like I discover something new at the museum every day—every minute!" Massimo said. "I mean, I could look at that Etruscan bronze chandelier all day and still find something new about it. And then on Thursday I was cataloging items from the Roman villa of Ossaia that date from the First Imperial Period to the Fifth Century. There's this big earthenware jug called a *glirarium*. You won't believe this, but it's where dormice were raised to be eaten."

"Oh, yuck," Luciana cried. "Mama, make him stop."

"Massimo," Veronica said, "we're still eating. Michele, tell us about what you're doing."

"Nothing nearly so interesting," Michele said. "I just keep the records of where Signor Martini takes clients. He's been busy. Just yesterday he took a couple to a bunch of old farmhouses, but some of them were falling down, so the people weren't interested. Then he took them to one with a tower that was built centuries and centuries ago. He said the woman who owned it doubled the price when she thought this couple was interested.

"And then he told me this funny story about how they went to one farmhouse where there were chickens running all over but they couldn't go inside because there was a black snake coiled up at the door."

"Mama!" Luciana cried, "make Michele stop. Right now. You know how scared I am of snakes."

"Well, that's what Signor Martini told me," Michele said.

"Did he take this couple anywhere else?" Veronica asked.

"Yes, he did. He took them to Bramasole."

SUDDENLY, BRUNO seemed interested. "I just heard from Giuseppe yesterday that there was a 'for sale' sign at Bramasole," he said. "I wondered if anyone was going to be interested in that old place. It's been empty for so long."

"Well," Michele said, "Signor Martini took these people there and when they got there, the woman liked it so much that right away she said, 'Perfect. I'll take it.' Then they went inside and Signor Martini pointed out the thick walls and the views of cypresses and green hills and other villas in the valley. He said they were especially impressed that there were two bathrooms that really worked. But there's dirt all over and a lot of work to be done. *'Molto lavoro,'* Signor Martini said. And that's just the inside. He said the work on the property might take months or years."

"I can't imagine," Veronica said, "anyone buying an old villa like that and fixing it up. Aren't there new places?"

"Of course there are," Bruno said. "But some foolish people think that old places are better. Just wait until the roof starts leaking and the plumbing stops."

"Michele," Massimo said, "do you know where these people are from?"

"Signor Martini said California."

"California!" Massimo said. "Why would somebody come all the way from California to buy an old villa for thousands and thousands of *lire* and then spend thousands and thousands more to fix it up? Insane!"

"That explains it," Rudolfo said. "I've always heard that everyone in California is crazy."

"And rich," Bruno added.

"Oh, and get this," Michele said. "Signor Martini said that the buyers teach at a university in California so they'd be here only during the summers."

"Now I know they're insane," Massimo said.

Someone asked Michele if he knew the buyers' names.

"Signor Martini said if they made a purchase it would be in one name. It's something like March or Hayes or Mayes. I've got it written down in

7

the office. OK, now I remember the first name, though. It's Francis. Yeah, that's it, Francis. And the last name is Mayes."

"Well, if this Francis Mayes really does buy Bramasole," Massimo said, "we'll change his name to Francesco and make him feel at home."

"So are they going to buy it?" Bruno asked.

"No, once they found out the price, they said no and went home."

The conversation stopped while Veronica and Analisa brought in more plates and removed others and Luciana shooed the cat from under the table.

"Well," Rudolfo said, "maybe there will be other people interested in Bramasole. Who owns it?"

"Signor Martini said some people remembered a painter from Naples living there once," Michele said, "but until last year it had been owned by five old sisters from Perugia. Then a doctor from Arezzo, Doctor Carta, bought it."

"Doctor Carta?" Rudolfo said. "That rich guy that I see driving around in an Alfa 164?"

"That's him. I saw him the other day. My God, I've never seen such an expensive suit. It must have been an Armani."

"So he's selling this villa?"

"Well, Signor Martini thought he was going to, but he may be changing his mind. He may want a higher price."

"Everybody who sells a villa wants more than it's worth," Bruno said.

"Signor Martini said that Doctor Carta and his wife had intended to live there as a summer place, but then he inherited property on the coast so he was going to use that instead."

"Ah yes," Massimo said. "Those that have money get more money."

"And those who don't, lose theirs," Bruno said.

Veronica reached over to her husband's arm. "Don't be bitter, Bruno. You'll get more work."

"I don't see how."

After everyone was quite full, Maria Elena returned to take care of her husband, Analisa and Pippino took their children back across the hall, and the others scattered.

Helping his wife with the dishes, Bruno broached a subject he'd been thinking about.

"Veronica, maybe I should just give up the tour guide business. I didn't have any customers last week, and only one the week before. People just don't want to come to Cortona."

"That's because they don't know how beautiful it is. Bruno, we'll manage. Really. Wait awhile and see how things go. OK?"

"I'll wait. I don't know how long a while is, though."

Bruno sat at the kitchen table and tried to revise the brochure about Cortona that he'd written seven or eight years ago.

Southeast of Florence, Cortona was conquered by the Etruscans who called it Curtun, and parts of the Etruscan wall can still be seen today. As a Roman colony its name was Corito. Now it is known as a medieval city with steep narrow streets. The highest point of the city, almost 2,000 feet above sea level, offers a spectacular view of the surrounding valley and Lake Trasimeno.

You can see art and artifacts from the Etruscan period as well as items from the medieval and Renaissance eras in the Museo dell'Accademia Etrusca, located in the Palazzo Casali. The Diocesan Museum includes a beautiful panel painting of the Annunciation by Fra Angelico.

The heart of Cortona is the Piazza della Repubblica, with the Palazzo Comunale, or town hall, overlooking the square. Nearby is Piazza Signorelli, named for the famous Renaissance painter who was a native of Cortona.

Among the beautiful churches of Cortona are the Church of Santa Margherita, named for the city's patron saint; the Church of San Cristoforo; the Church of Sant'Agostino, and the Church of Santa Maria Nuova, built by Giorgio Vasari in 1554, as a domed church with a centralized Greek cross layout....

"Boring, boring," Bruno thought. "Who would want to visit Cortona after reading this?"

He put the paper and pencil away.

When he went back to the office on Monday, Bruno received a telephone call from Michele, who said he needed to make a small correction to what he had said on Sunday.

"Papa, I made a mistake. That person from California who had been interested in Bramasole? The name isn't Francis, a man. It's Frances, a woman."

"A woman was interested in buying Bramasole?"

"Yes, and Signor Martini told me she's a poet and a writer. And she's also a professor at a university in San Francisco. Can you imagine?"

"Sounds very impressive."

"Well, Signor Martini said it's still up in the air. I think they're dickering about the price now."

It was only weeks later when Michele called his father with news. "Papa, the deal is done. That American woman, Frances Mayes, bought Bramasole!"

He went on to explain that Signor Martini had taken Frances Mayes and her friend Ed to a notary in Arezzo to finalize the transaction. He said Doctor Carta had some last-minute reservations about the price and wanted to ask for more, but the *notario*, a Signora Maniucci, kept on signing papers anyway.

Signor Martini had said that, in typical Italian fashion, Carta declared that he would claim that he received a lower amount for the house. He said, "That is just the way it's done. No one is fool enough to declare the real value."

Hearing this, Bruno just nodded. He'd heard this kind of talk before.

When Bruno revealed this information to his friends the following Saturday as they enjoyed their espresso at their usual tables outside Bar Sport, Tino was the most surprised.

"A woman is buying Bramasole?"

"Why not?" Bruno said. "It's 1990, women can do anything."

"Boh!" Tino said.

"Boh!" Cesare agreed.

Giuseppe smiled.

Also, Bruno said, the woman is a poet and a writer and a teacher.

"Madonna mia!" Tino said. "I bet she won't even talk to us. We won't be good enough."

"Now, Tino," Bruno said, "don't make judgments so soon. You don't know anything about her. Maybe she'll write something about Bramasole. Even Cortona. I guess people do that. Maybe for a travel magazine or something. Maybe then Cortona will be on the map and I can get some business."

REPORTS ABOUT BRAMASOLE and those strange new occupants from America continued to spread in Cortona as spring turned into summer. Giuseppe, speaking more often now, said he'd seen many workmen going up and down the hill to the villa when he visited the little shrine at the entrance to the old house every day.

"Sometimes," he reported to his friends, "I see a woman in the window. She looks nice enough. I don't think she sees me. I leave my flowers anyway."

But the conversation about Bramasole was temporarily forgotten one Saturday when their attention was drawn to two women buying vegetables at the farmers' market across Piazza Signorelli.

"Look at those girls," Cesare whispered. "What do they have on their heads?"

"They're scarves," Bruno said. "They're called a *hijab*."

"Why do they have their heads covered on a hot day in July?" Tino asked.

"They're Muslims," Bruno said. "Haven't you ever seen a Muslim before?"

"I don't think I have," Cesare said. "Where would I have seen one?"

"What are Muslims doing here?" Tino asked. "I thought they were only in Rome or Bologna or someplace. Now we're going to get Muslims in Cortona?"

Italy had established its first amnesty program for illegal aliens in the late 1980s, and as a result the number of foreign-born people in the country had increased dramatically. In 1985, the number of foreign-borns in Italy holding a residence permit was estimated at approximately 423,000. By 1990, that number had almost doubled.

"Never mind," Tino said. "I can remember when there were just people from Cortona here. Then we got all these people from Calabria. Then we got all these people from Albania. Now we're getting people from Poland and Hungary. I don't like it. I know I'm not supposed to say that, but I don't like it. Foreigners, that's what they are."

"Think of Cortona as being a little United Nations," Bruno said. "I think a lot of Poles went to Germany to find work but then there weren't any jobs there, so now they're coming here."

"*Boh!*" Tino said.

"I've seen some Polish workers going up to Bramasole," Giuseppe said.

"I've heard about them," Bruno said. "Michele told me that Frances Mayes wanted to have a long wall torn down, so Signor Martini sent over a contractor. The contractor hired three big Polish guys. Michele told me their names are Stanislao, Cristoforo and Riccardo or something like that."

"I've seen them around," Cesare said. "Big guys. Don't speak Italian, but they seem nice enough."

"Father Fabio lets them live in a back room of the church," Bruno said. "He even provides three meals a day, but he won't let them work on Sunday. Anyway, Michele said they tore down the wall like nothing. Frances Mayes told Signore Martini they were carrying hundred-pound stones like watermelons. She was very happy. She said they were even singing while they were working."

"In Polish?"

"I guess so," Bruno said. "What else? Well, after they tore down that wall, they built another. Just like that. Then they did a lot of work inside, washing down the walls. And you know what? They found a fresco on the walls!"

"I bet it was by that painter from Naples," Cesare said.

"Or maybe someone famous!" Tino said. "Maybe Giotto?"

"You know," Bruno said, "those Poles should be getting a lot more than they're being paid. I bet that contractor isn't paying them a decent wage at all. But it's probably more than they'd get at home, so they're happy."

"I think I know that guy," Tino said. "It's just like him to rip off people who don't even speak Italian."

"Sounds like you're sympathetic to these Polish guys, Tino," Bruno said.

"I just don't like people being ripped off. I don't care where they're from."

"I wonder if Frances Mayes knows about this," Bruno said. "Well, it looks like they're fixing Bramasole up good."

IF 1990 AND 1991 WERE BAD for Pezzino Tours, business was worse in 1992 and didn't improve in 1993. On the average, Bruno had one or two tours a week. Usually, these were small groups, which let him save money by using his smaller car but didn't provide the daily income he needed. Not to mention that he didn't get many tips.

Veronica was pleased that he didn't talk about quitting the business anymore. At fifty-six, how could he find something else to do? Somehow, they would manage with their savings. She didn't tell her husband that their son Rudolfo and their son-in-law Pippino were quietly filling an envelope with *lire* in a kitchen drawer every week.

Not even the visit by Pope John Paul II, the "Polish pope," to Cortona in May 1993 helped to improve tourism. When the rest of the family urged Bruno to capitalize on the visit, Bruno thought about ways for a long time. But then he pointed out that the pope would be in town only for an hour or so and probably at night since he had a big Eucharistic celebration in the stadium at Arezzo and other activities there earlier in the day.

"He's only going to be talking to people in front of the Church of Santa Margherita and then praying before her tomb in the church," Bruno said at one of the family dinners in April. "There won't be time for people to take tours, too."

"Well," Veronica said, "I'm excited about the pope coming. He's never been in Cortona before. We'll have to get there early because I'm sure there's going to be a mob of people."

"We?" Michele asked. "We? Are we all going?"

"Of course we're all going," Veronica said. "What are you thinking? How often do we get to see a pope?"

"But hardly anyone in this family even goes to Mass," Massimo said. "Well, you do. And Papa sometimes. And you drag Luciana and Silvio along."

"I don't drag them along," his mother said. "They want to go, right?"

"I only go to see Margherita's body in the tomb," Silvio said. "It's gross."

"Yuck," Luciana said. "I hate looking at dead bodies."

Of all the saints of the Catholic Church, Margherita of Cortona had one of the most interesting biographies. Born in 1247, she suffered under a cruel stepmother after her own mother died and her father remarried. As a teenager, she became promiscuous and ran away with a rich young man when she was seventeen. She lived in his castle near Montepulciano as his mistress for ten years and bore him a son.

When her lover was murdered, Margherita began a life of prayers and penance. She tried to return home, but her stepmother wouldn't accept her, so she took her son to the Franciscan friars of Cortona and he eventually became a friar, too. Margherita joined the Third Order of Saint Francis and somehow was able to establish a hospital in Cortona.

After her death, the Church of Santa Margherita was built in her honor and her body is preserved there. She was canonized in 1728.

"I think," Massimo said, "somebody made that whole story up."

"And did you know," Pippino said, "that she ate only bread and vegetables."

"Yuck," Luciana said.

Pippino had more to say. "You know how the church says a saint is the patron saint of something? Well, I read a list of what Margherita is the patron saint of. Listen to this. She is the patron saint of people who are falsely accused, the homeless, the insane, orphans, midwives, single mothers, stepchildren, hoboes, tramps and reformed prostitutes. She must be very busy answering all those prayers."

"Come on," Michele said, "Hoboes, tramps and reformed prostitutes? Well, I guess they need a patron saint like anybody else."

"All right," Bruno said, "let's change the subject. What's new at Bramasole, Michele?"

"Signor Martini says they're still doing a lot of work. Frances Mayes and her friend Ed go back to teaching in California and then come back here in the summer. I think those Polish guys are still doing work there."

"It still amazes me that they're doing all that work on that place," Bruno said. "It must be costing a fortune."

"Signor Martini says they are budgeting their money very well," Michele said. "And they've got good workers."

Despite the resistance of some of the children, Bruno and his entire family did go to see the pope on May 23, climbing up the steep hill to the church with hundreds of other pilgrims. Michele found himself standing next to a small crowd of Polish workers who had come to cheer the first Polish pope in history. He looked up and saw the three Polish workers he had heard so much about, Stanislao, the oldest, then Cristoforo and Riccardo. They were neatly dressed in sport shirts and slacks, waving small Polish flags and shouting, *Viva Papieza! Viva Papieza!*

Michele got into the spirit of the evening and started shouting *"Viva Papieza!"* too.

The pope told the crowd that Santa Margherita was a model for marriage and the family because she loved the father of her baby and eventually began a new life in penance, prayer and the exercise of charity toward the poor. Then he went inside to pray before her silver casket and everybody went home.

When they arrived back at their apartment Bruno took out paper and pencil, and Veronica asked what he was doing.

"I think I should have a new brochure," he said. "I've been using that old one for years and it doesn't seem to be doing any good."

"What will you put in it?"

"I'm thinking of something like 'Cortona: The Home of Santa Margherita.' And then I can write about her life and the fact that she had a baby even though she wasn't married and that the church canonized her anyway. And then I'll have a photograph of her tomb and say something like 'Come to Cortona and see the body of a saint.'"

"Do you think people will come to Cortona to see a saint's body in a church?"

"I don't know. Can't hurt to try, right?"

UNFORTUNATELY, the body of a saint wasn't much of a lure for tourists, and Bruno saw little change in his business in the next years. His friends noted that he seemed more and more depressed each time they met on Saturday mornings, and tried to cheer him up with little jokes. Even Giuseppe told stories about the Polish workers who were finishing up at Bramasole.

"It looks like it's done, as far as I can tell," he said. "I haven't seen the owners for a while, though. They must be back in California."

"Michele says Signor Martini says they really like the place, though," Bruno said. "They're going to spend a lot of time there."

Although his tourist business was still stagnant, one thing that always cheered Bruno was a visit every other month from his nephew Piero from Florence. Since Piero was a lawyer—Bruno called him "a big shot lawyer"—he claimed to know everything that was going on in Florence.

When Piero arrived and they all gathered around the big table for the

Sunday dinner, he didn't need much prompting to tell them bits of gossip about wealthy Florentines. But then he paused.

"Now," he said, "I have a surprise."

"What?" Michele asked.

"You're going to move to Cortona," Massimo said.

"No."

"You bought a Lamborghini," Michele said.

"No."

"You're getting married again," Pippino said.

"No."

"You won the lottery," Silvio said.

"I wish," Piero said. He pulled out the package he'd been sitting on and tore off the wrapping.

"Look! Frances Mayes has written a book. About Bramasole! About Cortona! About the people who live here!"

"Oh, my God!"

"I know you can't read English," Piero said, "and I don't read it very well either, but I was in a bookstore near the Duomo that sells English-language books. It's called the Paperback Exchange and it's really good. I've bought three or four books there over the years. It helps me improve my English.

"So I was in there the other day and I was looking around and suddenly I saw this book with a villa on the cover. And I thought, 'That looks sort of familiar.' Well, I looked closer and I knew it was Bramasole. And then I finally read the title. *Under the Tuscan Sun.* That's what this says. And there's a subtitle, *A Home in Italy.* And down here, 'By Frances Mayes.' Look, here's her picture on the back."

"That's her!" Michele shouted. "The woman who bought Bramasole. Signor Martini told me once that she was writing something about Bramasole, but I didn't think she would actually write a whole book."

"A whole book," Silvio said. "A whole book about Bramasole."

"And Cortona," Luciana said.

"Here, I'll pass it around,"

Carefully, the book was passed from hand to hand. Everyone touched the photo and traced their fingers on the letters. When it reached Maria

Elena, she began to cry. "Oh, I wish Luigi could see this. I'm going to take it to him."

She carried the book to her husband in the bedroom. For once he was awake but of course he couldn't see anything. "Touch this, Luigi. It's a book about Cortona. All about Cortona. Imagine."

She put his hand on the book, and the old man's sightless eyes began to tear. Maria Elena kissed him on the forehead and brought the book back to the table, where it continued to make the rounds until it returned to Piero.

"Well, as I said, I don't read English very well but I'll try to tell you some parts. Here in the preface she writes about how the book began just with her notes about flowers and projects and recipes. And then she writes about how restoring the house and the grounds and finding the links between food and culture helped her to learn another kind of life.

"Then she starts the book with how she signed the contract to buy Bramasole. Signor Martini is there…"

"Signor Martini is in the book?" Michele said. "Wow! He's going to be surprised."

"…and Doctor Carta. She quotes Carta as saying that he won't claim the full amount and he says, 'That is just the way it's done. No one is fool enough to declare the real value.'"

"Signor Martini said those are the exact words Doctor Carta said," Michele said.

"Then," Piero continued, "she says Cortona was the first town they'd ever stayed in and they kept coming back here. She talks about walking around town and the Bar Sport…"

"Bar Sport!" Bruno said. "I'll have to tell Giuseppe and Tino and Cesare. They're going to be so surprised."

"…and then she writes about visiting Bramasole and how Carta showed her the views and turned on a faucet to impress her with the fresh water. Let me find what she says. Oh, here it is. 'When I first saw Bramasole, I immediately wanted to hang my summer clothes in an *armadio* and arrange my books under one of those windows looking out over the valley.'

"Then she writes about the three Polish workers who were hired to help and how they lift big stones like watermelons. She says Riccardo is twenty-seven and Cristoforo is thirty and Stanislao is forty."

"They all look the same age to me," Bruno said.

17

"And she writes how they work from seven until noon and then they drive off in their Polski Fiat and come back at three o'clock for five more hours."

"My God," Analisa said. "I can't imagine Italians working like that."

"Frances Mayes obviously knows that the Poles are being paid less per hour than Italian workers," Piero said, "but she writes that they're pleased because before their factory in Poland closed they earned less than that in a day."

"They were still taken advantage of," Bruno said. "That's not fair. It's probably illegal, but who's going to say anything?"

"She writes about a lot of things," Piero continued. "How she shops at the market and takes walks around Cortona. She hires two carpenters, Marco and Rudolfo…"

"I know them!" Massimo said. "They did some work at the museum. They were very quiet."

"That's what Frances Mayes writes. She wanted a big table built for outside and they did that."

Bruno took the book from Piero's hands and paged through it. He tried to recognize a word here and there, but finally gave it back to Piero.

"Besides writing about Bramasole and Cortona," Piero said, "she also has some chapters that give recipes."

"In a book like that?" Analisa asked.

"Yes. Here's one for Baked Peppers with Ricotta and Basil. Here's one for Hazelnut Gelato. Here's one for Bruchette with Pecorino and Nuts."

"Piero," Veronica said, "do you think you could translate them for me? I could try them. Not the gelato, but the others."

"I may get the measurements wrong, but I'll try. But I've kept the best for last. Bruno, you know your friend Giuseppe?"

"Of course I know Giuseppe. He's one of my best friends. Is he in there?"

"Not by name, but I'm sure she's writing about him. She calls him the man with the flowers. I'm going to go slow, but here's what she writes:

"A sprig of oleander, a handful of Queen Anne's and fennel bound with a stem, a full bouquet of dog roses, dandelion puffs, buttercups, and lavender

18

bells—every day I look to see what he has propped up in the shrine at the bottom of my driveway."

"That's him!" Bruno said. "That's Giuseppe."

"She writes that sometimes she's working outside and sees him approaching:

"He pauses in the road and stares up at me. I wave but he does not wave back, just blank stares as though I, a foreigner, am a creature unaware of being looked at, a zoo animal."

"I'm sure," Bruno said, "that Giuseppe doesn't think she's a zoo animal. He would never think that way. That's just the way he is."

Piero continued. "She writes that once she saw him in a park and she said something to him, but all he said was *'buongiorno.'* She says that he had taken off his cap and his bald head was 'as bright as a light bulb.'"

"It is, it's that bright," Bruno said. "But he hardly ever takes off his cap."

"Here's what I find most interesting," Piero said. "Let me find this. She doesn't know who he is, but she imagines all sorts of things about him. She thinks he might be an angel because his coat hangs around his shoulders. I guess I don't understand that. Maybe she thinks the coat hides his wings, I don't know. But then she fantasizes that his mother was a great beauty who stepped out of carriages right where the shrine is, or that his father was cruel and forbade him to enter the house. Or that he visits the shrine to thank Jesus for saving his daughter from surgeons in Parma. She imagines all these things because she's so curious about him."

"Some imagination," Massimo said. "How do writers come up with stuff like that?"

"She writes that she doesn't touch the flowers that he leaves and that she doesn't even dust off Mary's face in the shrine."

"Well," Bruno said, "if Frances Mayes knew why Giuseppe walks all that way every day to bring flowers to the shrine she'd have a better story."

"I've always wondered why he did that," Rudolfo said. "Why does he?"

"I don't think he wants people to know," Bruno said. "They might think he's crazy."

"No," Veronica said, "they wouldn't think he's crazy. They'd think he was a very fine gentleman. Tell them the story, Bruno."

"Well," Bruno said, "you shouldn't really repeat this because he never talks about it, but here goes. From what I've heard, this happened a long time ago. There was a beautiful young girl, Felicità, and all the boys wanted to go out with her. She refused them all until she met Giuseppe. He was a couple of years older, and was a teacher in the school. She was just out of school and working for a seamstress who made fancy clothes for wealthy people. Giuseppe and Felicità fell in love. Madly in love. They went out for almost a year, and one Sunday afternoon Giuseppe drove her out to the countryside near Arezzo. They had a picnic and Giuseppe took out a ring and proposed marriage. She accepted, and they were very happy. They had never been so happy.

"Well, they were anxious to tell their parents and were driving home when they were rounding that curve right in front of Bramasole. You know how dangerous it is there. Just like that, a big hay wagon came out of nowhere from the other direction and slammed into them. Smashed the car to bits. Felicità was killed instantly. Giuseppe was thrown from the car but had only had a few bruises.

"Giuseppe was so upset he couldn't teach for a year, just kept in his room and hardly spoke to anyone. One day he got the idea to build a little shrine at the curve right where the accident happened. He did that and started taking flowers there every day. He's done that every morning after Mass ever since, no matter if it's pouring rain or blazing sun or freezing cold. For fifty years. But he never talks about it."

"He always seems so sad," Michele said. "I don't think I've ever seen him smile."

"He has a few times," Bruno said, "but not very often. He'll go to his grave like that."

Suddenly, no one seemed interested in talking about *Under the Tuscan Sun* anymore. Piero put the book down.

"I'll leave this here in case anyone wants to look at it," he said. "Do you think somebody should tell Frances Mayes the real story of this old man?"

"No, no," Bruno said. "Giuseppe wouldn't want that."

SINCE FEW PEOPLE in Cortona could read English and since *Under the Tuscan Sun* hadn't been translated into Italian, the book became a topic of curiosity but not much conversation in Cortona.

"Did you hear about that book by that woman from Bramasole?" someone would ask. "I hear it's very good."

"I've heard about it, but I can't read it," was the usual answer.

That, however, was not true in America where, to the author's surprise, the book suddenly became a best-seller. It soared to the top of *The New York Times'* best-seller list and remained on the list for two-and-a-half years.

American readers were fascinated by the story of Bramasole and, by extension, about Cortona itself. They'd never heard of the city before, but it sounded like one so untouched by tourists that they would be the first to discover it.

Bruno was surprised to get a phone call late one night.

"Hello. I'm calling from Chicago. Are you the man who has a tourist business in Cortona?"

"Yes."

"It sounds like an interesting place. We'll be in Florence in two months and we'd like to visit Cortona, too. How can I arrange a tour?"

That was just the first. It was followed by a call two days later from Philadelphia and by a third the following day from Houston. By the end of the week, Pezzino Tours had booked six excursions, a total of twenty-eight people, for the coming month.

"This is fantastic," Bruno beamed at dinner the following Sunday. "And it's all because of that book."

"Praise God for Frances Mayes!" Veronica cried.

In the next weeks, Bruno took visitors from Cleveland, Des Moines, Kansas City and Seattle on tours of Cortona. At the end of each tour, the visitors wanted to see Bramasole. Bruno was hesitant. He wanted them to see the Etruscan museum, the churches—especially the Church of Santa Margherita with the body of the saint—and to just guide them around the beautiful city.

Reluctantly, he agreed to just walk small groups by the entrance to Bramasole, pointing out the little shrine that was so reverently described in the book.

"Can you tell us about the man who puts flowers at the shrine?" someone invariably would ask.

"No, I don't know much about it," he would say. "Now let's get back in the bus and continue our tour."

The tourists seemed satisfied. A few were astonished when Frances Mayes herself happened to be coming or going at the same time. They were even more amazed when she stopped to talk.

One cheeky visitor shouted, "How much did you pay for this?"

Frances Mayes smiled.

A few months later, in the group from Milwaukee, someone mentioned that he recognized the narrow street off Piazza Signorelli because he'd seen the photo "online."

Bruno asked him what he meant. He said "the web."

Bruno didn't want to show any more of his ignorance, but he called Piero that night.

"He's talking about the World Wide Web," Piero said.

"What in the world is that? It sounds like something terrible."

"No, but it's something new," Piero said. "If you have a computer you can look things up and they appear on your screen. People put all sorts of things on it. Sometimes they do put photographs on, so somebody must have put up photos of Cortona and that's what this person saw."

"That's amazing," Bruno said. "I don't even have a computer."

"Well, you'll have to get one soon," Piero said, "or the world is going to pass you by. Maybe someday, if I can figure it out, I can put something up on it to advertise your tours. You can have your own page on the web."

"A page on the web? Piero, I can't even get used to this mobile phone."

"They're called cell phones now, Bruno. But here's one thing I'd suggest now. I'd change the name of your business. 'Pezzino Tours' doesn't tell anybody very much. How about 'Under the Tuscan Sun Tours'?"

"Really?"

"Why not? Why not capitalize on that name? People know it now. And it's not as if it was copyrighted. It's just a descriptive term. We all live in Tuscany and we're all under the sun."

Bruno tried the name out on his friends when they had coffee the following Saturday at Bar Sport.

"I don't know," Tino said. "Sounds kind of fancy. How about 'See Cortona.'"

"Not very descriptive," Bruno said.

Cesare and Giuseppe both liked the new name, though Giuseppe worried that people might want to see that old man who took flowers to the shrine every day.

"I promise you, Giuseppe," Bruno said, "I promise you I will never take anyone near Bramasole in the mornings when you're bringing the flowers. Never."

"OK. Thank you."

On about his sixth or seventh tour, Bruno was asked a question he'd never heard before.

"Bruno," a man from Pittsburgh said, "that story about fixing up Bramasole was very interesting. Are there other old villas around here for sale?"

It didn't take long for Bruno to think of at least three, the old Santucci mansion to the west, the Filippo villa to the south and the Montanini farm on the way to Arezzo.

Could Bruno take the man to one of them?

Bruno thought about it. No, real estate wasn't his field, and he didn't have a license. He called Michele. Would Signor Martini like to give a man from Pittsburgh a tour?

That was just the start. *Under the Tuscan Sun* soon became responsible for a wave of foreigners descending on Tuscany and elsewhere in Italy looking for old villas to rent or buy. Naturally, prices went up. Inevitably, many of the villas were in such terrible condition that some of the new owners gave up and went home.

And in a side development, there was a flood of books by the new owners writing about their own efforts, often futile, at restoration and inhabitation. None of the books achieved fame like *Under the Tuscan Sun*.

One Sunday evening, as the 1990s neared an end, Bruno and Veronica enjoyed a quiet moment after the rest of the family had scattered and only the cat was left to keep them company.

"Just think of it, Veronica. In 1990 I was ready to quit because the tourism business was so bad. We might have had to give up this apartment."

"And now your tours are booked almost constantly. You've got two more tour guides to help out, and Massimo and Michele do some work on weekends. I've heard that Cortona's population has even grown now that people know about it."

"You know what, Veronica? I don't think I want any more business. I don't think I could handle it."

"You've got quite enough now, Bruno. Oh, do you know what I heard today? I heard they're going to make a movie of *Under the Tuscan Sun*."

ELION

The horrific experience of Albanian refugees on the ship Vlora to Bari made front-page news in 1991 but had a heart-breaking ending.

EVEN THOUGH their weekend excursion wasn't until August, Davide and Sofia had started making plans in May. It had been three years, not since 1988, since they'd been able to get away together for even a few days. Something had always come up, for Davide at the carpentry shop, for Sofia at the hospital, and they didn't want anything to prevent it this time.

"You'd think we were going for a month," Davide said as he inspected the pile of things on their dining room table ready to be packed.

"I can't wait," Sofia said. "Solento was so beautiful the last time we were there. Those white beaches, the beautiful caves."

"And remember the water? I've never seen water so clean and warm. We could have spent the days just swimming."

They had been told about the Solento region by friends fifteen years earlier and had fallen in love with the region the first time they visited. It was a long drive from Florence, down the eastern coast of Italy to the very foot of the boot, going past Ancona, Pescara and Bari before getting to their destination.

"People are discovering it, though," Sofia warned. "Especially Bari. I hope we get there before the crowds come."

For many in Italy, August, the hottest month, was a time to escape to the sea. Davide and Sofia knew there might be a heavy influx of tourists, but they also knew that Solento in August was especially beautiful.

Friday, August 9, finally arrived, and they packed and were ready to go. Davide washed the breakfast dishes and Sofia straightened up the living room, keeping the television on in the background. She was singing softly to herself until she caught sight of something on the television screen.

"Oh my God," she cried. "Davide, come here, come here quick!"

Putting the last cup to dry, Davide rushed in. "What happened? Are you OK?"

"It's not me. Look at the TV."

They could hardly believe their eyes. A cargo ship was so laden down with people that the ship itself could barely be seen. Passengers filled the deck and hung from the masts and derricks. They were everywhere. The ship looked like an anthill. And the people were yelling something.

Davide put down his dish towel. "Who are these people and what are they crying?"

The sounds became clearer. *"Italia! Italia!"*

"Shhh. Listen," Sofia said. They settled back on the couch.

"These are live pictures," the announcer said. "You are seeing the ship Vlora at the port of Bari. A few days ago it returned from Cuba with ten thousand tons of sugar and arrived at the port of Durres in Albania. Yesterday, it was being unloaded when hundreds of men, women and children began storming aboard. They said they wanted to get out of Albania. More than ten thousand people, maybe as many as twenty thousand, are on board. Who can possibly count this many people?

"They ordered the captain to take them to Italy, and so the ship was forced to head due west through the Strait of Otranto. It tried to stop at Brindisi but the officials there refused, so it sailed up the coast and now it has come to Bari."

"Bari!" Sofia said. "That's on the way to where we're going."

"Oh, my God!"

The television cameras continued to focus on the ship and the refugees. Many, mostly young men, began diving into the Adriatic Sea and swimming to the dock.

"Oh no! They're going to drown," Sofia whispered.

Soon there seemed to be hundreds in the swirling waters. Rescue ships marked *Guardia Finanza* picked up some of them.

"This is incredible," Davide said. "Those poor people."

Then the television switched to an office where a man with flowing white hair and wearing a dark suit was seated at a desk. He held papers in his hand and looked over rimless glasses. A scroll at the bottom of the screen identified him as Professor Franco Mantini.

"This is an extreme part of what we now call the Albanian exodus to Italy," he said to the camera. "The economic situation in that country has been so bad for years that many Albanians have been trying to leave. Since last year many have gone to Greece and now they are attempting to come to Italy. Remember in March of this year? More than twenty-four thousand of them docked in Apulia at that time. They started in small groups, in fishing boats. Then the boats got bigger and bigger and more people came.

"What did Italy do then? Italy welcomed them. In fact, Prime Minister Giulio Andreotti suggested that families 'adopt' Albanians. The Italian politicians claimed that Italy and Albania were part of a common Adriatic culture, and so we had special bonds and obligations to them. The government started a program designed to integrate these people into Italian life, and they even got work permits. They had to get a job in four months or go back home. Many, many of them found jobs.

"Will this happen again, now in August 1991, with this group of people? I'm afraid things have gotten even worse in Albania, but we must also consider that attitudes have changed in Italy in just a few months. There is now a lot of suspicion and resentment towards Albanians. And there are so many on this ship! No, I don't believe these people will be welcomed."

Now the cameras, obviously from a helicopter, showed the ship being tied to the dock and a flood of people pouring out. Some of them jumped into the water to get there faster.

Soon hundreds, even thousands, of people milled around or stretched out on the concrete, exhausted.

The announcer came on again. "Police officers don't seem to know what to do. They are giving out a few bottles of water but there isn't nearly enough. These people left Albania last night and haven't had anything to eat or drink since then."

The refugees held up their arms to the cameras in victory signs.

"They think they're safe now," Davide said. "I wonder. Look, there's a man in a suit watching. Must be the mayor or somebody. That doesn't look good."

27

"Oh, and over there," Sofia said, "there's a young man limping. Something's wrong with his foot. How on earth did he get on the ship and then get off?"

"But there are so many still on the ship. Look, some guys are sliding down a rope to get to the water."

"Now even more are climbing up on the dock. Oh, my God, Davide. It's filled. There's no room for another human being there. And I don't see anyone helping them. Some of them look sick. They're carrying that boy. He's practically naked. And there's another boy stretched out. Who's helping them?"

"Nobody. There aren't any medical people. The heat must be terrible. Most of the guys don't have shirts on. Oh now, finally, somebody is bringing bottles of water."

Sofia turned the volume up. "There's another man carrying a young boy."

"Finally, here comes an ambulance. It says *Mater Dei* on the side. They're putting the boy inside."

"The dock looks so dirty, Davide. It looks like there are piles of coal dust."

"I can't believe we're watching this as it happens. The television crews must be all over."

"There are more people stretched out. Looks like they're passed out. That man won't even take water. Good God! These people need help!"

"Sofia, what do you think?"

"Davide, we have to go. Now."

SOFIA HAD BEGUN HER NURSING CAREER LATE, after she married Davide in 1979, and immediately upon graduation she got on the staff of the Ospedale di Santa Maria Nuova. Founded in 1288, it was the oldest hospital in Florence and, with its location in the center of the city, known for its service to the poor.

Sofia excelled in her job. She had a soft and comforting manner with patients and became skilled in a variety of nursing specialties. For the last four years she had been assigned to the I.C.U., a position she requested because she loved to treat emergency patients.

"You should have been a doctor," Davide often told her.

"No, this is just fine. I love what I'm doing."

Turning off the television set, she went into the bedroom and put on her white uniform and even added her cap. Davide changed into a dark green shirt and pants because "it looks sort of like a uniform."

They emptied their refrigerator and took cans and packaged foods from their shelves.

"I wish we had stocked up more," Davide said. "This isn't going to last very long. Maybe we can find something on the way."

"It didn't look like those people had any food at all," Sofia said, "but what we really need are some medical supplies. We'll have to stop at the hospital."

Davide parked illegally at the Ospedale di Santa Maria Nuova while Sofia ran in and found the supply room. She came back with three big plastic garbage bags filled with bandages, antibiotics, painkillers and other supplies. She had four blankets draped around her shoulders.

"One of the guards tried to stop me," she said as she tossed everything into the back seat, "but I told him there was an emergency."

With everyone escaping to the sea on this Friday, traffic was heavy going out of Florence, but they crossed the mountains to the Adriatic coastal highway and headed south.

After relinquishing the driving to Davide, Sofia wanted to know more about the political and economic climate of Albania. "I have to confess that I haven't been following the news from Albania very well," she said.

"I don't know that much either," Davide said. "But remember the family that our carpentry shop helped when they came here in March? They had come from Albania. The shop found them a place to live and the father Mergim is a good carpenter."

"So tell me all about Albania in twenty-five words or less."

"It will take more than that," Davide said, "but since I've gotten to know Mergim and his family, I've read more about it. Well, for decades, starting in 1944, there was a Communist dictator in Albania named Enver Hoxha. He was ruthless. He had a secret police force, and found out who the 'enemies of the people' were. The borders were sealed and people couldn't leave. They had to watch Italian television in secret. And the economy was in shambles. There were food shortages. He died in 1985, I think."

29

"With a big sigh of relief from the people, I'm sure," Sofia said.

"Students tore down a big statue of him in the square at Tirana. Well, a guy named Ramiz Alia succeeded him. He had been Hoxha's right-hand man. And so there were still lots of crackdowns, purges and executions. It was like Russia under Stalin. My God, he even buried enemies alive."

"Nice guy."

"Well, naturally the country continued to be in turmoil."

"I can't believe this was happening."

"So finally Alia introduced some reforms. He even eased restrictions on religion and on civil liberties. But the government began to crumble a couple of years ago when the Soviet and Eastern European Communist governments began to collapse. Alia tried to cling to power. He granted amnesty to political prisoners and promised some democratic reforms."

"Sounds like an about-face," Sofia said.

"It was. Sort of. But it didn't work. Everyone knew that Albania was the most backward, the poorest country in Europe. There was one crisis after another. The economy was dying. There were violent protests, and people fled. That's what caused all those people to flee to Greece and Italy earlier this year, as that professor said on television."

"And that's why all these people are fleeing today."

"Exactly."

"Well," Sofia said, "that was more than twenty-five words, but I learned a lot. And I feel so bad for those people. Having to live under those conditions and then to be crammed on a ship for hours and hours and who knows what's going to happen to them now."

"Like that man said on TV, I've noticed that Italy's mood has changed in the last months," Davide said. "I hear comments about Albanians all the time. They're still called strangers, *gli stranieri*. I don't think these people are going to be welcomed with open arms like Mergim and his family were. Who knows what's going to happen. They may even be sent home somehow."

Sofia thought about this, but she also thought about the people lying on the dock.

"Davide, I think we should bring water. Those people are dehydrated. And get some fruit."

"There's an *Autogrill* in a few miles. We can stop there."

Paying more *lire* than they expected at the crowded shop, they bought as many cases of bottled water as they could carry and stuff into the car. Then they went back and purchased dozens of oranges, apples and grapes.

"I knew we should have bought a bigger car," Davide said. "I don't think we can get another orange in here."

On the way out, they saw people gathered in front of a television set. It showed more scenes of desperate people on the dock at Bari.

"Stupid people," one onlooker said. "They think they can come here and take our jobs."

"Foreigners!" another man yelled. "Go back home."

"There's enough of your kind here," a third muttered.

Davide and Sofia rushed back to their car.

"Well, now we know what kind of welcome they're going to get," Davide said.

As they neared Bari they were able to get reception from a local station on their radio. The commentator was taking calls about the "invasion" of the immigrants.

"…more than in March or any other time," one caller was saying. "It's true. There must be a half million of them on that ship."

"I don't think the ship would hold a half million," the commentator said.

"Well, there are a lot. Where are they going to go? I'll tell you where they're going to go. They're going to spread all over Italy like a plague."

"Thank you for your comments. Now, another caller?"

"Hello? I just want to say that I have relatives in Albania and it's been terrible there. Maybe they shouldn't come here, but they are having a terrible time there. Thank you."

"And thank you for your comments."

Davide turned the dial. "Maybe we can find out what's happening now."

"…and now the police have moved in. They're forcing the crowds to get together. A few young men are resisting and the police have pushed them back. Now they've stopped resisting. There's a big tanker truck backing into the crowd. Maybe it's water. Now there's another ambulance from *Mater Dei* and two men are carrying another one into it. There's a man stretched out on the concrete. He looks unconscious. I don't know if he's even alive. People are just walking past him as if he wasn't even there.

There are more young men stretched out. There's a policeman with a boy over his shoulder like a sack of potatoes.

"There are still people swimming from the ship to the dock. Now the police are herding the people into one area but this dock isn't big enough for everyone. And it's so hot here. The sun is beating down. And the smell. All these people sweating. And the sea! And besides that, there aren't any bathrooms. They're using pails or going in the water. I think I'm getting sick and I'd better stop. I have to say, this seems like something out of Dante's *Inferno*."

"Oh, my God," Sofia said. "Can you drive faster?"

"Not with all this traffic."

The streets near the port were dense with cars, and it took Davide almost an hour to find a parking place.

"We'd better walk from here. We can use that cart in the trunk to carry the water and the other stuff. We may have to make a couple of trips. Are you ready?"

"I'll have to be."

THERE WERE SO MANY PEOPLE in the streets that it took another hour for Davide and Sofia, pushing the cart filled with supplies, to make it to the dock.

"These aren't Albanians," Sofia said, looking at all the other people around them.

"No, they're Italians who just want to see what's going on."

"And maybe prevent the Albanians from going any farther?"

"Maybe. I hope this doesn't get ugly."

Barricades were set up at the docks, perhaps to keep the immigrants in, perhaps to keep the Italians out. Sofia found a young guard at a locked gate.

"Hello," she said. "As you can see, I'm a nurse. We're here to provide water and some assistance to these people. May we come in?"

The guard looked them over and reluctantly unlocked the gate. Immediately upon seeing Sofia's white uniform, dozens of immigrants, talking loudly in a language she didn't recognize, surrounded them. Then one spoke in Italian.

"Please. My name Rezar. You have water?"

"Yes!" Davide dug into the cart, pulled out a case and began distributing bottles. Without being asked, everyone shared.

Sofia noticed a woman with white hair who had a deep cut on her arm. Rezar translated.

"She says she fell on ship. She used handkerchief but bleeding won't stop."

"I have bandages," Sofia said, dipping into the cart for Mercurochrome and long strips of white cloth. The woman winced as the antiseptic was applied but smiled broadly when Sofia had completed her work. Her two front teeth were missing.

"No food," Rezar said. "Run out of food."

Sofia handed out apples, grapes and oranges.

"I'm sorry, but this is all we could fit in our car."

Again, the people shared.

Davide, meanwhile, was talking to more people. He had learned a few words from his Albanian friend in Florence.

"Why did you come here?" he asked a few of them.

"Freedom! We want freedom!"

"We want out of Albania."

"Italy is beautiful!"

Rezar touched Sofia's arm. "Come."

He led her to a space where a young man had apparently passed out. He had no shirt and his arms and chest were covered with mud. His face was flushed and his forehead felt like a hot iron.

"Davide! More water!" she cried.

She washed the man's face and after many attempts got him to suck on the wet cloth. He was then able to sip from the bottle.

"There," Sofia said. "You'll be fine. Sit up, but don't move. God, I wish there was some shade."

Rezar took Sofia's hand. "Come."

A man about fifty years old was bent over, vomiting into a pail. A woman held him.

"She say her husband has terrible headache," Rezar said. "She say he gets them often. They no have medicine left. He very sick."

Recognizing a migraine, Sofia dug into her medicine bag and found her strongest painkiller. "He needs to rest in a dark place, too. Take off his shirt and put it over his head. And please cut up this orange and give it to him."

One after another. A man with a broken wrist. A woman with a sprained ankle. A boy cut around his arms. Two men overcome with the heat. A delirious old woman. An old man holding his head and moaning. She made the rounds, and then made the rounds again. Their food was running out and Davide went back to the car to get more.

After coaxing a woman into eating some grapes, Sofia saw a young couple and a small boy behind her. The young man was shaking the boy and yelling at him. The girl was yelling, too, and the boy was sobbing.

The man's head was shaved and sweat glistened on his bare chest. The girl had red-dyed hair and a heart tattoo on her left arm. Neither looked older than eighteen. The little boy wore a tattered plaid shirt and tan shorts. He had a thin scar running from his right ear to his chin and a big brown bruise on his left arm. He had the blackest eyes and the whitest teeth Davide and Sofia had ever seen. Uncharacteristically, Sofia suddenly wanted to pick him up and hug him.

"Excuse me," Davide said. "Is something wrong?"

"Elion says he wants some water," the man said. "Well, tough shit. We don't have any water."

"Here," Sofia said, taking a bottle out of the cart and giving it to the boy. "Drink this."

"*Grazie,*" the man said, grabbing the bottle and drinking from it before giving it to the boy. "Oh, my name is Loran and this is my girlfriend Marsela. Oh, and this is Elion."

Elion grinned and shook Davide's and Sofia's hands. "I'm from Albania!" he said.

They began to talk, and Davide and Sofia learned that the couple hadn't finished high school and couldn't find any jobs in Albania. They had secretly watched programs from Italy and when they heard friends saying they were going on the Vlora they decided to join them. They had no idea that there would be thousands of people on the ship also seeking refuge in Italy.

"We want to live here," Loran said. "That is our hope. We don't want to live in Albania. It is terrible there."

Elion made a contribution. "I watch cartoons on television. They are funny. Signor Davide, want to hear a joke?"

Loran pushed the boy aside. "Elion, don't bother the man. Go stand over there."

"I don't mind," Davide said. "Sure, Elion, tell me your joke."

Elion grinned again. "Knock, knock."

"Who's there?"

"Iva."

"Iva who?"

"Iva sore hand from knocking! Get it? Iva sore hand from knocking!"

The boy collapsed in laughter and Davide patted him on the head.

"That's great, Elion," Sofia said. "How old are you?"

"I'm eight. My birthday is the day before Christmas! I'm going to stay in Italy!"

"Well," Sofia said, "I hope you do." She looked at Davide, who looked away.

Loran pulled the boy away. "Let's go. I think something may be happening over there."

After they had moved to another part of the dock, Sofia whispered to Davide. "Such a strange young couple. They're not even twenty. That can't be their kid."

"They don't seem to be treating him very well."

"Poor kid."

They would have thought about it more, but Rezar poked Sofia's arm and summoned her to another case of heat exhaustion. It was now nearly 6 o'clock, and they could only hope that the sun would set soon.

"Davide, we're all out of the fruit and I'm running low on bandages. What are we going to do?"

"I don't know, hon."

"And what's going to happen tonight?" Sofia wondered. "Are they all going to sleep here? There's hardly room to stand. How will they all lie down?"

"We're going to have to stay and find out," Davide said.

Although police cars moved in and out of the area, forcing the people to scatter, the officers themselves didn't have answers. They mainly talked to one another as if awaiting orders.

Davide went up to one of them. "What do you think will happen to these people when it gets dark? Will they have to stay here?"

The policeman shrugged.

"Are there any plans to bring them some food or water?"

The policeman shrugged again.

"Are more medical people expected?"

The policeman walked away and began talking to another officer.

At the edge of the dock, Davide saw a sudden flurry of people talking excitedly to one another.

"What's going on?" he asked one of them.

"We heard some reports," the man replied. "We must go to an office in the morning and get permits to stay here."

"Really?"

"And then we can go anywhere in Italy and find work."

"Really? Are you sure?"

"You don't think this is true?" the man asked.

"Well," Davide said, "I just can't say. Who can predict what the Italian government is going to do?"

"I'm going to believe it. My cousin came in March. Everyone welcomed him. A man and his wife gave him a room. He got a work permit. Now he is working on a farm near Modena. He told me to come, so here I am. I will get a permit and I will get a job. Then I will tell my wife to come. Italy will be paradise."

"Good luck," Davide said.

The man next to him added, "My neighbor came in March, too. Big guy. Strong as an ox. He was walking on the street in Caserta. A car stopped. 'You want a job?' the man asked him. My neighbor said yes. The man brought him home, fed him for two weeks. Now he drives truck for a big company. I'm going to get a job like that."

Another man spoke. "My brother come and found job washing dishes in restaurant. Then he found another job and then another. Lots of jobs in Italy."

Davide reported the conversations to Sofia, who was bandaging a young man with a deep wound on his scalp.

"I'll believe it when I see it," she said. "Meanwhile, we've got thousands of tired, hungry people who have just endured a terrible boat ride and now are suffering intolerable conditions here. These people need help now, and nobody seems to be doing anything. Where are the medical people? I've seen only about a dozen nurses here. And not many ambulances. Where are the people bringing food and water? Where are the officials taking charge? I'm so tired I could lie down myself and go to sleep."

Davide put his arm around her. "Hold on, Sofia. Something must be going to happen soon. It has to."

"Right."

With nightfall, the putrid smells from the pails increased. There was still no sign of movement. The few policemen told people to stay where they were for the night. Tomorrow, they said, maybe there will be answers.

"Tomorrow?" Sofia cried. "How can these people last until tomorrow? No food, no water, babies crying, people sick. What are we going to do, Davide?"

"We need a miracle. Someone who can multiply loaves and fishes."

"Except that we don't have any loaves or fishes."

STRETCHED OUT on the concrete, jammed among so many smelly bodies, Davide and Sofia hardly slept all night. Shortly after 1 o'clock a man about fifty feet away began yelling.

"My wife! My wife!"

Sofia scrambled over bodies to reach him. The woman was retching.

"She sick," the man said. "She going to have baby in two months."

"Oh dear."

Sofia had no medicine or other remedy for this condition and just hoped that the baby wouldn't decide to come early. She gave the woman some water and sat on the concrete to let the woman rest her head on her lap. Eventually, the woman fell asleep. Sofia crawled back to her space and dozed off next to Davide.

An hour later, they were both awakened by someone screaming nearby and got up to look. A man about thirty years old was doubled up, holding his side.

"Pain, pain," he kept saying.

Sofia gently rubbed his abdomen.

"Have you had this long?"

"No. Since I got here."

"It is sharp or dull?"

"Sharp," the man moaned.

"Is it steady or does it come and go?"

"Steady. Ohhhh."

Sofia took a guess. "You may have something like gallstones. I'll see if I can get an ambulance to get you to a hospital."

One had just returned from Ospedale Generale, and Davide flagged it down. They helped the attendants move the man into the ambulance, which drove swiftly away.

"How many more of these people are going to get so sick?" Sofia wondered.

Eventually, the sun rose to another scorching day. Davide wandered around, trying to pick up information. Around 8 o'clock, he returned and took Sofia aside. She had been making an inventory of the few bandages and painkillers she had left.

"Sofia, I just heard something," he whispered. "They're not going to take these people to get permits. They're going to take them to the Vittoria Stadium. It's not far away. It can hold twenty thousand people."

"Why?"

"Because then they're going to be put on ships and airplanes and sent back to Albania."

"Oh, my God. Are you sure?"

"One of the policemen told me."

"And these people are so excited about staying here. What will happen to them?"

"They'll have to go back to their miserable conditions, I guess. I wonder if we can find Loran and Marsela and Elion again."

"Why?"

"Sofia, I'm worried about them, especially Elion. They seem so young and innocent."

"Well, young at least."

"I keep thinking of what will happen to them when they get back, especially that little boy. What's it going to be like living with those two? What's it going to be like growing up there?"

"I can't imagine, Davide. But I know it will be horrible."

They looked at each other hard, and each knew what the other was thinking.

"Sofia, what would you think about taking them back to Florence with us? I could see if I could find some sort of job for Loran."

"I don't know. They're going to be illegal, Davide."

"Lots of people are illegal."

"And we might get in trouble, harboring illegals."

"We can face that when it happens. If it happens."

Sofia put her hand on her husband's arm. "Well, we can't leave them here, can we? Let's find them."

A line of buses had arrived and people were pushing and shoving to get on. Policemen tried to keep order but mainly just pushed the Albanians onto the buses. Davide saw the young couple and boy in the middle of the crush. He grabbed them and pushed them to the side.

"Listen," Davide told them. "Come with us."

"But we have to get on the bus!" Loran said.

"Please come. It's important."

Loran and Marsela, holding Elion's hands, followed Davide and Sofia to the end of the dock.

"Please don't get on the bus," Davide said. "It's not true. They're not going to take you to get permits. They're going to take you to the stadium and then they'll put you on ships and airplanes and send everyone back to Albania."

"No!" Loran cried. "They told us! They promised us!"

"Don't believe them," Sofia said. "The fact is, the Italian government doesn't want you here."

"But they promised!" Marsela gripped Loran's hand. "We don't want to go home. We can't go home!"

Elion began to cry, and Sofia bent down and hugged him.

"Look," Davide said, putting his hand on Loran's shoulder, "why don't you come with us to Florence? We can find you a place to stay and I can try to find you a job. Then let's see what happens."

Now both Marsela and Elion were crying.

"You would do that?" Loran said. "Why?"

"Yes," Sofia said. "We would. Because...because we care about you."

Loran put his arm around Marsela. "All right. We go. Come on, Elion."

Elion grabbed Davide's hand.

"Are you taking us to your house, Signor Davide?" the boy asked.

"Yes. I think you'll like it there."

"Will I have my own bed?"

"I don't know," Sofia said. "Would you like to sleep on pillows?"

"Pillows! Can I? I love pillows!"

The boy chatted all the way to the car.

"Signor Davide! I have a joke."

"What's the joke, Elion?"

"Why do birds fly south in the winter?"

"Hmm. That's a hard one. I don't know."

"Because it's too far to walk! You like that, Signor Davide?"

"I like it a lot, Elion. Let's go."

WITHOUT THE SUPPLIES they had distributed on the dock, there was room for Marsela and Sofia to sit in the back of the Fiat with Elion on Sofia's lap. Loran sat in front with Davide.

Marsela was so exhausted she fell asleep right away and Loran was absorbed in the scenery. Elion talked nonstop.

"Signora Sofia, do you know why the boy brought the ladder to school?"

"No, why?"

"He wanted to go to high school!"

Sofia laughed.

"Signora Sofia, what has a face and two hands but no arms or legs?"

"Let me guess. Well, I give up."

"It's a clock! Get it, a clock!"

"Oh, of course. A clock. I'm so dumb."

"You not dumb, Signora Sofia. You smart."

"Well, not as smart as you, Elion. Now, should we look at the scenery for a while?"

"OK."

But soon the boy was back with his riddles and jokes. "What has to be broken before you can use it?" "What has a neck but no head?"

Davide offered to let Sofia drive, but she declared that she was actually enjoying Elion's chatter. He really was a sweet boy, and very smart. She almost envied Loran and Marsela. She wondered, though, why such a young couple had an eight-year-old boy with them.

It was late when they arrived in Florence, but Elion was wide awake and ready to explore every nook of Davide and Sofia's apartment.

"Look out this window! You can see the cars down there!" "Come see this closet! It's huge!" "This television is so big!"

"He's such a cute kid," Sofia told Marsela.

"He gets on my nerves," Marsela said. "Talk, talk, talk. He won't stop talking. Drives me crazy."

Meanwhile, Davide and Loran removed boxes and furniture from the guest room, made up a bed for Loran and Marsela, and threw down some pillows for Elion. Then it was time for baths, which Elion resisted.

Since they had taken all their food with them, there was almost nothing to offer their guests.

"Here's a bag of chips if you want them," Sofia said. "It's been opened so they're probably stale."

"I love chips!" Elion said.

When their guests had retired, Sofia collapsed on the living room sofa, and Davide brought out a bottle of a beer.

"It's the last one. We'll have to split it."

They pointedly did not turn on the television set.

"Well, so much for our vacation in Solento," Sofia said.

"There's always next year."

"Or the year after that."

They paused to sip their beer. The only sounds were whispers from the bedroom.

"Davide, do you think we did the right thing, bringing them back here? We're really taking chances with their lives."

"I don't know. I hope so. I guess it could only be better than what they had."

"Think you'll be able to find Loran a job?"

"I'll have to ask around."

"And where will they stay? They can't stay cooped up in here forever."

"I'll have to ask about that, too."

An ambulance screeched by, siren wailing.

"Poor Elion," Sofia said. "What a cute kid. I wish we knew his story. That scar? And that big bruise? Where did those come from?"

"I suppose a lot of stories will start to come out."

ELION WOKE UP first in the morning, ready to tell anyone more jokes. Davide said he would stop for groceries and take Loran to his carpentry shop and see if anyone had ideas about employment.

"And maybe a place for them to live," Sofia said.

Alone with Marsela in their apartment, Sofia avoided the news programs on television but found cartoons for Elion and put the cappuccino maker on. There was no bread to make toast.

"You've had a hard life," she told Marsela.

"Yes. Terrible. Thank God we're out of there."

"What did you do in Durres?"

"Nothing. I hated school, so I quit. Loran had a part-time job working in construction, but then he got laid off."

"So it was just you two and Elion."

"Yes."

"Such a nice boy."

"If you think so."

"Is he...is he a relative?"

"Well, you should know this stuff, I guess."

"Come sit down."

They sat at the kitchen table, and Sofia poured cappuccino for both of them.

Marsela began her story, recounting it without emotion, as if it had happened to someone else. She began picking off the bright red nail polish on the fingers of her left hand.

"When our mother died, it was just me and my sister and her husband and Elion in the house," she said. "We never knew where our father was, he was drunk all the time anyway. We were getting along OK, but then my sister and her husband were in this accident. They were driving back from Elbason. That's where the Chinese built a steel mill. You may have heard about it."

"Vaguely."

"Anyway, Drita and Faton, that was my sister and her husband, were driving back when they missed a curve and hit another car. Faton was killed on the spot, Drita lived for a few more days."

"Oh, how terrible. I'm so sorry. Was Elion hurt?"

"He wasn't with them. He was home with me."

"Poor little kid."

"As I said, Drita lived for a few more days. I went to the hospital every day. The last thing she said to me was, 'Take care of Elion.'"

"Oh, Marsela, how sad. And what a burden for you."

"That was almost two years ago. He was six. So then I met Loran and he moved in with me and we've been taking care of him."

"The poor kid must have been traumatized, his parents killed like that."

"He woke up screaming sometimes after the accident. He doesn't scream now, but he whimpers and calls for his mama and I have to go in and stay with him and he squirms and bounces and I don't get any sleep. I'm exhausted in the morning."

"He seems so happy."

"Loran says he hides what's really going on in his little head. Maybe that's why he talks so much."

"What a responsibility for you, and you're so young!"

"It's hard work sometimes. Really hard work."

"But you like the little boy, don't you?"

"He's my sister's son, what can I say? But we can't go out, we can't do anything. We always have to stay home with him. All our friends go out all the time, dancing and movies. I get so mad I could scream."

"I'm so sorry."

"Look, we brought him along because we couldn't very well leave him behind."

"No, of course not."

Marsela was now scraping off nail polish on her right hand.

"OK, I need to tell you this. The real reason we brought him is we hope we can find a family here who will take him. It's just too much for us. We tried to find someone in Albania but no one would take him. No one. So we're stuck."

"But you wouldn't give him up, would you?"

"Well, he's not my child, you know. I shouldn't have promised my sister. I'll regret that till the day I die."

"He seems to like you two."

"He's afraid of Loran."

"I guess that's natural. Loran isn't his father."

Sofia poured another cup of coffee for Marsela and this time she needed another one, too.

"Loran has some problems. He gets really mad sometimes, he can't control his temper and he thrashes about. He's never hurt me though."

"That scar on Elion's face, and the bruise?"

"Elion got scared about a month ago when Loran was having one of his outbursts. He ran and he stumbled down the stairs and hurt his face."

"Oh my. And the bruise?"

"That was just last week. Loran grabbed him too hard."

"Oh, my God. Has that sort of thing happened before?"

"A few times."

"Marsela, I'm so very sorry."

Marsela had now finished with her nails. "I'm going into that room and lie down. I didn't sleep very well last night."

She turned around at the door. "And if we can't find a family, do you think you could find an orphanage where we could put him?"

"Oh, my God," Sofia whispered. She was still shaking when she joined Elion on the couch as he watched *Candy Candy*.

"That's a funny show, isn't it, Elion?"

"I love this show."

Sofia put her arm around the boy's shoulders and he rested his head on her side. She wondered why she was crying.

When Davide returned home with Loran that afternoon, he had good news. One of the carpenters said a maintenance man was needed at one of the apartment buildings he had refurbished, and there actually was an apartment available there.

"It's very small, though. Elion will have to sleep on the couch."

"Davide," Sofia said, "I want to talk to you about something, but let's wait until tonight."

Davide had brought supplies for supper, and afterwards they all gathered around the television set to find out what was happening in Bari today. Elion sat between Davide and Sofia on the couch.

The cameras showed people boarding a military airplane.

Elion piped up. "Why are those people getting on that airplane, Signor Davide?"

"They have to go back home."

"Why?"

"Because Italy doesn't want them to stay."

"Why?"

"I don't know, Elion. I don't know."

"Do we have to go back?"

"No," Sofia said. "You are going to stay in Italy."

"Can I stay with you?"

"Here, with us?"

"Yes."

"I don't know, Elion. I just don't know."

"I want to stay here."

AFTER THEIR GUESTS had gone to bed, Davide and Sofia again sat on the couch, but they didn't turn the television on.

"Davide," Sofia said, "I talked to Marsela today. I'm really upset."

The whole story about Marsela and Loren and Elion came out, and by the end of it Sofia was wiping tears away. She rarely cried.

"They want to get rid of that little boy?" Davide said. "How could they do that? He's such a good little kid. That's terrible."

"I'm trying to think what I would have done if I was sixteen years old and suddenly I had to take care of my sister's little boy, if I had a sister. I don't know what I'd do."

Davide threw his newspaper down. "Well, you wouldn't put him in an orphanage, I know that. Sofia, the more I think about this, the madder I'm getting. They can't do that! They can't give that boy away! Goddammit! It's criminal! There must be laws against this."

"What are we going to do, Davide?"

"We can't talk them out of this?"

"No, I don't think so."

"We can't tell them to get some help, somebody to look after the boy?"

"They could never afford that."

Davide began to shout as he paced the floor. "Well, something's got to be done! We can't let this happen!"

Sofia had never seen her husband so angry. "Davide, don't shout. You'll wake the others."

"OK, OK."

He wiped his forehead, picked up the newspaper and threw it at the wall, and then stared out the window.

"Do we know anyone? We must know someone."

"I've been thinking all day, and I can't think of anyone. None of our friends are going to want to raise a little boy."

"What about…what's her name…Flora, that woman at the flower shop that we go to sometimes? She's young, and she's married, isn't she?"

"I think her husband just dumped her."

They thought for a long while. Davide was now pounding on the window frame.

"What about that young nurse at the hospital?" he said. "You've talked about her. Does she have kids?"

"Anita? I don't know. The way she talks about her husband, I don't think they get along very well. What about you? What about that Albanian family you know? That would be a logical match, wouldn't it?"

"Mergim and his family? I think they're barely making it. They've got four kids already. I don't know if they'd want another mouth to feed."

"Well, maybe they'd know somebody. You can ask, right?"

"And you can ask that nurse?"

Sofia was on the early shift the following day, so she was home early to find Marsela waiting at the door.

"Sofia, I'm going crazy in here. I've got to get out for a while. Elion's watching TV. OK?"

"Well, sure. Of course. Why don't you walk down toward Ponte Vecchio. Turn right at the corner. There are a lot of shops you can browse in. Here, take some money. Buy something for yourself, something nice. After all this, you deserve it."

She gave her a handful of *lire*. "Take your time. Elion and I will be fine."

Sofia found the boy engrossed in another cartoon, but he jumped up when he saw her. "Signora Sofia! You are home!"

He ran into her arms and kissed her cheek.

"Oh, Elion, what a nice greeting. Look, let me change, and then we can do something together, OK?"

"OK!"

Now in an old shirt and jeans, Sofia brought the boy into the kitchen. "How would you like to make some cookies?"

"Really? I have never made cookies. Can I?"

"Sure. Let's see what we have."

She found a box of gingerbread cookie mix and wiped off the kitchen table. She brought out a big bowl and a mixer, and eggs from the refrigerator.

"Have you ever cracked an egg, Elion?"

"Me? No! Can I?"

Some of the shell got in the bowl, but otherwise he got a "Good job!"

For the next hour, Elion, with a towel tied around his neck for an apron, chatted nonstop as he helped Sofia mix the dough, roll it out and make seventeen gingerbread men with a cookie cutter. Their little candy eyes and belly buttons weren't quite where they belonged, but Elion was pleased, especially when Sofia let him lick the spoons.

After sliding the cookies into the oven, he talked about his teacher in Albania and his friend Pieter and Pieter's dog Leka. He talked about what he hoped to get for his birthday. "Some candy!" He talked about the two boys he met on the ship.

"They weren't very nice. They were fighting."

"Do you ever fight, Elion?"

"My mama told me to never fight."

"Elion," Sofia said, "do you miss your mother and dad?"

The boy grew quiet. "Sometimes. Sometimes I see my mother in my dreams. She is always smiling at me."

"And your father?"

"Sometimes he's there, too. He's watching the soccer games on television. He lets me sit with him."

"Elion, I'm sorry you don't have them anymore."

"I know. I'm sorry, too."

Sofia feared that they were both going to cry, and she hugged him.

47

"You know, Signora Sofia, you kind of look like my mama."

"Really? How?"

"You have short hair like her. Marsela has long hair. I don't like it. And you don't put paint on your face and your fingers. My mama never put paint on her face and her fingers."

Sofia hugged him again. "Elion, Elion. What a funny boy. Well, let's put these men on the counter and let them cool. Then you can have one, and Signor Davide can have one when he comes home soon."

Davide did arrive an hour later, with bad news. The Albanian family wouldn't be able to take Elion and they didn't know anybody who would. Sofia reported that Anita also declined to take the little boy, "not with all the stuff going on in our house now."

The next day they went to see their parish priest to see if he knew of anyone willing to adopt a child.

"I can't think of any off the top of my head, but let's see," Father Stefano said, pulling out a dusty, leather-bound book from a shelf behind him.

He began running his finger down the page.

"Accorsi," he began. "They're kind of young. He's trying to be an actor so they don't have much money and they probably need to get settled. Let's see who else."

He ran his finger down another page.

"Buffone…Buffone…why do I know that name? Oh, right. He was just sent off to prison for robbing that bank. I know he took the rap, though. It was really his cousin Pietro."

More pages.

"Filippi. Hmmm. Possible. Fosca and Massimo. They're such a great young couple, so in love. They've been together for years. They really want to have a baby and are trying hard. So far, no luck. I'll mark them down."

He wrote their name and phone number on a piece of paper and continued his search.

"Let's see. Locatelli. I don't know them too well, but I remember Betina saying that she wished she could have a child for years but there had been problems. She was going to see a doctor."

He wrote their name and phone number down.

More pages, more pages, more pages. And more mumbling. Davide and Sofia tried to stay calm, but Davide noted that his wife's hands were shaking. And then he noticed that his were, too.

"Palmissaro....Palmissaro. No, no, no. What was I thinking?"

More pages.

"Santini. Luigi and Giuseppina. That's possible. They come to church every Sunday and even put a little in the basket. They have three children, I think. They're not that young."

He took down their information.

More pages, more pages. He closed the book.

"OK. Three names. Filippi, Locatelli and Santini. I'll contact them. If that doesn't work, I'll go through the book again. Give me a day, OK?"

"Father, we are so grateful," Davide said as he shook the priest's hand. "You don't know how relieved we are."

"Well, don't count your blessings yet. I haven't talked to these people."

"One of them will surely be interested, right?" Sofia said. "Surely?"

"Pray to Saint Jude," the priest said. "He's the saint of lost causes."

Although they rarely prayed, Davide and Sofia said they would.

Prayers didn't do any good. Father Stefano had distressing news the next night when Davide and Sofia again visited. Fosca and Massimo had told the priest they were moving to Spain to work for an automobile factory; Betina Locatelli was so excited because she was going to have a baby! And Luigi and Giuseppina Santini were going to have their fourth child.

"I went through the book two more times and I tried some other people, too," Father Stefano said, "but no luck. They all had reasons not to do this."

"Well, that's that," Davide said. "You tried. We appreciate your efforts. Let's go, Sofia. Thanks again, Father."

"Wait, don't go yet. I was wondering. How long you two have been married."

"It will be ten years in October," Sofia said.

"Nice. And no sign of children?"

"Oh, we've tried," Davide said, "but the doctors said it's not possible because, well..."

"You don't have to go into details. I was just wondering. Just wondering."

"What are you suggesting, Father? No! No! Don't even think about it. No! Come on, Sofia."

SOFIA ALWAYS KNEW when Davide was angry or upset. He walked fast. He kept his hands in his pockets. He looked straight ahead and sometimes bumped into people.

"Davide, wait. I can't keep up with you."

They had left the Church of San Salvi and were walking on Via della Scala. Davide finally stopped at the Piazza della Repubblica and they found a bench near the carousel.

"Davide, I know what you're thinking, and I agree. We can't adopt Elion. It would be impossible. We're too old. We both have jobs. We have no idea how to raise a child."

"Right."

"We would have to be committed to him all the time. We wouldn't have a life of our own."

"Right."

"We would have no idea how to help him with his homework."

"Right."

"And we wouldn't be able to play soccer with him, or any other sport."

"Right."

"None of our friends have little kids so who would he play with?"

"Right."

"And imagine watching cartoons all the time."

"Right. Let's go home."

Sofia still had trouble keeping up with Davide, who was walking really fast with his fists in his pockets.

At home, Elion sat absorbed in another cartoon on the television set.

"Signor Davide! Signora Sofia!"

He plunged into their arms and wouldn't let go.

"Did you have a good day, Elion?" Sofia asked.

"It was OK. I watched cartoons."

"All day?"

"They were funny. Want to hear a joke they said?"

"Of course."

"Knock, knock."

50

"Who's there?"

"Stopwatch!"

"Stopwatch who?"

"Stopwatch you're doing and open this door!"

Elion jumped up and down. "Stopwatch you're doing and open this door! Get it! Get it!"

"That's very funny, Elion," Sofia said. "Well, I think Signor Davide has a headache so he's going to lie down for a little while. Let's just sit here and I'll read *Pinocchio* again."

Sofia read from the book, but her mind wasn't on Geppetto and his wooden puppet. She finished two chapters and put the book down.

"I think I have a headache, too, Elion. We'll read some more tomorrow night, OK? I think I'll lie down, too."

Elion put his hand on her forehead. "Are you sick, Signora Sofia? Can I get you a glass of water? Or a glass of milk? I can get you a glass of milk from the refrigerator."

"Thank you, Elion, that's very sweet, but I'll be fine. You can watch more cartoons if you want."

"That's OK. I think I'll just look at this book."

Before Sofia got up, Elion hugged her tight and kissed her. "I like your hair, Signora Sofia."

"Thanks, Elion. I'll come back later to put you to bed."

Sofia found Davide lying on the bed and staring at the ceiling.

"Elion OK?" he asked.

"He's fine."

Sofia busied herself folding sheets and towels from the laundry.

"We can't do it, of course," she finally said.

"No, of course not. It's out of the question. We can't even think about it."

"And it's not as if he's our responsibility. It was all an accident. We just happened to see Loran and Marsela on the dock and he was with them. It's their responsibility. She told her sister that she would take care of him."

"I know that," Davide said.

"How could we ever learn to be parents?" Sofia said. "We're not young anymore. I'm thirty-four, you're thirty-five."

Davide got up and blew his nose. Hard.

Sofia turned her back and looked out the window. "Then why are we both crying?"

"Sofia, I've been going round and round and round. I think one way and then I think the other way."

"Yeah. Me, too."

"Come sit here."

They sat on the side of the bed, holding hands.

"Davide, we can't let them put him in an orphanage. It would be terrible for him. What if nobody adopted him and he'd have to stay there? We always hear these horror stories about orphanages. I don't think I could stand it thinking about him in an orphanage. And what if he were adopted by people who didn't love him?"

"We've tried, Sofia, we've tried. We couldn't find someone else. No one."

"I know."

Then Davide started to laugh.

"What's so funny?"

"I was just thinking. My mother would be absolutely delirious if we did this."

"Grazia has always wanted a grandchild. I think she blames me for not having a baby."

"That would not be a reason for doing this, of course."

"Of course not."

"Look," Davide said, "we know all the arguments against this. Sofia, let's think about the arguments for it."

Against the backdrop of noise of traffic from the street below, they tried to think of all the reasons why—for heaven's sake—it might be possible for them to actually adopt Elion. It didn't take long.

"There's really only one reason," Sofia said. "It's because he is the sweetest boy who ever lived."

"And he loves us and we love him."

"What other reasons do we need?"

"None that I know of!" Davide kissed Sofia and they went hand in hand into the living room.

"Guess what, Elion! You're going to stay with us! You're going to be our son!"

"Really?"

He leaped into their waiting arms.

"Yes!"

"And I can stay here forever?"

"Yes!"

"Really? I love you, Signora Sofia."

"I love you, Elion."

"I love you, Signor Davide."

"I love you, Elion."

"Can we stay up late tonight? Want to read a book? Want to hear a joke?"

LUCA THE FLAG THROWER

I've always loved watching groups of flag throwers. They seem to bring medieval times back to life—their bugles, their drums, their costumes, their agility. I wanted to write about them and I also wanted to set a story in the beautiful village of Pienza. Imagine my surprise to find that Pienza has a flag throwing group, the Gruppo Sbandieratori a Musica Pienza.

FOR ANY THIRTEEN-YEAR-OLD BOY, a minute, a second, can seem like an eternity, so Luca Marceri was getting very annoyed that his friend Mauro was taking forever to get ready.

"Mauro! We're going to be late!"

"We won't be late," Mauro called from the bathroom. "I'm almost ready. You know it never starts on time."

"Sometimes it does. And we want to get good seats."

"We will. Besides, the cheese contest is first and we don't have to see all of that."

Luca often wondered why he still called Mauro a friend. He was always keeping him waiting and he thought he knew everything about everything because he was fourteen. But if Luca didn't have Mauro as a friend he wouldn't get to see Mauro's sister. Gabriella was thirteen but because she was a girl she was, well, more developed. Luca liked the way she walked, the way dimples appeared when she smiled, the way her long blond hair waved in the wind. When Gabriella said, "Hi, Luca," his mouth dried up and he couldn't speak.

"All right, I'm ready," Mauro Gatti said as he slicked his hair down one last time. "Don't I look great?"

Mauro had spent what seemed like an hour combing his black hair forward, ending in a peak on his forehead.

Mauro thought it was cool. Luca thought it was stupid.

Their ear buds in, their phones in their hands, they set off on Corso il Rossellino to Piazza Pio II. They wore yellow scarves tied around their necks.

With only two thousand residents, the Renaissance town of Pienza in southern Tuscany was proud of its famous—at least biggest—event for tourists, a celebration every September of its most illustrious product, cheese. One highlight of the *Fiera del Cacio* was a competition in which teams rolled a round of cheese on the cobblestones of Piazza Pio II toward a spindle. The team that got the cheese closest won, to the cheers of residents and hundreds of visitors.

The other highlight was a performance by the *Gruppo Sbandieratori a Musica Pienza,* the town's flag throwing group, and that's why Luca couldn't wait to get to the piazza.

Crowds had already lined all four sides of the piazza when the boys arrived, but they made their way to Palazzo Piccolomini where people were hanging out from the leaded windows all the way up to the third story.

Luca noticed Gabriella with a group of girlfriends in the second row.

"Hi, Luca," she said.

Luca's face turned red and he managed a weak smile.

They had just found places in front of the Cathedral of Santa Maria Assunta when an elderly man wearing a black scarf around his neck announced that the games were about to begin. Tensions were rising as he pointed to the foot-high painted spindle at the center of the piazza. Teams with six members each from Pienza's six *contrade* stood ready.

The contest began. One player at a time knelt on a rug in the corner and, with many detailed instructions from a coach, set a round of cheese rolling toward the spindle. The pavement was uneven and there were holes in the bricks so the cheese took unexpected turns.

"To the left!" someone shouted.

"To the right!"

"Roll it faster!"

"No, slower!"

The crowd became more boisterous, and it was clear that some onlookers had stopped at one of the wine bars before arriving.

Each player was allowed three pitches, and a large board on one side of the piazza kept track of the score for each *contrada*. Each effort was greeted by loud cheers and boos.

Mauro was busy texting and Luca found all this increasingly boring and began to stand up, sit down, stand up.

"Sit down!" the people behind shouted.

At last the contest was over and the *Contrada il Prato* was declared the winner. The team captain accepted the large trophy, and the jubilant winners, all wearing green scarves, were carried off to the nearest bar in triumph.

The crowd milled around as the spindle was removed, the pavement swept and pieces of errant cheese picked up.

"Why aren't they starting? Why aren't they starting?" Luca wanted to know.

"Luca, don't get your ass in a sling," Mauro said, not looking up from his phone.

"I don't want to miss anything."

After too long a wait, he finally heard the sounds over the din of the crowd. The drum beats became louder and louder and Luca could feel his heart racing as the crowd quieted and then began to cheer.

The elderly man stepped to the center again and shouted, *"Gruppo Sbanieratori e Musici Pienza!"*

From under the arches of Palazzo Comunale a dozen young boys filed in, two by two. They wore long red vests over white shirts. Their black tights had a white stripe down the right leg. They beat their drums loudly, then softer, then loudly again. The crowd erupted.

As the drumbeats continued to reverberate against the stone buildings around the piazza, the boys lined up on one side. Then a dozen older boys marched in. Their uniforms were the same, but they carried huge flags with four large squares, two in red and two in white. They gathered, four on four, in the middle and began to twirl their flags and then toss them in the air, over and over.

"Ohhhhhhhh," the crowd murmured.

"Ahhhhhhhhh."

The flag throwers tossed their flags even higher.

"Ohhhhhhhhhh."

Now they threw them at an angle so that their partners across the way caught them and threw them back.

"Ahhhhhhh."

Never once was a flag dropped. Each was caught with a deft twist of a wrist.

Luca was jumping up and down, ignoring the complaints of those behind him.

"Did you see that?" he kept asking Mauro.

Mauro was still texting.

When the boys had completed their performance they were replaced by four men who did the same routine, only the flags were thrown to their partners higher and more often.

"Ahhhhhhhhh."

The four returned to the side and everyone looked at the arch where the others had entered. Then a tall man, clearly the leader of the group, strode in, bearing a single flag. His head was bald but he was not old, perhaps forty. He marched to the center of the piazza and stood in the circle just used for the cheese contest.

"Papa!" Luca cried. "Papa!"

Two young men followed, each bearing a flag, and stood at the side. The crowd exploded in cheers and applause, knowing this was the highlight of the afternoon. Even Mauro took out his ear buds and put his phone away.

"Papa! Papa!"

If Guiseppe Marceri heard his son's cries, he ignored them. He stood still for a moment, then began twirling his flag around and around before sending it into the air with his right foot. He whirled it again and again, throwing the flag higher each time.

"Ohhhhhhhhhhh."

His aide brought him a second flag and he spun both, round and round, up in the air. Higher and higher.

"Ahhhhhhhhhhh."

Now a third flag was deftly caught and all three were twirled, swirled, thrown and caught. Over and over. With one long continuous motion, he never stopped for an instant, never seemed to take a breath.

Finally, he tossed two flags back to his aides and with a mighty lunge aimed the third one so high it was on a level with the papal coat of arms carved in the apex of the cathedral.

Clearly, he was one of the finest flag throwers in the world. The crowd stood and cheered as Guiseppe Marceri strode off the piazza, but not before he gave a slight sideways smile to his son.

The man next to Luca slapped him on the shoulder. "Next year you'll be out there, right?"

IT WAS LIKE A PUNCH TO THE GUT. Luca had been enjoying the day so much and now it was ruined. It was time to go home.

For so long, Luca had been trying to forget that when he turned fourteen next March he could begin training to be a flag thrower himself. He didn't have a choice. Whether he wanted to or not, it was universally assumed that he would continue the legacy of his father and his brother.

Especially since his brother was dead.

His parents never said this out loud, but he knew that his mother, grieving over the loss of her older son, would be comforted knowing that Luca was following in Alfonso's footsteps. One day he stood in the hall and saw her take Alfonso's flag thrower uniform out of its box in the closet. She held it closely and then, with tears flowing, put it back.

"Oh, Luca," she said. "I didn't see you there. I was just looking at... looking at..."

"It's all right, Mama."

His father, the experienced and celebrated flag thrower, never said anything either, and he certainly didn't offer to teach him a flag thrower's maneuvers.

"It's up to him. I don't want to push him. When he's fourteen he can go to the training school and learn how to do it. Or he can decide not to. Whatever he decides is fine."

Luca often found his father looking at him in a strange way but he didn't ask why.

Alfonso was always in the back of their minds. The boy had everything to live for. At eighteen, he was bright, good-looking, with tons of friends. And perhaps most notably, Alfonso had graduated from the *Piccoli Bandierai,* the school for young flag throwers, and had joined his father in the *Gruppo Sbanieratori e Musici Pienza.*

More than joined. He lived for it, and he quickly became noticeable even in what is always a team presentation, with no stars.

No one who was there would ever forget his final night at the *Fiera del Cacio*. After taking part in the group performances Alfonso strode to the circle. He bowed to the four sides and then twirled and tossed his flag around and around. Never stopping, he threw it up into the air, higher and higher. The crowd went crazy. Then Alfonso bowed and saluted his father with his flag.

Guiseppe came forward, bowed to his son, and completed his own solo act. Then Alfonso strode to his side, flag over his shoulder. Together they twirled and flew their flags alone and to each other. Guiseppe tossed his flag high. Alfonso threw his higher. Again and again. Finally, arms around each other's shoulders, they bowed. The cheers and applause reverberated against the ancient palaces in the piazza, and there were cries that they should form a team, the *Padre e Figlio Sbandieratori*.

A month later, Alfonso died instantly when he tried to avoid an oncoming truck and his motorcycle swerved off a rain-soaked Highway 146 from Montepulciano. The photo on his tomb in the crowded village cemetery showed the smiling boy in his flag thrower uniform.

Luca, who had adored his older brother, knew immediately that he would be expected to also become a flag thrower. Worse, that he was supposed to be as good as his brother. He knew he couldn't. He was too scrawny for one thing. For another, he would always compare himself to Alfonso. And so would everyone else. Yet Luca knew that he would honor his brother if he joined the group.

Every night before he went to bed he picked up Alfonso's photo on his dresser, the same picture that adorned his brother's grave. Luca touched his fingers to his lips and then touched the photo.

After many conversations with his parents—"I will, I won't, I will, I won't"—Luca could not make a decision. His parents weren't much help.

"Maybe we should see Doctor Bruni?" Maddalena asked her husband.

In the early years of their marriage, Maddalena and Guiseppe had problems common to other couples and sought the help of one of Siena's most noted psychologists. After a couple of months, they felt immensely better.

"I'll make an appointment," Guiseppe said.

Doctor Bonavento Bruni's office was on via Salicotto near Vestri Palace in Siena and they had trouble finding a parking place. His office was sparsely furnished, but a huge Botticelli print hung over a fireplace. With long white hair and beard, Doctor Bruni seemed to personify a psychiatrist.

The doctor said he was pleased to see them again and hoped that he would be able to help.

"And this is Luca? I'm very glad to meet you. How are you doing?"

"OK, I guess."

"That's good. OK is very good. I'm happy to hear that."

Guiseppe explained that they had asked for an appointment because Luca was having trouble deciding whether to become a flag thrower.

"He feels that he would be honoring the memory of his brother if he became one, but he would also feel the burden of his brother's legacy. He fears that people will always compare him to Alfonso, and that even he would compare himself to Alfonso. He fears he wouldn't be as good and would get discouraged and resent Alfonso's abilities. It's all very confusing."

As he always did, Doctor Bruni paid no attention to a fifty-minute time limit and discussed their situation kindly and with great empathy. He remembered his own experiences with his younger daughter when her older sister died suddenly and how he himself struggled to help her.

"Well, it's all complicated, so let's talk about it," Doctor Bruni said. "Do you want to talk about it, Luca?"

Luca shrugged.

"Are you thinking about this a lot?"

Luca shrugged.

"Guiseppe, Maddalena, maybe Luca and I should have this conversation by ourselves?"

Luca's parents hesitated and then left the room.

"Luca, would you like a Coke? I have some cans in the little refrigerator over there."

Luca nodded.

"Good. I think I'll have one myself."

Luca stared at the ceiling and Doctor Bruni sipped his Coke.

"Luca can you tell me how you and Alfonso got along? Were you good friends?"

Luca nodded.

"Did you do things together? Play sports, for example?"

"We kicked a ball around. He was always better than me."

"Well, he was bigger, right?"

"Yes."

"Did you play any board games?"

"We played Monopoly sometimes. And checkers. I always beat him at checkers."

"You beat him?"

"All the time!"

"Oh, that's great. What did Alfonso do then? Did he get mad? Did he get upset?"

"No. He just said, 'Good job.'"

"Good job? Well, that's great. It shows that he respected you. And you must have respected him."

Luca nodded and his eyes welled up. Doctor Bruni tried to change the subject.

"Luca, did you go to see your brother when he performed at the *Fiera del Cacio?*

"Yes, every year."

"What did you think when he performed with your father a few years ago?"

"He was so good! I couldn't believe it! My Papa is really good, some people say he's the best in the world, but Alfonso was good, too. He kept up with our Papa really well. Everybody said so."

"Did you talk to Alfonso after it was over?"

"I told him how good he was and he hugged me."

"He hugged you, you didn't hug him?"

"Well, we both did."

"And did he say anything?"

"He said…he said…he said that someday…that someday I would be as good as he was."

Tears streamed down Luca's cheeks and Doctor Bruni gave him a couple of tissues. They sat quietly for a long time.

"Luca, would you like to become a flag thrower?"

Luca looked around the room, at the ceiling, at the Botticelli, at the floor. "Yes." His voice could hardly be heard.

"Why, do you think?"

"I think I'd like to learn all those things. The way they throw the flag and catch it and then throw it to each other. It's so complicated but it's so beautiful. It's like watching a movie. I think if I could do that, then I would know that I could do something nobody else could. Well, not a lot of people."

"And the cheers of those who saw you? Would you like that?"

"Yes, that, too."

"So it wouldn't matter that your father and brother had done this, you would be doing this on your own?"

"Yes."

"Luca, I imagine you would compare yourself to Alfonso sometimes. But remember that Alfonso was Alfonso. And your Papa is your Papa. You are you. So I think you should try to think of this as a new adventure. Enroll in the school and see how it goes. Learn the techniques, learn the maneuvers. And practice, practice, practice. And when you do something that's really good, something that you can be proud of, think of Alfonso looking down and saying, 'Good job!' You'll be fine, Luca. You'll be fine."

DEEP IN THEIR THOUGHTS, Guiseppe, Maddalena and Luca remained silent on the way home and then sat at the kitchen table. Each had a note pad.

"I'm glad you decided, Luca," Guiseppe said. "And remember you can always change your mind. But for now you should start thinking about *Piccoli Bandierai*. It starts in March, right after your birthday, about five months from now. So there's time for two things. First, you have to gain some weight. You should gain at least ten pounds. That will get you up to almost one hundred and ten, which is probably what the other boys in the school weigh."

"I'll be in charge of that," Maddalena said. "You know how I love to make pasta and we can start off every meal with pasta. We can have a different kind every night. Farfalle, tortellini, macaroni, rigatoni, spaghetti, bucatini, cavatelli, fettuccine. Oh there's tons."

"Won't you run out?" Luca asked.

"Never."

"OK," Guiseppe said, "and the second thing is you have to build up some muscles and strength. You should use the treadmill in the study. Start at twenty minutes and build up. And you should start running. Start slow, only a mile or two, and then build on more. Also, you know how *sbandieratori* toss and twirl and throw their flags? They can't do it without strong wrists. I'll show you some exercises and you can squeeze a tennis ball whenever you have a chance."

Fortified by plenty of pasta and having registered hours on the treadmill and in exercises, Luca gained more than four pounds by the end of November and he felt stronger.

"Great!" Maddalena and Guiseppe said when they looked at the scale.

"Want to ease up?" Guiseppe asked.

"No! I'm good."

Because of the route he took, Luca's three-mile run every day took him past Mauro's house. That route was planned, of course, because Luca hoped Gabriella would be out in front talking to her girlfriends. On some days she was.

"Faster! Faster!" she would call, and Luca would grin and speed up a little. It was the highlight of his day.

Near the end of December Luca had gained another pound and a half and the family took a break to enjoy Christmas in Pienza.

In Piazza Pio II they toured the stands and little markets. They bought panini and gelato and sat on the stone benches to enjoy a jazz band and a children's choir. After admiring the large nativity scene in the nearby Church of San Francesco, they emerged to witness the lighting of the Christmas bonfire in the piazza. Then it was time for what Guiseppe always called "the stupidest game on Planet Earth."

It was an ancient game and no one knew why it was still being played. Yet here they were, six teams from the town's *contrade* ready to compete in *Il Gioco del Panforte*. With almost no rules, contestants threw the traditional round Christmas cake called *panforte* across a table, trying to get it as far as possible without it falling off. That was it.

"I can't believe they still do this," Guiseppe said. "Climate change is ruining us, Italy's government is falling apart again, migrants are being turned away from our shores and here we have grown men and women watching other grown men and women throw a cake across a table."

"Oh, lighten up," Maddalena said. "This has been going on for centuries. It takes our mind off bad things for a little while."

"I hope nobody eats that thing," Luca said. "I hate it. It's too sweet."

"That's because it's made of so many spices and dried fruits and nuts," his mother said.

The first contestant stood at the end of a long table, holding a six-inch round *panforte* wrapped in white paper. He lobbed it across the table and it landed five inches from the end, a fact duly noted by the scorekeeper, an elderly woman wearing a bright red dress and green scarf. Another young man stood, threw the cake too hard and it skidded off the table. Loud boos ensued.

There were cheers each time the following throws saw the cakes just reach the end of the table. After a half hour, the team from *Contrada del Gozante* had won the requisite six points and the crumbling *panforte* was tossed in a nearby garbage can.

Guiseppe, Maddalena and Luca walked away with the rest of the crowd.

"OK," Guiseppe said, "enough of that. Let's have a little tour of the piazza."

In a region famed for its postcard-ready hill towns, Pienza stood out as sublimely perfect. It was designed that way.

Originally known as the village of Corsignano, Pienza was the birthplace and home of Enea Silvio Piccolomini, a Renaissance humanist, poet and politician who became Pope Pius II in 1458. As pope, he used his money, power and influence to commission the rebuilding and renaming of Corsignano into Pienza. With astonishing architecture and art, it has been called an outstanding example of a perfect Renaissance town.

Centered on the piazza named for him is the pope's own home, Palazzo Piccolomini, with magnificent loggias on all three floors and the Piccolomini Museum on the first. (Scenes from Franco Zeffirelli's "Romeo and Juliet" were filmed here). Behind the palace are the exquisitely trimmed Piccolomini hanging gardens, itself a tourist attraction. Circling the piazza are Palazzo Comunale, or city hall; the Bishop's Palace with another beautiful museum, and the Cathedral of Santa Maria Assunta with its own museum. Nearby are Palazzo del Tesoriere and Palazzo Lolli, not to mention Palazzo Tommaso Piccolomini and Palazzo Salomone Piccolomini, once homes for the pope's relatives.

The family stopped at each until their eyes glazed over.

"OK, enough of the Renaissance for a day," Guiseppe said after the last stop. "Let's go home."

On the way, Guiseppe explained the six *contrade* that make up Pienza. The districts, he said, were created only in 1962 by a grass roots organization that wanted the town to have more personality. Each *contrada* has its own color.

"We live in *Contrade del Casello,*" he said. "Our color is yellow and that's why we wear yellow scarves. That announcer at the *Fiera del Cacio* wore a black scarf because he lives in *Contrada del San Piero,* and the scorekeeper at that stupid *panforte* game wore green because she lives in *Prato*. Those in *Case Nuove* wear purple, those in *Gozzante* wear red, and those in *Le Mura* blue.

"But obviously, Pienza was inspired by the seventeen ancient *contrade* in Siena. Siena's are famous because they inspire such an identity for the residents. They have their own banners and symbols and slogans. They even have their own little churches and museums.

"And there's a fierce rivalry, especially when each district has an entry in the Palio, the horse race that's run in the main piazza twice a year."

"I remember when we went there," Luca said. "I was only six but I remember."

"Yes, and Alfonso was thirteen."

At the mention of his name Maddalena gripped her husband's hand tighter, Luca fell behind and no one spoke until they were safe at home.

WITH THE WEATHER OFTEN BLISTERY in the new year, Luca gave up his outdoor run and added some time on the treadmill. He only saw Gabriella in a hallway at school now, but he did notice that every time she saw him she smiled and said, "Hi, Luca." He could barely concentrate in the next class.

By the end of February he had gained eleven pounds, slightly over the goal his father had set, so his fourteenth birthday was especially memorable:

A chocolate cake, but more important, a drone with an HD camera that captured live video.

"Oh, wow, oh, wow, oh, wow!"

"The ad says it's for adults but I think you can figure it out," Guiseppe said. "Don't expect me to help, though. I can barely work my camera."

"I've always wanted one of these!"

"Always? They've only been out a few years."

Luca began counting the days until the start of *Piccoli Bandierai* on the twentieth of March. He helped himself to more pasta every night and stayed on the treadmill longer. His parents looked on with some trepidation.

Luca knew he was forcing himself, and every once in a while he thought: "What if I mess up? I can't mess up."

The day finally arrived and after hugs from his parents he set off for the school in an abandoned warehouse on via Santa Caterina. He was early, but so were twenty or so other boys. Luca didn't know any of them, which was odd in a town of two thousand people, but he never did make friends easily.

One boy edged closer.

"Hi. My name is Francesco. Francesco Muti. What's yours?"

"Luca. Luca Marceri."

"Marceri? Are you the son of Guiseppe Marceri? The most famous flag thrower in the world?"

"Yes."

"And Alfonso Marceri was your brother?"

"Yes."

"Hey!" Francesco shouted. "Listen up! This guy's the son of Guiseppe Marceri! And his brother was Alfonso Marceri!"

Luca was soon surrounded by a dozen boys asking him what it was like to be the son and brother of such famous flag throwers. Luca blushed and made up a few answers.

Then one of the boys said, "I saw your brother twice. He was really good. Wasn't he killed in an accident?"

"Yes."

"I bet you're going to be just as good as your brother," the boy said. "The rest of us won't have a chance."

Luca blushed and didn't say anything. He edged out of the crowd and stood against a back wall.

"It's starting," he thought.

Fortunately, the instructor arrived then, a tall man, about sixty years old, with closed-cropped hair and bulging muscles.

"*Buongiorno!* My name is Vito Capelli. I was once the captain of *Gruppo Sbandieratori a Musica Pienza* but I found the need to retire four years ago. That's when Guiseppe Marceri took over and I have to say he's a better flag thrower than I ever was. Now, let's see who's here."

Vito began to call the roll. When he got to Luca Marceri there was much whispering, and Luca's face became almost as red as the flag on the wall.

"Marceri?" Vito said. "The son of Guiseppe? I am honored to be your mentor but I'm certain your father could be a better teacher. And the brother of Alfonso? I knew your brother well. A fine young man and a fine flag thrower. A tragedy that he left us. You can be proud of him."

Everyone now stared at Luca and a few applauded. Luca felt his eyes sting.

"I'm gonna mess up. I'm gonna be terrible."

"All right," Vito said. "In order to be a flag thrower you must first understand the history of this great tradition."

Flag throwers, then known as flag wavers, were used at the end of the Fourteenth century as "signalers" during the many wars between municipalities in Italy, he said. They were used to communicate between various regiments, waving their banners to indicate the best moments to attack, what movements should be carried out and the important phases of the battles.

The flags were made of fabric or leather in different colors, sometimes many colors, so that they could be recognized by their troops.

"Only good soldiers could be entrusted with the flags," Vito said. "They had to be faithful and imaginative and know different languages so they could understand the enemies. If they were captured, they could not reveal secrets or the signals they used. Upon pain of death."

"Death?" one boy asked.

"Yes. You know flag throwing was actually taught in military academies at that time. But when the wars ended—finally, thank God!—the tradition of flag waving was not abandoned. Instead, groups were formed to preserve the heritage. Now they are accompanied by drums and bugles, they wear colorful costumes that reflect the Middle Ages, and they perform intricate and elaborate maneuvers that thrill crowds. Just like you're going to do with the *Gruppo Sbandieratori a Musica Pienza.*"

Vito asked if there were any questions. There were none.

"You know," he added, "you can be proud to be part of this group. There aren't many *sbandieratori* in Italy now, and most of them are in Tuscany. Pienza may be the smallest town anywhere to have a group."

The boys exchanged proud looks.

"All right. We're not going to be throwing any flags today, but you need to get used to some things. First, you need to learn how to carry a flag and march with it."

He handed each boy a well-worn flag and tapped his phone until the sounds of drumbeats rang throughout the room.

"These flags are old, but they'll do. Now hold the flag over your right shoulder and start marching single file. OK, not so fast. Don't raise your knees so high. Backs straight. Hold the flags firm, don't let them droop. Keep a steady pace."

The boys marched around the edge of the room six times and then Vito asked them to walk in pairs. There was much confusion before they got into the rhythm. Then in threes. Then fours.

"OK, let's do it all over again. First single file, then in pairs, then threes, then fours. Good!"

The most that could be said was that they were better when they finished than when they started.

"All right, that's enough for today. Put the flags on the table over there and I'll see you again next Saturday."

As the boys milled around, Luca could see some of them pointing at him and he heard his brother's name whispered. At the door, a freckle-faced boy stopped him. "Are you really Alfonso's brother? Wow!"

Maddalena and Guiseppe didn't understand why Luca was so quiet when he came back home.

"Was the first day good?" his mother asked.

"Yes."

"Did you meet a lot of other boys?" his father asked.

"Yes."

"Well, next week will be better."

That night Luca turned his brother's picture against the wall.

WHEN MADDALENA cleaned Luca's room the next day she saw Alfonso's picture turned away and, being an intuitive mother, quickly deduced what was going on.

"Guiseppe," she said when her husband returned from work, "what we feared would happen is already happening. Luca's being identified as Alfonso's brother at the school. I guess he's going to have to live with that."

"Poor kid. I didn't think this would happen so soon."

"What should we do?"

"I don't know. If we coddle him he's not going to get the confidence he needs, not just now but in the future. Remember what Doctor Bruni said. Alfonso was Alfonso. Luca is Luca. I think he'll come out of this."

"After a rough start."

Maddalena suggested that perhaps Guiseppe could coach their son a little on some of the basics, but Guiseppe was adamant.

"He needs to do this on his own. He can't have his father teach him. Vito is a great coach. Luca will be fine."

They didn't get to talk to Luca after his school ended because he went off with Mauro to do more testing of the drone and its camera. Happily, Gabriella came along, which made Luca so nervous he could barely manage the controls.

"Wow, this is so cool," Gabriella said. "Can I try?"

That meant that Gabriella held the controls while Luca stood right behind her holding her arms. He could barely stand it and he was sure she could feel his heart beating. Mauro made obscene gestures.

The drone kept them occupied in the next days, but on Friday night Luca's parents noted that he disappeared after dinner. Washing the dishes in front of the window to the backyard, Guiseppe saw something move outside.

"Maddalena, come here."

Under the pale glow of a lamplight, Luca had a broom pole over his shoulder and was marching all around the perimeter. He stumbled on the grass or a rock every once in a while but generally walked smoothly with his back firm. When he came in a half hour later his mother looked up from her book.

"What were you doing outside?"

"Nothing."

"OK. Have a good time tomorrow."

Vito began the class on Saturday by calling the roll, and again Luca felt the eyes of the other boys on him when his name was read. Vito then distributed the old flags and had the boys march around the vast room singly, in pairs and in threes.

"And today," he said, "we're going to learn some basics."

He told the boys to form a large circle, separating themselves by six feet and about ten feet from the wall.

"Now, stand firm and look straight ahead. The flag pole should be on your right shoulder. Don't move."

He put on the tape with the drum beats.

"Now, in a quick gesture, kneel on your right knee. Just the right."

More boys than could be expected didn't know their right leg from their left and there was much bouncing around until everyone got it right.

"Now stand and hold the flag out in front of you, raised just a little. Your hand should be about ten inches from the end."

Some boys had trouble figuring out the correct distance and looked from one to another.

"Now slowly twirl the flag around and around. Good. Carlo, you're going too fast. Antonio, look ahead, not at the flag. Luca, you're going good. Really good."

Vito told the boys to stop and had them repeat it all again. And again. Some boys still weren't getting it right.

"Luca, you seem to have the hang of it. Come over here and demonstrate."

"Me?"

"Yes, please."

Reluctantly, Luca moved to the middle and Vito turned the drum beats louder.

"OK, do the routine."

Luca went through the drill five times and Vito patted him on the back.

"Good job. Must be in your genes."

The drills continued. Vito had the boys turn and face the wall and repeat what they had just done, the kneel, the flag out front, the twirl. Again and again.

"OK, let's take a break."

Two boys came up to Luca.

"I'll bet you know all this stuff already," one said. "Your Papa and your brother must have taught you."

"No. They never taught me anything. I didn't even think I wanted to be a flag thrower until after the *Fiera del Cacio* last year."

"Really? Come on."

When they returned to their places Vito told them to team up in pairs. Immediately four boys approached Luca.

"Can I be with you?"

Looking down, Luca pointed at the first boy.

"OK," Vito said, "let's do the same as before but this time synchronize your movements so that the two of you are doing the same thing at the same time."

Much confusion and then over and over. Luca had to wait for his new partner to catch up to basic movements.

"OK, that's it for today. Next time we'll go outside and learn how to throw a flag. See you next week. Luca, could I see you for a minute?"

Vito put his arm around Luca's shoulder. "Luca, I know you're bearing the fame of your father and brother. You don't need to. You're showing some excellent talent. You have the right skills and knowledge. You know the moves. It will take a while, but I think you're going to be one of the best members the *Gruppo Sbandieratori a Musica Pienza* has ever had. OK?"

"OK!"

Luca smiled all the way home.

"How'd it go today?" his father asked.

"Great!"

He turned Alfonso's photo back around.

WITH THE DRONE to occupy Luca's time, not to mention being near to Gabriella, the week went quickly, and Saturday soon arrived. Vito told the group to go into a large field a block away. The boys cleared out some rocks and debris and formed a circle.

"All right," Vito said, "Now start as you did inside last week with the kneel. Then stand and twirl your flag back to front, back to front."

Many flags scraped the ground and many more were dropped. Vito patiently gave them time to get used to handling these awkward extensions of their right arms.

"Now twirl them front to back."

More confusion.

This went on for forty-five minutes until a break. The boys on either side of Luca told him he had better control than they had.

"Thanks."

"All right," Vito said, "let's try an actual throw. Start by twirling the flag as you just did and then faster and faster and when you feel you've got enough speed and momentum let it go into the air."

The boys did just that, and all the flags fell on the ground.

"OK, that's good. Let's do it again."

After two hours, Vito called a halt. "Next week, we're going to try to actually catch them."

Vito slapped Luca on the shoulder as he was leaving. "Good work."

"Signor Capelli, can I ask something?"

"Of course."

"Can I take a flag home to practice?"

"Well, sure. No boy has ever asked that before."

Under the lone light in the back yard, Luca learned in the following week not only how to improve his throw but actually catch the flag a couple of times.

It was now May. In successive weeks the boys learned to catch their flags—most of the time—and move on to throwing them higher and then to throwing them to each other.

Vito cheered them on. "You're doing great! All of you!"

School ended the second week of June and Luca could spend days as well as nights practicing. It consumed him.

He rarely saw Mauro any more. Although Mauro had been fourteen for more than a year, he refused to join the *sbanieratori*.

"Those tights are girly," he declared.

The real reason, Gabriella told Luca, was that Mauro was so uncoordinated he would have absolutely no ability in twirling a flag, much less throw and catch one.

"But you're going to be one?" she said. "Oh, Luca, I'm so proud of you! You're going to be so great! I'll come and watch!"

"Better yet," Luca said, "why don't you come on over and I'll teach you some of this."

Much to Mauro's disgust, he was left behind as Luca and Gabriella practiced in his back yard. With an extra flag that Luca obtained, Gabriella actually had a knack for this, and together they formed a precision team.

"Luca," she said one night, "do you think they'd let me join the *Gruppo Sbandieratori a Musica Pienza?*"

"A girl? As a *sbandieratori?* I've never heard of such a thing. But I could ask."

Vito scratched his head when he heard Luca's question.

"Well…well…well, a girl? Well, why not? But I think I should see what she can do first."

The other boys winced when Gabriella arrived. On the one hand, she was a girl. On the other hand, she was a *girl.*

Luca and Gabriella went to the middle and began to perform. Luca threw his flag high and Gabriella threw it higher. He threw his to her, she threw hers to him. The boys were amazed, and at the end Vito told Gabriella to "stand over there with the others."

In the middle of August, with the *Fiera del Cacio* fast approaching, Vito told the group he would distribute uniforms the following week so that adjustments could be made.

"Guiseppe," Maddalena said, "Alfonso's uniform is still in a box in the closet. I could trim it in for Luca, it wouldn't be a problem."

"I don't think so. Luca has done all this on his own. I think he has left Alfonso's shadow behind. This would only bring it back."

On the Saturday of *Fiera del Cacio* Guiseppe and Luca put on their uniforms and paraded around the living room. Maddalena took selfies and the three of them headed off to Piazza Pio II. The cheese competition seemed interminable, but then the sound of drums could be heard under the arches of Palazzo Comunale. The drummers filed in and the dozen young *sbandieratori* followed, two by two. The uniforms looked freshly cleaned, long red vests over white shirts and black tights with a strip down the right leg. They carried huge flags with four large squares, two in red and two in white. As always, the cheers were deafening.

At first Maddalena, seated with friends in front of Palazzo Piccolomini, couldn't find Luca among the dozen boys marching in. Then she saw him next to a *sbandieratori* with long blond hair.

"My God," she whispered. "He looks so much like Alfonso. But no, Luca is Luca. And that must be Gabriella! She's beautiful!"

The performance began. Four on four, the young flag throwers moved to the middle and began to twirl their flags. Then they tossed them in the air and then to each other, catching them proudly and firmly. Over and over and over.

"Ohhhhhhhh." "Ahhhhhhhhh." "Ohhhhhhhh."

As always, there were no stars, no one who stood out because this was a synchronized, precision team event. But that didn't stop Luca from smiling when the performance was over. He knew he had done well. He knew that he might not be better than everyone else, but he was just as good. Next to him, Gabriella gave him a slight elbow to the ribs and he smiled.

Luca saw his father standing alone under the arches. He was looking at Luca and pumping his fist. From high above the piazza Luca thought he heard a voice.

"Good job."

LETTERS FROM THE FRONT

Italy's involvement in World War I was disastrous. More than 650,000 Italian soldiers were killed and more than one million were seriously wounded. But the story can probably best be told through a single soldier.

FIRST LETTERS

15 May 1915
On the train to Venice
Cara Lucia,

We are on the train to Venice and I have a few hours to write. In Venice we will board transports to take us north.

Although it has been only a few hours since we left Florence, I miss you so much already. I can still see you waving as the train left the Santa Maria Novella station. You became smaller and smaller as I watched until you disappeared altogether.

Lucia, I am very sorry we had the argument yesterday. I know you don't understand the reasons why I enlisted. I know there are many people who don't understand. But when I joined with the other students in Bologna it was because we wanted to help Italy. We wanted to drive those bastard Austrians back and reclaim our territory. This is just continuing the efforts at national unification that Garibaldi and Cavour began a half century ago.

I know you say you don't like to talk politics. But, Lucia, this is not about politics. This is for Italy's solidarity and its future!

Here on the train, a group of soldiers has begun to chant, "Trento and Trieste!" They want to reclaim these territories from Austria. They belong to Italy! We know the king didn't want war. The politicians didn't want war. The Church didn't want war. But the people wanted war! They demanded war!

That's why I joined the army. I know I am only one person, but I want to do my part. I am ready to fight!

Lucia, please don't cry. I can't stand it when you cry. I love you so much. We have been together for three years now. When this is over let us talk about our future together. We need to be settled before we can make any decisions.

I don't think this war will last very long. Italy has a strong army with strong commanders. I can't wait to get involved! "Trento and Trieste!"

Now I want to write a letter to my Mama so I can send these when we get to Venice.

Lucia, I love you so very much. I am so happy that you will wait for me until I get back. I hope that will be soon.

I will enclose the address where you can write to me.

Ti voglio tanto bene,
Filippo

22 May 1915
Florence
Caro Filippo,

I received your letter today and will write right away.

Filippo I miss you so much. When I was standing on the platform watching the train leave I began to cry. I think of you all the time. When I'm alone at night I long to have your arms around me and I just want to hold you again.

No I still don't understand why you joined the army. Pietro next door said he didn't join and he tells everyone he's not going to join and get killed. He called you a "fool" for joining. I know you are not a fool, but I wish you had just stayed in school and got your law degree. Then you could practice law after we are married.

Filippo sometimes I think about the apartment we will have. I have even decorated it in my mind! There will be a small kitchen where I will make your dinners when you come home from work and I will bake the cookies that you like. We will have a little sitting room and you can read your books while I knit something. (Perhaps it won't be long before I will knit some small clothing!) And of course there will be our bedroom. I think it should have a blue bedspread, don't you? It makes me so happy to think we will be together in our little home.

As soon as you come home, we will go to the priest and make the arrangements. My Mama and Papa said that they will be glad when I am married and they won't have to worry about me anymore. I don't know why they worry about me.

Filippo, I will wait for the postman every day until I receive another letter.

Con tutto il mio amore,
Lucia
xxxxxxxxxxxxxxxxxx!

—————

15 May 1915
On the train to Venice
Cara Mama,

Mama, I am writing on the train to Venice. Then we will go north.

Can you believe that I will be in Venice! I have seen so many pictures and it looks so beautiful! Maybe I will be able to see St. Mark's Square and Santa Maria della Salute from the train. I remember your stories about going to Venice on your anniversary and having coffee in St. Mark's Square. I know you and Papa were so happy then. I miss him every day.

Mama, I know you didn't like it that I joined the army but please do not worry. Italy has a big army and I am sure I will be safe. I may not even get to the front. They will probably put me in a dining hall to serve pasta!

I will write you again when we travel some more. Please take care of yourself. Walk around Florence. It will do you good to get out sometimes. Go to a museum. Keep busy. I will enclose the address where you can write to me.

Il tuo figlio affectuoso,
Filippo

22 May 1915
Florence
Caro Filippo! Filippo, Filippo, Filippo!!!
Mio Caro!

I received your letter today and my hands were trembling so much I could hardly open the envelope. My sister Angelina was here with me and she held my hand when I read your letter. I was crying all the while and she hugged me.

I am glad you will see a little of Venice. Me and your Papa enjoyed our few days there and I remember everything we did. Someday you and I will go there and we will have coffee in St. Mark's Square.

I miss your Papa very much. First he goes and now you go. But I am glad he is not here to know that you have gone off to fight. I don't understand why you did this. You have always been so stubborn Filippo. There have been many times I have cried myself to sleep because you have different opinions than I do. I just want you to stay home and have a nice job and get married and have children. Is that too much for a mother to ask? You are only 22 years old, you have your whole life ahead of you.

I know you don't like it when I say these things, but I am your mother and I love you so much. You are all that I have.

Angelina says I should not think about the war. She wanted me to go to her house when the grandchildren were there but I get sad when I see other peoples' grandchildren. I want to have grandchildren of my own. So I stayed home and said the rosary.

Filippo writing this has tired me out. Is there any way you could come home soon? Maybe you could get a leave or even a discharge? Did you tell them about your eyesight, that you have to wear glasses? Tell them. Please tell them.

Please, please write again soon.

La tua affectuoso madre,
Mama

SECOND LETTERS

10 June 1915
Monfalcone
Cara Lucia,

We are now in this town called Monfalcone. They say it is in a region called the Carso. It is high in the mountains and south of us is Trieste. When we got here we thought we could get to Trieste in two weeks. Now we don't think so.

Lucia, I didn't know we would be seeing terrible things so soon and I find it hard to write about them. But I think I should let you know about these things because you will be my wife. It is not pleasant, I warn you.

When we got off the train at the Mestre station in Venice there was so much confusion. And the noise! And the smells! There were hundreds of wounded soldiers waiting to be taken to hospitals. They had come from the front. Some of them were crying and screaming and others looked like they weren't conscious. You could smell the blood, and worse, everywhere.

One soldier must have been out of his mind because he kept getting up and screaming for his rifle and they kept pushing him back down. Another one had made a mess in his uniform and nobody took care of him.

I felt so bad. I went up to one of them on a stretcher and offered my hand but then I saw that he didn't even have a hand. The captain pulled me away.

We had time to walk a little around Venice. You wouldn't believe it! It looked like nothing that my Mama and Papa had described from their visit on their anniversary years ago. It is empty because of the bombings by the enemy. People don't go out and there is no light at night except for candles. What if people fell into the canals? The hotels have been turned into hospitals and the shops are closed and St. Mark's has been hidden by planks. It looks like a warehouse. I can't tell my Mama this.

We could have looked around more but the captain ordered us to start marching. We crossed the Isonzo River on 5 June. It is a medium-sized river with a tremendous current. We reached Monfalcone on 8 July. But we found that the Austrians had evacuated. So there will be no fighting here! There are some villagers still here but the shopfronts are shuttered. People are starting to come out now.

There was a rumor that a sweet shop had opened but the soldiers wanted liquor. They found a store that sells liquor and they put the owner in a back room and stole cases of the stuff. Lucia, the soldiers in my unit drink a lot. They say they have to in order to fight. You know I never touch the stuff. I met another guy from Florence, Franco, and he doesn't drink either.

Yesterday the soldiers started ransacking the town. They said they wanted souvenirs so they stole pictures and tablecloths and even clothes. There was one old woman screaming at a soldier when he tried to take something from her shelves. She was beating him with a broom. I thought we were here to fight. I didn't think our soldiers would act this way.

The people of Monfalcone don't seem to welcome us as liberators. The newspapers said that they would cheer us when we arrived. Instead, a lot of the people ignore us on the street. We wonder if we are the heroes we thought we would be.

Lucia, I thought I was so brave when I joined the army. Now I don't think I'm so brave. But when I become fearful I take out your picture and look at it and I know that you love me as much as I love you. I can't wait until I get back.

I know that it is going to be hard soon. I wish you would write me things about what is happening there so that I can think of nice things instead of bad things.

Con tutto il mio amore,
Filippo

22 June 1915
Florence
Caro Filippo,

I received your letter two days ago. I started to read it then, but it made me sad so I put it aside. I tried two or three other times but I couldn't read it all the way through. I told Papa to read it and tell me anything I needed to know.

Filippo, you don't have to tell me all these things. Can't you write about the scenery or the food or something? I can read about the battles and everything in *La Nazione* if I wanted to. Papa reads the paper every day and I ask him what is happening in the war but he doesn't answer me.

You asked me to tell you what is going on here so I will tell you what I have been doing. Yesterday Bianca and me went to Ponte Vecchio and looked at all the beautiful necklaces and earrings and rings in the shops. We kept asking each other which one would we buy if we had all the money in the world. Bianca found diamond earrings, the dangling kind, that must have cost a fortune. She asked the shop owner how much they were but he just looked at her and turned his back.

I was looking at engagement rings. Some of them are soooooo expensive, but I found one that is very simple with just one diamond in the middle. I asked the shopkeeper how much it cost but he didn't answer me either. Anyway, I'll keep an eye on it and maybe it will be still there when you come home.

Three days ago I saw your mother in the *mercato* buying vegetables. I was going to say something to her but she didn't look at me.

Do you know yet when you will be coming home? You've been gone almost two months now. I miss you so very very very much!

Con molto amore,

Lucia

xxxxxxxxxxxxxxx

━━◦◦◦━━

10 June 1915
Monfalcone
Cara Mama,

Now we are in this ancient town of Monfalcone. I was able to read about it and I learned that it goes back to the 800's. Imagine! It was once on the trade route from the Black Sea to the Adriatic. Isn't that interesting? There is a big fortress called the Rocca and a big church dedicated to Saint Ambrose but I didn't have time to go in. On the plaza there is a tower built by the Venetians about 500 years ago. I am seeing so much of Italy that I didn't know about.

I hope you are well and keeping busy. Don't worry about me, Mama. I am fine.

Il tuo figlio affectuoso,

Filippo

22 June 1915
Florence
Caro Filippo! Filippo, Filippo, Filippo!!!
Mio Caro!

I thought you would never write again. I have been waiting and waiting. Angelina comes over every day and asks me if I have received a letter from you and every day I have to say that I didn't. But then today I have received a letter!

You didn't say anything about Venice. Isn't it beautiful? I am glad that you are in a nice town called Monfalcone. I have never heard of it, but it sounds very interesting. I am glad that you have time to see the sights. Maybe they don't keep you too busy.

I have been going to different churches to pray for you. The Duomo, of course. Santa Maria Novella. Santo Spirito, Santa Croce, San Marco, San Lorenzo. There are so many. Some of them are far away and my legs hurt by the time I get there and I'm out of breath and I have to sit for a while. I hope you come home before I run out of churches.

I say the rosary three times in each church and I light two vigil candles, one for Papa and one for you. At night I say the rosary again. Filippo, I think about you all the time. Are you sure you are telling everything that is going on? You know how I worry, but you don't have to hide anything from me.

The other day I saw that girl Lucia when I was buying vegetables in the *mercato*. I know you have been seeing her and I know you don't want me to know. I don't think she saw me and I didn't stop. She was wearing a bright red dress and she had a lot of red lipstick. I never use lipstick.

Don't worry about me. Just take care of yourself.

La tua affectuoso madre,
Mama

THIRD LETTERS

15 July 1915
Monfalcone
Cara Lucia,

They brought a stack of mail yesterday so I will answer.

I've started a diary and after all this maybe I will write something about what I've seen and heard here. If you don't mind, I would still like to write things in my letters to you. You can let your Papa read them if you don't want to. I can't write these things to my Mama.

We are back in Monfalcone after some very bad days. I thank God I'm still alive and haven't been injured.

The captain said our goal was to capture Mount San Michele on the Isonzo River. We had to take it in order to get to Trieste. You might think it is one mountain, but it is actually four hills in one. We started on the morning of 1 July at the village of San Martino del Carso near the river. There had been a thunderstorm and it was still raining and the woods were muddy.

The captain had us stop for a few hours to dry out. Then all of a sudden I heard the sound of a trumpet and we started climbing up the hill. Someone shouted "Savoy!" and another one shouted "Trento and Trieste!" and everyone joined in. We heard the enemy shout *"Zivila Austrija!"* That means "Long Live Austria." We were only 100 or 200 meters apart.

I never thought we would go into battle with the sound of a trumpet. It seems like something they would do in ancient days.

We fought hard but they outnumbered us. The Austrians are far better equipped than we are. Their trenches are deep and ours are shallow. When we got close they began firing machine guns. We had only a few 149-millimeter guns. Men went down one after another. This was the first time I had seen men get killed right in front of me. The captain forced us to continue.

The captain asked for reinforcements from the High Command but it refused. It said "The time is not yet ripe." I don't know what that means. I suppose it means they don't have reinforcements so we're left on our own.

So we fought on. I kept running but I had to jump over dead bodies. Dead bodies of men I had eaten with just a few hours before! And then it started raining again. We retreated and went back to our trenches. We have lost this battle but the captain said there will be others.

At night, the captain ordered us to bring back the bodies. I was with my friend Franco and we were both crying. Carlo. Luigi. Alfonso. Our friends. We had to dig through the hard clay to bury them and our shovels kept breaking. There were a lot of dead horses out there too. We didn't try to bury them. The stench is unbearable.

The nights are long. We try to sleep on top of our capes. We can smell dead things in the bushes by the side of the road. We have all been infested with lice and we can't get rid of them.

These days my friends talk about what happened. Somebody asked if we hated the enemy and another fellow said no, we were just under orders. War is war, he said. It's very strange. We fight against each other but then we realize we are all human, Austrians and Italians. We took some prisoners and sent them down to Italy to work. We heard that when the Austrians take our men they offer them good food because they know we have nothing.

This is a strange war, Lucia. I don't think I will ever understand.

Lucia, I will never be able to afford a ring from the Ponte Vecchio but we will find a place where we can buy one. I can't wait to put it on your finger!

Lucia, I don't know if you can read this. My hands are still shaking. I have to end this now.

Con tutto il mio amore,
Filippo

25 July 1915
Florence
Caro Filippo,

I received your letter of 15 July but I couldn't read it. It was too sad. My Papa said that *La Nazione* called it the Battle of the Isonzo. He said there were 15,000 Italian casualties. I can't even imagine how many that could be! I am so glad you were not one of them.

Here is more about Florence. I have to tell you what Bianca and me did last week. We went to Ponte Vecchio again and there is a new tradition started. It is under the statue of Cellini in the center of the bridge. You know where it is, we have been there many times. Remember we kissed for the first time there! I will never forget it.

Anyway it is now a tradition for lovers to put padlocks on the fence in front of the statue with their initials on it. Then they throw the key into the Arno. That means that their love will last forever. Well Bianca had two locks and she wrote her and Nico's initials on one of them and put it on the fence and locked it and threw away the key. She said that means that she and Nico will get married. She is going to tell him soon.

She gave me the other lock so I wrote our initials on it—F.M. and L.S.—and I locked it and put it on the fence and threw the key into the river. That means that you and I will be lovers forever! Waiting for you!

Con molto amore,

Lucia

xxxxxxxxxxx!

15 July 1915

Monfalcone

Cara Mama,

We have been to the village of San Martino del Carso. I have to thank the Italian government for letting me see all these pretty little villages. I wouldn't have seen them otherwise.

Il tuo figlio affectuoso,

Filippo

25 July 1915

Florence

Caro Filippo,

Caro Filippo, you write such short letters! I wait and wait for your letters and when they come they are so short! And they don't tell me much about how you are! I imagine you are busy now with the war going on. I see *La Nazione* on the newsstands and I see the big headlines but I don't ever buy the paper. I don't want to read about it because I'm afraid they will say something about where you are.

Last week I went to see the priest and told him how worried I am and I can't sleep at night and I don't want to eat anymore. He said I should try to be calm and to pray more. But I pray all the time! I go to the church here every morning for Mass and afterward I go to all those churches I told you about. I started making a novena for your safety and I know the Virgin Mary will answer me.

The priest said I should try to eat more, too, but I don't have any appetite. My dresses are starting to be too big for me. Angelina said it was good because I could stand to lose some weight. But I am naturally big. I always was even as a girl. And what does she know she's thin as a rail.

Filippo I think I have some good news. Angelina told me about some friends of hers who live over near Santa Maria Novella. She said they have a lovely daughter named Nina. She is 19 years old and finished high school and is going to nursing school. Angelina showed me her picture and she is very beautiful. Angelina said she would introduce me to Nina's parents. Who knows?

I will close now because I need to take in my new black dress so that it fits better.

Take good care of yourself *caro* Filippo. Did you tell your officer about your eye problems?

La tua affectuoso madre,
Mama

FOURTH LETTERS

18 August 1915
Monfalcone
Cara Lucia,

It has been a month since we tried to take Mount San Michele again and it is only now that I am able to write about it. Lucia, it was hell. Even now when I think about it sweat is pouring down my face and my hands are shaking.

It was on 18 July. We were making good progress climbing up the hilltop and everyone was yelling "Savoy!" and we felt we had a chance. We stormed it on 20 July and the Austrians fell back. For the first time we celebrated. Everyone seemed to have a bottle and everyone else drank, some of them too much.

Our captain asked for reinforcements but again we didn't get them and the Austrians began a counterattack the next day. I was with Franco and there were all these craters in the ground and we tried to shoot and run at the same time. We kept falling and getting up. Everyone was. Sometimes rifles went off when we were falling. I saw one soldier shoot another man from our unit by mistake. He shot him in the back!

Then they began shelling us besides shooting. Big canisters that exploded. Franco was hit. Lucia, I watched as he fell and his stomach poured out of him. I can still see it now. I vomited and tried to help him but the captain said we had to fall back.

The captain said we shouldn't take chances, but I couldn't let Franco out there so I went out to get him late that night and I cried all the way back, He was so small I carried him on my shoulders. I buried him as best I could in the hard rocks and I put a little cross over it.

We took the hill twice on 26 July but we weren't able to hold it. So we're back where we started. Again. And the Austrians have the hill.

Lucia, the heat was unbearable and the smells! From the corpses and from—I won't tell you what else there was. It was all over. We're so thirsty all the time. We get a liter of water every day but we suck it dry so fast. Our tongues are swollen, so are our fingers, and our eyes burn.

We lie in our trenches on top of bodies because there is nowhere else to bury them. I can't look at them. And I can't sleep. I try not to scratch the lice. We stare at the sky. The moon seems to be mocking us.

That is a nice custom about the locks on the Ponte Vecchio. Did you have to pay Bianca for the one she gave you? I hope soon this legend will come true!

Con tutto il mio amore,
Filippo

2 September 1915
Florence
Caro Filippo,

Filippo, I didn't want to hear it but my Papa read me *La Nazione* about the war. He said I should know what is going on. He said the papers are calling this the Second Battle of the Isonzo. They are calling it a bloodbath. They say there were 42,000 Italian casualties.

Filippo, I put my hands over my ears. I don't want to hear about this.

I started reading your letter and I gave it to my Papa to read but I told him I didn't want him to read it to me. I am sorry. I just can't.

Life in Florence is pretty much the same. I heard some people talk about the war the other day but I didn't listen. I hadn't gone out at night since you left and Bianca said I was a refuse, or something like that, and she insisted that we go to the cinema. So we went to see *Rapsodia satabuca*, a new film by Nino Oxilia. Oh Filippo it was so beautiful I can't stop thinking about it. It is about this old countess who sells her soul to the devil so she can be beautiful again. The devil makes her beautiful and she floats around in these thin veils in this beautiful palace and everything is so lovely. But then at the end the devil turns her back into an ugly old woman. It was so sad. I couldn't stop crying. Bianca was too. We were bawling!

Filippo the star of the film was Lydia Borelli. I just love her. Remember we saw her in *La donna nuda* last year? I liked it but you didn't. And we saw her in *Memoria dell'altro* and *Fior di male* too. I think I have seen all her films. She is so beautiful don't you think? I can't wait to see another film by her.

I saw your Mama the other day near Santa Croce but she started walking fast so I didn't talk to her.

Con molto amore,
Lucia
xxxxxxxx!

18 August 1915
Monfalcone
Cara Mama,

I am sorry I haven't written sooner but we have been busy. We go out in the day sometimes but then we come back here. We are still in Monfalcone. The moon is very bright tonight.

Please take care of yourself. Give my love to Angelina.

Il tuo figlio affectuoso,
Filippo

2 September 1915

Florence

Caro Filippo,

Another short letter? Well, I won't get upset because I know you are busy. I am just glad that you are well and that everything is going good there and that you can write to me. Every morning I wake up and I think will there be a letter from Filippo today?

I went to see the doctor. I was so surprised. Doctor Tagliani has retired! I was going to him for so many years and he was always so nice. So they sent me to this other doctor. He was so young not much older than you I think. I didn't like this young doctor poking and feeling me all over. I was so embarrassed. I told him about not eating much or sleeping and he gave me some pills but I don't think they help much. What does a young doctor know about pills and things?

I also told him how sometimes I get some little pains near my heart and he examined me and then he said he wanted me to have an "x-ray." I never heard of that. He said it was like a picture of my insides. Can you imagine? What won't they think of next?

He sent me down the hall and there was another young doctor there. Why aren't these young doctors fighting in the war? He had me go behind a curtain and I had to take my dress off and put on this flimsy gown. I felt so foolish. And then I had to stand in front of this screen and turn around front and back and side and side and I couldn't move and I heard a buzzing sound. And then he told me to get dressed and go home. So the first doctor called me a week later and said everything looked good and I should eat well and sleep well. But I can't.

I still get the pains but don't worry about me. You are busy.

I saw your friend Lucia near Santa Croce but I was in a hurry so I didn't talk to her.

La tua affectuoso madre,
Mama

FIFTH LETTERS

25 September 1915
Monfalcone
Cara Lucia,

I know it has been a while since I wrote but there has been a problem with the mail service and we can't mail letters.

I hope you are well. In your last letter you said you had gone to a movie. I remember *Memoria dell'altro* but not the others.

They say we are having a lull in the fighting. Sometimes the Austrians fire at us and we fire back, but we can go days without anything happening. The Carso is barren with lots of holes and it's dangerous to go out there. We have buried more bodies and we stay in our trenches. It seems like every time somebody sticks his head out the enemy fires.

All the people in the villages around here are fleeing. We see them pass by on the road behind us. They have oxcarts and mules and they take some furniture and other stuff. They all look tired and afraid. Yesterday there was a cart with an old man and an old woman and they were both crying. A soldier went up and let them drink from a bottle he had. The woman didn't want to but then she did. The old man downed the rest of the bottle. We all laughed. I know Franco would have liked seeing that. I still miss him.

It is starting to get cold on this mountain. They say the winters are very bad here. Night times are worse than days. It gets very quiet. We watch the moon go through the clouds. Sometimes we hear animals howling.

Lucia, sometimes I wish we would have another assault and get this over with. I hear they call this the Great War but I don't know anything great about it. I can't wait to come home and take you in my arms again.

Con tutto il mio amore,
Filippo

17 October 1915
Florence
Caro Filippo,

Your letter arrived yesterday and Papa read parts of it to me. I felt so sad after. Bianca said I should go to a cinema to feel better. I didn't think

I wanted to but we did. I know you like to hear about cinema so I will tell you about the film.

It was called *Assunta Spina* and it told the story of this laundress who lived in Naples. She was engaged to this butcher named Michele but a nice man called Raffaele was courting her. Michele got so mad he slashes her face and he was arrested. But she tells the jury he didn't do it. Well, I'm not sure what happens next. Something about his being sent to prison but then when he gets out he has to kill somebody. Bianca tried to explain it to me but I'm still thinking about it. I wonder if some day someone will invent something so that we can hear the people talk. Now it's hard to just read the words and sometimes I can't read them fast enough so I get confused.

Anyway, it starred Francesca Bertini. She is so famous. I read that she has made fifty films already. I think we have seen only one, *Histoire d'un pierrot*. I don't know if I like Francesca Bertini or Lydia Borelli better. They are both beautiful but I think their acting styles are different. Bianca says she likes Lycia Borelli better.

Bianca wanted to go to the movie with Nico and she didn't want me to go alone so Nico brought his brother Rico.

I know you are busy, Filippo, but write when you can.

Con molto amore,
Lucia
xxxxxxxx!

25 September 1915
Monfalcone
Cara Mama,

I am sorry that it has been a long time since I wrote to you but we are having some problems with the mail. But I am fine. Don't worry about me.

We are still in Monfalcone. They say it will get colder in winter but we have heavy coats, so we will be warm.

How are you feeling? Are you still having pains around your heart? Should you see the doctor again? Why don't you talk to Angelina about this and she can take you.

Il tuo figlio affectuoso,
Filippo

17 October 1915
Florence
Caro Filippo,

Your letters seem to be getting shorter and shorter but I know you are busy there. I read them over and over and then Angelina comes over and we read them together. I am saving all of them in a pretty box on my dresser. It is next to the photo of your Papa.

Filippo I am going to send you Papa's winter gloves. They are woolen and thick and he hardly ever wore them. They will keep your hands warm. I still have so many things of your Papa's and he's been gone now for almost seven years. I remember it like yesterday when he fell down those stairs. I always have to take out my handkerchief when I think about it.

Yes, I am still having those pains. Angelina says I should go to the doctor again but I don't like to do that. I don't want to go to that young doctor and have to take my dress off again. Maybe he can give me an examination without taking my dress off.

The newspapers here are full of news about the war but I don't read them. Angelina says I shouldn't read them if they make me have pains around my heart.

I have been going to the Chiesa di Sant'Ambrogio every day now because that's where the miracle of the wine that turned into blood occurred. There were so many tourists in the summer but now it's more quiet. I go to the Cappella del Miracolo and say my rosaries for you and then I walk around and look at the works of Filippo Lippi and Sandro Botticelli and Giovanni della Robbia and so many others. I think I like the Botticelli best. It gives me great peace. Your Papa liked to go there, so I say a special prayer for him too.

I don't like to say this but Angelina told me that two times she saw your friend Lucia with that boy Rico. One time was in the *mercato* and the other time was near the Duomo. Angelina said Rico and his brother are not of good stock. That's what she said. I don't know what it means.

I am hoping to meet that girl I was telling you about, Nina. Angelina is going to take me to her house.

Please, Filippo, be careful. I worry so much about you I can't sleep at night. Don't worry about me.

La tua affectuoso madre,
Mama

SIXTH LETTERS

26 December 1915
Monfalcone
Cara Lucia,

Perhaps this letter will not be as sad as all the others I write. There is still a lull in the fighting and I want to tell you what happened on Christmas eve.

Remember how we read that there was this Christmas truce between the Germans and the British and the amazing thing that happened on Christmas eve last year? It was in all the papers.

The German and British trenches were only about fifty meters apart and the British soldiers could hear the German soldiers singing. They were traditional Christmas carols so everyone knew them and everyone started singing. Then the soldiers on both sides got out and crossed over to meet each other in the middle. They greeted each other and shook hands and talked and laughed, as much as they could understand each other. There were dozens of men getting together in broad daylight. Can you imagine? Some of them exchanged food and souvenirs. The Germans even had a few Christmas trees that they put up and somebody had a football and the two sides played a little. After that they went back to their trenches and a few days later hostilities resumed and the war was back on.

The Christmas truce of 1914 is a famous story. I imagine people will be talking about it for years.

Anyway, somebody suggested that we do something like that here because there is the lull in our fighting now and our trenches aren't that far apart. Every once in a while we can hear the Austrians shouting at each other. I think they drink as much as we do. Maybe more. But our commanders got wind of this and sent word that we were forbidden to do it. We'd be severely punished, they said. We heard the Austrian commanders did the same.

Well on Christmas eve we were talking about what we did at home on Christmas. Everybody had a story. A lot of them said they had the feast of the seven fishes on Christmas eve. My friend Antonio said he gave his girlfriend an engagement ring last Christmas.

Then we heard the Austrians singing. It was soft at first but then it got louder. It was Silent Night—*Stille Nacht*. We started singing it too. Then the Austrians started singing another Christmas song, *Still, Still, Still*. So our soldiers wanted to sing an Italian Christmas song back to them and someone started to sing *Gesù Bambino*. You know *Gesù Bambino*, everybody does.

Then we sang some other songs back and forth and somebody threw a snowball over to the Austrians and the Austrians started throwing snowballs back and we did that for a while. We were yelling and laughing and it was fun. Somebody on that side had fire crackers and they set them off. We were afraid to get out of our trenches though.

And then the clouds covered the moon and it got dark and we stopped. But Antonio's mother had sent some Christmas cookies so he gave me some. She sent them in November so they were stale but that was all right. He also had some *vin santo* stolen from the shop in Monfalcone so we had some of that. All in all it was a nice Christmas eve. I suppose last year the soldiers on both sides thought the war was going to end soon and that's why they got together. The war is still going on.

On Christmas day it was bright and sunny and we buried more bodies that had been out in what they call No Man's Land.

I hope you and your family had a nice Christmas.

Con tutto il mio amore,

Filippo

8 January 1916
Monfalcone
Caro Filippo,

Yes! This time I read all of your letter. Every word. I am happy that you had a nice Christmas. But I didn't like the part about what you had to do on Christmas day.

We had a very nice Christmas. Papa and Mama gave me a nice shawl and I gave Papa some tobacco for his pipe and Mama a pretty handkerchief. We had the usual feast of seven fishes on Christmas eve and on Christmas we went to Mass and then we had Mama's ravioli and chicken cacciatore and we had spumoni for desert.

Bianca and Nico and Rico came over in the afternoon and we sang Christmas songs. Of course one of them was *Gesù Bambino!* Rico brought some *grappa*. I had never had that before.

Everyone hopes you have a good and safe new year.

Con molto amore,
Lucia
xxxxxx!

26 December 1915
Monfalcone
Cara Mama,

I hope you had a nice Christmas. It was quiet here in Monfalcone. Some of my friends started singing Christmas songs and I learned some new ones. We played some games too and another friend had Christmas cookies from his mother and we talked and laughed.

What did you do for Christmas? I hope you are looking forward to a new year. Maybe the war will be over. Thank you for Papa's gloves. I will make good use of them.

Il tuo figlio affectuoso,
Filippo

8 January 1916
Florence
Caro Filippo,

I received your letter and am happy that you had a nice Christmas.

I felt bad when I read that your friend's mother had sent Christmas cookies. I could have sent some if I wasn't so stupid. I know how much you love them. I could have made *pizzelle* but I suppose they would have been crumbs by the time they got there. But I could have made *biscotti* or *amaretti* or *cuccidati*. Your friend would have loved them. Why didn't I think of this?

Christmas wasn't so happy here because for the first time I was alone. Papa gone. You off to war. I didn't know what to do with myself. I went to Mass in the morning but there were all those children running around and I couldn't pay attention.

I didn't put up any decorations. I didn't feel like it. The only thing was that little toy truck that you loved so much. Remember we used to put it under the tree. I put it by my chair.

Angelina came over and brought some chicken and trimmings they had for dinner. I waited until after she left to try it but it was cold by then. I made myself a nice bowl of Tuscan bean soup. That was enough for me.

Christmas is just another day. I hope and pray Filippo that you will be here for next Christmas. I don't know what I would do if you were not.

Angelina said she saw your friend Lucia walking along the Arno with that boy Rico on Christmas night and they were holding hands.

La tua affectuoso madre,

Mama

SEVENTH LETTERS

20 January 1916
Monfalcone
Cara Lucia,

Lucia, I am afraid this will be another sad letter.

We are not fighting because it's the dead of winter and we can't move and the Austrians can't move. It started snowing at the end of December and it has probably snowed every day since. We try to keep up with it. We try to dig out the trenches and throw the snow behind us but our shovels are small and useless. The snowbanks are getting very high. But the enemy is in front of us.

Sometimes we go back there and make snowmen. That is our only recreation. But we can't stay long because the Austrians sometimes see us and shoot. We're so thirsty we eat the snow but then we get even thirstier.

It seems like life is suspended. We know that once fighting starts there will be death and death and death.

We don't know why but we are not prepared for this winter. We don't have enough weapons. We don't have enough helmets. Our woolen uniforms are worn thin and our boots often have cardboard soles. We sleep in the hay or mud and pack against each other. We are covered with snow when we wake up.

Some soldiers have typhoid and cholera and the ambulances come every day to take them away them to hospitals.

The only hot meal we get is in the morning and by the time it gets here it tastes so bad we can't eat it. Anyway, it smells so bad here that we don't have any appetite.

And we all smell.

There are some soldiers from Sicily in our unit. They seem to be lost, and don't know what's going on. They're not used to the cold and they huddle together and try to sing but nothing comes out.

Lucia, we are fighting so many things, not just the Austrians.

I know this letter has been filled with complaints. I can't help it. Everybody says the same thing. They swear a lot. And they drink a lot. Sometimes somebody runs into the town and steals bottles and bottles.

I can't write any more. I am too tired, too sad. I can't wait to get out of this hell hole and in your arms again. I love you so much! You're the only thing that keeps me going.

Con tutto il mio amore,
Filippo

14 February 2016
Florence
Caro Filippo,

It is Valentine's Day so Happy Valentine! I received your last letter but as soon as I started reading it I gave it to Papa. He said it was very sad.

Filippo I had such a good time last Tuesday. You wouldn't believe it but they put a carousel in Piazza della Repubblica! And it is so beautiful. It's huge and has twenty horses all painted in blues and reds. It's just like in a carnival! And there's music! There was a long line when we got there and a lot of them were kids but not all of them. When we were going round and round people started clapping and cheering. It was so much fun!

Bianca and me went with Nico and Rico, they're brothers you know, and afterwards we had gelato. I had strawberry. And then we stayed and listened to a guitar player who played very romantic songs.

When you come back we will go to Piazza della Repubblica and take a ride on the carousel. I know you will love it!

Con molto amore,
Lucia
xxxx

20 January 1916
Monfalcone
Cara Mama,

I will write a few lines now when I have time. It is now very cold on the mountains and Papa's gloves give me extra warmth. Thank you! Whenever I wear them I think of Papa.

Mama I don't mind if Lucia goes to movies or for walks. I don't want her sitting home while I'm gone. I love her and trust her completely.

I hope you don't have any more pains. Take care of yourself. Have you seen a doctor again?

Il tuo figlio affectuoso,
Filippo

13 February 1916
Florence
Caro Filippo,

It is cold now in Florence but maybe not as cold as where you are. I wear my heavy coat, the brown one with the fur collar, when I go to the churches. Yesterday I went to Santa Croce. I don't know if I like that church very much. It is so big and all the tombs make me sad. I don't know why they had to bury all those famous people inside of a church.

I guess I am sad all the time now. Your last letter made me sad. Come home soon, Filippo.

La tua affectuoso madre,
Mama

EIGHTH LETTERS

20 March 1916
Monfalcone
Cara Lucia,

My hands are shaking but I am writing tonight because I can't get something out of my mind. I'm sorry to have to tell you about this but I have to tell somebody. I am sorry. Your Papa can read it if you don't want to.

I saw some things in the last week I thought I would never see. I always

thought that in a war there were the good guys and t'
thought the Italians in this war were the good guys. I

Last week some of us were ordered to go to a commu
not far from Monfalcone. Our commander had heard tha
were shooting at our men. I don't know how he heard that. The
aren't supporting the Austrians. They just want to be left alone.

The commander had no proof that this had happened and he didn't try to find out. It was just a rumor. He ordered all the men in the village to go to the central piazza. There were a lot of old men and a few young ones. He lined them up in front of the church. The men didn't know what was going on. The women were screaming and the little kids were crying.

Then he had three of our sharpshooters come up. He pointed out six of the men and ordered our soldiers to kill them. It was over in a minute. We learned later that one of the men was the deputy mayor. Other people from the village were sent off to an internment camp.

Then the commander heard that farmers around the villages of Caporetto and Tolmein were telling the Austrians where we were. Again, he had no proof, just rumors. So he ordered us to go to a central place and ordered about sixty men to line up. Again, the women were screaming. Their wives, old grandmothers, little children. He ordered every tenth man to step forward. Then he ordered our shooters to kill them. Again there were six of them. Then he ordered some of us to bury them right there.

Lucia, I couldn't do it. I couldn't. The women were trying to get at the bodies and the guy I was supposed to bury was younger than me. I couldn't look at him. I started to cry and the commander finally hauled me away and had some other soldier do it.

Lucia I can't get all this out of my mind. We killed innocent people! Oh, I can't wait until this war is over. Every night I think of you as I try to go to sleep. I can't wait to hold you in my arms again.

Con tutto il mio amore,
Filippo

P.S. The carousel in Piazza della Repubblica sounds like fun. We will go on it together when I get back.

rch 1916

ence

aro Filippo,

I received your last letter but as soon as I started reading it I gave it to Papa. He said it was very sad.

I will tell you about the last movie I saw. It was called *Gli ultimi giorni di Pompeii*. It was another movie about the last days of Pompeii. We saw one years ago. This one was about a statesman and there was a pagan priest and a blind beggar and also a beautiful woman. They live in the shadow of Mt. Vesuvius and at the end the volcano erupts.

I don't know. I don't like movies like that. I like romantic ones. The only thing interesting was that it was somehow colorized so that made it a little different.

Bianca had to stay home to babysit her little sister so I went with Rico.

Con molto amore,
Lucia

---

20 March 1916
Monfalcone
Cara Mama,

It is starting to become spring here and the weather is getting warmer.

Thank you for going to all those churches and praying for me. I think I can feel the prayers working. I hope you are well and don't have pains. And I hope you are eating and sleeping good.

Il tuo figlio affectuoso,
Filippo

30 March 1916
Florence
Caro Filippo,

Filippo I have to tell you that Angelina and me went over to her friend's house near Santa Maria Novella and we met Nina and her parents. Remember I told you about her? She is so nice Filippo. She was so interested in what you were doing. I brought your letters along and she had so many questions. She wanted to know where you were fighting and I couldn't answer because you never tell me anything about the fighting. But she knew about Mount San Michelle because she reads *La Nazione* every day. She is very smart. She said there were terrible battles there and I didn't know that. So I didn't know what to say and now that I think about it I feel very sad for you.

But she also asked about you and I told her how you had gone to the University of Bologna and was studying to be a lawyer but that you felt you had to join the army and fight for Italy. She was very impressed with that. She also wondered if you had a girlfriend but I said you didn't. I showed her your picture and she said you were very handsome. She said the glasses make you look intelligent. That's what she said. She said she liked your curly hair and your smile.

When she read your letters she told me I am very lucky to have a son who loves me so much. That made me want to cry.

She said she will get her nursing degree in two years and if the war is still on she would like to go to the front—that's what she called it—and help with wounded soldiers.

I don't think the war will still be on in two years. I hope it ends this year. What do you think Filippo? Do you think it will be over soon and you will come home? Now when you come home you will be able to meet Nina.

La tua affectuoso madre,
Mama

NINTH LETTERS

15 May 1916
Monfalcone
Cara Lucia,

Our unit is angry because two soldiers cut themselves on purpose so they could go to hospital and not have to fight. I've heard of other soldiers doing this but I didn't know anyone who actually did. One cut his arm badly and will be in a sling and the other one almost cut off a finger—his trigger finger as it happens.

That kind of thing demoralizes us all. It's bad enough that we don't have enough soldiers but now we'll have even less. And it seems like an odd way to get out of fighting. Meanwhile the rest of us have to do more of it.

We are still having skirmishes with the enemy. We make some headway and then we have to fall back. Soldiers, sometimes friends of mine, get killed and we bury them and then we fight again. I do it, but I won't ever get used to it.

We thought this was going to be a short war but it is dragging on and on. We get so discouraged. Soldiers are deserting and then they're caught and then they face a tribunal and then they're sentenced. If it's bad enough they could even be sentenced to death. Meanwhile we don't have enough soldiers to fight and the High Command doesn't send replacements.

You know how I felt when I enlisted Lucia. "Trento and Trieste!" and all that. Sometimes I can't believe I felt that way. We've been living in these trenches now for months. Terrible heat and rainstorms in summer, terrible cold and snow in winter. We live in mud and filth. And fight the lice. And we spend a lot of time just waiting around.

Am I afraid? Of course. We all are. But we don't talk about it. I hope that if I am killed it will be quick. I don't want to be injured and have to spend the rest of my life as a cripple.

Lucia the only thing that keeps me going is knowing that you love me and are waiting for me. I hope we will be in each other's arms soon.

Con tutto il mio amore,
Filippo

1 June 1916
Florence
Caro Filippo,

When I opened your letter and saw it was going to be sad again I had Papa read it and he said it was really sad so he didn't read it to me.

I like to tell you happy things to cheer you up so I will tell you what Bianca and me did last week. We went to her aunt Elisabetta who lives over by Santa Croce. She has a beautiful apartment overlooking the Arno and we could see people in *barchetti* sailing up and down. It was so beautiful.

But we went there because Elisabetta is a hair dresser and you know how Bianca and me have always had long hair all the way down our backs. But mine has always been longer than hers. Anyway, we were looking at magazines and all the girls had very short hair. They call them bobs. So we had Elisabetta cut our hair really short like that! You won't believe it. There was a ton of hair on the floor but this is so much cooler and easier to manage.

Nico told Bianca that he liked hers and Rico told me he liked mine.

Con amore,

Lucia

15 May 1916
Monfalcone
Cara Mama,

It has been pretty quiet here lately. Sometimes we play cards. I'm getting pretty good at *scopa!*

Mama, Nina sounds like a nice girl but you know that I am in love with Lucia and I know she loves me. We are practically engaged.

Il tuo figlio affectuoso,

Filippo

1 June 1916
Florence
Caro Filippo,

I received your letter and I have to say Filippo that I was a little upset about what you said about Nina. I think she is a very nice girl and would make you very happy but I am only your mother so what do I know what you want? We will talk about this more when you come home. I hope that is very soon!

La tua affectuoso madre,

Mama

TENTH LETTERS

15 August 1916
Venice
Cara Lucia,

I am in hospital in Venice. A nurse is writing this for me. On 29 June Austrians set off 3,000 cylinders of a mixture of chlorine gas and phosgene. We did not see it coming. I had a gas mask on but many others did not. They keeled over left and right. They said 2,000 men died. My friend Antonio was one of them.

I was lucky. My eyesight is really bad now and they are treating me for some scar tissue on my lungs but I am alive and I feel better than I did when this happened. They don't know if I will ever be all better.

Discharge papers should come soon. I will be back in Florence by 15 September.

All of this has made me want to hold you again even more. We will be together soon, my darling.

Con tutto il mio amore,
Filippo

25 August 1916
Florence
Filippo,

Filippo when you come home I think we have to sit down and have a talk.

Lucia

15 August 1916
Venice
Cara Mama,

I have good news! I will be out of the army and back in Florence by 15 September.

I have written to Lucia, too. I can't wait to see her again.

Il tuo figlio affectuoso,
Filippo

25 August 1916
Florence
Caro Filippo,

I am so excited! How wonderful that you will be home soon. I will start making the cookies you like so much and put them in the ice box. I know what kind of pasta and chicken and steaks that you like so I will go to Luigi's the week before you come and stock up. I will buy a bottle of good wine to celebrate.

As for Lucia, Angelina happened to be walking past Santa Maria della Tromba last Saturday and she noticed that a wedding party was coming out of the church. It turned out to be Lucia and Rico. Angelina said Lucia had a long white dress with a train and she had three bridesmaids. She said Rico's tie was all tangled and he looked like he had been drinking. She said that Lucia looked very much in the family way, if you know what I mean.

Filippo your handwriting looked different in your last letter but maybe you were tired.

Shall I invite Nina for dinner the first night you are home or should I wait a little? I can't wait Filippo!

La tua affectuoso madre,
Mama

A BABY IN THE CONVENT

Sometimes, bad behavior can be explained by a life-changing incident in the past.

BECAUSE HIS WIFE had died years ago and he had no children, the only mourners at Salvatore Cervelli's funeral in the Convento di Santa Illuminata were ancient widows and old men. Father Manfredo came from Siena to celebrate the Mass, speaking loudly so that the elderly nuns behind the screen could hear him. The priest talked of Salvatore's hard life, his good work and his devotion to the good sisters in the convent.

Afterwards, the funeral director's men loaded the casket into the hearse, Father Manfredo went back to Siena, and the nuns gathered in their meeting room. They had an important question that had to be answered immediately. How could they possibly replace Salvatore?

The meeting did not begin well.

"He should have been replaced years ago," the always redoubtable Sister Severina declared. "This place is a mess."

"Now, Sister," Sister Rosetta replied. "He tried. You have to admit he tried. And he was ill for so long. In the last years it was all he could do to sweep the floors."

It was true. Salvatore wanted to do more, but when the roof over the chapel began leaking he placed pails under the St. Joseph statue. The kitchen appliances were from another era. Every inch of every wall needed new paint. And there was much more.

"Well," Mother Augustina said, "let's forget about that and thank God for Salvatore's service—wasn't it forty-two years?—and pray for his soul. Now the important thing is to find a good replacement. I will write to the motherhouse tomorrow and ask that they find another caretaker."

"Not just a caretaker this time," Sister Clara said. "He'd also have to be a maintenance man."

"And an electrician."

"And a plumber."

"And a painter."

"And a gardener."

"And a roof repairer."

"And when one of us has to go to the doctor in Siena—and you know that's becoming more common at our age—he'll also have to be the driver."

Now it must be said that all of the women in the Convento di Santa Illuminata on the western edge of the commune of Monteriggioni south of Siena, were not exactly young. In fact, all were quite elderly. Sister Naomi, the youngest at seventy-seven, had come in 1966 because she didn't like the changes wrought by Vatican II. Sister Lucia, the oldest at ninety-four, spent her days just waiting "for God to take me."

There were now only fifteen left. Resistant to change, they still wore the black habits with the white coif that the Order of the Sisters of Charity of Santa Illuminata had worn for decades. And their days were always the same, rising at 2:30 a.m. to go to the chapel for Matins followed by meditation, some light work, Mass at 7:30, breakfast followed by more work, more prayers. In the afternoon, making holy cards that were sold to parishes throughout this part of Tuscany. At night, an hour of free time, followed by retiring at 9 p.m.

As a cloistered order, they never left the convent. Children in Monteriggioni saw only occasional movement inside the fortress-like building and so were convinced the place was haunted, a belief encouraged by their older siblings.

Now that Salvatore was gone, the only outsiders the nuns saw, except occasionally for the doctor in Siena, were the bearded Father Manfredo, who celebrated Mass on Tuesdays, Thursdays and Sundays, and Signorina Barbone, the cook for the last fourteen years after succeeding her mother who was there for thirty. The good woman came every weekday and prepared meals for the freezer for weekends, although they were not so frozen now that the refrigerator had become erratic.

Three months after receiving Mother Augustina's letter, the

motherhouse replied that it had been unsuccessful in finding Salvatore's replacement but would continue trying. "Patience," the motherhouse said.

"Patience!" Sister Severina replied when it was announced at the weekly meeting. "They wouldn't have much patience if they didn't have any heat because the furnace is broken."

If Sister Severina had been a schoolteacher, her students would have inevitably called her "the crabby nun."

The only solution, they finally decided, was that God would answer their prayers. So they went to the chapel and prayed even harder.

Then Signorina Barbone said she heard a rumor from Father Manfredo. The motherhouse had found a young man to fill the job. He would move into the tiny apartment in the basement in the next week. He would be paid—not much, but paid—to do repairs and the upkeep on the centuries-old building.

"It's going to be wonderful," Sister Clara said.

"I'm so excited."

"Imagine! A young person here! We're all so old!"

Predictably, Sister Severina remained dubious. "Isn't there a rule in our order that no young person can live in this convent?"

"No!" Sister Claudia said. "There's no such rule, and I'm sure we don't care as long as the work is done."

"But we're all old people here," Sister Severina countered. "Let us old people live by ourselves. We don't need a young person around. And besides, he's going to be right below me. I'll say one thing for Salvatore. He was quiet. Never made a sound. This new young man will probably play loud music all night. You won't have to listen to all the racket, but I will!"

Sister Severina got up and went back to her cell. She looked very sad, but she always looked sad. Unlike the other women, Sister Severina stayed by herself most of the time and never took part in the nightly crocheting and knitting sessions. She never talked about her past so no one knew much about her.

The other women shook their heads.

The following week when a big white moving van pulled up in front of the building, fifteen pairs of eyes eagerly peered through the lace curtains at every window at the front of the convent. The nuns in those cells had invited the women who lived in the back to join them.

"There are three men," Sister Benedicta announced as the movers began unloading. "I wonder which one is our new caretaker."

"Two of them are older, so it might not be one of them," Sister Mila said.

"I hope," Sister Severina said, "it's not that skinny red-haired kid. He doesn't look strong enough to fix the vacuum cleaner, much less the furnace."

Changing the subject, Sister Mila observed, "Look at that wonderful rocking chair. Mine is so old."

"And that big cozy chair," Sister Clara said.

"How will this all fit into that little apartment?"

Two hours after the van had left, a small black Fiat pulled up, and all the nuns were summoned to watch.

"My God!" Sister Philomena cried. "It is the skinny kid."

The young man had a reddish crewcut, freckles on his face and a small growth of hair on his chin. He wore a colorful shirt and denim shorts that were slightly ripped at the knees. They watched as he went to the passenger side and opened the door.

"There's a woman!"

"My God," Sister Naomi cried. "There's two of them!"

The young woman had curly black hair that fell to her shoulders. She wore a similar shirt tied at the waist and jeans with holes in the knees. She kissed the man on the cheek and they held hands as they gazed at their new home. The couple unloaded two bicycles from the back of the car.

"They must be a married couple!"

"Let's hope so," Sister Severina said. "We don't want people living in sin here."

"Remember when we were that young?" Sister Naomi asked. "Were we ever that young?"

"I don't think so," Sister Severina said. She looked even sadder.

They watched until the couple had locked their car and entered their apartment."

"She's so young," one sister said. "And so beautiful."

"And," another whispered, "he's quite handsome, too."

THE FOLLOWING DAY, the couple made a point of visiting each of the nuns, introducing themselves and talking about their background. Most of the sisters gushed and said they would pray for them.

The young man explained that his name was Chris O'Toole, he was 24 years old, and he came from Springfield, Illinois, "in the middle of the United States." His father was an engineer for a company there and his mother did data entry for the same firm. He had two younger brothers still in high school.

He came to Italy after college four years ago and traveled around Europe on a motorcycle and "just fell in love with Italy."

"And then I met Patrizia and I really fell in love with it. We've been married six months."

Chris put his arm around his wife and she pinched his cheek.

Patrizia said she was 21 years old and from a town called San Ferdinando not far away, "an old medieval town that gets a lot of tourists." Her father did occasional odd jobs and her mother worked in a *trattoria*. Patrizia had studied at the Florence Academy of Art but became bored and decided to take a motorcycle trip to Germany.

"We met at a hostel in Hamburg and we haven't been apart since."

They grinned at each other as they moved closer together.

Only one sister was not as welcoming as the others. Sister Severina mostly conduced an interrogation.

"So your parents, Chris, don't mind that you married an Italian girl?"

"No, no, of course not. They want to come over and meet her someday. They didn't come for the wedding."

"Why not?"

"We didn't tell them."

"Oh. And you, Patrizia, your parents didn't mind your marrying an American?"

"No! They love Chris!"

"Oh."

Sister Severina noticed something on Chris' wrist.

"What's that?"

"This? It's a butterfly. Isn't in beautiful? Blue and yellow and pink."

"I have one, too," Patrizia said. "Look! We decided to get these little tattoos instead of buying wedding rings."

"A friend did it," Chris said. "People are always losing wedding rings, but we'll never lose these!"

They touched their wrists together and smiled.

Sister Severina could be seen rolling her eyes.

Chris' first job the next day was to replace all the burned-out light bulbs in the convent. Some hallways were so dark, Mother Augustina told him, that she feared some nuns would trip and fall. After a short inspection, Chris returned.

"Mother, I'd like to replace all the lights in the building with LED lamps."

She had never heard of the term.

"They're new," he said. "Well, sort of new. I'll put it simply. They're made differently so they last much longer than these incandescent lamps you have. And they are much more efficient. They're a little more expensive, but in the long run you'll save money."

How interesting, Mother Augustina thought.

"And," Chris continued, "we have to think about our climate, which as you know is in a crisis."

Mother Augustina was only vaguely familiar with global warming problems.

"LED bulbs also help reduce air pollution. So that makes the air healthier to breathe for people who suffer from asthma, heart disease and many respiratory ailments. Did you know that most household energy still comes from coal-burning power plants? A LED bulb uses seventy to ninety percent less energy than a standard bulb, so there isn't a need to burn much coal."

"My goodness. How in world do you know all this, Chris?"

"I don't know. I just do. Young people these days know that we have to protect our planet or terrible things are going to happen."

Without television or newspapers, and only limited use of the radio, the good sisters of the Convento di Santa Illuminata were only dimly aware of the threats brought about by a changing climate. Chris thought he should start doing some educating.

Patrizia found that she should do that, too. That afternoon, the cook, Signorina Barbone, invited her to go shopping with her at the big new supermarket that had just opened outside Monteriggioni "to see what they have that we don't have in our garden."

Patrizia was wary of big enterprises like this, but wanted to see what a supermarket had. Both were overwhelmed by the rows and rows of kitchen supplies, laundry detergent, baking ingredients and so much else besides the meat, vegetables and fruit. By the time they got to the produce section, Signorina Barbone had her cart full but picked out some broccoli, carrots and cauliflower. When the clerk put them in plastic bags, Patrizia made a face.

"Don't they know," she told Signorina Barbone as they left the store, "how dangerous plastic bag are? I just read this: The buildup of plastic in our oceans is so great that some ten thousand marine animals suffocate on bags. Imagine!"

"But I don't throw the bags in the ocean!" Signorina Barbone cried.

"No, but you probably throw them in a garbage bin and they eventually get into the ocean, right?"

The cook was silent. This was too much to consider.

"Listen," Patrizia said, "when we get to the convent, do you have any old nun habits that are just lying around?"

"Two of our sisters died recently so their clothes are still in their cells."

"OK. I'm going to take them and I'm going to make you some big shopping bags. Then you can take them to the supermarket, and you can use them over and over and you never have to use a plastic bag again."

The following day, after Chris had repaired the long-broken washing machine, he watched as Signorina Barbone loaded it.

"Signorina," he said, "how about turning the temperature down to twenty degrees? Your clothes aren't dirty, so that's warm enough. And don't put too many in. The water and detergent need room to swirl around."

Signorina Barbone did as she was told, and Chris complimented her for hanging clothes on the line to dry, the nuns' undergarments modestly concealed inside pillow cases.

The couple turned to improving the looks of the building, and Patrizia began her big project: Painting the walls in all fifteen cells occupied by the nuns. Instead of the institutional gray that had been used for a hundred years, she asked each nun to choose a new color. Delighted, they selected pink, light blue, pastel green, rusty orange. Sometimes they chose a contrasting color for one wall.

"Oh my goodness, oh my goodness" could be heard throughout the building as the nuns returned to their cells after the painting was completed.

In the weeks that followed, most all of the sisters delighted in having the young couple around, fixing something here, making suggestions there. The elderly women were very interested whenever they encountered the young couple in the halls or coming in all sweaty from a bike ride. They fluttered and twittered and asked all sorts of questions.

Sister Severina was particularly observant. When she saw Patrizia pulling weeds in the garden wearing only a bikini top and shorts, she immediately reported this to Mother Augustina. When she saw a shirtless Chris chopping wood, she again went to her superior, though she watched for a good half hour before doing so.

"They're so nice," Sister Lucia told the others. "It seems like they've been here forever."

Sister Severina didn't say anything.

She did say something, though, when the nuns discovered that the young couple planned to adopt a puppy.

"A dog!" Sister Severina said. "Here? In a convent? Salvatore never had a dog."

"Now, Sister," Mother Augustina said, "don't you think a dog will add a little life to this place?"

"No! This is supposed to be a quiet place. We're cloistered after all. A dog will be yelping and barking all the time. It will be a great disturbance."

"Now Sister…"

"And the mess! He's going to do his duty all over the front lawn and little children will play in it, and the postman will step in it, and it will be just awful."

The other sisters were surprised by Sister Severina's reaction when Chris and Patrizia brought up a fluffy tan-and-white cocker spaniel to be introduced.

"Her name is Rosie and she's three months old," Chris said.

"Isn't she adorable?" Patrizia said.

As if on cue, Rosie yelped, ran around the room, climbed up on a chair and then, still yelping, headed for Sister Severina. The dog paused at her feet, then jumped on her lap. Sister Severina made a face and tried to shoo the puppy off. Then she started petting Rosie.

"I had a dog just like this when I was little," she said.

ABOUT SIX MONTHS after Chris and Patrizia had moved in, the women, who were careful to watch their every move, noticed something different. Chris and Patrizia weren't riding their bicycles anymore. Instead, they took walks with Rosie, Chris holding his arm around his wife's waist. Sometimes they stopped and just embraced.

"Isn't that sweet?" Sister Clara said as she looked out the window with the other nuns. The women spent a good deal of time at their windows when Chris and Patrizia were outside.

"Hmmm," Sister Mila said. "Do you suppose?"

"I just wonder," Sister Elisa said.

Then a few weeks later, Sister Lucia stopped and talked with Patrizia in the hall. Even at ninety-four, Sister Lucia rushed upstairs to tell the others.

"You won't believe this," she wheezed. "I just saw Patrizia. She looked pale. I asked her if something was the matter. She said nothing was the matter. She said, she said…"

"What did she say? What did she say?" all of the other women cried in unison.

"She said…she said…" Sister Lucia wheezed, "she said she was fine, but that she was going to have…" Sister Lucia paused again. "She was going to have a baby!"

Sister Lucia collapsed on the sofa in the hall.

"A baby!!!!" all of the women cried.

"A baby here!!!"

"A baby in the Convento di Santa Illuminata!!!"

The women hugged each other, all except one.

"A baby?" Sister Severina said. "All that crying and screaming? Right below me? The Convento di Santa Illuminata is never going to be the same."

"How can you say that?" Sister Rosetta asked. "A baby, any baby, is a blessing!"

Sister Severina didn't answer and went back to her cell. The other women thought she was crying and didn't say anything else. They quickly went back to their own cells and closed the doors behind them.

But during the evening free times in the next weeks and months, there was much activity. Sister Elisa dug out the old knitting bag from back on a closet shelf and began to knit again. Sister Rosetta, who was an excellent seamstress, began to sew something on the ancient machine in the meeting room. Sister Antonella found her crochet needles and began to make something small and delicate.

Everyone was busy with some sort of small task, except for Sister Severina. But one day she went deep into a trunk in the closet and took out a small pink box tied with a pink ribbon. She opened the box, looked inside, tied it up again and put it back in the trunk.

The first weeks of December were cold, and the women observed that Chris and Patrizia wore heavy coats when they took Rosie outside. Patrizia's coat didn't conceal her condition.

Two weeks before Christmas as the nuns gathered for their nightly meeting, they heard a car door slam and the Fiat screech around the corner.

"They're going to the hospital!" Sister Lucia said. "It's time."

They gave up their knitting and reading and went to the chapel to pray.

In the morning, with no sounds from the apartment below, they silently smiled at each other as they passed, and visited the chapel more often.

At noon, they heard the car pull up, then heard Rosie barking.

"He's taking the dog for a walk," Sister Elisa whispered. After all these months, the nuns kept track of the couple's every move.

When they heard the apartment door close again, Mother Augustina whispered that she would go down. She found Chris hunched over the sink, his shoulders shaking.

"Chris?"

He lowered himself deeper into the sink, his whole body shaking.

"Chris?"

When he turned around, she saw tears running down his freckled face. "Oh, Chris."

It was not the custom for members of the Order of the Sisters of Charity of Santa Illuminata to hug someone, but customs could be ignored.

"Thank you, Mother."

Mother Augustina found water and a can of coffee and set a coffee pot to boiling. At the kitchen table, she waited until Chris was ready to talk. They were on their third cup.

"We knew it was going to be difficult. The doctor had told us that the baby was in the breech position—that means bottom first instead of head first."

"I know that."

"So they had to...they had to do a Cesarean. Do you know what that is?"

"Of course. Chris, I was a nurse before I entered the sisterhood."

He drained his coffee cup and she poured another.

"Poor Patrizia is so tired, she's just exhausted. She had such a hard time. For a while the doctors didn't think she'd make it. Mother, I couldn't do anything! Nothing! I just sat there holding her hand. Then they gave her something and she went to sleep.

"And the baby. Mother, she's so little. I could have held her in one hand, but she's in an incubator. So little. We're going to call her Natalia because it's so close to Christmas."

He began to cry again, and Mother Augustina massaged his shoulders.

"I'm going back. I don't know how long they'll be in the hospital. I just came home to walk Rosie."

"Chris, don't worry about Rosie. Signorina Barbone will take care of her, walking and feeding. You just stay with your wife and daughter."

He got up but didn't seem to know what to do. She helped him put his coat on.

"Take care of yourself, too, Chris. We'll all be praying for all of you." She hugged him again.

"Thanks."

The nuns heard Chris come back a few times in the next eight days, but he quickly left. They prayed harder.

On December 23, fifteen pairs of eyes watched from the windows as the Fiat stopped in front of the convent. Holding their collective breaths, they followed Chris as he opened the door for Patrizia. She was clutching a bundle in a pink blanket close to her chest.

"Oh, my goodness!"

Many of the ladies had tears in their eyes. They looked at Sister Severina, but she was staring straight ahead and they couldn't tell what she was thinking.

"Well," Sister Lucia said, "we can't go visiting now. We have to wait to let them get settled."

"Yes," Sister Rosetta said, "we'll have to wait until tomorrow."

"Yes, yes," everyone agreed.

It seemed strange, then, that exactly one hour later, fifteen elderly women stood outside the door of the basement apartment. Sister Severina was the last in line.

"I thought you were going to wait to visit until tomorrow," Sister Albertini said.

"Oh, I have to go to the doctor tomorrow," Sister Lucia said.

"I have to start my novena to Saint Philomena," Sister Benedicta said.

"I have to do my laundry," Sister Elena said.

Soon, there was a great deal of snickering and bickering and then the door of the apartment flew open.

"Well, ladies," Chris said. "How nice of you to visit us. Do you want to see little Natalia?"

"Little Natalia!" the women cried in unison.

Chris led them inside where Patrizia was holding little Natalia in the big chair next to a small Christmas tree. Sister Severina watched at the side as one by one, the other women went up and looked at the baby, who had inherited her father's red hair and faint freckles and her mother's fine features.

Some of the nuns gently touched the pink blanket and presented their little gifts, toys, dolls, handmade booties, sweaters, caps, blankets, so many things. Patrizia and Chris opened all the boxes and exclaimed over every one of them.

"Do you want to see little Natalia, too?" Patrizia asked Sister Severina. The nun slowly went up to the baby and looked down.

"I'm afraid I don't have a gift for her," she said.

"Oh, Sister," Patrizia said. "We weren't expecting gifts. We're just glad you're here."

Sister Severina touched the pink blanket.

"She's so beautiful."

EVEN IN A CLOISTERED CONVENT, Christmas was always a special day. Father Manfredo wore bright red vestments for midnight Mass, an abundance of flowers decorated the altar and the tiny figures of the *presepe* were under the Virgin Mary window. As the youngest, Sister Naomi placed the Baby Jesus in the manger at exactly midnight.

After Mass, Mother Augustina kept the nuns together to make an announcement.

"I know that the rules of our order forbid us from having outsiders come inside for meals, but I am taking it upon myself to, well, bend those rules a little. I have invited Chris and Patrizia and the baby to have Christmas dinner with us."

Gasps and laughter echoed throughout the building. The nuns returned to their cells but no one could sleep. At 5 a.m., abandoning the usual schedule of the day, four sisters volunteered to help Signorina Barbone with the turkey and pasta and vegetables. Two others began making pies. Three others started decorating the Christmas tree and stringing lights around the dining room. Two practiced carols on the pianoforte in the meeting room, and the others swept and cleaned and polished.

"We've never had such a Christmas," Mother Augustina said. "They'll be here at 1 o'clock so let's hurry."

At 1:35 the young family arrived. "Sorry we're a little late," Chris said. "Had some trouble finding stuff."

Patrizia went from sister to sister showing off little Natalia. She stopped when she reached Sister Severina.

"Would you like to hold her?"

"Hold the baby?"

"Yes. She won't break."

"No, no, I couldn't." But then she added, "Maybe later."

Natalia was remarkably patient during the dinner, demanding to be fed only once, during dessert. Patrizia went into an adjoining room to nurse her.

It was a leisurely meal, accompanied by nonstop murmurs and chatter and laughter, and soon the plates were clean with enough leftovers to last for days.

Carrying glasses containing *vin santo*, everyone moved to the meeting room where the chairs were more comfortable. Patrizia sat in the biggest chair with Natalia, and Chris sat on the arm.

It was now late afternoon, and the sun had set and stars began to shimmer in the cold winter sky. Sister Rosetta got up to turn on the lights, but looked at Chris and instead lit the tall candles around the room. Sister Clara went to the pianoforte and the nuns' sweet voices filled the room.

Tu scendi dalle stelle
O Re del Cielo
E vieni in una grotta
Al freddo al gelo.
E vieni in una grotta
Al freddo al gelo.

You come down from the stars
Oh King of Heavens,
And you come in a cave;
In the cold, in the frost.
And you come in a cave;
In the cold, in the frost.

This was followed by *"Gesù Bambino," "Mille Cherubini in Coro," "La Canzone di Zampagnone,"* and so many more.

Then, except for little Natalia's baby sounds, there was silence.

"Well," Sister Severina said, "I think it's time I told you something." She was seated on the only straight-back chair in the room, fumbling with a rosary in her lap.

The other nuns stirred, and Chris and Patrizia straightened.

"Do you want us to leave?" Chris asked.

"No, no. I want you to hear this, too."

The elderly nun's voice, usually strident, could barely be heard.

"You don't know much about me, if anything, so I'll start from the beginning. I came from a very wealthy family. We had a large villa outside of Lucca. My father was a banker, my mother, well, she mostly took care of me. I was an only child and my parents gave me everything, fine clothes, beautiful dolls. They had me take art lessons, piano lessons. They loved me so much. I guess I was spoiled.

"I didn't have any friends. Maybe the other girls at school were jealous of me or something. So I mostly stayed in my room and if it was nice I liked to read under a big chestnut tree in the garden. One summer, I became friendly with the son of the gardener. His name was Marco. He was sixteen years old, I was fifteen.

"I'm sorry to say I started flirting. He didn't pay any attention at first, maybe because he was afraid of what my parents would say. Then after a while we started talking. We didn't have much in common, but I found out he was very smart. He liked to read, too, so we talked about books. Then we started going on walks when his father wasn't around and my parents were in the house. We went farther and farther. We found a little place in the woods near a creek where it looked like no one had ever been before."

Sister Severina stopped, took out a handkerchief and wiped her eyes.

"I remember the first time we kissed. It was so lovely."

Several nuns gasped loudly, but Sister Severina continued.

"Well, we spent more time there. Sometimes we would just lie there, holding each other, looking at the sky. Oh, Mother, I loved him so!"

"I'm certain you did, dear Sister."

"Well, I guess you can imagine what happened." She paused, closed her eyes and continued. When I found out I was pregnant I knew I should have been ashamed, but I wasn't! It was a symbol of our love! I wanted that baby so much!

"Foolishly, I thought my parents would be happy for me. Oh, I was so naïve. There was a great scene. I had destroyed the family. Marco had to go. His father had to go. And I had to go!"

"You?" several nuns said together.

"My parents decided I would go to a place near Pisa that took girls like me. I would have the baby but I would have to leave it there. Oh, I was so upset, but what could I do? So I went to this place, and the nuns were kind and all, and I had the baby. It was a girl, a beautiful baby girl. I wanted to name her Angelica. She looked like a little angel. But the nuns let me hold her for only a few minutes and then they took her away. And then they sent me home. I never saw little Angelica again."

Her voice seemed strangled, but she continued.

"When I came home, my father wouldn't even speak to me, or even look at me. My mother didn't know what to do. So they decided that I should be a nun. I would come here, far from home, and enter the Order of the Sisters of Charity of Santa Illuminata. And that's why I'm here."

Suddenly her voice rose.

"Mother, I didn't want to be a nun! I never wanted to be a nun! I didn't have a choice. They made me. If I had stayed at home everyone would find out what I had done. I could never go out. So I've stuck it out because that's my fate. I committed a terrible sin and I'm being punished for it. All these years."

Her voice broke and she covered her face with her hands.

"Oh, Sister," Mother Augustina said. "Who's to say you committed a sin? You and this young man loved each other and love is the most important thing in the world. Only God can say something about you and this boy."

The mother superior got up and went to Sister Severina, who was now bent over, sobbing. She lifted her up for a long embrace. The other nuns tried to look away.

"You didn't have to tell us all that, but I'm very proud of you," Mother Augustina said. "We are all proud of you. And we love you."

The other nuns murmured their ascent.

Through tears, Sister Severina looked around the room. "And I want to apologize to all of you. I know I've been a nasty, nasty person. I've always been so, I don't know, angry. Angry at what I'd done. Angry that I was here. So I took it out on you. Honestly, I don't know how you could stand to live with me all these years. I'm sorry. I'm truly sorry."

"No!" Sister Lucia, as the oldest, declared. "Sister, we love you. Thank you for telling us this. We understand now."

"No!" Sister Severina said. "Don't forgive me. I don't deserve it. I have been a terrible human being. And I'm so so sorry."

She was still in Mother Augustina's arms.

"Sister, you are not a nasty person. You are not a terrible human being. We understand how you were affected by all this. Sister, you are a lovely person and God loves you, I know."

Sister Severina sat down again. "Well, I just wanted you to know, finally. Seeing little Natalia has brought this all back to me. You know, I have never seen a baby, any baby, since Angelica. She's so precious!"

Patrizia held the baby up so everyone could see her.

"And now," Sister Severina said, "I have a little something for her."

She took out a small pink box from the folds of her long sleeve.

"I bought this at a shop in Lucca when I found out I was going to have the baby. Little Angelica. I've saved it all these years, not knowing what to do with it. Now Natalia can have it."

She gave the box to Patrizia, who took out a tiny glass angel that sparkled in the candlelight.

"It's beautiful," Patrizia and Chris said together. "Thank you so much."

After a moment, Patrizia said, "Sister, would you like to hold Natalia now?"

"Oh, my, may I?"

The baby was placed in her arms, a tiny pink bundle against a severe black habit. Sister Severina smiled and wept.

"I've thought about my little Angelica so much over the years," she said. "I thought about how she would be sleeping in my arms, how she would smile. I wondered what her life would be like. If her new parents would love her like I loved her. I only held her for a few minutes, but I still miss her so much."

She smoothed Natalia's curly hair. "There, there, lovely child."

The nun thought the baby smiled.

No one knew what to say. Then Sister Clara went to the pianoforte and the nuns began the Christmas hymns again.

Nell'umile capanna
nel freddo e povertà
é nato il Santo pargolo
che il mondo adorerà.

In the humble hut,
In cold and poverty
The Holy infant is born,
Who the world will adore.

"Sister Severina," Patrizia said after Sister Clara closed the lid on the pianoforte, "I have an idea. I want to start working around here again and I have errands to run, and Chris is busy all the time. I wonder if we could ask—I know this would be a big imposition and I know you have other things to do—but I wonder if we could ask if you would like to come down a few afternoons a week and look after Natalia. It would be a great gift for us. Would that be all right for Sister to do that, Mother?"

"Of course! Of course!"

"Oh, my," Sister Severina said. "I don't know what to say. I would be so happy to take care of this beautiful baby. Thank you!"

"No, thank *you,* Sister," Chris said. He went back to the dining room for the last bottle of *vin santo* and poured a little in everyone's glass.

"Buon Natale!" they all said.

THE *STAFFETTA*

Even in Italy, the legacy of the women who fought with the partisans during World War II remains largely forgotten. Yet records show that of the 200,000 Italians who participated in the Resistance, at least 55,000 were women.

WHEN SHE SAW the return address of the commune on the envelope, Rina Sartori thought it must have something to do with taxes. Taxes, always taxes. And for what? Well, she thought, she'd paid them on time and she wasn't going to pay another blasted *euro* to those people who never did anything anyway. Like fix her sidewalks.

But when she sat at her kitchen table and read the letter she could only lean back and stare at it.

"Oh, my."

The letter was short and to the point.

"*Gentile* Signora Sartori. We are pleased to announce that because of your heroic work as a *staffetta* during World War II you have been named Woman of the Year for 2010 by the Commune of Sant'Alfonso. A recognition ceremony will be held on International Women's Day on 8 March 2010 at 1300 hours in the town hall of Sant'Alfonso. We look forward to seeing you there, and of course you may bring guests."

For some people, the reaction upon getting such a letter might be: "Well, it's about time. It's only been sixty-five years since the war ended. What took you so long?"

For others, it might be: "Well, since the mayor and all the members of the commune council are male, who did you have to ask to find a woman to nominate? Your wife? Your mistress?"

But Rina Sartori simply thought, "Well, isn't that nice?"

Rina had to read the letter three times to get all the details firm, and she wrote the date, time and place on the calendar on her refrigerator. It was still two months off.

She had no one to invite. She had no close relatives and the other *staffette* were gone. Maria. Francesca. Isabella. Alicia. Serafina and all the others. Gone. And at 92, she was certain she would be joining them shortly.

She read the letter yet another time. The kitchen table. This was where it all began.

Two weeks after receiving the letter Rina received a telephone call.

"Signora Sartori? My name is Teresa Tinucci. I am a reporter for the Pistoia edition of *La Nazione*. My editor would like me to interview you about the honor you will receive for National Women's Month. May I come visit?"

Well, Rina thought, if she doesn't even know the correct name of the honor, this might not be a good idea. But she agreed.

Teresa Tinucci turned out to be even younger than expected and wore a white blouse and black pants. Rina hated pants on women.

Settling at the kitchen table, Teresa unpacked her tape recorder, opened her notebook and began. "Thank you for allowing me to talk about this great honor, Signora. I have a basic question. Can you tell me what…what…*stufore* means? It sounds like something my Nonna makes at Christmas."

Rina gently took the notebook from the girl's hand.

"Why don't you start your tape recorder and I will just talk and you will have it all on tape and you can write your story from there. Is that all right?"

"Shouldn't I ask some questions? My editor said I should ask some questions."

"I think you'll have enough on the tape recorder."

Rina proceeded to tell Teresa that *staffette* was the name given women who took major roles in the Resistance during the second world war. She talked about how they started by putting out pamphlets and flyers and little newspapers. She talked about how they then became couriers, delivering food, clothing, medical supplies and even arms to the partisans in the hills. How they kept watchful eyes on Germans and Fascists and reported movements to partisans. And how they took care of injured men and buried some of them. And many other things.

"Some of us did some things," Rina said. "Others did other things."

At the end of it, Teresa could only say "Thank you, Thank you, Thank you," but before leaving she impulsively kissed the old woman's withered cheek. The headline on her article read "Local Woman a Heroine in WWII." Rina didn't read the story.

Wearing her best black dress, Rina arrived on time on 8 March. The ceremony, in the town hall that had been rebuilt after the bombing in the war, was short. Children from the local school sang the famous *"Bella Ciao: The Song of the Partisan,"* and Rina wiped away tears when she heard the opening lines, *"Una mattina mi son svegliato; O bella ciao, bella ciao, bella ciao ciao ciao...* One morning I woke up; *O bella ciao, bella ciao, bella ciao ciao ciao..."*

The mayor, with a tricolore sash across his portly chest, gave a little talk indicating that he knew even less about the *staffette* than Teresa Tinucci, and presented Rina with a medal and the traditional bouquet of yellow mimosa. Rina went home and treated herself to a dish of spumoni.

Six months later, after the medal and the newspaper clipping had long been stored in a drawer, Rina received another telephone call.

"Good afternoon, Signora Sartori. My name is Carla Tambulino and I am with Progetti Internazionali. We are a production company that makes television documentaries for RAI in Italy and the Organization for Public Television in America."

"Yes?"

"We read about your honor from the Commune of Sant'Alfonso and we were so fascinated with the *staffette* that we began to do some research. We were amazed at how important you women were to the partisans' cause, and we would like to film a documentary about it. We would like to focus on the work you and others did around Pistoia and of course we would like to interview you and have you be an important part of this piece. Would you agree?"

Rina sat down. On television? What would she say? Her memory was fading. There were others who knew more. She would get everything mixed up. And it would bring back so many memories, things she didn't want to remember.

"Oh, all right, I guess."

"Wonderful! When can we come to visit?"

TWO WEEKS LATER, Carla Tambulino arrived promptly at 2 o'clock accompanied by another young woman who was introduced as Carla's assistant, Beatrice Palumbo. Both wore tailored suits with pants and very high heels. Rina frowned at the pants.

After the greetings the three of them sat at the kitchen table and Carla explained something about her company.

"We have produced a number of documentaries now, most of them having to do with important situations in Italy. Our 'The Children of Naples' won the Critics' Choice award two years ago. In America, the Organization for Public Television put 'Vatican Intrigue' on a DVD and offered it as a reward in their membership drives."

"Of which they have a lot," Beatrice added.

"We were pleased that many new viewers were able to see it."

Carla opened her laptop.

"I want you to know, Signora, that Beatrice and I and our staff did some research, first on the war, then on the partisans and then on the *staffette*. So we know a little, but of course we need to know much more."

"Yes," Rina said. "There is so much to say."

"We've done research at the University of Bologna, the University of Milan and the University of Florence. We've read the memoirs by Ada Gobetti and Lidia Menapace. We've read the online accounts by Anita Malavasi and Giacomina Castagnatti and Giovanna Quaderi and others."

"Some of the women have their own particular experiences," Rina said.

"Yes, we realize that, and that's why we want to talk to you, to get your first-hand involvement in the Pistoria area."

"If I can remember anything. Things get hazy after a while."

Carla tapped a few keys on her laptop and pulled up a map of Italy.

"We'll have to assume, at least for those in the United States, that we should show a map of Italy first. So after a voiceover introduction, we'll show this map and then have a flyover going north. Naples, Rome, Siena, Florence, swing west to Pisa and back to Lucca and finally Pistoria. We'll have a drone loom over its famous walls, the Duomo, the Ceppo Hospital, Palazzo Panciatichi and then some of the modern shopping districts.

"Then we'll zoom in on the hills around Pistoria and all the little villages. Agliana, Alto Reno Terme, Cantagallo, Marliana, Montale, Quarrata, Sambuca Pistoiese and, of course, Sant'Alfonso."

"Let me see Sant'Alfonso."

"Here."

"It's so small!"

"Yes, I'm afraid it is. But lovely."

Carla said that at this point there would be a short introduction about the German occupation of Italy and the incursion north. It will be given by a professor of World War II history from the University of Bologna. She tapped a few keys and the image of a woman seated at a desk in front of a book-lined wall appeared.

"This is Professor Lucia Germanetti," Carla said. "She's very well respected and an expert on the war. By the way, we are only using women as our experts in this program."

"Good," Rina said.

Professor Germanetti began speaking.

"Let's begin by talking about Italy in World War II. Italy watched while Hitler's troops overran parts of Europe, and at first its flamboyant dictator, Benito Mussolini, remained neutral. But on May 22, 1939, Italy and Germany signed what was called the 'Pact of Steel' that officially created the Axis powers. The following year, as the Nazis plowed through France, Mussolini announced Italy's entrance into the war. But the Italian Army was unprepared for war, and struggled to fight on many fronts, from the Balkans to Russia.

"In 1943 Italy was in chaos. On July 25, 1943, with the war turning against Italy and with the Allies landing in Sicily, Mussolini was deposed and arrested. In September, Prime Minister Badoglio announced an armistice with the Allies before fleeing along with the king into their custody. Germany, aware of this development in advance, quickly invaded and disarmed the Italian Army and occupied the country. German armies were all over Italy.

"But the Allies, after invading Sicily, entered the boot of Italy and slowly pursued the Germans north. In June 1944, they captured Rome, a decisive victory. But as they fled north the crazed Germans killed and terrorized people in cities and villages."

Carla tapped a key and the screen went blank.

"There's so much more that could be said, but we've found that our audiences have limited attention spans."

"Very limited," Beatrice said.

"That was such a terrible time," Rina said. "I was so happy that my Papa and Mama didn't live to see it."

"We'll have to get all that down," Carla said, "but today we'll just show you what little we've done so far. Now after Professor Germanetti's presentation we'll show these clips of Germans occupying the cities and villages of Italy, of Germans fighting Allied soldiers and of the Allies bombing Italian cities. There will be some voiceovers."

The clips were in black and white, often grainy but very explicit. Rina was having a painful time watching this and turned away. "I can't watch. Go to another speech."

"Of course. I'm so sorry. We feel we have to show how horrific this all was so that people can understand how courageous the partisans and the *staffette* were. Don't you think?"

"I suppose so." Rina murmured.

The next presentation, Carla said, would be by Professor Sylvia Messina, the director of the *Istituto Nazionale per la Storia del Movimento di Liberazione in Italia* in Milan. Professor Messina appeared on the computer screen, a tall white-haired woman in a long brown coat. Large photographs of armed partisans formed the background. She approached the camera and began to speak.

"After September 1943, with the Germans occupying the entire country, groups began to form to resist them. They were called the partisans. At the same time, Fascists who supported Mussolini became active. The Germans and Fascists were everywhere, including in the hills, and so that's where the partisans formed, too.

"Partisans were actually fighting three types of wars. First, there was a civil war against Italian Fascists, sometimes in their own families. Brother against brother, cousin against cousin.

"Then there was a war of national liberation against the German occupation, and finally a class war, led by Communists, against the ruling elites. Besides that, there were terrorist groups in the cities that began strikes in industrial areas and sabotaged war production.

"The numbers vary, but according to most sources, partisan membership grew from some 20,000 in May 1944 to more than 200,000 by the end of the war in April 1945. It is also estimated that German and Fascist forces killed some 70,000 Italians, including both partisans and civilians, for taking part in Resistance activities."

Carla shut down the laptop.

"Well, again that's a lot, but I think there's some general background for the viewers. Do you agree?"

"It all seems so, what can I say, impersonal, like a university lecture."

"And that's why we want you to give your own account. Tomorrow, we'd just like to talk about your background, get to know you a little. We won't even start filming yet."

Rina couldn't sleep that night. The images on the computer screen and the words of the women lecturers filled her mind. She got up after midnight and made some chamomile tea and sat at the kitchen table. This table, this table.

When she returned to bed, her sleep was marred by the sounds of far-off gunfire and explosions, by the sight of torn bodies.

CARLA AND BEATRICE arrived the next morning accompanied by Felicità, a young woman they said would be taking notes. She stayed in a corner while Carla and Beatrice sat at the table and Rina poured coffee for everyone.

"This is such a lovely home," Carla said. "How long have you lived here?"

"All my life. I was born in the bedroom upstairs."

"My goodness. Can you tell us all about that? This isn't for the film. I'm just curious."

"My Papa and Mama bought the house when they got married. That was in 1916, so it's going on a hundred years old and the house is showing it. There are so many problems with the plumbing, with the electricity. The roof leaks and the floor in my bedroom tilts. But I'm not going to put any money into it, even if I had some. Why should I? I'm not going to be here much longer. I'm 92 years old, for God's sake."

Beatrice got up to examine the walls.

"There are so many nice features," she said. "I love this paneling and the shelves for your beautiful dishes and that cute little pantry back there."

"That's where I made ravioli. When I made ravioli. I don't anymore."

"I wish you did," Carla said. "I'd love to have some."

"Anyway, soon after my parents bought the house Papa was called up to serve in World War I. He served in the Second Battle of the Marne. You've probably heard of it."

"I'm afraid not."

"No. Why would you? Nobody cares about history anymore. All they care about...never mind."

"I'm sorry," Carla said.

"Anyway," Rina continued, "the Italian army stopped the German advance and that was a turning point of the war. Even though some nine thousand Italian soldiers died out of some twenty-four thousand."

"Really? I never knew that."

"Papa came back, but he wasn't the same. He'd been gassed and couldn't work. But Mama got pregnant and I was born a year later. I never knew my father. He died when I was two. My mother brought me up by herself."

"She must have been very strong."

"She wasn't. She was sickly and then she became depressed. When I got older I took care of the house and then I did the shopping and the gardening. I dropped out of school when I was fifteen."

"And you're such a small woman. With all those responsibilities."

"I survived. But I'm telling you this because it's what the Germans did to us that made me so angry when they invaded my country in the second war. I don't mean the German people, I mean the German army and Hitler and all of them."

"I can understand that."

"My mother died when I was seventeen. She just got sicker and sicker and she wouldn't go to a doctor. She said she wanted to be with my father. I got a job in a *trattoria* so I was fine. I had friends. People said I was pretty and I had a few boyfriends. Nothing serious."

"Did you ever marry?"

"No, never married. No, I never married."

Rina seemed to suddenly be off in another world.

"You lived all alone in this house all these years?" Carla asked.

"Yes. Alone."

"May I ask, have you ever been lonely?"

"Not really. I have a nice radio and I read. I don't need a television. It's funny, as I get older the time seems to go by faster. I look at the calendar and it's Sunday and I say, how can that be? It was just Sunday yesterday."

"You know," Beatrice said, "that's happening to me, too."

"And I did keep in close contact with the other *staffrette*. We talked a lot on the phone. We got together every month. Of course, they're all gone now."

Rina got up to pour more coffee.

"And you're surviving OK, Rina?" Carla asked.

"I'm fine. My parents left me a little money. I have a nice garden. My neighbors look after me. They do what shopping I need."

"And may I also ask if your health has been good?"

"Well, for an old woman I'm pretty good. I've had some pains in my chest lately but I'm not going to worry about them."

"What does the doctor say?"

"Doctor? I'm not going to see some old doctor who would just give me some pills. Anyway, he's in Pistoria and I'm not going there."

"Rina, we'd be happy to drive you. Really, it wouldn't be a problem. It's not that far. Why don't you…"

"No, no. I'm not going. I'll live with this."

Rina paused to finish her coffee.

"Let's take a break," Carla said. "I know this is tiring for you. In fact, why don't we call it a day. This seems to be a good point where we can start filming your recollections. Would that be all right?"

"I guess so."

"OK, let's wait until tomorrow."

Rina made a cup of chamomile tea even before she went to bed that night but she still couldn't sleep. She got up, took a chair and lifted a cardboard box from the top shelf of her closet. It was labeled "G." She sat with the box in her lap but couldn't open it. Yet.

HAVING SLEPT SO LITTLE, Rina was groggy when she opened the door to Carla, Beatrice, and Felicità, plus a young woman introduced as the videographer, and a young man, her assistant.

"I was just making coffee," Rina said. "I need it. I didn't sleep well last night."

"I'm so sorry," Carla said. "We'll try to make this as painless as possible."

They discussed the plan for the day. Rina would just sit at the kitchen table, coffee cup and a glass of water handy, and talk about how she began as a *staffetta*. She would only talk about the beginnings today and save other stories for other days.

"Other days?" Rina asked. "How long is this going to take?"

"I'm not sure. Maybe five or six days? Do you think you can do that?"

"Five or six days? I don't know. We'll see."

"But we're going to have very short days, Rina. Just a few hours each time. We don't want to tire you out and we have all the time in the world."

Carla said it would have been preferable to have a makeup person along but she knew the kitchen was too small to hold any more people. So she did the job herself, using a brush to give a little glow to the well-worn face."

"You'll never hide all the wrinkles," Rina said.

"Wrinkles are good. Yours follow your smile so you must smile a lot."

"I don't think I do."

Carla gave a signal to the videographer, Stefania, who leaned against the sink and turned on the camera.

"Now, Rina," Carla said, "you can just start talking when you feel like it. If you could start with what was happening in your area during the war, Mussolini and so on. And then you could talk about how the *staffette* began. And feel free to stop and go back when you like. I may interrupt to ask some questions, but no worry. We'll be editing this later."

Rina took a long sip of coffee and stared out the window. Since it was summer, the apples on the trees were ripening and sunflowers glowed in a field beyond. She saw her neighbor hanging her wash on the line. After a couple of false starts, she began.

"Under Mussolini life became so different. It was like a cloud over everything. It was like being at the edge of an ocean and the waves were coming closer and closer. We had to live our lives, but we didn't know from day to day how things were going to change. We had to resist."

"Of course, the Resistance," Carla said.

"The Fascists were coming out of the woodwork. Their signs were everywhere and the Blackshirts were marching in the streets, and if people didn't take part in their activities, well, watch out.

"Suddenly families were being split apart, for and against the Fascists. My friend Maria said that three of her cousins had taken up with the Fascists and the family was in turmoil. Big fights, bloody fights. Francesca, she was another friend, said that her own father joined up and wore a uniform and her mother cried all the time. And then our friend Alicia said one brother joined the Fascists and another one didn't and they fought all the time.

"Then young men in the village opposed to the Fascists were starting to take action. At first, it just seemed like pranks, but some people called it sabotage. They'd let out the air in the Fascists' cars. They'd drain their gas tanks. They'd write '*Fascista*' in big red letters on their houses. And they began to organize. They would meet in a cabin in the hills that they used for hunting wild boars and they'd plan what they would do that night."

Rina paused to sip her coffee.

"Regarding the *staffette*, we really didn't plan on starting anything. It just sort of happened. Every Saturday my girlfriends came over, Maria, Francesca, Alicia, Isabella and sometimes Betina and Mirella. They were from the villages near Sant'Alfonso, not far. We were all in our twenties and we all had jobs. We'd just talk and make a meal and enjoy a glass of wine. Sometimes we'd knit baby clothes for the nuns who ran the nursery in Cantagallo. That's a village near here.

"One thing that worried us all was how Jews were being treated. It got worse and worse. We heard of people being deported. When we saw posters offering rewards we tore them down. Alicia had a good friend that she hid in her basement until she could flee to her family in Switzerland. Isabella had a friend who asked her to keep all her books and things until after the war ended. She never saw the friend again. We felt so bad and we felt so helpless.

"Well, of course as the war went on we girls knew what the boys were doing and we were jealous. I remember Francesca saying, 'I'm tired of making booties. I want to DO something.' Well, we all did. Women had no rights, no voice, no equality. But what could we do? So we started making socks for the men.

"And then we heard about a new draft law. Young men who were born in 1925 and later had to register for the draft. Well, that meant Alicia's brothers and Maria's cousins and so many more were going to have to fight for the Germans. The boys were very upset and said they would never register. But we knew that there were lots of boys who wouldn't even know about this and the Fascists would round them up. We heard that they were going from house to house and taking the young men away. But to where?

"I don't remember if it was Alicia or Francesca, but somebody suggested that we write leaflets warning people and distribute them all over. Alicia said she knew of someone who had a small printing press in his basement and he could be trusted. So we wrote little leaflets. *"Attenzione!"* they said. We pointed out that if they were drafted they would be sent to Germany and would have to fight against their fellow Italians.

"We printed the leaflets and at night we would put them in mailboxes in our villages. We handed them out at factory gates. We tacked them up on poles and I guess people were afraid to take them down. I used to take them when I went to the markets and put them in the shopping baskets of women there. So I guess that's how the *staffette* was born. Right here on this kitchen table."

Once started, Rina had talked nonstop and her coffee was cold. Beatrice refilled it.

"Rina," Carla said, "that was just perfect. I have goosebumps. And look at my crew."

Stefania, the videographer, said her hands were shaking and she worried that the film was, too. Her assistant, Mario, blew his nose several times.

"Let's call it a day," Carla said. "I don't think any of us could stand any more today. Thank you so much, Rina. Would you by chance have any of those leaflets? We'd love to show them."

"They're in a box upstairs.

"That would be wonderful."

She kissed the old woman before they all left.

After she had her tea and before she climbed into bed, Rina opened the cardboard box from the closet and found the leaflets. She closed the box before looking at anything else but she traced her finger over the "G" on the cover.

RINA WAS STARING OUT the window and having her morning coffee when the television crew arrived the next day. Kisses for everyone, even for Mario. Rina gave Carla the leaflets.

"Perfect!" Carla said. "Are you ready?"

"I guess so."

Stefania turned her camera on and Rina sat down with a fresh cup.

"Well, the leaflets were so successful that we started printing other material. Pamphlets, flyers, posters. But we still felt helpless. I remember Francesca saying, 'I'm tired of printing posters. I want to do MORE.' Well, we thought we could help the young men who had been doing those pranks.

"They had decided to make that little cabin in the hills their headquarters and we helped them. Francesca got her sister's wagon and we loaded it with blankets and warm jackets and pots and pans and other stuff and we hauled it all up there, ten miles or so on a gravel path. We had to make several trips but the men were so excited and grateful. I remember one of them especially."

"Oh?" Carla said. "Do you want to tell us about him?"

"No."

Rina refilled her coffee cup and continued.

"By the end of September 1944 we heard that there were other groups of men in the hills above Pistoia. Each of them had up to twenty men. The men were from all different backgrounds. I remember that one group had a barber, a professor, farmers, factory workers, university students. They were stealing weapons, and they found soldiers who had fled the army show them how to use them.

"By now they had grown past letting gas out of cars. Now they were also stealing bombs and planting them on railroad tracks. They mined roads where the Germans and Fascists traveled. They blew up bridges. They ripped down telephone wires.

"Everyone knew this was happening, and now me and my friends wanted to do even more. We knew that we could go where men could not. Young men, after all, if they failed to report for military service were taken and sent to concentration camps. We women didn't have to register.

"And as women we could move freely. The Germans and the Fascists wouldn't stop us. So we became spies, although none of us liked to call ourselves that. It sounded so much like some stupid war movie and this wasn't a movie. When Maria and I would enter a village, for example, we would find out if there were any Germans or Fascists there so the partisans would know if it was safe to enter. Sometimes we'd be stopped, but mostly we just looked like simple Italian women with scarves on our heads and prayer books in our hands. We always told them we were going to church to pray for the end of the war. We dressed like we always did but we carried double-bottom shopping bags to store things.

"I think women were enjoying their new roles. They had some power at last. I remember a woman named Agnese. She wasn't like us, she obviously had money. Wore good clothes. She must have had a wonderful life, a good husband, a wonderful son. But now her husband had been taken prisoner and her son was somewhere with the partisans. She didn't know where. So she joined us because she knew she had to do something.

"I guess my name was out there because very day somebody would call me. 'How can I help? How can I help?' I told them to get a few women together and we would meet with them. So I got on my bicycle and Francesca got on the handlebars and we went over to Agliana or Mariana or Quarrata and told the women how they could help. We told them they should find a printer and put out leaflets and posters like we did. We told them they should keep an eye on the Germans and the Fascists and write reports on what they were doing, where they were going, and tell all this to the partisans in the hills. We told them they could also do things like letting air out of tires and draining gas tanks."

Carla held up her hand but signaled to Stefania to keep the camera running. "Rina, can I ask why you did all these things. You kept putting your life in danger. So did the other women. Why? Why couldn't you just stay home?"

Rina's face became flushed. "Oh, Carla, how could we stay home? The war was going on. So many were being killed. Not just our men fighting but innocent people in their homes, on their farms. Women were in this just as much as the men. We had to resist those Germans and Fascists. We had to fight. For our lives, for our children!

"It was hard, but it was something we had to do. We did so much walking. It was nothing to walk or ride my bicycle from here all the way to outside Pistoria and back again. My legs would get so tired. But the next day we'd be off again."

She took a sip from a glass of water.

"I see, I see," Carla said. "I just wanted to get it down."

"When we heard the Allies had invaded Normandy—that was in June 1944—everyone was so happy in the towns. The war was going to end soon! Well, it didn't. The fighting in the hills seemed to get worse. The Germans must have known that their time was running out. They were taking more chances.

"I always remember the time I was walking home with Francesca at night in Sant'Alfonso and we saw this big wooden box in front of a house where we knew some Fascists lived. It must have been just delivered. Well, we could hardly carry it but we got it home and the next day we put it on the wagon and I took it up to the cabin. It was full of machine guns!"

Rina smoothed her apron and seemed lost in thoughts. Carla let her have her moment.

"It seems like you went to the cabin often, Rina."

"Yes."

"Well, again, this is such a good segment. As you know, these documentaries have such short segments. I'm not sure how much of what you're saying we'll be able to use, but I have to say that it will be very hard to cut."

"I think I'd like to stop for today," Rina said.

"Of course."

Rina opened the cardboard box again that night and pulled out a packet of slips of paper tied in a blue ribbon. She opened one of them. It was stained with mud and grass. "My darling Rina," it began. "Everybody was so excited when they saw the machine guns. We can certainly use them! I think of you all the time and will write more later. With much love, Giorgio."

Rina tied the piece of paper with the others and closed the box.

RELIVING THOSE MONTHS from long ago, Rina's mind was filled with memories, all jumbled up. She worried she wouldn't be coherent and that she wouldn't be able to describe how important the *staffette* had been.

Carla assured her the next day that her stories were even more powerful than she expected and that she should just continue talking the way she had.

"Thank you so much for doing this," she said.

"I guess I have to thank you. People don't know about about the *staffate*, even people in Italy. Or they like to forget."

"I'm so glad we will be able to tell it. Should we get started?"

A fresh cup of coffee in hand, Rina began.

"I should have mentioned that we all went by different names. We had to because we didn't want to be identified. I took the name Filomena because that was my mother's name. I remember Alicia became Rosetta. I don't remember the others. Of course the partisans also chose new names, sometimes for animals like Lupo for wolf or Giraffa.

"So then we became couriers for our group of partisans and women did the same for other groups. In a few months, every group of partisans had its own couriers. We'd carry food, clothing, drugs, documents, messages, and then even arms and ammunition.

"I remember one time the leader of a partisan group on another hill wanted to get some rifles to our group in the cabin. They had some extras and the fighting had become more bloody all of a sudden. So they asked us if we could take them. We got a big piece of canvas, a tarp it was called, and put the rifles in and lugged it up to our men. They were so pleased.

"Another time our group of partisans asked Maria and me to help plant some bombs on a railroad track near Montale. We got there at night and we stayed the whole night to see what would happen. Well, the train arrived at six in the morning and it just had German troops and ammunition on it. The bombs went off and six or seven cars were derailed. I don't know how many Germans were killed."

Rina needed to stop and Stefania turned off her camera. After a few minutes, Rina signaled that she could start again.

"Then we began doing something else. We were making dinner one night, pasta and chicken, and somebody wondered how the boys in the hunting cabin were doing. How were they eating? We knew that sometimes they spent hours looking for food and only found potatoes and mushrooms. They could kill rabbits and squirrels but those didn't last long. And they had better things to do, like fighting, than looking for food.

"So we decided to do something. Every Saturday we would make a big meal, pasta and salad and baked chicken and fruit. We'd wrap it all in lots and lots of newspapers so it would keep at least a couple days. They had a stove there so they could reheat it.

"I remember at Christmas that year, 1944, we knew we had to send a very special meal. There were seventeen men in the cabin then so it was a big undertaking. We couldn't do the traditional seven fishes meal that's always done on Christmas Eve because of course everything was rationed, but we found some cod and calamari and even eel by begging the people who ran the markets. Then we made three big dishes of lasagna, a sausage and grape mixture that's a Tuscan specialty, a big pot of minestrone, another big pot of chicken cacciatore, eight loaves of crusty bread, a lettuce salad, a cheesecake and a bag of apples. Oh, my goodness! I'm telling you we worked all day on that meal and the girls brought their mothers and sisters to help.

"We also made Christmas cards and wrote notes on them. We knew the names of all of the men so they each got their own."

"Rina," Carla said, "can we ask who you wrote your card to?"

"No."

"Oh."

Rina refilled her coffee cup and continued.

"Since I had been at the cabin more than the others I always volunteered to take the meals up in the little wagon on Saturday nights. It was always overflowing but I managed to get everything in. The boys were so happy. It was late and dark by that time and I didn't want to go back to Sant'Alfonso so I stayed over until the next morning."

"You stayed with the young men?"

"Why not? It was perfectly safe, I can tell you."

"Well, that's amazing," Carla said. "Home-cooked meals in the forest."

"Maria took a photograph of us making the Christmas meal. I have it somewhere."

"Really! Oh wonderful! Do you still have it? We would love to include it. Please?"

"I'll try to find it tonight."

When she looked for the photo in the box that night she also found another slip of paper. "*Cara* Rina. Thank you for the wonderful meal. Let's always spend Saturday night together. Loving, Georgio."

FOR THE FIRST TIME in a long time, Rina had pleasant dreams that night. She pulled her blanket tight, imagining it was Georgio. And so she was smiling when she greeted the television crew the next morning.

"It's a lovely day, isn't it?" she said, opening the window to let a breeze come through.

"We love this part of Tuscany so much," Carla said. "It's so beautiful."

"And the food!" Beatrice said. "You wouldn't believe the dinner we had last night in Montale. It may be a small town but it has the best restaurant!"

"Well," Carla said, "Should we start again?"

Stefania turned her camera on and Rina began.

"The war got worse in the first part of 1945. The Germans were going from village to village massacring people for no reason. They always claimed that the people were helping the partisans. Actually, sometimes they were. But the Resistance was getting stronger. The partisans were all over northern Italy now, especially in Tuscany. There were so many groups and people were supplying them with weapons.

"Then we received a message from the commander of the partisans in our area. It was directed toward the *staffette*. If I remember right it said that from that moment we were not men or women anymore. We were partisans. We had to do what everyone else did, share duties like patrolling the area. It also said that we had to learn to handle weapons and care for them and load them and, most important, how to use them.

"Well, we wondered how far we had come in just a few months. A year ago we were just housewives—well, I wasn't married, of course—and now we were preparing to shoot people."

"Unbelievable!" Carla said. "I had no idea *staffette* were doing that, too."

"Some did, but fortunately, no one in our little group was ever called upon to shoot. But we did something else that we needed training for. And that was because the partisans' battles against the Germans and the Fascists were getting bloodier and bloodier. So many people were getting killed and so many wounded. It was horrible.

"I remember one battle that wasn't far from our partisans' cabin. The Fascists had found out about it and were on their way there when one of the partisans heard them. Franco, one of our partisans, led six of them into the forest and there was a fierce gun battle. They managed to kill all the Fascists but one of our men was killed and three were injured. They called us to come help and Maria and I went up there. We managed to get the injured men back to the cabin and tried to fix them up but we really didn't know how.

"And we couldn't leave the dead partisan out in the woods. Maria saw who he was and started to scream. His face was all mangled. He was the brother of a boy she had dated and she knew him well. We managed to get him into the wagon and took him to his mother in Quarrata. We took a picture of his body and put in on a poster with the headline '*Assassino!*'.

"But we realized that we needed training to help the wounded. We had to! Who else was going to take care of all these wounded partisans? One of the new members in our group, Julia, was a nurse so she helped us. Not just in taking temperatures and pulses, but also how to give injections and do resuscitation.

"We found so many cases where the men suffered bullet wounds and Julia showed us how to to apply pressure and how to wrap the bandages. She also taught us how to make stretchers by taking two poles and stretching a cloth over them. One time there was a group of soldiers infected with lice. Oh, that was something. Julia showed us how to shave their heads and she found some medicine to wash their scalps. Those buggers wouldn't die!

"It turned out that I did so many things that they called me Nurse Rina. But I wasn't that good, you know."

"I'm sure you were an excellent nurse," Carla said.

"The worst part was treating the young men. So many were still in their teens. They were so afraid even if their wounds weren't very bad. We made up an area of the cabin that we called the 'ward.' We would bring the injured boys there. If I wasn't doing anything else I would sit with them and hold their hand and tell them stories. I wouldn't talk about the war, I'd tell them stories about the little villages in the area where they were from. I knew things because the other *staffette* were from those towns.

"Sometimes, the boys—they were so young!—wanted me to put their arms around them. I'd have to look away when they started to cry. The other *staffette* would, too, but somehow I think the boys liked me best. I've never been a mother, but for the first time in my life I think I felt something of what a mother feels."

Carla signaled to Stefania, who turned off the camera.

"Rina, this is all so heart-breaking. I don't know how you did it."

"We had to. That's all. We had to."

Carla signaled, and Stefania turned the camera back on.

"So now all of a sudden the *staffette* were nurses, too?"

"Not real nurses, but we learned to do some things. And after we had helped a wounded partisan we had to notify the hospital about what we had done. The hospital was interesting and you know *staffette* helped put it together. A doctor in Pistoia had found an empty warehouse and he got the help of *staffette* to find supplies. The women went around to hospitals and clinics and begged for medicines, bandages, cots, sheets, blankets, blood pressure kits, everything, even bed pans."

"Oh, my," Carla said. "We're learning so much. This is going to be outstanding. Rina, have you ever thought about writing a book about all this? This is something people need to know!"

"No, no. I'm not a writer. Maria was, but she's gone."

"Well, I'm so glad we have your story and lots of people are going to learn from it. Thank you again, Rina. We'll go now but we'll be back tomorrow."

Rina went to sleep that night holding the cardboard box.

CARLA GAVE RINA an extra long hug when she arrived the next morning. She appreciated Rina's memories so much but wondered about one thing. Was it possible to be a little more personal? Would Rina like to say something more about how all of this had affected her? For example, how she felt like a mother?

"I know this is a lot to ask," she said, "but I think our viewers would be most interested in this. But it's entirely up to you."

Rina thought a minute. "I don't think so."

"That's fine. Rina, did you continue doing all this until the end of the war?"

"Yes. Nothing let up. We had to."

"Didn't you take a break? I can't imagine having all that pressure all the time."

"I took a few days off in the middle of March of '45. I had to."

"May I ask why?"

Rina got up and let cold water run in the sink. She took a cloth and washed her face.

"Excuse me. I want to get something upstairs."

When she returned she carried the cardboard box.

"I've never told anyone about this but I think you should know something that happened so you know more about me. Can you promise that what I say now will not be part of the documentary? If you don't promise I will take back everything I've said all week and you can go back to Florence."

Carla looked at Beatrice, who nodded.

"Rina, this must be very personal so of course we respect your wishes. None of what you tell us now will be part of the documentary. I promise. Truly."

Rina took off the cover of the box.

"I know you asked me some questions that I didn't answer, so I'll explain why. When I first went to that hunting cabin in the hills I met all the men, there were about six or seven then. They all seemed nice, but there was one who seemed especially nice. His name was Giorgio. He was 24, I was 23. He had blond hair and blue eyes, not like the others who were dark. Anyway, he was very appreciative of what the *staffette* were doing, and especially interested in why I was doing this.

"So I told him some things about me and he told me some things, how he grew up in Prato and went to the university and hoped someday to become a doctor. His father was dead like mine, and his mother worried about him but she supported him joining the partisans.

"I had dated other men but I didn't really have feelings for any of them. With Giorgio it was different. All of a sudden I knew we were matched and I know he loved me, too. So at first when I went up there on Saturdays I would eat a little with them and then Giorgio and me would go into a corner and talk. We had so much to talk about!"

Rina fiddled with the cover of the box.

"And after a few weeks we found a little room upstairs that nobody was using so we spent the night there. The other men knew what was going on. How couldn't they? But they didn't care. It was wartime.

"We had such a lovely time together. He was so caring, so gentle. When I think about it now I think my heart will break."

She paused to take a sip of water and look out the window for a long time.

"I knew that Giorgio was the leader of this band of partisans. His partisan name was Tigre. He wouldn't talk about it, but I knew that he led the group when they bombed the bridge at Cantagallo and when we derailed the train near Montale. And he led the partisans many times when they fought the Germans. They were bloody battles. Men on both sides were killed."

Rina closed her eyes tightly. Her lips quivered.

"When I brought the meal to the cabin on March 10, no one was there and nobody came back that night. It was late so I stayed. I was so lonely in that little room. And so worried. In the morning no one had still come back, but I had to get back to Sant'Alfonso, so I left. On Sunday night another partisan in the group came to my house. I knew right away that something was wrong and he had trouble getting the words out. Finally, he said that Giorgio had been killed. There was a battle over the next hill. The partisans were outnumbered but they managed to capture seven Fascists. But Giorgio was protecting a comrade who had fallen and he was killed instantly."

Rina wiped her eyes. "That's when I had to take a few days off."

The room was silent except for the sounds of muffled sobbing. Carla put her arms around Rina.

"Oh Rina, Rina. How very terrible."

Rina took a little box out of the cardboard box.

"They found this in his pocket. He obviously wanted to give me this when he got back."

She opened the little box to reveal a small diamond ring.

"I suppose people wondered why I've always worn black even though I was never married. Well, I could have been. It's just my way of honoring the love of my life."

She put the little box inside the big box and closed it.

"All these years I thought I was over all this, but talking about that time and all the things we did brought all these memories back. I had pushed all those things way back in my mind because I didn't think I could live with them. I hope now I can. I know I don't have much time left."

"Oh, Rina, Rina."

"I think I need to lie down for a while. Do you mind?"

"Of course not."

They made arrangements to meet again the next day.

CARLA THOUGHT it odd when Rina didn't answer her knock the following morning but since the door was never locked the crew walked in.

"Rina? Rina?"

They found the old woman slumped at the kitchen table, her head on the cardboard box and a diamond ring on her finger.

"Oh, no!"

Fleshed out with more commentaries from experts, footage of partisans fighting and photos of *staffette,* the documentary "A *Staffetta's* Story" was completed in 2017 and shown on television in Italy and America in 2018. It received unanimous praise from critics and won numerous awards.

A screen at the end said:

> Caterina (Rina) Sartori died in her home on August 2, 2010, at the age of 92. This film is dedicated to her memory and to all of the *staffette* who valiantly fought for the Italian Resistance in World War II. "If there hadn't been women," one of them wrote, "there wouldn't have been any Resistance."

ROBERTO AND GIULIANA

The year 1935 instead of the 1300s? Siena instead of Verona? Two rival contrade *instead of the mutinous Capulets and Montagues? A happy ending to the tragic Romeo and Juliet story? Why not?*

THE SCENE: Siena, September 1935

DRAMATIS PERSONAE:

SIGNOR and **SIGNORA CAPELLINI**, wealthy residents of *Contrada dell'Istrice*
GIULIANA, their daughter
PASQUALINA, her governess
SIGNOR and **SIGNORA MONTAGNI**, wealthy residents of *Contrada della Lupa*
ROBERTO, their son
MARCO and BENEDETTO, his friends
FATHER LORENZO, rector of the Duomo

PROLOGUE

Two *contrade*, both alike in dignity,
In fair Siena, where we lay our scene,
From ancient grudge break to a new serenity
Which none but God could have foreseen.

ACT ONE

SCENE 1. *Contrada dell'Istrice. Villa Capellini. Signor Capellini and Signora Capellini are in their study reading different sections of* La Nazione.

SIGNORA CAPELLINI

I don't suppose there's any good news in your section today.

SIGNOR CAPELLINI

Well, as a matter of fact there is. Listen to this. Mussolini is preparing twelve infantry divisions to send to Ethiopia. He's also getting heavy artillery and ground and air vehicles ready, so it looks like this will be a short war. The Ethiopians really don't have an army to speak of.

SIGNORA CAPELLINI

I don't think that's good news. Another war. Nazario, all Mussolini wants to do is salvage his pride from the last defeat.

SIGNOR CAPELLINI

That may be, but we'll also get Ethiopia's resources and we can use them.

SIGNORA CAPELLINI

At the cost of thousands and thousands of lives. War, war, war. That's all the Duce wants. And it's obvious that he's getting mighty close to that monster Hitler.

SIGNOR CAPELLINI

Isabella, you have to look at the good things he's done. He's built railroads and sports stadiums and schools and bridges. All that construction helped solve the unemployment problems. And he's given industries more money for steel and iron production. And...

SIGNORA CAPELLINI

And he's abolished elections. And taken away free speech. And suppressed opposition parties and unions. His only use for women is to bear children.

SIGNOR CAPELLINI
But…

SIGNORA CAPELLINI
And listen to what's in the paper today about what his friend Der Fuhrer is doing in Germany. They've passed something called the Nuremberg Laws and it has to do with Jews. Here's what the paper says: "Jews are denied the rights of citizenship and reduced to the status of 'subjects.' Marriages between Jews and 'Aryans' are forbidden. They are also forbidden to shop in gentile stores or gentiles in Jewish stores. They cannot attend movies, theaters or stroll in public parks." This is terrible! I'm sure this is only the first step of what he's going to do. What's going to happen to the Jews? Oh, Nazario, I think something terrible is going to happen.

SIGNOR CAPELLINI
No, no. Nothing worse is going to happen. Hitler knows what he's doing. And people will rise up if he attempted anything bad. If word got out the whole world would attack Hitler. I'm sure of it.

SIGNORA CAPELLINI
Oh, sure. Just like people are protesting now in Germany and just like Italians are protesting what Mussolini is doing. Are you so naïve? Nazario, I just wish you wouldn't follow this guy without any questioning. I'm getting more and more afraid. Aren't you? Thank goodness we don't have any sons to send off to war.

SIGNOR CAPELLINI
Yes, thank goodness. And why isn't Giuliana up?

SIGNORA CAPELLINI
She's with Pasqualina somewhere. She stays in her room a lot and I don't see her.

SIGNOR CAPELLINI
Letizia, don't you think Giuliana is a little old for a governess? She's sixteen.

SIGNORA CAPELLINI

No. I wouldn't know what that girl would be doing if Pasqualina wasn't watching her every minute. She'd be out with some strange girls—or boys—and who knows what she'd be doing or where she'd be going.

SIGNOR CAPELLINI

She'd better not be going far. Especially if she's going to marry Patrizio.

SIGNORA CAPELLINI

Oh, for goodness sakes. This isn't the Middle Ages, you know. You can't tell her who she's going to marry. And anyway, she's only sixteen. She has lots of time to decide.

SIGNOR CAPELLINI

I hope she'll like him. He has a good job in the bank. And that beautiful Ferrari.

SIGNORA CAPELLINI

And he's thirty years old with a reputation for liking young girls.

SIGNOR CAPELLINI

Age won't make a difference after a few years. And it means uniting two of the oldest families in *Contrada dell'Istrice.*

SIGNORA CAPELLINI

That's another thing. Nazario, you are always so caught up in the affairs of our *contrada.* We live in Siena! Does it really matter what *contrada* we live in?

SIGNOR CAPELLINI

Of course it does! How could you even ask that question? Each of seventeen *contrada* in Siena gives its people a special identity. In our *Contrada dell'Istrice* we have our own colors, our own flag, our own uniforms. We have our own headquarters on via Camollia. We have our own chapel, San Vincenzo e Anastasio, with our own museum next door.

SIGNORA CAPELLINI

Not to mention that we have our own symbol. A porcupine! Imagine having a porcupine as a symbol! With a motto of "I only sting for defense"! Nazario, isn't this all rather medieval, too?

SIGNOR CAPELLINI

Letizia, you know that I love traditions. And you can be proud that our *contrada* beat *Contrada della Lupa* in the Palio last month. That was sweet revenge. *Contrada dell'Istrice* beat our bitter rival.

SIGNORA CAPELLINI

After they beat us in the Palio in July.

SIGNOR CAPELLINI

I still think that horse race was fixed. I wouldn't be surprised if Signor Montagni had something to do with bribing the jockeys.

SIGNORA CAPELLINI

Just like you had nothing to do with our *contrada* winning last month. Right?

SCENE 2. *Contrada della Lupa. Villa Montagni. Signora Montagni and Signor Montagni are in their kitchen making pasta. She is rolling out the dough, he is cutting it into long narrow strips.*

SIGNORA MONTAGNI

Alberto, I think you're cutting the pieces too big. We want to have enough. You know how Roberto devours linguini.

SIGNOR MONTAGNI

Maybe we should have a couple of his friends over. It would take their minds off last Friday.

SIGNORA MONTAGNI

I can't believe our *contrada* lost in the Palio.

SIGNOR MONTAGNI

Especially after we won the one in July.

SIGNORA MONTAGNI

Our horse wins in July, theirs in August.

SIGNOR MONTAGNI

I have to believe this race was fixed. The *Contrada dell'Istrice* would do anything to win. I bet Signor Capellini had something to do with it. Bastard.

SIGNORA MONTAGNI

Lupa will win again. Remember, it's had twenty-eight victories, all the way back to 1696.

SIGNOR MONTAGNI

1696? I didn't know that. You should be the *contrada* historian.

SIGNORA MONTAGNI

I know. A lot of women wouldn't be interested in the *contrade* or the Palio but to me, this is what makes Siena great.

SIGNOR MONTAGNI

And you're ready to recite the whole history at a moment's notice.

SIGNORA MONTAGNI

Of course. I know that the *contrade* districts go back to the Middle Ages and now every important event—baptisms, deaths, marriages, church holidays—is celebrated in their own districts.

SIGNOR MONTAGNI

Remember the celebrations after our victory in July? Tables set up in the streets, a party every night. It was wonderful.

SIGNORA MONTAGNI

I love going to our museum and our chapel and I love our symbol. A female wolf nursing twins, just like Romulus and Remus.

SIGNOR MONTAGNI
Certainly better than a porcupine like the *Contrada dell'Istrice.* Imagine a porcupine! Our motto is better, too. *"Et urbis et senarum signum et decus"* "The symbol and honor of Siena and its people."

SIGNORA MONTAGNI
Let's not bring up that *contrada* again if we can help it.

    Enter Roberto

SIGNOR MONTAGNI
Well, he's home at last. Where did you go, son?

ROBERTO
Just around.

SIGNORA MONTAGNI
With your friends?

ROBERTO
Yeah.

SIGNOR MONTAGNI
What did you do?

ROBERTO
Nothing

SIGNORA MONTAGNI
We'll be having dinner soon.

ROBERTO
I'm not hungry. I'll skip.

SIGNOR MONTAGNI
Is something the matter?

ROBERTO
No. Nothing.

Exit Roberto

SIGNOR MONTAGNI
What's the matter with him?

SIGNORA MONTAGNI
He's eighteen years old. That's all.

SCENE 3.
A garden at Villa Capellini. Enter Giuliana and her governess, Pasqualina.

PASQUALINA
You slept late again, my darling.

GIULIANA
(*yawns*) Some days I don't want to get up at all.

PASQUALINA
But you have everything to live for! You're young, you're beautiful. And it's such a lovely day today. What would you like to do?

GIULIANA
You know what I'd like to do but you won't let me.

PASQUALINA
Now, now. You know I have to follow the rules your parents gave me.

GIULIANA
All the time?

PASQUALINA
Yes, all the time. Now, would you like to go for a walk?

GIULIANA
Boring.

PASQUALINA
Then what would you like to do?

GIULIANA
(sighs) I don't know. Nothing.

PASQUALINA
Well, we can't sit here all day.

GIULIANA
You could go inside and read.

PASQUALINA
No, Giuliana, I'm not allowed to let you alone. I know what we can do. I think this is really exciting. I was reading in a newspaper about how they found the remnants of a building right near the square where we were the other night, Piazza dei Paparoni.

GIULIANA
Where I was talking to this cute guy Tonio and…

PASQUALINA
Before I pulled you apart. Anyway, this building was once a palace and a family named Bandinellli lived there and that's why the piazza is named like that. The paper said the palace was built in 1218. Imagine! That was the Thirteenth century and…

GIULIANA
Pasqualina…

PASQUALINA
The Bandinelli family was very powerful and in 1159—I think I got that date right—one of their members Rolando, well actually Rolando Bandinelli Paparoni who was made Pope Alexander the Third and it happened right here in the Duomo and…

GIULIANA
Pasqualina!

PASQUALINA
All right, all right. I just thought this was such an interesting story and you would like to go to see what's left of this famous palace but I guess you don't.

GIULIANA
Boring.

PASQUALINA
Well, another thing today is that the choir from the Duomo is going to give a concert in the *contrada* chapel this afternoon and I know how you love music so we could go there and...

GIULIANA
Not that kind of music.

> *They remain silent for a long time.*

GIULIANA
Pasqualina, can't we go somewhere that's fun?

PASQUALINA
And what, dear girl, do you consider fun?

GIULIANA
You know.

PASQUALINA
Yes, I know, but you're too young to go to a place where there are boys and loud music. I shouldn't have let you talk to that boy Tonio the other night.

GIULIANA
Pasqualina, I'm sixteen years old. All the other girls are going out with boys now. This is 1935. Things are different than when you were a girl.

PASQUALINA

Well, your parents don't want you to. They want you to get to know Patrizio.

GIULIANA

Patrizio? That old man? I wouldn't marry him if he were the last man in Siena.

PASQUALINA

Giuliana, he's very rich. He could give you anything you want.

GIULIANA

And he's a lecher! And anyway, I won't be getting married for years. Maybe I'll never get married. No boy will ever find me. I'm stuck in this villa. (*She begins to sob.*)

PASQUALINA

Oh Giuliana, don't talk like that. Let's decide what we should do today.

GIULIANA

Boring, boring, boring.

There is another long silence.

GIULIANA

Oh, all right, if we have to do something. Let's go to via Montanini again and look in the shops. That will waste some time.

PASQUALINA

Those shops are very expensive.

GIULIANA

We don't have to buy anything, just look.

PASQUALINA

And you know that via Montanini is the boundary line between *Contrada dell'Istrice* and *Contrada della Lupa* so there will be some of *those* people there. You are not—NOT—going to talk to anyone from *Contrada della Lupa*, understand?

GIULIANA
Of course not.

SCENE 4.
The Piazza Salimbeni in Contrada della Lupa. *Enter Benedetto and Marco, two friends of Roberto.*

BENEDETTO
So where the hell can he be? We've looked all over.

MARCO
Hiding again. He doesn't want to see us.

BENEDETTO
More likely he doesn't want us to see him.

MARCO
It's about time he got over it.

BENEDETTO
Her.

MARCO
Whatever. We used to be three good friends, doing everything together.

BENEDETTO
Getting into trouble together.

MARCO
Well, if he doesn't show up soon let's go play some damn pool.

Enter Roberto, downcast.

BENEDETTO
Well, here he is now, looking happy as ever.

MARCO
Biggest smile I've ever seen.

ROBERTO
OK, OK. You can stop it now.

BENEDETTO
Roberto, isn't it about time you forgot about her?

MARCO
It's been three weeks, Roberto. Time to move on. Want a smoke? *(lights a cigarette.)*

ROBERTO
No.

BENEDETTO
She's not worth it.

MARCO
You know she cheated on you.

BENEDETTO
Over and over.

ROBERTO
SHE DID NOT!

MARCO
Oh, Roberto, were you blind? She's such a bimbo. She was always flirting with Stefano and Dante and Giovani and…

BENEDETTO
And Luca and Sergio and…

ROBERTO
STOP IT!

MARCO
Roberto, Concetta dumped you. Face it.

ROBERTO
She did not! She just…she …

BENEDETTO
She dumped you.

(Roberto rushes at Benedetto and punches him in the stomach. Benedetto punches Roberto back. Marco tries to intervene but the three of them keep punching each other until they are rolling around on the cobblestone pavement. Finally, Marco and Benedetto lie sprawled in front of Palazzo Tantucci and Roberto sits in front of Palazzo Spannochi, his head on his knees. Marco and Benedetto go over to him.)

MARCO
OK, had enough?

ROBERTO
Why did she leave me? I just don't understand.

BENEDETTO
Look, just forget about Concetta. She's not worth it.

ROBERTO
I can't.

MARCO
You will. I know I got over Bettina and Lilla and Serena.

BENEDETTO
And I got over Marcella and Donata. Just like that.

ROBERTO

I'm going to get out of Siena. I'm going to join the *Avanguardisti.*

MARCO

The *Avanguardisti?* Mussolini's youth group? Roberto, you're crazy! You hate Mussolini.

BENEDETTO

And besides you're too old. That's for boys under eighteen. And you're eighteen.

ROBERTO

Then I'll join the army. I'll go to Ethiopia. And get killed. Then she'll be sorry.

MARCO

Right. Go fight for damn Mussolini and get killed.

BENEDETTO

Concetta will be totally upset.

MARCO

Better solution. You're free now to look for another girl. We all are. So let's do it. All three of us. Let's go find a girl. Yeah!

BENEDETTO

And the first one who finds one wins a prize.

MARCO

What?

BENEDETTO

Hmm. I don't know. We'll figure it out. Where do we start?

MARCO

How about here in the piazza. Look at those two girls over by Palazzo Tantucci.

BENEDETTO

I don't know. The taller one looks OK, but the shorter one looks a little, um, pudgy.

MARCO

More than pudgy. How about those two girls eating lunch on that bench over there. The blond one has big boobs.

BENEDETTO

The other one doesn't have any! *(Benedetto and Marco laugh uproariously. Roberto is silent.)*

MARCO

How about that girl feeding the pigeons? She's hot! When she bends down you can see damn everything!

BENEDETTO

Nah.

MARCO

Or that one over there? She has a great ass.

BENEDETTO

Nah.

MARCO

Roberto, aren't you going to look? Come on!

ROBERTO

I'm not in the mood. Nobody is ever going to replace Concetta.

BENEDETTO

Well, you never know. You might meet some girl and fall in love right away.

ROBERTO

No. I won't. Nobody falls in love right away. That's only in movies.

MARCO

Sometimes they do. Come on. Let's blow this place.

BENEDETTO

How about the shops on via Montanini? There are lots of dames there. Beautiful ones. I've seen them.

MARCO

But via Montanini is the boundary line between *Cantrada della Lupa* and *Contrada dell'Istrice*. There will be girls from *Contrada dell'Istrice* there. We can't talk to them!

BENEDETTO

We can't? Let's go.

SCENE 5.

The shops on via Montanini. Giuliana and Pasqualina enter at one end.

GIULIANA

Isn't this great? Look at all the people here.

PASQUALINA

Stay close to me. I don't want you out of my sight.

GIULIANA

We can just stay on the sidewalk and look in the windows. Like here. God, those purses are gorgeous! Have you ever seen anything like them?

PASQUALINA

Giuliana, your father would have a fit if you brought one of them home.

GIULIANA

Well, I can look, can't I?

Giuliana and Pasqualina whisper in front of the shop window. At the other end of the street Roberto, Marco and Benedetto enter.

MARCO

Why did we think of coming here? All these things are too damn expensive and these girls wouldn't even look at us.

BENEDETTO

What's wrong with us? We're young, we're healthy, we're good looking. At least I am.

MARCO

And Roberto here is the height of fashion. Button-down shirt, neat pants. Any girl would fall for you, Roberto. Roberto? What are you looking at, Roberto?

ROBERTO

Let's walk down a little. I want to look at those purses in that window.

BENEDETTO

You want to look at the purses? Roberto, I didn't know you were interested in purses.

They make squeaky noises.

ROBERTO

Never mind. I'll go by myself.

He walks to where Giuliana and Pasqualina are looking in the window. Roberto and Giuliana look at each other. Pasqualina sees this and pulls Giuliana away.

PASQUALINA

Giuliana, let's go inside and look at the purses.

ACT TWO

SCENE 1.

The garden of Villa Capellini. Pasqualina sits on a bench, Giuliana is pacing.

PASQUALINA

But Giuliana if you would just listen…

GIULIANA

Don't talk to me.

PASQUALINA

But darling…

GIULIANA

Don't darling me.

PASQUALINA

I was only trying to protect you.

GIULIANA

Protect me from what? In the middle of via Montanini?

PASQUALINA

I didn't think he looked like the kind of boy you should be talking to.

GIULIANA

Oh for God's sake. "Looked like the kind of boy"? What is that supposed to mean? He was dressed right, his face was washed, his hair was combed. For goodness sake! (*She bursts into tears.*)

PASQUALINA

Oh, my darling. (*She attempts to put her arms around Giuliana but Giuliana pushes her away.*)

GIULIANA

Let go of me. Go away!

PASQUALINA

I'm so sorry, Giuliana. I'm so sorry.

GIULIANA

We were just about to say something to each other and you pulled me away.

PASQUALINA

I thought it was for best. I thought of what your father might say.

GIULIANA

I don't care about what my father says. I wanted to talk to him.

PASQUALINA

I'm sorry.

GIULIANA

I never saw such a nice looking boy like that before. Ever!

PASQUALINA

He was rather pleasant looking.

GIULIANA

Pleasant! He was so handsome! Such a nice face. Such dark curly hair. The bluest eyes I've ever seen.

PASQUALINA

I did notice that.

GIULIANA

And nice broad shoulders. And strong arms.

PASQUALINA

You noticed all that in the five seconds you were together?

GIULIANA

It doesn't take long. I felt I wanted him to hold me.

PASQUALINA

But Giuliana, you don't know anything about him.

GIULIANA

And now I never will. But I'll never forget him.

PASQUALINA

And you don't even know his name.

GIULIANA

And I never will.

PASQUALINA

There, there. I'm sorry, but I think this is all for the good.

GIULIANA

I think I'm going to die.

PASQUALINA

I think you're being too dramatic. You're acting like somebody in a play.

GIULIANA

Plays are about real people.

SCENE 2.

The office of the rector of the Duomo of Siena. Father Lorenzo sits at his desk. Roberto enters.

FATHER LORENZO

Good afternoon, my son. Welcome! Move those books and have a seat.

ROBERTO

Um, good afternoon, um, Father.

FATHER LORENZO

I go by Father Lorenzo. And your name is?

ROBERTO

Roberto. Roberto Montagni.

FATHER LORENZO

Ah, the son of Alberto Montagni, I assume?

ROBERTO

Yes, sir, Father.

FATHER LORENZO

Of the *Contrada della Lupa,* right?

ROBERTO

Yes, that's right.

FATHER LORENZO

I know your father well. He's a fine man. Your mother, too. He always sends me a bottle of wine from his vineyards at Christmas. And what brings you to this musty old office on this beautiful September day?

ROBERTO

Um, I think I have a rather strange request, Father.

FATHER LORENZO

I get strange requests every day. I doubt if yours is any stranger. Let me decide.

ROBERTO

Well, I was wondering. You have been here a long time, right?

FATHER LORENZO

Oh yes. I'll have been at the Duomo thirty-two years next January.

ROBERTO

And you know a lot of people in Siena.

FATHER LORENZO

Well, yes. I can't say I know a lot of them well, but I am acquainted with many of our fine Sienese.

ROBERTO

So, if I told you a name, do you think you might know something about that person?

FATHER LORENZO

Perhaps. It depends on what you want to know.

ROBERTO

Well, the thing is, I only know a first name.

FATHER LORENZO

Just the first?

ROBERTO

Yes, Father.

FATHER LORENZO

And you expect me to know somebody in this city of more than thirty thousand people just by their first name? Do you know how many Pietros there are? And Marias? And Marios? Not to mention Robertos?

ROBERTO

I know this is a wild goose chase but I'm kind of desperate.

FATHER LORENZO

I'm guessing this is a girl.

ROBERTO

Yes.

FATHER LORENZO

And that you saw her once and just heard her name and you are in love with her.

ROBERTO

Yes.

FATHER LORENZO

That sound you just heard is a long sigh. Well, tell me the name and tell me what she looks like and I'll use my magical powers and see if I can come up with something.

ROBERTO

Well, her name is Giuliana and she's about this high (*raising his arm*) and she has long blond hair and she has the greenest eyes I've ever seen and she has…she has…a very nice figure.

FATHER LORENZO

I think I know what you mean. You don't have to go into detail. And how old do you think she is?

ROBERTO

Oh, she's at least seventeen. Maybe eighteen. I'm eighteen and maybe she's as old as me.

FATHER LORENZO

And you fell in love right away?

ROBERTO

Father, I just wanted to take her in my arms and hold her.

FATHER LORENZO

And you were with her for how long?

ROBERTO

It seemed like an eternity. Maybe five seconds.

FATHER LORENZO

Five seconds. And how did you find out her name?

ROBERTO

She was with this old lady and we were outside a shop and the old lady said, "Giuliana let's go inside" and so they did and I waited around for a long time but they didn't come out and my buddies said we had to leave. So we did.

FATHER LORENZO
And where was this shop?

ROBERTO
It was on via Montanini.

FATHER LORENZO
Ah, via Montanini, where people from your *contrada* and those from *Contrada dell'Istrice* can encounter each other. But they'd better not.

ROBERTO
Yes, Father.

FATHER LORENZO
Let me think.

There is a long silence.

FATHER LORENZO
Roberto, I hesitate to say this, but Signor Nazario Capellini has a daughter Giuliana. I know that because we are on a committee that arranges the flag throwers' parade ahead of the Palio and he talks about her. Now I can't say for sure. There may be thousands of Giulianas in Siena.

ROBERTO
Really? Wow!

FATHER LORENZO
I did see her once when she came to a meeting. She is blond and, well, she matches those other features you mentioned but maybe a little younger.

ROBERTO
It's her! It's her! I know it's her!

FATHER LORENZO
Maybe. They live in a villa on Via Vallerozzi.

ROBERTO
Oh wow. I can find that. Father, I can't thank you enough. I can take it from here. Thank you, thank you!

FATHER LORENZO
Well, Roberto, you'd better hold your thanks. The Capellinis' villa is in *Contrada dell'Istrice.*

SCENE 3.
The garden of Villa Capellini. Nightfall. Roberto enters.

ROBERTO (*Stumbling.*)
Oops. Pretty dark here.

A light appears in an upstairs window.

ROBERTO
What's that light? Hello?

No answer.

ROBERTO
Hello! Hello!

Giuliana appears in the window.

GIULIANA
Who's out there?

ROBERTO
It's me.

GIULIANA
Who are you?

ROBERTO
Roberto.

GIULIANA
Roberto? Roberto? I can't see you, Roberto.

He goes directly under the window.

GIULIANA
It's you! The guy from via Montanini! I can't believe this! How did you find me?

ROBERTO
Father Lorenzo told me your name.

GIULIANA
Good old Father Lorenzo. He knows everybody. But why did you come?

ROBERTO
Because I'm in love with you.

GIULIANA
Really? Really?

ROBERTO
Yes.

GIULIANA
Roberto, you know what? Ever since we saw each other in via Montanini I can't stop thinking about you.

ROBERTO
And I can't stop thinking about you. I can't sleep at night.

GIULIANA
Me neither. My governess thinks I'm sick.

ROBERTO

My buddies think I'm crazy. Marco says I should borrow Cupid's wings and fly, something like that. He says odd things sometime.

GIULIANA

I'm so happy you found me. But I don't know anything about you.

ROBERTO

Well, I've finished high school and I'm looking around for a job. I'm really good at making things. And I'm eighteen years old.

GIULIANA

Really? I thought you were nineteen or twenty. I'm sixteen.

ROBERTO

You're kidding. I thought you were eighteen or nineteen.

GIULIANA

I guess I look older. Maybe it's the way I wear my hair. I'm still in school and I don't know what I want to do. My mother says I should be a nurse. My father says I should get married. He even has somebody in mind but I'm never going to marry that guy.

ROBERTO

Why not?

GIULIANA

Because he's ancient! Anyway, I won't marry anyone unless I loved him.

ROBERTO

Me neither. A girl, I mean.

GIULIANA

Roberto, what does this remind you of?

ROBERTO

What?

GIULIANA

Me up here at the window, you down there talking to me? Don't you remember reading that Shakespeare play in high school?

ROBERTO

Which one?

GIULIANA

The one about Romeo and Juliet. They're young lovers. There's a scene where Romeo stands below Juliet's balcony and they say sweet things to each other.

ROBERTO

I thought that was pretty sappy.

GIULIANA

Oh come on. Everybody says it's the most romantic play ever written. That scene—I've read it so many times I swear I could say it by heart. Don't you remember

> *But, soft! what light through yonder window breaks?*
> *It is the east, and Juliet is the sun.*
> *Arise, fair sun, and kill the envious moon,*
> *Who is already sick and pale with grief,*

Oh, I could just cry.

ROBERTO

I guess I remember something like that. I don't know if I'd compare Juliet to the sun, though. What does that mean?

GIULIANA

And later she says:

> *O gentle Romeo,*
> *If thou dost love, pronounce it faithfully:*
> *Or if thou think'st I am too quickly won,*

I'll frown and be perverse and say thee nay,
So thou wilt woo; but else, not for the world.

Oh, that's so romantic. I could cry.

ROBERTO
I remember reading that umpteen times and I still couldn't understand it.

GIULIANA
I just love it. I wish somebody would put the play on here so I could play Juliet. I'd love to meet my Romeo.

ROBERTO
Don't they both die at the end?

GIULIANA
Yes.

ROBERTO
I didn't like that part. Why couldn't he just have had them get married and live happily ever after?

GIULIANA
Because they were from opposing households and they weren't supposed to even be with anybody from the opposite one. That's so crazy. Something out of ancient history.

ROBERTO
Well, maybe it's not so crazy.

GIULIANA
Why?

ROBERTO
Because I'm from the *Contrada della Lupa.*

GIULIANA

Really? Oh, it's just like Romeo and Juliet! I love it! They were from different households and they were rivals and we're from different *contrade* and we're rivals. This is so awesome!

ROBERTO

Won't it make a difference?

GIULIANA

No, not for me. But my parents will have a fit. They'll forbid me to see you.

ROBERTO

Mine, too.

GIULIANA

What are we going to do?

ROBERTO

We won't tell them.

GIULIANA

They'll find out.

ROBERTO

Then we'll lie.

GIULIANA

Oh, Roberto, we've got to figure something out.

ROBERTO

OK. But let's not worry about it now. Giuliana, I love you!

GIULIANA

And I love you, too!

ROBERTO

I want to see you all the time. I can't live without you, Giuliana. How about going out this weekend? We could go to a movie.

GIULIANA

I haven't been to a movie in ages!

ROBERTO

"*Territorial Militia*" just opened. It's supposed to be very funny.

GIULIANA

Oh, I'd love to! And we can hold hands in the dark.

ROBERTO

And maybe something else.

GIULIANA

Like what?

ROBERTO

We'll figure it out. But we'd have to go to a movie in a *contrada* on the other side of the Campo so we wouldn't be seen.

GIULIANA

Oh Roberto, I would love to do that, but I could never leave here. My governess watches me like a hawk.

ROBERTO

Doesn't she sleep?

GIULIANA

She's sleeping right now. Can't you hear her snoring? But sometimes she wakes up.

ROBERTO

Maybe you could give her something so she wouldn't wake up.

GIULIANA

I don't think I have anything…wait, I know.

ROBERTO

What?

GIULIANA

I have the sleeping potion my mother gave me when I was sick. I have lots left. I'll give her that.

ROBERTO

OK, do that, and I'll come by tomorrow.

GIULIANA

Oh Roberto, "*Good night, good night! Parting is such sweet sorrow, that I shall say good night till it be morrow.*"

(They blow kisses.)

ACT THREE

SCENE 1.

Over the next months, Giuliana occasionally climbed down a nearby ladder to go to a movie with Roberto while her governess was sleeping, but mostly they stayed in Giuliana's room. They talked and laughed and did other things that young people do. Soon, Roberto was sleeping over, escaping just before dawn to return to his own bed. Eventually, the expected happened. By February, Giuliana was showing and this was discovered by Signora Capellini. Signor Capellini ordered his wife, his daughter and her governess to meet in the villa's study.

SIGNOR CAPELLINI

All right, young lady, explain how this happened.

GIULIANA

I don't know. It just happened.

SIGNOR CAPELLINI

Governess, how did this happen? Weren't you watching my daughter all the time?

PASQUALINA

Yes, sir, yes, sir. All the time. Every minute. I don't know how it happened.

SIGNOR CAPELLINI

But I assume you weren't watching her in your sleep, were you?

PASQUALINA

No, sir.

SIGNOR CAPELLINI

And you slept lightly so you would have heard something?

PASQUALINA

I was having trouble sleeping so dear Giuliana was kind enough to give me a nice sleeping potion and that helped a lot. Now I can't go to sleep without it and I don't wake up.

SIGNOR CAPELLINI

And you never saw a boy going in and out of her room?

PASQUALINA

No, sir, no, sir.

SIGNOR CAPELLINI

Oh hell. What are our neighbors going to think? We'll be the laughingstock of the *contrada*. Isabella, is it too late to do something about this?

SIGNORA CAPELLINI

Yes, Nazario, it's too late.

SIGNOR CAPELLINI

All right, Giuliana, who is the father of this…this…

GIULIANA

Um, I don't know.

SIGNOR CAPELLINI

You don't know? Then how did it happen?

GIULIANA

It was a miracle?

SIGNORA CAPELLINI

Giuliana, answer your father. We won't be angry with you. Really. We just want you to be safe, and we want the baby to be safe. Now what is the father's name?

GIULIANA

(Whispering.) His name is Roberto.

SIGNORA CAPELLINI

Roberto. That's a nice name. And he is a nice boy?

GIULIANA

Oh, yes. And, mother, I love him so much! And he loves me so much!

SIGNORA CAPELLINI

I'm sure you do or this wouldn't have happened. Now, does Roberto have a last name?

GIULIANA

(Hesitating.) It's Montagni.

SIGNOR CAPELLINI

(Shouting) MONTAGNI!

GIULIANA

Yes.

SIGNOR CAPELLINI
The son of Alberto Montagni?

GIULIANA
Yes.

SIGNOR CAPELLINI
Damn!

SIGNORA CAPELLINI
Now Nazario…

SIGNOR CAPELLINI
From *Contrada della Lupa!*

GIULIANA
Yes.

SIGNOR CAPELLINI
Damn! Damn! Damn!

SIGNORA CAPELLINI
Nazario, calm down. You're going to have another heart attack.

SIGNOR CAPELLINI
The son of our mortal enemy. I can't believe this. Damn!

SIGNORA CAPELLINI
There's not much we can do about it now, Nazario. We'll just have to wait it out. Giuliana can stay indoors and nobody will notice and after the baby is born, well, we'll just see. There are some very nice adoption services in Siena.

SIGNOR CAPELLINI
We're not going to wait it out! We're going to take care of this now! Let's see what Alberto Montagni has to say about this! Let's go.

SCENE 2.

The office of the rector of the Duomo of Siena. Father Lorenzo sits at his desk. Also present are Signor and Signora Capellini, Signor and Signora Montagni, Giuliana, Roberto and Pasqualina.

FATHER LORENZO

I'm sorry we're a bit crowded here and we don't have enough chairs. Roberto, why don't you sit on the floor next to…is this Giuliana?

GIULIANA

Yes.

FATHER LORENZO

You're just as lovely as Roberto has said.

GIULIANA

(Blushing) Thank you. *(She holds Roberto's hand.)*

SIGNOR CAPELLINI

Father, let's get right down to business. This Roberto here has taken advantage of my daughter and we want to know what you're going to do about it.

FATHER LORENZO

Me? You expect me to do something about it?

SIGNOR CAPELLINI

Well, you're the church and the church has things to say about illegitimate children.

FATHER LORENZO

Yes, it tries to make illegitimate children legitimate. But first, let's hear from these young lovers. They should have a say in this. Roberto, what have you got to say?

ROBERTO

I love Giuliana! I want to marry her!

FATHER LORENZO
And you, Giuliana?

GIULIANA
I love Roberto! I want to marry him!

FATHER LORENZO
Well, that seems simple enough. What's the problem?

SIGNOR CAPELLINI
Roberto is from *Cantrada dell'Lupa*.

SIGNOR MONTAGNI
And Giuliana is from *Contrada dell'Istici*.

FATHER LORENZO
So this isn't so much about Giuliana and Roberto having a baby than it is about the fact that Giuliana and Roberto belong to two different *contrade*. Is that right?

SIGNOR MONTAGNI
Not just different, Father.

SIGNOR CAPELLINI
Opposing! Rivals! Bitter rivals!

FATHER LORENZO
Ah. You know, ever since I was assigned to Siena and especially since I was made rector of the Duomo more than thirty-two years ago, I have been struck by the rivalry among all the *contrade* in the city. Now don't get me wrong. I like a lot of things about the *contrade*. I like the pageantry and the customs and the colors and the symbols—well, most of them—and the museums and churches and of course the feasting. And how all of this comes together in the Palio. But mostly I am overwhelmed by the pride and solidarity among the people of each *contrada*. There's nothing like this in the whole world.

SIGNOR CAPELLINI and **SIGNOR MONTAGNI** (*together*)
We're very proud of our *contrada*.

FATHER LORENZO
But I have always been alarmed when things get out of hand. When there are brawls and fights between members of two opposing *contrade*. Bitter words. Recriminations. Revenge. And I think, is this something to be proud of? Is this something that people in this day and age should be doing? I'm asking you.

There is no response.

FATHER LORENZO
I have always hoped, and prayed, that people from one *contrada* could get along with those from the others, especially those from the *contrade* that have been decreed by the city to be rivals. They would visit, have meals together, go to church together, perhaps even marry each other.

SIGNOR CAPILLINI
Marry, Father? I can't remember the last time anyone from *Contrada dell'Istrice* married outside the *contrada*. It just isn't done.

FATHER LORENZO
Well, Signor Capellini, it's 1936. The world is changing, and these are frightening times. Hitler is riding roughshod over Europe and doing terrible things against the Jews. Italy is living under a dictator just like Hitler. Mussolini has conquered Ethiopia and is about to drag us into a war that I fear will be far worse than we can ever imagine. Our freedoms have been taken away. The Blackshirts are marching around and that blasted banner with the eagle is everywhere. People are worried, no frantic, about what is going to happen to their lives and their families. Signor and Signora Capellini, Signor and Signora Montagni, this is a time to come together. It's not a time for people from one area of Siena to be rivals with another. Don't you agree?

There is silence in the room.

FATHER LORENZO
Continuing) I'm sure you do. And what better way to bring people together than in the holy sacrament of matrimony? In particular, this loving couple, Giuliana and Roberto, and in the symbol of new life, a baby. We need a sign of hope, of joy!

SIGNOR CAPELLINI and **SIGNOR MONTAGNI** *(together)*
What? Giuliana and Roberto married?

SIGNORA CAPELLINI and **SIGNORA MONTAGNI** *(together)*
Oh, how lovely!

GIULIANA and **ROBERTO** *(together)*
Oh, wow!

PASQUALINA
Yes! Yes! Let's do it!

FATHER LORENZO
Wonderful! And by the way, Giuliana and Roberto, what do you plan to name your precious baby?

GIULIANA
If it's a girl, Father, we'll name her Angela because she will be an angel sent from heaven.

ROBERTO
And if it's a boy we'll name him Matteo because that means Gift from God.

FATHER LORENZO
Giuliana and Roberto, the church can be proud of you. We are all proud of you. And you, Signor and Signora Capellini and Signor and Signora Montagni, aren't you excited that you will be grandparents? You'll have a baby to spoil! But you'll have to do it equally. That means Roberto's parents and Giuliana's parents can't spoil the baby more than the other. You can show to all Siena that the bitter rivalry between *Contrada dell'Istrice* and

Cantrada dell'Lupa is at an end. Signora Capellini and Signora Montagni, please embrace.

The women hug each other in a long embrace.

FATHER LORENZO
Now, Signor Capellini and Signor Montagni, shake hands.

SIGNOR CAPELLINI
Do we have to?

FATHER LORENZO
Yes.

The men shake hands, Signor Montagni forcing the handshake to last a long time.

SIGNOR CAPELLINI
OK, but we're still going to compete at the Palio, right?

SIGNOR MONTAGNI
Of course.

ROBERTO
Father?

FATHER LORENZO
Yes, Roberto?

ROBERTO
Can Giuliana and me kiss?

FATHER LORENZO
Of course!

They do.

FATHER LORENZO

All right, let's do it now. We're all here. Let's go to the little Cappella della Madonna del Voto. It's my favorite part of the whole Duomo, going all the way back to the Seventeenth century. All of the *contrade* pay homage to the Virgin Mary there every year so you're familiar with it. So come, come with me, and we will make short work of this as the holy church incorporates two lives into one. And may this alliance turn your households' rancor into pure love.

All exit.

EPILOGUE

Never was true love ever so
Than this of Giuliana and her Roberto.

A PROTEST IN PISA

The feminist movement suffered a setback under Mussolini but then came back with public activism over such issues as divorce and abortion. It became more prominent during the administration of Prime Minister Silvio Berlusconi, focusing on the objectification of women on national television shows and politics.

ELENA WAS AFRAID she was going to run out of alibies. On Tuesday last week she said she had to go to a meeting of international students. On Thursday, she said she was meeting a friend to buy a textbook. On Tuesday it was to meet another friend to study for an exam. Now here it was Thursday again and she was having trouble coming up with a story her host family would believe.

She also wondered if they suspected anything was strange since these meetings always occurred at 3:30 p.m. on Tuesdays and Thursdays.

But they seemed to believe her. She was, after all, from a good family in America and seemed to be doing well in her classes at the Scuola Normale Superiore in Pisa.

Now it was Thursday again and she hadn't thought of a reason. Well, she'd have to say something. She found her host mother in the kitchen making *pizzelle*.

"Signora Coppelletti, that textbook I bought was wrong. I'm going to exchange it."

"All right. Be careful. And Elena, don't talk to strangers."

Bumping into other students, Elena ran all the way to Piazza Dante. The bench in the corner was empty so she'd have to wait. After a half hour, she texted. "Francesco. I am here."

Forty-five minutes later. "Are U being held up?"

Elena didn't know why she tolerated Francesco's tardiness, even absences. She had met Francesco when she had run into him, literally, in Piazza Dante on the second day of classes. Two minutes later they were buying gelato cones at the outdoor stand. Fifteen minutes later they were on a bench talking about their classes. She was taking Ancient History courses, he was studying civil engineering. An hour later they were in a secluded spot near the Arno discussing all sorts of things.

Francesco wasn't like any of the boys she had dated in Minneapolis. He was tall, had black curly hair and even blacker eyes. He always had the top buttons of his shirt unbuttoned to reveal chest hair and a medal of the Virgin Mary on a gold chain. Elena thought he looked like a young Marcello Mastroianni.

She waited another hour and when most of the students had gone home texted again. "R U coming today?"

At 6:30, she gave up. "Going home. Text me tonight. Love U!"

Again?

She found her hosts, Angelo and Carlotta Coppelletti, eating their desserts when she returned home.

"Oh, my goodness," Carlotta said. "We thought you must have found some friends and already had dinner. Did it take that long to exchange the textbook?"

"Textbook? Oh, um, yes, it took a while."

"Let me get you something. You must be starving."

"Just a little pasta, maybe. I'm not very hungry."

Carlotta and Angelo decided to stay at the table with her, "just to keep you company."

Elena couldn't have asked for a nicer couple to live with during her first year in the university. Middle-aged, they'd been married for twenty years and were childless because "there are too many children in the world."

Still, they relished having a young person living with them for eight or nine months. They had one a few years ago but even though "that didn't turn out too well," they decided to have another now, in the fall of 2019.

"Elena," Angelo said, "we've been so eager to talk to you about this. You know how Italians are fascinated with politics in the United States. We can't get over the things your president says."

"I wouldn't call him my president."

"Well, do you think he's going to win again next year?"

"Who knows? It's getting scarier and scarier."

"Isn't there any Democrat who could beat him?" Carlotta asked.

"I don't know. I'm going to work for Elizabeth Warren. She's progressive, but also very practical. But I don't know if a woman could be elected president."

"What about that Black woman?"

"Kamela Harris? It would be hard enough to elect a woman, much less a Black woman."

Elena ran down a list of other Democratic hopefuls, shaking her head about each one.

"What about," Angelo said, "Joe Biden? He's been around a long time. He's got a good record, hasn't he?"

"Biden? He's too nice. Trump would demolish him. I'm going to stick with Warren."

Elena had finished her *tagliatelle* and Carlotta put a dish of gelato in front of her.

"Elena," Carlotta said, "there's something else we wanted to ask. Why did you choose Italy to study abroad?"

"I absolutely love Italy! My grandparents on my father's side were born in a little town near Perugia. My mother's parents were born in Austria, but we don't seem to have an attachment to that. Anyway, they took me to Italy when I was ten and we went to a bunch of cities, Rome, Venice, Florence, Milan, even Naples, but I was too young to appreciate it.

"But then when I was a sophomore, four years ago, we went back and I couldn't get over how everything was so beautiful. The scenery, the architecture, and art works, the food! We mainly stayed in Florence and Siena—oh, how I love Siena!

"When we got home I started watching Italian movies, some of the old ones. 'La Dolce Vita,' 'Roman Holiday.' But you know what my favorite movie is? 'Under the Tuscan Sun'! I know, I know, some people say it's schlocky, but the scenery! I think that's one of the main reasons why I wanted to come to Tuscany to study."

"Elena," Carlotta said, "I hope you won't be too disappointed in what you'll find here. There are a lot of, well, bad things in Italy now. People are so upset about migrants coming from Africa and other places. The politicians shout at each other and don't get anything done. It seems like we get a new prime minister every other week. We turn off the television. Italy isn't like some romantic comedy."

"Oh, I know. I can understand if there are problems. But I know I won't be disappointed."

"And, Elena," Angelo added, "there's another thing, and I say this as a man. Be careful of the men in Italy. Not all of them, certainly. Most of them are just fine, they respect women. But there are some that don't. They treat them as objects. Just be careful."

"Oh, I will. I'm nineteen years old. I can take care of myself."

When she looked at her phone before going to bed there still wasn't a text from Francesco.

ONE REASON Elena had chosen the Scuola Normale Superiore, commonly known as "*la Normale*" in Pisa, for her freshman year abroad was because it was small. It only had about six hundred undergraduate and postgraduate students.

Another reason was because it was in Piazza dei Cavallieri, far enough away from the Leaning Tower and the Duomo so that she could avoid the mobs of tourists.

When they looked at the university's literature her mother was impressed that it was founded by Napoleon and her father was impressed that among its graduates was the famed physicist Enrico Fermi, often called the architect of the atomic bomb.

Elena was more impressed that another graduate was Massimo D'Alema, who served as prime minister from 2006 to 2008 and was the only former Communist prime minister of Italy.

"Elena," her father teased, "why do you always find some left-wing angle in what you do?"

"Just because."

Sometimes, her parents thought she had spent more time protesting various causes than she spent in class at her high school.

When she was a freshman in 2015 she joined other students marching in front of the Minneapolis City Hall to observe the one-year anniversary of the killing of a Black teenager, Michael Brown, by a white police officer in Ferguson, Mo. She made a "Black Lives Matter" sign out of cardboard and a thick Sharpie.

When she was a sophomore, she organized a group to pray in front of the American Indian Center in Minneapolis. She told the students that they needed to join in solidarity with teenagers fighting the Dakota Access Pipeline, which would have cut through the Standing Rock Sioux Reservation.

In January 2017, she and five friends boarded a Greyhound to go to Washington to take part in the Women's Rights March and to protest the inauguration of Donald J. Trump. She carried a hand-made sign saying "No One Is Free If Others Are Oppressed." Her friends carried other signs with words she couldn't report to her mother. Elena couldn't stop talking about the weekend for weeks.

As a senior, she organized a sit-in at her school on March 24, the day students in Parkland, Fla., held a March for Our Lives protest for gun control after a gunman killed seventeen students and faculty members at their school.

"Haven't you run out of causes?" her father asked after that one.

"Hardly. We're going to do something with migrants, with gay rights, with climate change, so much more. And then I'll get involved in the 2020 election."

"Aren't you going to be in Italy then?"

"I'll be home by June. And maybe I'll find something in Italy that would be exciting."

Elena's mother wondered where her daughter got all this passion. At her age she was happy to work on a veterans' assistance program and that was enough.

Six weeks after she arrived in Pisa, she was itching for a new cause when she noticed a sign on a bulletin board. It was headed by the words *"Ni una nemos."*

"What's that about?" she asked the young woman next to her.

"You don't know? Oh, right, you're from America, aren't you? *Ni una nemos* means 'Not One Less.' It means not one woman less and it's a huge feminist movement seeking to end male violence against women. There have been big demonstrations around the world, especially in Latin

America and in Europe. But I suppose the United States as usual is a little behind on these things."

"No, that's not true! I went to the Women's Rights March in Washington two years ago. There were thousands and thousands of people there."

"Did they talk about violence against women?"

"Um. I think a little."

"OK. My name is Claudia."

"I'm Elena."

Claudia took her arm. "Let's sit down. This is a long story."

They found a quiet spot outside the cafeteria.

"Well, Elena, on October 19, 2016, the *Ni una nemos* collective organized a mass strike in Argentina, the first ever by women. It was in response to the murder of a girl in Mar del Parta in Argentina, her name was Lucia Pérez. She was abducted outside her school by a gang who drugged her, repeatedly raped her and sodomized her, and she died the next day. Two men had left the body at a hospital and tried to say she was the victim of a drug overdose, but doctors said she had been subjected to extreme sexual violence.

"Women in Argentina were furious. They dressed in mourning for what was called *Miércoles negro,* which is Spanish for Black Wednesday. Soon there were street demonstrations in Chile, Guatemala, Peru, Bolivia, El Salvador, Paraguay, Uruguay and Mexico and then they spread to Spain. Surely you've heard about all this."

"The news in the United States now is all about Trump."

"On March 8, 2017, *Ni una menos* took part in the International Women's Strike. Actually, the strike was spearheaded in the United States by the leaders of that Women's March on Washington that you went to. They said *Ni una menos* was an inspiration."

"I wish I could remember that."

"Well, anyway, there have been many many demonstrations in Italy since then. They have been about the violence against women but speakers also talk about how women are treated in Italy, how they are disrespected, how their wages are less than men."

"That last part is true in the United States, too. But nothing seems to change."

"Sometimes countries have specific goals. Female genital mutilation has caused an outcry in Africa and Asia and the Middle East."

"I can't believe that's done!"

"Well, it is. It's a fact of life in those countries."

Elena watched the line of students hurrying from class to class.

"It all seems so hopeless. What can one person do?"

"Elena, that sign over there? It says that there will be a meeting Wednesday night to organize a march in Pisa. Do you want to come?"

"Do I? Of course!"

SURPRISINGLY, Francesco was even a little early when he arrived in Piazza Dante on Thursday afternoon. He had put on his best cologne and unbuttoned another button on his shirt. He was tired of the mumbling and fumbling at the river bank and planned, after weeks of her refusals, to take Elena back to his apartment.

"This time she's gonna come," he said as he dusted a little hairspray on his curls.

Elena arrived breathless, barely giving him a peck on his cheek. "Oh, Francesco, I have so much to tell you."

"Elena, can we get a gelato?"

"Francesco, I went to the most amazing meeting last night. They had it in Palazzo dei Congressi."

"You went to the Palazzo dei Congressi? That big convention hall on via Matteotti? You went there by yourself? At night?"

"Good grief. I went there with my friend Claudia. They had reserved a room for two hundred fifty people, but so many people came they moved it to one for five hundred and there were still people out the doors. It was packed! Teenagers, students, young married women, grandmothers, nuns! Even some men."

"Elena, can we get a gelato?"

"Oh, Francesco, there's this marvelous movement called *Ni una nemos,* which means 'Not One Less.' It began in Argentina but now it's all over the world. Well, not so much in America but I swear I'm going to start something when I get back next year. I know some friends who will help me."

"Elena, slow down. What's the point of this 'Nobody but Us'?

She sat on the bench next to him, got up and sat down again.

"It's 'Not One Less.' Well, its main purpose is to stop violence against women, like murder, rape, assaults and lots of other things, like forced sexual acts or child sexual abuse or human trafficking. Plus psychological abuse. So many, many things."

"So how are you going to stop it? You can't stand on a street corner and yell 'Stop raping that woman!'"

"Of course not. There has to be stronger laws. The police have to do a better job of making arrests. Judges can't be so lenient. Francesco, did you read the report that just came out? Two men were cleared of rape charges in Ancora because the judges said that the victim was not 'appealing' enough to be raped or pursued sexually. Can you believe this?"

"Come on."

"It's true. This happened in 2017 but it was just revealed. And the three judges were women!"

"Well, then."

Elena ignored him and began pacing in the tiny piazza.

"Francesco, you probably have never even heard the word 'femicide.'"

"Fem…?"

"It's a term for a sex-based hate crime. In other words, intentionally killing women or girls because they are female. But there are so many ways women are subjected to violence. That's what they were talking about last night."

"Elena, I've never seen you so worked up. I like it!"

"And women have to be more willing to report abuse. Often they're afraid to. They think there's a stigma or shame to it. There was a report at the meeting that said that one of three women and girls in Italy experiences physical or sexual abuse, and most of the time it's by a partner. And that more than ninety percent of domestic violence cases go unreported."

"Want to get some gelato?"

"No, Francesco, I do not want to get some gelato. Have you heard a word of what I've said?"

"Of course I have. I just don't see what it has to do with me. It sounds like a women's thing."

It wasn't warm, but Elena was sweating. "It's NOT a women's thing! Do you know that the World Economic Forum ranked Italy seventy-fourth out of one hundred thirty-four countries in gender equality? That's the worst in Europe and behind such countries as Ghana, Malawi and Vietnam."

"Elena, can you sit down? Can we just talk?"

Elena had just begun. "One woman," she said, "gave a report last night showing that many women get fired for being pregnant."

"That's not legal, is it?"

"Of course not. But sometimes employers demand that women sign an undated letter and they use that. Also, even though abortion is legal in Italy some doctors refuse to perform an abortion because they don't want to lose their jobs in clinics run by the Catholic church."

"I suppose next you're going to bring up Berlusconi."

"He was such a joke. Such a misogynist. And he's how some people picture Italy. At home I read an article in Newsweek. They called Italy the 'Bunga-Bunga Nation' because of his misogynist antics. A great prime minister you had."

"Now I suppose you'll bring up the #MeToo movement."

"It goes without saying. God! Many women last night talked about how they were harassed at work and how they never reported it. And then they got into the Italian machismo thing."

"Ah yes, the Italian machismo thing."

"I wasn't even aware of it until I got here last month. Now I notice it everywhere."

"Like what?"

"Francesco, I can't walk down the street without some guys in a car honking and catcalling, 'Hey, Beautiful! You're looking good. Come on with us, we'll have a good time.'"

"Elena, you shouldn't wear short skirts."

Elena punched him in the arm. "I don't wear short skirts! They're no shorter than anyone else's."

"It's just a harmless flirtation, Elena."

"It's harassment, Francesco. It's treating women like objects. Like all those women on game shows. Last night one woman yelled, 'Look at all those bimbos! They don't have anything on!' Everybody booed."

"Hey, I like those girls. I was watching the other night and there was one girl who took a shower with hardly any clothes on. The guys in the audience went crazy."

"A lot of women think it's disgusting."

"Disgusting? People love to watch those shows. That's television. Anyway, those girls wouldn't be doing it if they didn't want to. I bet they get paid millions of *euros.*"

"Francesco, you just don't get it. The treatment of women is a worldwide problem. That's why there's a *Ni una nemos* movement."

"Elena, why don't we go back to my apartment and we can talk about this more?"

Elena sighed and lowered her voice. "OK, let's get personal about this. It's also how you treat me. You're always late for our meetings. Sometimes you don't show up at all."

"Hey, I'm here today, aren't I?"

"You don't respond to my texts."

"What?"

"I see how you look at other women when I'm talking to you. That's very rude."

"Oh, God."

"I'm just another of a long line of girlfriends, right, Francesco?"

"No, no. I really like you, Elena. Really. I've never been with an American girl before. All my buddies are jealous."

"Oh, so I'm your trophy American girl."

"No! No!"

"Well, maybe I'm your last. I have to go, Francesco. I have to help plan the march on Saturday. Have a good time."

"Elena!"

HUNDREDS OF PEOPLE, including some men, joined the *Ni una nemos* march on Saturday. It began in Piazza San Sivestro near the Museo Nationale, wound along the Lungarno Mediceo on the Arno, then up via San Frediano to the university and Piazza Dante. Elena saw Francesco standing near their bench among other onlookers. He looked forlorn. Then the marchers proceeded on to Piazza dei Miracoli with its huge Duomo and the Leaning Tower.

The milling crowds of tourists stopped and stared as many of the marchers carried *"Ni una nemos"* signs and other banners that said *"Basta violenza sulle donne"* (Enough violence against women), *"50/50 non una di meno"* (50/50 no less), *"Sono una donna soggetto"* (I am a subject woman) and *"La violenza non è forza ma debolezza"* (Violence is not strength but weakness). Elena's said *"Libera menti donna"* (Free woman's minds).

A makeshift stage had been set up on the expanse of grass near the tower and Elena saw her hosts, Angelo and Carlotta Coppelletti, at the front of the crowd holding signs. Speaker after speaker described *Ni una menos*, called for an end to violence against women, urged passage of new legislation, denounced sexism and urged everyone, men as well as women, to join the cause. There were a few catcalls, but many of the tourists applauded. They had no idea this was going on in Italy.

When the marchers returned along the same route, Elena saw Francesco still standing in Piazza Dante. But this time he was alone and holding a sign, *"Il futuro è femminile"* (The future is female).

Elena waved.

NONNA'S HOUSE

In late February 2020, Europe faced its first major outbreak of Covid-19 when Italy reported that cases suddenly grew from five to more than 150.

IF DANNY HADN'T noticed the large white envelope stuck in the pile of junk catalogs and pleas from charities, his mother wouldn't have opened it and they'd still be living in Pittsburgh, Pennsylvania.

"Mom! Is this for me?"

"I don't think so. Let me look." Elizabeth Donato cracked another egg in the bowl and wiped her hands on her apron.

"It's for me, right?"

"No, afraid not. Odd, though. It's from Italy. Look at the great stamps, Danny. Maybe your father can help you start a stamp collection."

"Really?"

"Who could be writing from Italy? The address says Calvi e Bandettini. *Avvocati di diretto*. Lucca' A law firm in Lucca?"

It took ten minutes to find the letter opener that someone had artfully concealed in the drawer with plain envelopes and stamps. She slit the envelope open.

"What? What? Is this real?"

"Mom, what is it? Mom, what happened? Why are your hands shaking?"

Four of the six pages fell to the floor but Elizabeth continued reading from those in her trembling hands.

"I can't believe this!"

"Why are you crying, Mom? Did somebody die?"

"This can't be true."

"Who died, Mom? Who died?"

205

"Danny, where are your father and your sister?"

"They're raking leaves in back. Why are you crying? Mom, please!"

"Go get them, Danny."

Elizabeth sank into a kitchen chair, almost knocking over the bowl on the table. Sniffling, Danny ran out the back door, returning in a minute with his father and Sarah.

"What's up, hon?" Stephen said. "Why is Danny crying? He said somebody died. Who died?"

Sarah started sobbing, too. "Who died, Mom? What's going on?"

Elizabeth handed the pages to her husband.

"Really? Oh my God!"

Elizabeth and Stephen had gone to Italy for the first time on their honeymoon, landing in Rome, then driving north to Florence, Milan, Venice and then circling down to northern Tuscany. Stephen wanted to discover the village of San Martino where his father was born and to meet his grandmother.

The visit went beyond their wildest expectations. Ever since her son and his wife were killed in an automobile accident in America, Nonna had never dreamed that she would see her only grandchild.

"Stefano! Stefano! Santa Maria! Venire qui! Dammi un bacio! Dammi un abbraccio!"

Having taken an Italian course at a Pittsburgh technical college in preparation for the trip, Stephen knew that he should give her a kiss and a hug, which he did, except that it went on and on, and then the whole thing was repeated with Elizabeth.

"Elizabetta! Elizabetta!"

Skipping any attempt at conversation and always presuming that everyone is always hungry, Nonna practically pushed them into chairs at the table and proceeded to bring out plates and bowls and platters. Ravioi, chicken in a red sauce, an omelet, a vegetable torte, fresh lettuce, tomatoes, celery, crusty bread, cheeses.

"Mangiare! Mangiare!"

Throughout the meal Nonna told stories about how she was born in this very house and how she met her husband, Stephen's grandfather, at the start of World War II. He was, she said, such a wonderful, beautiful man and they were so much in love. But in 1944 he joined the Resistance fighting the Germans and Fascists in the hills just above San Martino. Her voice began to break and Stephen and Elizabeth waited quietly.

Then, she said, just before the armistice, her husband and the other partisans were preparing their weapons when the Nazis surrounded them and killed them all. The bodies were returned to the village and buried in the church cemetery. Nonna was seven months pregnant.

"Bastardi! Bastardi! Bastardi!" she exclaimed.

Seeing the tears running down his grandmother's cheeks and wanting to change the subject, Stephen said, "Nonna, please tell me about my father."

Nonna said how little Pietro was a perfect baby, but as he grew older he became a *mascalzone*—a rascal—and was always getting into trouble with the teachers. But she still loved him so much and she was devastated when he decided to go with some friends to America. Only nineteen years old—*un giovane!* Nonna never saw him again.

She showed Stephen the letters his father had written her, describing how he was working in a factory in Pittsburgh. Nonna said she didn't even know where that was. And then he wrote that he was getting married. She also showed Stephen and Elizabeth the letter informing her that her son and his wife were killed when an airplane crashed on the way back from Florida where they were vacationing.

"I miss Papa and Mama every day," Stephen said. "I was twenty-three years old and about to get married when that happened. Elizabeth saved my life."

Nonna's handkerchief was wet and she took out another from her apron. *"Mio figlio. È morto. Morto."*

Elizabeth tried to comfort her. "You must have been very brave living here all alone all these years."

Nonna shrugged. "No, no, no."

When they said their *"Arriverdercis!"* three hours later, after visiting his grandfather's grave in the church cemetery, after going through photo albums and scrapbooks, and after eating too many cookies, there was an abundance of kisses and hugs and promises to return.

"Presto!"

For months, Stephen couldn't forget the image of his little grandmother standing in the doorway and waving goodbye.

The second visit was six years ago, a few months after Sarah was born. *"Bel bambino! Bel bambino!"* Nonna cried. She gave the baby a porcelain doll that she had been saving for the daughter she never had.

Sarah was two and Danny was just born when they visited four years ago. They stayed two weeks this time because Stephen wanted to do some repairs. Tiles were cracked on the roof, the electricity was haphazard and the outside balcony needed bolstering. The house, Nonna said, was built by her great-grandfather so of course there were always things that had to be done.

The visits became annual. They would stay for two weeks, Stephen would do repairs, Elizabeth would take cooking lessons from Nonna, and the family found good friends in the neighbors next door, the Lucchesis, Fredi and Francesca and their children, Marco and Livia. The couple taught the Americans how to play *scopa* and *briscola* and what to buy at the little *mercato* in the center of the village.

Each year, the children counted the days before they flew to their great-grandmother's and wrote her little letters when they returned. Sarah said she wished Nonna had Zoom, but her father said she didn't even have a computer.

Nonna clearly wasn't feeling well on their visit last year. Instead of the extravagant meals she had always prepared, she offered a frozen pizza.

"Sono malato," she said.

"We're so sorry," Elizabeth said. "We love you, Nonna."

Stephen didn't want to talk about it, but Nonna said she knew she wouldn't have long to live and didn't know what would happen to her house.

Someone would surely buy it now that it was in better shape, Stephen said.

Nonna said she didn't want strangers living in her house. And that ended the conversation. When they left that time, both Stephen and Elizabeth knew it would be their last visit to San Martino. They would never see her again.

Last August, Francesca Lucchesi called and, with her voice cracking, said that Nonna's body was found on her kitchen floor. She'd been trying to bake bread and had a heart attack. The family couldn't attend the funeral, but went to Mass at their local church the next day. Elizabeth made Nonna's ravioli in tribute and they shed many tears.

"Well," Stephen had said, "maybe we'll go back to Italy someday, but there's not much reason now, is there?"

WITH THE KIDS shooed out to the backyard to play with their new kitten Rosie, Stephen and Elizabeth sat at the kitchen table, the pages of the letter spread before them.

"I can't believe she did this," he said.

"She said she didn't want strangers living in her house, but I never thought…"

"You'd think she would have asked us."

"You know Nonna. She wasn't the kind to ask. She just did it."

Stephen put down his coffee cup and stretched.

"Poor old lady. I can just imagine her worrying and worrying about what would happen to the place. And then she died like that."

He shuffled the pages around, as if hoping there was some other explanation. There was not.

"Well," he said, "I'll call the lawyers tomorrow to see if they can find a real estate agent for us. I don't think it will be too hard to sell. It's a nice house. Old, but nice. Let me wash up."

"It shouldn't be hard. Dinner's almost ready."

The letter sat on the mantel after dinner as a sort of silent sentinel while the family played their nightly game of Monopoly. Sarah held Rosie in her lap and Danny was caught cheating, again. When the children went to bed—Sarah still holding the kitten—Danny stopped on the staircase.

"Mom, why did you cry when you got that letter today?"

"Well…um…we'll talk about it tomorrow."

The parents soon followed.

"Tired?" Elizabeth asked as they got into bed.

"Yes. Maybe I'm getting too old to rake all those leaves."

"Stephen! You're only thirty-three!"

"Then maybe I'll cut some of those trees down. That'll solve the problem. Good night, hon."

"Night."

Within minutes, both were fast asleep.

It could have been the shaft of moonlight that struck the bed after clouds had parted. It could have been a bare tree branch switching against the window. Whatever it was, Stephen suddenly woke and stared at the dark ceiling.

He turned over. And again. And stared at the ceiling again. Then he poked his wife.

"Hon?"

"I'm awake. Couldn't sleep."

"You're not thinking what I'm thinking."

"Um. Maybe."

"We can't, right?"

"No, we can't."

"Dumb idea."

"Really dumb."

"Go back to sleep."

"Night."

At 2 a.m., they were both lying on their backs, staring at the ceiling.

"The kids would have to make new friends," Stephen said.

"Danny might like it but Sarah would scream bloody murder if she had to leave her friends here."

"Of course they'd have the Lucchesi kids, Marco and Livia.

"Right."

"You'd miss your students, too," Stephen said.

"I'm sure I would," Elizabeth said.

"Of course, I can do my online stuff anywhere."

They were silent for another fifteen minutes.

"We've always loved San Martino," Stephen said.

"The people are so friendly."

"Not much to do, though."

"The *mercato* takes ten minutes."

Another long silence.

"I do like the house now that you've fixed it," Elizabeth said. "I love the kitchen cupboards. And the second bathroom was really needed."

"Nice big windows."

"The stove is old."

"It can be replaced," Stephen said.

They thought some more.

"There's been so many murders in Pittsburgh lately."

"Hardly any over there."

"That tiny village just seems so safe."

"Let's sleep on it," Elizabeth said. "We can think clearer in the morning, OK?"

"OK."

Since neither had slept much, both came into the kitchen badly needing morning coffee.

"Mom," Danny said as soon as he saw his mother. "What did that letter say? Who died?"

Elizabeth and Stephen exchanged glances and sat down.

"Now," Stephen said, "you know how you loved to go to see Nonna in Italy?"

"Yes."

"Well, as you know, she died about eight months ago…"

"And we couldn't go to the funeral because Mom was teaching and you had a deadline," Sarah said.

"Right," Elizabeth said. "Well, Nonna's only relative is your father."

"Because," Danny said, "Daddy's parents were killed in that airplane crash before we were even born."

"So," Stephen said, "she didn't have anyone to leave her lovely house to, so, guess what? She left it to us!"

"Really?" Sarah said.

"Wow!" Danny said.

"So," Elizabeth said, "at first we just thought we'd sell it. But we've been thinking all night and we think, maybe, just maybe, we could move there! What do you think?"

"To San Martino?" Sarah asked

"Yes."

"And leave here?" Danny said.

"Yes."

There was a long silence as the children stared at the table, at each other, and at their parents.

"When?" Danny asked.

"Well," Stephen said, "we'd have to wait until the semester is over, so it would be over the Christmas break."

"I wouldn't go to my school?" Sarah asked.

"No."

"I wouldn't see my friends?"

"No."

"Then I'm not going!" Sarah shouted.

"Sarah!" Stephen said.

"I'm not going!" Sarah picked up Rosie and ran to her room.

"Oh, Oh," Elizabeth said. "I was afraid of something like this."

For the next ten days, there were screams and sulks, stomps and silences. Elizabeth and Stephen attempted conversations but they were aborted. Sarah would make new friends, they told her. Italian schools were supposed to be very good. She liked playing with Marco and Livia. There was a very nice playground. They could go to the *mercato* every day.

Sarah said she didn't want to talk about it. Her parents shrugged. "She'll come around," Elizabeth said.

"I hope so."

Danny, meanwhile, packed and unpacked his little suitcase eleven times.

Elizabeth gave notice at her school, saying she would complete the semester teaching second grade but a successor would have to be found after that. The principal expressed his gratitude and said her little students would miss her very much.

Stephen notified his clients that he would complete their current projects but he would wait until late January to take on others.

He called the law firm in Lucca and had a long conversation with Signor Calvi about the transfer of the property. Since Nonna had left a formal will *(Testamento)*, the lawyer said, the house could be turned over to the Donato family immediately. They would have to pay a tax, but they could afford that.

Again, Stephen and Elizabeth sat down with Sarah.

"You know," Stephen said, "you've always liked going to San Martino and we've only been able to stay for a little while. Now we could stay for a long time, maybe forever."

Sarah grimaced.

"The weather's so much nicer than here," Elizabeth said. "You could play outdoors for much longer. You could go up in the hills to those secret hiding places you and Livia found."

Sarah closed her eyes.

"And think of having Christmas in Italy! Remember those picture books that showed all the beautiful decorations? We could go to the shops in Lucca and they have such wonderful treats. And Midnight Mass in that quaint church? Oh, Sarah!"

"And Easter's special, too," Stephen said. "Processions! Fresh *panettone* bread! Chocolate eggs!"

Sarah held Rosie tighter.

Stephen saved the best for last.

"Listen. I called Alitalia and guess what. We can take Rosie. She'll have to stay in her carrier under your seat but she'll be with us all the while. Isn't that perfect? I just bet Rosie will love Italy."

Sarah kissed Rosie.

"OK," she whispered.

"Great. Now we just have to sell this place."

There was work to be done, and they made a list: Plastering, painting, wall papering, electrical work. Contractors came in and out for weeks. When it was finished, they put the house up for sale. It was a seller's market in Pittsburgh then and they received three offers. It wasn't hard to pick one.

Their friends were truly sad to see them leave. Stephen and Elizabeth had made many friends in the eight years they had lived in Pittsburgh. Stephen was an umpire for the Little League and had four good golfing buddies. Besides teaching second grade at McKinley School, Elizabeth belonged to two book clubs and a knitting group.

But they were probably better known for their performances on the cello (Stephen) and violin (Elizabeth). The "Donato Duo" often performed in schools and retirement homes and had even been featured in a story in the Pittsburgh Post-Gazette. Sometimes, they went out on their front lawn and performed duets. Even neighbors from the next block came and sat on the grass and applauded.

They wondered about taking the instruments, but Stephen said, "What the hell, we'll regret it if we didn't take them."

"What the hell," Elizabeth added.

213

On an unusually warm night just before Christmas they gave their last concert, consisting entirely of Christmas carols and ending with "Ave Maria." All the neighbors came up afterwards for hugs and kisses.

Their friends threw a big going-away party in the church hall right after Christmas. The hall was decorated with Italian red, green and white streamers and every family brought at least one Italian dish. Spaghetti was the most common.

Someone played the accordion, and a number of people danced. At the end of it, Johnny Greco, Stephen's best friend, got up on a table and raised a glass of beer.

"To our dear friends, the Donatos. We're very sorry to see you go. We're gonna miss your concerts, but mostly we'll miss you, Stephen, Elizabeth, Sarah, Danny. You are Family Numero Uno! But, hey, what could be better than going to Italy in 2020?"

WITH ROSIE STOWED under her seat on the long flight to Pisa, Sarah spent much of the trip kneeling on the floor and poking her fingers into the cage. Danny fell asleep soon after takeoff and Elizabeth and Stephen were so nervous and/or excited they couldn't finish their cold dinners, couldn't read, couldn't sleep. They just held hands.

"It's going to be great," Elizabeth said.

"We're going to love it."

"Of course."

A million thoughts—and fears—went through their minds.

They managed to get two kids, a cat, five suitcases, a cello and a violin into the rental car.

"Look at those trees," Elizabeth said as they approached San Martino and saw the ancient cypresses standing like tall guardians on the sides of the road.

"They never change," Stephen said. "Just like everything else here."

"Except," his wife said, "now they're going to have a new young American family as permanent residents."

"They're so lucky."

Unlike the picturesque hilltop villages seen on countless calendars and in movies, the nondescript San Martino consisted of a range of houses mostly built after the village was bombed by the Nazis during World II and a few, like Nonna's, that had somehow survived for a couple of centuries.

A massive church, much too large for the village, stood in the middle alongside a creek that was mostly a trickle. The business "district" consisted of the *mercato* and a *bar* for coffee and sweets. A canning plant at the edge of town provided some employment.

"I love this place," Stephen said.

"You know," Elizabeth said, "it feels like home already. It's so quiet, so safe. We're not going to have any worries here."

"Let's hope not."

They felt even more at home when they pulled up to what would always be called "Nonna's House" and saw the big sign stretched between two poles in front:*"Benvenuti Americani!"*

"Oh, wow," Stephen and Elizabeth said together.

They had barely opened the car doors when they were engulfed by the hugs and kisses of their new neighbors, the Lucchesis.

"We've been watching from the window all morning," Francesca said as she hugged Elizabeth and Sarah together.

"We hardly slept all night." Fredi shook Stephen's hands and grasped his shoulder as the children smiled shyly at each other.

Everyone helped unload the car and carried it all inside.

With their neighbors' help, Stephen and Elizabeth unpacked a few things and then enjoyed the bottle of Rosso di Montelcino that Fredi had brought.

"Welcome to Italy," Fredi said. "May you always find love, happiness and good health here."

Francesca gave Stephen a sealed envelope: *Caro Stefano ed Elizabetta.*

"Nonna gave me this to give to you after your last visit," she said.

"Look," Stephen told Elizabeth, "she says, '*Dio ti benedica nella tua nuova casa.*' God bless us in our new home. She knew then she was going to give it to us."

"God bless her," Elizabeth said.

"We're so glad she did," Francesca said.

"We talked about this," Fredi said, "and we said we would never let anybody but you all to live next to us."

Unpacking took much of four days, with some things lost forever and only minor damage to the cello and violin. Stephen thought he could restring and tighten.

Stephen set up an office in an alcove on the second floor and Elizabeth enrolled Sarah in the bright new school in the neighboring village of San Mateo and told the principal she could start teaching in the fall. Rosie found a nesting place on a window sill where she could observe the variety of birds in the back yard.

The children spent much of their time with Marco and Livia and a bunch of other kids at a well-equipped playground that had swings, slides, jungle gyms, trapezes and even a playhouse.

Tears were shed whenever they found something of Nonna's—a piece of jewelry, her hand-written recipes on index cards, photos of her and her young husband.

One afternoon they visited Nonna's grave at the cemetery. Amabilia Bianchi, 1934-2019. Her marble tomb was next to her husband's, Stefano Donato, 1922-1943.

"Look, Dad," Danny said, "you were named after your grandfather."

"I know. My parents thought he was a hero, killed by the Nazis like that. And notice that your grandparents had different last names. That's a custom in Italy, the wife keeping her maiden name."

"I'm going to keep my name when I get married," Sarah said.

They gathered close to examine the little photographs in glass frames on top of the tombs.

"Nonna looks fierce," Danny said.

"And Daddy's grandfather looks very young." Sarah said.

"He was."

Stephen and Elizabeth had met some of the villagers on their previous visits and found that the community represented a larger range of backgrounds and lifestyles than they might have expected. Apparently, some people preferred San Martino's isolation.

All of the neighbors on the Donato's street were elderly. Signora Franchi was Nonna's good friend and they had visited each other every day. Next to her, two elderly men who had been harassed in Pisa had moved to San Martino for safety and isolation. Then a retired teacher who had volunteered in Nigeria. Then a Chinese importer, Signor Chen, who made frequent visits to Codogno, a town in Lombardi.

There were many traditional families, some with elderly parents sharing the home with young grandchildren. A few widows made daily visits to the cemetery and some old men gathered in front of the *mercato* every morning to gossip and play cards.

For the first few weeks, all of them greeted these newcomers with good wishes and sometimes with home-made meals. They reminisced about "poor old Nonna" and wondered why in the world a young family would leave a big city in America to live in a tiny Italian village with no movies, no restaurants, no soccer team.

"Sometimes we wonder ourselves," Stephen said.

They earned even more friendly comments when they began playing little concerts from their balcony. Once a week they unpacked the cello and violin and soon the strains of something familiar, like "Musetta's Waltz" from "La Boheme," or something obscure like Goddard's "Aubade" filled the air. People came out on their own balconies and cheered and applauded when the concerts ended.

Friday night was reserved for playing *scopa* with the Lucchesis and they alternated houses. Toward the end of the evening in late February, Francesca wondered if Stephen and Elizabeth had seen the news recently.

"Afraid not," Elizabeth said. "We've got so many projects going."

"Well, there's something strange going on. They're talking about a new disease that's baffling doctors. It was found in a man in Codogno."

"Isn't that where Signor Chen goes to buy things?" Stephen asked.

"Yes," Francesca said. "But this man was 38 years old and he was having respiratory problems. The doctor said he had the flu and prescribed some medicine. But the man got worse, and he went to the hospital there."

Fredi continued the story. "The doctors found it interesting that the guy recently met an Italian friend who had been in China. Now this disease was first reported in China, so the doctors tested the man and his pregnant wife and they tested positive for this disease."

"What's scary," Francesca said, "is that this man had a lot of friends and may well have infected others, so the disease may be spreading. He's now in a clinic in Pavia."

"That's about 35 kilometers south of Milan," said Fredi, who was obsessed with maps.

"Anyway," Francesca said, "this thing has a very odd name."

"When I first heard it," Fredi said, "I thought it was a name for a new planet. It's called Covid-19. But we don't have to worry. This is in Lombardy. We're nowhere near Codogno."

A FEW DAYS LATER, Stephen suggested watching the news to see if there was anything new about this disease.

"We should get used to finding out what's happening in Italy," he said. "Probably nothing as exciting as a Steelers game."

All four lined up on the couch.

"There are now," the announcer was saying, "79 confirmed cases of the coronavirus. Of the new ones, 54 were found in Lombardy, 17 in Veneto, eight in Pavia, two in Emilia-Romagna, two in Lazio and one in Piedmont."

"This is so sad," Elizabeth said.

"It's spreading all over," Stephen said.

While Sarah clutched Rosie, Danny grabbed his mother's hand.

"What's happening, Mama? What's going on?"

"It's OK. There's a bad sickness going around up north, but it's far from here. We'll be fine."

"Are people going to die?"

"No, no. I don't think it's that serious."

The next night the announcer reported that there were 984 confirmed cases and that two government officials in Emilia-Romagna had tested positive.

"Even government officials," Stephen said.

The news was even grimmer the following night.

"We can now report," the announcer was saying, "that the first deaths have occurred because of Covid-19."

"Deaths?" Elizabeth whispered. "There have been deaths?"

"Mama!" Danny cried. He leaned against her.

"The first was a 77-year-old woman from Casalpusterlengo, who visited the same emergency room as that 38-year-old man from Codogno that we've mentioned. She died in Lombardy. There was also a 78-year-old man who died in Veneto, so we now see the coronavirus in both the northwest and northeast parts of Italy."

"Oh, my God," Elizabeth said.

"But people are dying?" Danny said.

"It's fine, Danny, it's fine. Don't worry."

"Are you sure?" He climbed on his mother's lap.

"Yes, Danny, it's fine. Let's listen to the man on the TV."

The man on the TV was continuing.

"There have been many cases reported in other countries, even in the United States."

"The United States? It's happening there, too?" Stephen said as he pulled out his phone. "I'm going to text Johnny."

His hands were shaking so it took a couple of tries.

"Hey! Bad virus around here. There?"

"Hey! No prbls here. Pres says under control. Only 15 ppl with it. Only one sick others fine."

"Really?"

"Yeah. Pres said going to be miracle. Going to disappear."

"U believe in miracles?"

"Why not?"

Stephen had long ago learned not to talk to Johnny about the president of the United States.

"Take care, Bud."

When Stephen put the phone away he noticed that Sarah was staring straight ahead, not even looking at the TV.

"You OK, honey?"

When she didn't respond, Stephen put his arm around her.

"Don't worry, Hon. It's not something near us. We're going to be fine. Hey, how's Rosie doing? She always looks so happy. I think she's gotten bigger since we've been here, don't you? Hon? Don't you? Such a good kitty."

He patted the cat. Danny, meanwhile, hugged his mother. Elizabeth stroked his back.

"Well," Stephen announced, "it sounds bad, but I'm sure it's not going to spread very far. Not here anyway."

BY MARCH 1, the death toll in Italy had climbed to 40 and with Danny tight against Elizabeth and Sarah staring straight ahead, the Donato family sat transfixed in front of the television every night as the announcer listed the victims.

A 68-year-old woman in Crema. An 84-year-old man in Bergamo. An 88-year-old man in Codogno. An 80-year-old man in Milan. A 62-year-old man in Como. An 84-year-old man in Nembro. A 91-year-old man in San Fiorano. An 83-year-old woman from Codogno.

"You see," Stephen said, "these are all old people. Eighties, nineties. And they're all far away. No need to worry."

The announcer continued. "Also, a 26-year-old Norwegian man who has been living in Florence has tested positive."

"Good heavens," Elizabeth said as she adjusted Danny, "this guy is 26, younger than we are, and he's in Florence, which isn't that far away."

"We've also," the announcer said, "had reports of young people who have tested positive, A 4-year-old girl from Castiglione d'Adda, a 15-year-old in Bergamo, two 10-year-olds from Cremona and Lodi, a 17-year-old from Valtellina who attended a school in Codogno, and a school friend from Sondrio.

"Mama," Danny whimpered, "we're all gonna die!" Tears ran down his pink cheeks.

Elizabeth grabbed the remote and turned the TV off.

"Time for bed, kids."

Sarah and Danny were at her heels as she ran up the stairs.

After she had put the kids to bed and returned to the living room she found that Stephen had turned the TV back on. She turned it off again.

"OK," he said. "why is Danny obsessed with death?"

"He's always been that way. Remember after we found out about your grandmother's death? He came into our bedroom every night with his teddy bear wanting to sleep with us. And when we got the letter about the house the first thing he said was 'who died' and began crying."

"Well, you were crying. But what's up with Sarah? I don't think she's said three words in the last week."

"She retreating. She does that. This is a bad time, Stephen, and it's going to get worse."

Elizabeth told Stephen that she didn't want to watch the news anymore, but Stephen said they had to be aware of what was going on.

The news was always bad.

"This is like watching a horror movie," Elizabeth said.

"Except that we don't know how it's going to end."

"Badly, I'm afraid."

Italy began to take steps to protect its citizens since it couldn't control the virus. The first lockdown at the end of February covered ten municipalities of the province of Lodi in Lombardy and one in the province of Padua in Veneto. About 50,000 people were affected, including 16,000 in the most affected town of Codogno.

"I wonder if Signor Chen still goes there," Elizabeth said. "I hope not."

On March 4, the government closed all schools in the country. Elizabeth had mixed feelings about that. Sarah was having trouble adjusting to the school in San Mateo, and now she'd be taking classes online. How was she supposed to learn?

On March 8 Prime Minister Giuseppe Conte announced the expansion of the quarantine zone to cover much of northern Italy, affecting more than sixteen million people. Penalties for violations of the quarantine ranged from a $231 fine to three months in prison and police were ordered to enforce it. Regional train service to the most affected areas was suspended, with trains skipping stops at Codogno. The last two days of the Venice Carnival were called off, major league soccer matches were canceled, and the famous La Scala theater in Milan was closed. Shops were reporting empty shelves.

At the time of the decree, more than 5,800 cases of coronavirus had been confirmed in Italy, with 233 dead.

"Oh my," Elizabeth said.

Sarah hugged Rosie and stared straight ahead. Danny began sobbing.

"Mama," he cried, "What does that mean? Is everybody going to die?"

"No, no," Stephen said. "It just means that people should stay inside so they are safe, so that the disease doesn't affect them."

He took Elizabeth aside. "I think we're going to be quarantined soon. We'd better stock up."

"Agreed."

There was no point going to the little *mercato* in San Martino so the next afternoon they drove to the supermarket in San Mateo. Dozens of other people had the same idea and Stephen and Elizabeth witnessed two arguments that almost resulted in fistfights over a bottle of wine.

Although they filled two shopping carts, mostly with frozen foods, they also found shortages.

"Look, there are only six packages of toilet paper left," Elizabeth said. "Take three."

At home, two of Stephen's four clients in the United States said they were canceling because they couldn't afford his design work for now. They reported that there were 1,300 cases now in the U.S., and Stephen texted Johnny Greco.

"Hey. How u?"

"No prblm. Pres said will go away."

"Really?"

"He says summer coming and heat will drive away."

"Heat will kill virus? U believe?"

"Course."

"Take care, Bud."

Stephen put the phone away.

THAT EVENING, they watched on television as the prime minister expanded the lockdown to the entire country. Italy, he said, was the first country to implement a national quarantine as a result of the Covid-19 outbreak.

"Tell the kids what that means, Stephen."

"Well, the rule is '*Restate a casa*'—stay at home. We have to stay indoors all the time except that we can go to a grocery store or a pharmacy once a week. Many other stores will be closed. There won't be any Masses in churches. We need to carry ID cards. Oh, and we have to wear masks outside."

"I can't play with Marco?" Danny said.

"Afraid not," Stephen said.

"We can't go to the playground?" Sarah said in her first words of the day.

"No," Elizabeth said. "You can play with Danny on the balcony."

"We can't go to the *mercato* and buy candy?" Danny said.

"Not for a while."

"We're in a prison!" Sarah shouted.

Elizabeth, who was not known for being religious, began fingering a rosary they'd found in Nonna's jewelry box.

"You know what I've been thinking, hon?" she said. "I've been thinking how terrible all of this would have been for Nonna. She was always out and about, talking to all the neighbors. I'm glad she isn't here for this."

"One of the few things we can be grateful for, I guess," Stephen said.

The next day, pointing to 118,000 cases in more than 110 countries, the World Health Organization declared Covid-19 a pandemic.

Unfortunately, a talking head on TV then said that Italy was being menaced by a *mostro silenzioso*—a silent monster.

"A monster!" cried Danny, who had been terrified of the creatures for all of his four years. "A monster is going to get us? Mama!"

"No, no."

"But he said a monster, Mama!"

"It's OK, it's OK, honey. Stephen! Turn off the damn TV!"

THE FAMILY ENTERED entered a time of tears and tensions. Danny was permanently attached to Elizabeth's pants leg. Sarah tried to put her doll's clothes on Rosie, who didn't cooperate and Sarah fled under the bed. With the TV virtually banned, Stephen spent hours online with *la Repubblica*, *Corriere della Sera*, *La Stampa* and CNN. Elizabeth tried to occupy the time by doing paint-by-number with the kids and gave up when they weren't interested.

Soon, the days seemed endless and nerves were frazzled.

"I thought you were going to empty the dryer."

"I thought it was your turn. I did it yesterday."

"No, I did it yesterday. It's your turn."

"OK, OK, OK."

Or:

"I thought this was your night to supervise the baths."

"That was last night."

"OK, OK, OK."

Or:

"Didn't you pay the phone bill?"

"Sorry, I forgot."

Sometimes Stephen and Elizabeth passed in the hall without speaking.

Both Sarah and Danny crawled into their parents' beds during the night and Stephen and Elizabeth let them stay. They were soon joined by Rosie. Everyone was crabby in the mornings.

Dinners, which had always been a time for sharing the news of the day, became a time of silence or arguments.

"Mom, this hamburger isn't cooked," Sarah said.

"Should I reheat it, hon?" Stephen asked.

"Why the hell don't you cook it yourself?" Elizabeth shouted. "In fact, why don't you cook all the bloody meals?"

"OK, OK, I will."

Stephen's pasta the next night was denounced by the children as hard, cold and inedible. Elizabeth had skipped dinner.

Elizabeth and Francesca took to having daily phone calls, waving at each other from their kitchen windows, their children at their sides.

They talked about the times when they were allowed outside.

"It's so strange," Francesca said after a shopping trip to San Mateo. "I saw two people being ticketed just because they were talking to each other in the piazza."

"I've noticed," Elizabeth said, "That people try to avoid eye contact. You think the next person you meet might get you infected."

"Or arrested," Francesca said. "This is so hard. Italians are so gregarious. We hug, we kiss—on both cheeks! Now we can't even go outside."

They worried about their neighbors, all of them elderly.

"Poor Signora Franchi," Francesca said. "She was always going out and she had some other old ladies in every week to play cards. Now she has to stay in all the time. She must be going crazy."

"Those two men who live in the next house," Elizabeth said, "I wonder how they're doing. They always seemed so nice."

"The came here because people were commenting on how they were living together in Pisa. And now this."

"What are they doing for food?"

"I see the kid from the *mercato* put something on their doorstep every day at 5:30. Not that I'm watching or anything."

"What about Mr. Chen?" Elizabeth asked. "Is he still going to Codogno to buy things?"

"Yes. I know he shouldn't but Fredi says that's his job."

They talked about their lives.

"I cook, I clean, I take care of the kids," Elizabeth said. "I'm so stressed."

"I'm not used to having Fredi home all the time," Francesca said. "I wish he'd help with the kids more."

"Tell me about it," Elizabeth said.

On her own laptop, Elizabeth tried to find out how to talk to children about the pandemic.

"Nobody knows!" she told Stephen later. "Be honest, they say. Correct misconceptions. Support your child. Follow a routine. Good grief! This is all so obvious. Have any of these people ever had children?"

"It's sort of good advice," Stephen said.

"How would you know? You're up there on your computer all day."

"Elizabeth, I'm not…"

"You don't have to deal with Danny and Sarah. I don't know what to do with them. They're freaking out."

"But I am helping…"

"I'm so tired. I can't sleep at night so then I'm tired in the morning."

"I know, hon."

"Well, I WISH TO HELL YOU'D HELP OUT MORE!"

When she burst into tears Stephen tried to hold her hand but she brushed him away and ran upstairs, followed, of course, by Danny and Sarah.

STEPHEN AND ELIZABETH made up that night—sort of. Elizabeth said she was sorry she had bitten Stephen's head off, and Stephen said he knew that they were under such strains now and he would help more with the children.

"Are you sorry we moved here?" he asked as they were lying in bed after returning Danny to his own bed.

"I don't know. We can't go back."

"I sure don't want to go back to Pittsburgh. Johnny said there were two more murders overnight."

"We've been in lockdown for three weeks," Elizabeth said. "When will it end?"

Stephen suggested that they have a family meeting—one the kids called a family council—to discuss what was going on. They gathered around the dining room table.

"We know," Elizabeth said, "that this has been a very hard time for all of us, but we have to live together so let's make the best of it."

"How about," Stephen said, "if we had a routine. Then we could manage things better because we would know what to do and when we had to do it."

They took out notepads and made out a schedule. Breakfast followed by online class time from her school for Sarah while Stephen and Danny made birdhouses. Then a treat and then more class time for Sarah and a board game for Danny. Lunch would be followed by a cleanup time.

"And everybody is going to clean," Elizabeth said, not looking at anyone in particular.

Then they all would work on a 2,000-piece Hogwarts jigsaw puzzle they'd barely started on the dining room table. Then the kids could read or play with Rosie on the balcony and then all four would help make dinner. At night, the kids could play the Superclips videogame and then Stephen and Elizabeth would bring out the cello and violin and play. Maybe Sarah and Danny could learn some simple songs.

"And once a week," Elizabeth said as she posted the schedule on the refrigerator, "you can have a Zoom session with Marco and Livia. I've talked to Francesca and she loves the idea. They're making up schedules, too."

"Remember how we used to go camping and we stayed in a tent?" Stephen asked. "Well, let's pretend that this is a tent and it's raining so we can't go out for a while, OK?"

"Well, OK," Sarah and Danny replied, not very enthusiastically.

Elizabeth sighed.

The system worked well enough, but sometimes it fell apart. Sarah accused Danny of hogging the console for the videogame and Danny threw it at her. Danny threatened to push Rosie off the balcony and Sarah screamed. No one paid attention to the jigsaw puzzle for days because the kids said it was "too hard."

The news that Stephen saw online continued to be bad. On March 23, Italy led the world with a death toll of 5,476.

"I don't want to set a record," Elizabeth cried. "I just want this to be over."

"It's OK, Mama," Danny said. "It's OK."

Elizabeth was alarmed when she received a call from their neighbor.

"Francesca, why are you whispering?" Elizabeth asked.

"Listen, don't tell the kids but you know Signor Chen has been going to Codogno and three days ago he wasn't feeling well and he went to a doctor who put him in the hospital. He's there now."

"Oh, God! Is he OK?"

"I don't know. Don't tell the kids, OK?"

Elizabeth took Stephen aside to tell him.

"Well," he said, "I guess it was just a matter of time before San Martino had a case. Now we really have to stay inside."

Danny was suddenly tugging at Elizabeth's apron. "Mama! What's going on? Did somebody die?"

"No, honey, no one died. Let's work on the puzzle, OK?"

While they did that, Stephen opened his phone to text Johnny.

"Hey. How U?"

"OK."

"Just OK?"

"Getting real bad here. 40,000 ppl positive in PA. 1,500 dead."

"What pres say?"

"Said drink disinfectant."

"What? U kidding?"

"What he said."

"No!"

"Yes."

"How U feel?"

"Sad. Scared."

"Not sick?"

"Not yet anyway."

"Take care, Bud."

Four weeks into the lockdown, Stephen and Elizabeth wondered how to celebrate Easter, traditionally a bigger feast than Christmas in Italy with festivals and processions and fireworks.

"In Florence," Stephen told the children, "they have a big cart that explodes with fireworks and people come from all over to watch. Maybe we can go next year."

"We're never going to go anywhere," Sarah said. "We're stuck here forever."

Ignoring her, Elizabeth said that she found a cake shaped like a lamb and two chocolate eggs in the supermarket and they'd have them on Easter.

"And after that we can watch the pope give his Easter message, and there's a concert by Andrea Bocelli from the Duomo in Milan and…"

"Big deal," Sarah said.

AT THE END OF APRIL, there were finally a few reasons to be a little optimistic. Francesca reported that Signor Chen had returned from the hospital and had to stay in quarantine but was feeling better. Stephen read online that the Norwegian student who had tested positive in Florence had recovered. And CNN said that Italy had posted its lowest number of new coronavirus cases in seven weeks and that Prime Minister Conte would make an announcement that night.

"OK," Stephen said, "I think we can watch television for this."

They lined up on the couch again, Danny still sitting close to his mother and Sarah hugging Rosie and staring ahead.

Conte appeared on the screen, a tall man with black hair.

"After 56 days," he said, "I am pleased to announce that Italy will cautiously begin easing restrictions on May 4."

"Oh, thank God," Elizabeth said. "Thank God!"

"Can we go out again?" Sarah asked. "With Rosie?"

"Can we go to the playground?" Danny asked.

"Can we go to the the *mercato* and buy candy?"

"Yes, yes, yes."

Television stations seemed relieved not to be reporting new cases and death tolls. Instead, when the day came, they showed clips of the country coming back to life: A couple buying ice cream, kids playing soccer, people singing on their balconies. Once again Italians ventured from their homes, and even though they wore masks and stayed at safe distances, cautiously resumed the traditional evening walk of the *passegiatta*.

In a phone call soon after the lockdown had ended, Francesca asked Elizabeth why she and Stephen had stopped their balcony concerts.

"Oh, I don't know. I guess we just didn't feel like it. I think we can start again now."

The next night, with Sarah and Danny turning their pages, their concert was a celebration: "Greensleeves," Beethoven's "Moonlight Sonata," a waltz from "Sleeping Beauty," Bach's "Minuet" and finally, "Amazing Grace."

All the neighbors listened from their own balconies, even Signor Chen in his bathrobe, and their thunderous applause could probably be heard in San Mateo.

Stephen reached over and put his arm around his wife. "We're going to be OK, right?"

"I guess for now. But I'm still worried that it's going to start up again."

"I know. A second wave."

THE TOUR GUIDE

A tour guide named Marcello was my driver/interpreter (and my friend) on many trips to Italy. He lost his job because of the pandemic.

ANOTHER NIGHT. Yet another night. Again with no sleep. Tommaso turned over on his left side, then his back, then his right side, then his stomach.

"Tommaso," his wife said, "what are you doing?"

"Trying to get some sleep."

"Well, you're keeping me awake."

"OK, OK."

Tommaso slipped out of bed, grabbed a robe and went down the hall. The balcony was cool and quiet this early in the morning. Stars and a crescent moon would soon give way to the slowly brightening horizon in the east. Lights were beginning to shine in the homes down below, and far in the distance the skyline of Florence twinkled. That was one reason why he bought this house in Fiesole, so that he could enjoy Florence's ever-changing skyline.

Adjusting the cushions on the lounge, Tommaso leaned back and closed his eyes although he knew he would not fall asleep.

When is this ever going to end? When will there be relief?

"Tommaso? Why are you out here?" His wife was in the doorway.

"Couldn't sleep. Just getting some fresh air."

"Well, you woke me and now I can't sleep." She went into the kitchen and turned the cappuccino maker on.

Oh boy, Tommaso thought, it's going to be a long day.

He knew he shouldn't, but whenever he was depressed like this he thought back to the good times he'd had last year. It was an exceptional

231

year for tourists—the government said 62 million—and as one of the most popular tour guides in Florence and elsewhere in Italy, he was completely booked from April until November.

Tommaso Tomaselli Tours was known far beyond Italy, and he could have taken on even more clients. There was a time in April and another in October when he actually had to refer a few to another tour guide. He didn't like to do that because he knew that Romolo gouged people right and left, adding generous tips for himself to the bills for dinners and rooms.

Perhaps he was popular because he was so attentive to his clients' needs. Since he knew a smattering of languages, he was able to have good conversations and make a point of finding out personal information like family origins and educations and occupations. He went out of his way to find the best hotels at the most reasonable prices, restaurants that would serve memorable meals and visits to unknown places far away from the Michelangelos and daVincis.

Sometimes, he later regretted voicing his strong opinions about the Vatican scandals, corrupt politicians and the influx of refugees from Africa. His clients usually didn't know what he was talking about.

Anita came in with a cup of coffee and toast, put it on the table near him, and turned and left.

"Thank you," he said.

Tommaso sighed and nibbled his toast. He had hoped this year would be a good one, too. There had been no reason it wouldn't be.

Then the coronavirus struck. Italy was one of the first hit and the hardest. Rome declared a strict quarantine for parts of the country and then a lockdown for all of it. Travel to the country was banned, which meant that he had no customers.

He and Anita stayed in their home, or at least he stayed on the balcony and she remained in the living room reading and knitting with her three cats at her side. They didn't talk much.

When Italy opened its doors to other European countries on June 3, he did have a few clients, a French teacher and a Spanish writer, but both wanted only a day tour of Florence. It was now the end of June and he was still waiting, and not sleeping.

"Why don't you try to find some other work, even part time?" Anita frequently asked.

"I think business will pick up soon," he would say.

"When?"

"I don't know. Stop asking."

Tommaso had been a teacher before he became a tour guide and he knew, at 54, that he couldn't go back to that. He seemed to have no other options.

What he really looked forward to were the Americans. They would surely come soon. Americans were known to spend easily and tip generously. Once again, Tommaso would have an income and he and Anita would not have to depend on the little money she got cleaning neighbors' apartments.

The sun had now risen and from this view in Fiesole, the dome of Florence's famous Duomo seemed to glow. Anita brought out today's *la Stampa* and Tommaso hoped there would be good news. Yes! A main headline read: "E.U. Sets New List of Approved Travel Partners."

Tommaso had been eagerly awaiting this announcement because he knew that only visitors from countries that had controlled the coronavirus pandemic would be allowed to enter European countries. Surely the United States would be on the list.

He read the list of countries that were allowed: Australia, Canada, Georgia, Japan...

"Where is the United States?"

Then he read the list of countries that were still not allowed: Brazil, Russia, United States.

"The United States? No Americans? Damn!"

THE NEWS set Tommaso off for the day. He snapped at Anita, kicked at one of the cats and slammed the door behind him when he left to have coffee with his longtime friend Luigi. Since the lockdown had been lifted they had resumed their almost daily morning get-togethers at their favorite *bar*, Franco's, just off Piazza Mino.

"I heard the news," Luigi said. "I'm sorry."

"Damn E.U," Tommaso said.

"Well, they wouldn't want people with the infections to come, right? We're not completely over this ourselves."

"We're almost over it."

"Better not take chances," Luigi said. "And who knows? It might come back."

"Damn E.U."

As always, Luigi was optimistic. "Maybe the ban will be lifted when they review it in two weeks. That's not too long to wait."

"Damn E.U."

"Let's look at the papers."

Tommaso had brought his *la Stampa* and Luigi brought *la Repubblica* and it was their custom to go through them together.

"Here's an interesting story," Luigi said after turning a couple of pages. "An Italian village is selling homes for just one *euro*."

"Must be a catch."

"It says the town of Cinquefrondi in Calabria hopes to attract new residents with this low price. It says it has lost many young people to cities to find work."

"I see the Calabrians on the streets all the time," Tommaso said. "They can't find jobs there and now they try to take the jobs northerners have."

"It says the homes have been abandoned."

"They're probably falling down and not even worth a *euro*. Damn E.U."

Luigi sighed. "Tommaso, why don't you find a story?"

Tommaso turned page after page trying to find something that interested him.

"OK, here's one from London."

He began to read. "'Thousands of demonstrators gathered in London on Saturday in a largely peaceful protest against the death of George Floyd and of systemic racism in the United States and around the world.

"'Activists braved bad weather to fill Parliament Square during the day, but more heated scenes unfolded in the evening when protesters clashed with police outside Downing Street, the official residence of Prime Minister Boris Johnson.

"'Meanwhile, sizable crowds chanted Floyd's name and 'Black Lives Matter,' at one point all taking a knee in unison outside Parliament.

"'One protester said, 'It's a worldwide issue, no matter where you are. It's an issue everywhere, we all need to rise up.'"

"Good God," Tommaso said. "Now this thing is spreading around the world. Why? Why should we care what happened in some town in Minnesota?"

"It's not just Minnesota, Tommaso. This Black guy was choked by a white cop for more than eight minutes. Eight minutes! It just an example of how Blacks are treated. So this has raised consciousness everywhere. Even in Italy."

"We treat Blacks very nice," Tommaso said. "I see them in Florence all the time. If they don't bother me I don't bother them."

Tommaso and Luigi had had this argument many times and Luigi knew he couldn't win.

"Find another story, Tommaso."

Tommaso turned to the international news.

"Damn. Listen to this," he said. "It says that Columbus, Ohio, has removed a statue of its namesake, Christopher Columbus, from City Hall as part of a nationwide call to replace statues of colonizers, slave owners and other controversial historical figures. What? They took down a statue of Columbus? Christopher Columbus?"

"Read some more, Tommaso."

"It says the mayor declared that the statue does not reflect the city and represents patriarchy, oppression and divisiveness. I can't believe this. What next?"

"I've read," Luigi said, "that Columbus treated Native Americans brutally. I guess people are starting to look at his whole life, not just his voyages."

Tommaso slammed the paper down.

"Christopher Columbus! They're ignoring what Columbus did! That's...that's...a sacrilege! He discovered America! Where would all Americans be if it wasn't for him?"

Luigi tried to make light of it. "In Spain?"

"I think I'll go for a walk," Tommaso said. "See you in a couple of days."

THREE DAYS LATER, Tommaso had calmed down at least a little when he met Luigi for coffee. He had resigned himself to the lack of business and had taken a part-time job at Anita's church. Now that Masses had resumed, the place needed a janitor.

235

"Only ten more days and the E.U. will review its ban on United States visitors," Luigi said as they stirred more sugar into their little cups. "I bet there won't be a problem this time."

"No, I think there will be."

"Why?"

"I got an email from a former client in Michigan. He said things are getting worse in the United States, not better. There are now more than 2,700,000 cases and about 130,000 deaths."

"That's terrible!"

"And there are new hot spots. California, Texas, Florida."

"What the hell happened?"

"Their president let the states have control and some of them opened too early and people were tired of the lockdown so they took chances. Didn't wear masks, didn't stay apart. Of course more people got infected."

"Why did the president do that?"

"Who knows. I don't understand American politics, not under this president."

"Sick, sick, sick. So you don't think you will get any American customers for a while?"

"Not for a very long while, Luigi. Maybe there'll be some from Spain, France, England. Not from Germany. The Germans drive so they don't need me."

"Well, let's see what's in the papers."

They put their coffee cups aside and opened *la Stampa* and_*la Repubblica*.

"Well," Luigi said, "you'll enjoy this story."

"What?"

Luigi put on his glasses. "Sardinia Blocks Americans Who Land in Private Jet."

"Really?" Tommaso said. "Read the story."

"OK." He spread the paper out in front of him. "It says that officials on the Italian island of Sardinia prevented a group of Americans who arrived in a private plane from Colorado from going to their summer house because the European Union has banned travel from the United States."

"Ha! So they tried to sneak in and got caught," Tommaso said.

"Let me go on. It says that the group of about ten people landed at the

Sardinia airport on Wednesday and after several hours they were ordered to go back on the plane. They flew back to the United States."

Luigi put the paper down. "Well, we know one thing. Italy is enforcing the travel ban."

"Damn E.U. I'm never going to get any Americans."

"You will," Luigi said. "It'll just take time. Let me find another story. Oh, here's one. 'Italy OK's Rescue of 180 Migrants from Mediterranean.'"

"What? What?"

Luigi began to read. "It says that Italy has authorized the charity vessel Ocean Viking to transfer 180 migrants rescued in the Mediterranean to a ship in Sicily for quarantine.

"It says that those on board exploded with joy at the announcement that their ordeal amid the cramped conditions on the ship would soon be over. It says the migrants, who include Pakistanis, North Africans, Eritreans, Nigerians and others, were picked up after fleeing Libya in four separate rescues. The migrants include twenty-five children."

Luigi put down the paper. "That makes me feel good. Italy did something right about the migrants for once."

Tommaso didn't say anything.

"OK," Luigi said, "here's another. 'Italy to Grant Amnesty to 600,000 Illegal Migrants.'"

"That's insane!" Tommao said.

"It's true. It says that Teresa Bellanova, Italy's pro-mass-migration agriculture minister, signed the bill which grants six-month residency permits to illegal migrants working in the agricultural and domestic sectors. It said she cried tears of joy."

"Well," Tommaso interrupted, "millions of Italians are going to be crying, but not in joy."

Luigi continued. "Here's a quote from Matteo Salvini. You know, the right-wing former deputy prime minister. He said, 'Minister Bellanova's tears for the poor immigrants, with no reference to the millions of unemployed Italians, do not move anyone.'"

"He's right," Tommaso said. "I agree with him. Migrants are taking our jobs."

Over the years, Tommaso and Luigi had frequent discussions—some would say arguments, others would say battles—over the the migrant issue. Thousands of migrants from Libya, Eritrea, Somalia, Nigeria, Ghana and elsewhere had died trying to enter Italy, and scenes of migrants in overcrowded, ill-equipped boats had horrified people around the world.

Tommaso at first was sympathetic, especially when 250 migrants drowned off the coast of Lampedusa on March 27, 2009.

But as the number of migrants in Italy swelled to more than a million, he and many others began to resent their presence. They were, the opponents said, costing Italy too much to take care of them and they were also taking jobs away from Italians. A poll found that seventy-one percent of Italians wanted fewer immigrants to be allowed in the country.

"Listen," Tommaso said, "we've lost so many jobs during the lockdown and now we're going to let more of these people in?"

"'These people,'" Luigi said, "are human beings. Remember what Jesus said, 'Whatever you did for one of the least of these brothers and sisters, you did for me.'"

"Yeah, yeah. He didn't have to look for a job. Now I'm a part-time janitor."

"Tommaso, you always talk like the migrants are one big mob. These are individual people who are escaping terrible conditions in their own countries. Do you know any migrants?"

Luigi couldn't offer any response to that, and they soon finished their coffee for the day.

"See you when I see you," Tommaso said.

AT HOME, Tommaso watered the cats, trimmed weeds in his garden and picked up a book. Back on the balcony, he tried to analyze his opinions about migrants. He really resented them taking jobs from Italians, especially now when the unemployment rate was so high. But maybe Luigi was right. Maybe he should think about migrants as individuals, not as a horde.

He had to admit that he didn't know any. There was a young sad-eyed woman with a baby begging every day on the steps of Chiesa di Santa Maria Assunta in Fiesole. Everyone said he shouldn't put coins in her plate, and so he always walked on and soon forgot about her.

"The migrants probably planted her there," he thought.

Unable to resolve the issue, he decided to check his emails, not that anyone wrote to him anymore.

Someone did!

"Tommaso Tomaselli Tours: You have been recommended to me by a colleague who was impressed with your services when you took him to the graves of Keats and Shelley in Rome. You may remember him."

"What? Of course, I remember him. That professor who didn't want to go to the Vatican or anywhere else in Rome and just wanted to go to the Protestant Cemetery. He was such an ass. He recommended me?"

"I am a professor of anthropology at Oxford and would like to go to the village of Sant'Angelo as part of my research on the SPRAR project there. You may know the project as the Protection System for Refugees and Asylum Seekers.

"I would like to arrive on the fifteenth of this month and spend three weeks there. It will be necessary that you accompany me throughout this time because of my limited knowledge of Italian. Accommodations are provided, there is a small stipend and I have a grant to take care of all your expenses.

"Please let me know at your earliest convenience if this is acceptable.

Sincerely,

K.L. Anderson, Ph.D

Tommaso read the email again. And a third and fourth time. This was incredible. He had a job! Three weeks! All expenses paid! This would be enough for him and Anita to get by for several months. He wouldn't have to be a janitor any more. And maybe by then Americans would be able to fly to Italy.

He quickly Googled "Protection System for Refugees and Asylum Seekers." He'd never heard of it.

The SPRAR project (Protection System for Refugees and Asylum Seekers) is financed by the Ministry for the Interior through the National Fund for Asylum Policy and Services. Its aim is to support and protect asylum seekers, refugees and immigrants who fall under other forms of humanitarian protection.

The services consist of: accommodation in a small house; supply of food vouchers for board; orientation in relation to local services; support of a linguistic mediator, assistance in procedures to access social, health and educational services (Italian language courses for adults, enrolment in school for minors).

It also provides orientation in relation to employment, enrolment in training courses, professional re-training, and support in looking for a job and a home.

SPRAR works in the villages of Vaiano, Carmignano, Poggio a Caiano, Montemurlo, Bagno a Ripoli, Sant'Angelo and S. Casciano Val di Pesa. Each can offer support to a maximum number of 50 people. There is a waiting list.

Tommaso read the entry again and again. So this was a government service that places refugees into little villages and supplies them with food and board, teaches them Italian and gives them support to start new lives. Hmmm. There must be a catch. He'd be living with migrants? Well, he needed the job. He'd never been to Sant'Angelo, but he knew where it was because tourists liked to go to Castelnuovo di Garfagnana, which was nearby.

He would reply to this Professor Anderson and tell him he would accept.

ANITA WAS, of course, pleased that Tommaso had a job. Three weeks would provide a good income for a while, not to mention that he would be out from under foot. They both knew they needed some time apart.

"Have fun!" She gave him a peck on the cheek and he loaded the Fiat Panda with three suitcases. For some reason, he always packed as if he was going to be away for three months.

In a subsequent email Professor Anderson had said that the British Airways flight would arrive at Amerigo Vespucci Airport in Florence at 3:20 p.m., and Tommaso, as always, was early.

The plane didn't land until 3:42 and by that time Tommaso had become more and more worried as the passengers retrieved their bags and left the terminal. He kept looking for what he assumed would be a tall, professorial-looking gentleman, perhaps with white hair and a beard, but no one matched that description.

At last, only one person was waiting, a very short, 30-something woman wearing a dark blue pantsuit and carrying a large tote bag. Her blond hair stretched in a long braid down her back. She saw Tommaso first.

"Signor Tomaselli? From Tommaso Tomaselli Tours?"

"Yes?"

"I'm Karen Anderson. So pleased to meet you."

"But…but…"

"You thought I'd be taller."

"No…no, I just thought…"

"I should have used my full name. So sorry. Shall we go? I can't wait to see Sant'Angelo."

Karen Anderson had only one suitcase plus her tote bag and they were soon on their way. They drove northwest, going through Prato, Pistoia and Lucca before entering the rugged part of Tuscany called the Garfagnana.

Tommaso pointed out the snow-capped mountains, the little streams, the small villages.

"This is gorgeous!" his passenger said. "I've never been in this part of Italy."

"It's my favorite part, Professor Anderson."

"Please, call me Karen."

"Karen it is."

Along the way, Karen told Tommaso that she was born in Leeds, the only child of a medical doctor and a nurse practitioner. When she was young, under ten, her parents went to Zambia where her parents helped operate a clinic.

"Fortunately, the main language was English, but I did learn a little of the native languages, Nyanja and Bemba. I don't know if I remember any of that now. But I did learn to love the people so much!"

Living with the natives, she said, aroused a lifelong desire to work with the peoples of Africa, and she received a doctorate in African Studies at Oxford. She was fortunate to join the faculty after that and was now an assistant professor.

"I hope my research here at Sant'Angelo will be the last thing I need to get a promotion," she said. "And you, Signor Tomasselli? Tell me about your life."

"Call me Tommaso, please. Not much to tell. I'm from a little town near here. I was a schoolteacher for many years but then I couldn't take the kids anymore and a friend asked me to join him in the tourist business. I did, and eventually bought him out. My first wife died sixteen years ago and I married Anita ten years ago."

"How lovely! To find love again!"

"Yes. And you?"

"No, no. A few relationships but nothing that lasted."

They were now winding through the town of Castelnuovo di Garfagnana, and Tommaso pointed out the castle ("Twelfth century"), the Duomo ("Sixteenth century"), the fortress ("late Sixteenth century").

"This is so terribly beautiful," Karen said. "I wish I could have lived back then."

"If you lived in the Fourteenth century, you might have died in the Black Death. Of course, we just lived through Covid-19. At least I hope it's over."

"Knock on wood."

A few miles north of Castelnuovo di Garfagnana, they were on the outskirts of Sant'Angelo and then, because it was so small, they were in the middle of it.

"Oh my," Karen said. "I just didn't expect anything like this."

"Beautiful, right?"

Sant'Angelo looked like other towns in the Garfagnana. Small stone houses with red-tiled roofs flanked the narrow main street. A few shops displayed vegetables and fruits outside. At the center, a church, a two-story municipal building, a tall tower and what might be called a palace surrounded a small piazza.

Unlike other villages, however, not all of the people who filled the streets talking and shouting looked like typical Italians. Their skin was dark and they wore very bright clothes.

"From what I've read," Karen said, "the people are from all over, Eritrea, Nigeria, Somalia, Sudan, Syria, Gambia, Bangladesh, Liberia, Ghana. Isn't this a lovely mix?"

"Um. I don't know. I guess I'll have to get used to this."

Tommasso was startled when he saw a very black hand knocking on his window. He rolled it down. The man, well over six feet and very thin, wore a dazzling red shirt emblazoned with yellow suns. When he smiled, his white teeth contrasted sharply with his dark skin.

He reached out a hand. "Hello. I am Maduka. Welcome to Sant'Angelo."

TOMMASO AND KAREN were assigned rooms on the second floor of the municipal building, now converted into a bread and breakfast. The rooms were small but adequate, nothing like the luxurious hotels where

Tommaso had stayed in Rome or Milan. They were told that dinner would be served shortly in the restaurant.

The Ras Dashen Canteen, remodeled from its previous life as a convent, was a blast of colors with abstract murals on the walls and bright tablecloths. The tables were set safely apart even though Sant'Angelo had welcomed few visitors during the pandemic and had, miraculously, not had a single case of Covid-19.

Tommaso and Karen were seated with their greeter, Maduka, who said he was from Nigeria, plus Father Aloysius, whose parish helped to sponsor the program, and Gamal, a teenager from Syria.

They had just finished the introductions when Amukusana, a striking middle-aged woman in a long flowered dress, began serving their meal.

"This is what we call *nshima,*" she said. "We eat it all the time in Zambia. It is made from corn that is processed into a fine white powder called 'mealie meal.' It is basically a very thick porridge and as you can see, it is served in lumps. And, oh yes, it should be eaten with your hands."

While the others proceeded to dig in, Tommaso stared at the concoction in front of him. He had never seen anything like it before. He had never eaten with his hands before. And yet it smelled awfully good.

Watching to see how it was done, he grabbed a portion and rolled it into sort of a ball, and then took a bite.

It tasted nothing like the pasta he was used to. It was delicious.

The others talked about what they did that day, but Tommaso was too absorbed in a second helping and heard only parts of the conversation.

Father Aloysius was forming a new choir with immigrants, Maduka was finishing a table in a wood-working class, and Gamal said he met a girl from Syria and they were going to watch the outdoor movie in the piazza that night.

An hour later, Karen nudged Tommaso. "I'm beat. Want to call it a night?"

He did.

AFTER SLEEPING straight through for the first time in months, Tommaso joined Karen for a briefing from Father Aloysius and Maduka. The project, the priest said, had begun five years ago and usually involved thirty-five families on a rotating basis. They learned trades, the Italian language, reading, writing, how to prepare for a job, and simply how to get along better in a foreign country.

"What we want to do here," the priest said, "is to help these people live a normal life. They've been through so much trauma in their own countries. You can't even imagine it. And then the terrible sea crossing in which so many died, many of them family members. We try to help them find the right path, the way they want, not the one we want for them."

The priest showed them photos of migrants studying, cooking, working in a farm field.

"There is no question," he said, "that the anti-immigrant prejudice has grown. It says all migrants are bad and dirty and stealing jobs, which isn't true. If all our immigrants left Italy tomorrow, the country would descend into chaos."

Tommaso could feel his face getting red.

After going through scrapbooks and ledgers, Karen and Father Aloysius went off to talk to others, and Maduka offered to give Tommaso a tour of the village.

They stopped first in the kitchen of the Ras Dashen Canteen where a dozen women, ranging from Italian grandmothers to migrant teenagers, were at oversize stoves stirring pots that gave off delectable aromas.

"We teach," one of the women explained, "migrant women how to adapt their cooking to Italian patrons. Then they can get jobs in restaurants and in catering businesses in the nearby towns."

A woman offered Tommaso a spoonful of what was in a pot.

"We are serving this tonight," she said. "It's called *kubbah safarjaliyah*. It is from Syria. It consists of stuffed meatballs cooked with a quince-based soup."

After swallowing, Tommaso couldn't wait until dinner.

Maduka led the way to an old villa behind the restaurant.

"They say this was built in the Fourteenth century," a receptionist at the entrance said, "but now it is used as a clinic. There are classes in meditation and stress relief, but we also have two psychiatrists. We all know that many migrants have suffered severe trauma. Some are suicidal. A young woman took her life last year. She had been raped and tortured in Libya."

Tommaso winced.

From there, they went to what was once a barn where women were sewing aprons, men were making little bookcases and men and women formed necklaces from brightly colored stones. Maduka explained that the items would be sold at a shop in Florence.

Tommaso saw a young man finishing a necklace.

"That's beautiful! My wife would like one of those. I wonder...I wonder if I might come here and make something like that."

"Of course," Maduka said. "You can start tomorrow."

At another ancient building, Maduka explained that this was used as a classroom where the Italian language was taught.

As they returned to the piazza, Tommaso was overwhelmed by the sights and sounds. Men, women and children in brilliant African clothing talked and shouted in their native languages and in Italian. Smartphones blared hit tunes from Syria, Nigeria, Ethiopia. Exotic cooking smells filled the air.

"I've been to many Italian villages," he told Karen later, "but nothing like this. I never use this word, but you know, I think this is fantastic."

TOMMASO HAD BROUGHT a bagful of books along, thinking that he would read when Karen didn't need him for translations. Instead, he could hardly wait to get out every morning to meet people, listen to their music and learn a little of their languages. In between, he began making the necklace for Anita.

From his work translating the migrants' hesitant Italian to Karen, he met Shadi, who had escaped kidnapping during the civil war in Syria. He met Asida, a Rohingya Muslim woman who had been raped in Bangladesh. He met Mustafa, who had fled the revolution in Tunisia and landed on the island of Lampedusa.

Makin, a teenager from Syria, said he was on a boat with 200 migrants that capsized when people moved to one side of the vessel. Fifty-six survivors were taken to Italy.

"My brother...my brother. I hold on to his shirt. He told me to let go, to go back. But he got away. He went into sea. Now I am alone."

Everyone had a story and every story was heart-breaking. Tommaso often found himself bleary-eyed and needing to go back to his room for a rest.

Every night there was a new adventure in dining. The stuffed vine leaves called *dolma* from Syria. The raw marinated meat called *kitfo* from Ethiopia. The medley of beans and rice called *waakye* from Ghana. The soft cake called *doolshe buuro* from Somalia. Tomasso wondered if could make these things if he got the recipes, but decided against it.

Maduka had become his good friend. They walked together each night in a sort of international version of a *passeggiata* and then sat on a bench and talked. When Maduka asked him about his tourist adventures, Tommaso told him stories about his customers.

The American couple who clearly didn't understand papal protocol and wrote: "We are arriving on the Nineteenth. Please arrange a private meeting with the pope at 2 p.m. on the Twentieth."

The Parisian man who countered anything Italian with something better in France. Viewing daVinci's "Last Supper" in Milan, he had said, "But we have the Mona Lisa in the Louvre."

All the sulking teenagers who refused to eat anywhere but McDonald's.

But also all the friends he'd made, so many of them American. The grandmother and her family who were enchanted in Florence by the armor collection at the Stibbert Museum, the perfumes in the Santa Maria Novella Pharmacy and the flea market in Piazza dei Ciompi.

The elderly rabbi from New Rochelle who needed help researching his relatives killed in the Ardeatine massacre in Rome in World War II.

The Wisconsin author who wrote a series of novels set in Tuscany and who came back again and again for what he called "research."

The young family from Delaware that had promised the kids they'd see Rome at Christmas.

Individuals and groups, school classes and senior citizens, he'd had so many over the years.

Maduka was fascinated, but changed the subject every time Tommaso asked about his own life.

Each night, Tommaso met with Karen, who reported that her interviews filled forty-three files in her laptop. She was exhausted but exhilarated.

"This has been wonderful," she said on the Friday of their last week, "but I'm ready to go home."

"I don't want to, but I guess we have to."

First, they met with Father Aloysius and told him how grateful they were to have received such a warm welcome from everyone in Sant'Angelo. The priest noted that the Protection System for Refugees and Asylum Seekers was planning a similar project just north of Florence in the village of San Domenico and was seeking applicants.

Tommaso immediately thought of someone.

"There's a young woman in front of Chiesa di Santa Maria Assunta in Fiesole every day. I'll tell her."

"You might also be interested in knowing this," the priest said. "They're looking for people to teach and do other things at this place. It doesn't pay much, but enough. They're kind of desperate."

"Really?" Tommaso said. "Really?"

"Do you think you'd know of anyone?"

"I might."

His thoughts tumbled. He wouldn't have to worry about the lack of American tourists. Maybe Anita could join him. It would be a short drive. And he'd be working with migrants. He would call next week.

After loading the Fiat, Tommaso said he wanted to talk to Maduka one more time.

They sat on their bench and after hesitating, Tommaso said, "Maduka, I have spent a lot of time talking about my life but you haven't told me anything about yours. I know you went through a terrible time. If you don't want to talk about it, that's fine. But I'm your friend. I'm interested."

Maduka looked into the distance, then leaned his long body forward and held his shaking hands.

"Is not a good story."

"I understand."

He paused.

"You know of Boko Haram?"

"A little. A terrorist organization in Nigeria."

"Terrible. Terrible. Murderers. Rapists. Suicide bombings by young girls. Terrible. Terrible."

"I've read some," Tommaso said.

"You know what happened in 2014?"

"Yes. I remember. Terrible."

Maduka took a deep breath and continued.

"They kidnapped 276 girls."

"From a school, right?"

"The Secondary School in the town of Chibok."

"Yes."

"To become sex slaves."

Maduka took another deep breath.

"My daughter...my daughter...Ginika..."

"Go slow, Maduka, go slow."

"She was one."

"Oh my God."

It was another five minutes before Maduka could continue. His whole body shook, and sweat poured down his face. Tommaso put his hand on Maduka's shoulder.

"My wife. My wife, she go crazy. Cry all the time. Hysterical. Hide under covers. I could do nothing. Nothing."

"Oh, Maduka. My friend."

"One night, I couldn't find her. I look everywhere. I go all over village. I go down to river. I find her body in the...in the water."

Maduka let his tears fall. Tommaso stroked his back and they sat silently for a long time.

When he had gained composure, Maduka said that he learned later that their daughter had died soon after her arrival in the Boko Haram camp, and he was actually grateful.

"No sex slave. She is in heaven. With her mother."

"And you?" Tommaso asked.

"I run away. Fast as I can."

Maduka got up and walked aimlessly around, toward the church, toward the tower, toward the palace, and sat down again.

"You married, Tommaso?"

"Yes."

"Children?"

"No, no children."

"Love your wife, Tommaso. Love your wife."

Maduka dug into his pocket and brought out a small gold piece.

"See the picture of the tortoise, Tommaso? In Nigeria, the tortoise

248

brings good luck. You give this to your wife and she will be happy and you will be happy. You will have good luck."

They stood up. The tall man from a foreign country and the short, stocky Italian. Color didn't matter. Where they came from didn't matter. They hugged.

A BELL RANG AND FOUR MEN DIED

This was my most personal story because it is based on an actual event that involved a distant relative. It was also the most difficult to write because few details are available about that event. Because I wanted to write a tribute to these neglected heroes, I could only imagine what their lives were like and what happened on that terrible day.

A bronze plaque on the wall of the cemetery at San Martino in Freddana northwest of Lucca features four photos. Under glass and surrounded by olive leaves, the photos show four men wearing suits and ties, as if they were going to a wedding. The inscription says they were martyrs, murdered by the Germans for freedom, on September 8, 1944, during World War II.

A pamphlet, written for the dedication of the plaque a year later, gives brief biographies of the four victims as well as a description of the massacre. But since not many details are given, the following is a (mostly) fictional account based on what we know about them.

ANTONIO POLI

We know that Antonio Poli was born in Carignano, near Turin, the son of Lorenzo Poli and Angela Bernicchi on July 20, 1870. We do not know the name of his wife, but the pamphlet says that of their ten children, three died, three went to America and one became a priest, actually the pastor of the church at San Martino in Freddana. So what follows is speculation about the life of this man.

EVEN IN A VILLAGE with large families, Antonio and Maria Poli's brood stood out. When they marched in a single file, according to age, to church for Sunday Mass, the neighbors smiled. They looked, they thought, like the line of ducks in the creek that ran through San Martino in Freddana.

Other children laughed, but their parents could not help but admire this loving and affectionate family.

Angelo was the oldest, and then came Benedetto and then Carlo.

Then came Gabriella and Daniella.

Then Pietro and Filippo.

Then Giacomo and then twins Francesca and Isabella.

After that, Maria told Antonio: *"Basta!"*

Antonio suggested that maybe they should talk to the priest first.

"No!" Maria replied. "Ten is enough!"

Antonio and Maria were married in September 1890 when he was 20 and she was 18. Angelo arrived the following May and the others in roughly two-year intervals. All were welcomed.

"Another boy!"

"Another girl!"

Their house, on Via Camaiore at the edge of San Martino and on the road to Lucca, was never designed for so large a family. The kitchen and dining room were narrow, and what was called a parlor barely had room for two small couches and a chair. Upstairs, Angelo, Benedetto, Carlo and Pietro had bunk beds and Filippo and Giacomo slept on cots on the floor. In the second bedroom, Gabriella, Daniela, Francesca and Isabella crammed into two single beds. Antonio and Maria's room was not much bigger than a closet.

On Sundays, they stretched out over an entire pew, Antonio on one end and Maria on the other. The younger children scrunched together and Maria held one or the other twin on her lap. Even the youngest held a prayer book, sang the hymns and paid attention to the priest's sermons.

At home afterwards, the girls helped Maria finish preparations for the big Sunday dinner and the boys set the table with a lot of jousting as they bumped into one another.

Everyone bowed their heads when Antonio said the blessing. "Thank you, Lord, for the abundance of food and for all the blessings you have given our family. And thank you for giving Maria and me so many wonderful children."

Antonio rarely complained. He had a back-breaking job at the Ondulato cardboard factory in nearby Monsagrati, had to walk a mile to work, and came home exhausted from running the heavy machinery.

The job paid enough when they only had a few kids but not when others came along. Then, Maria found work at Filanda, the silk factory at the other end of the village, part of the thriving silkworm industry based around Lucca. Even though she wore gloves, her hands became blistered and bloody handling the delicate silkworms and extracting the tiny threads.

But no matter. According to Antonio, the family was blessed.

Every night after dinner, Antonio insisted that they read a few pages of *La Sacra Bibbia*, an Italian translation of the Bible, and the younger children were allowed to read *Strega Nonna*, about the Christmas witch, or, for the older ones, Alessandro Manzoni's *I promessi sposi*, about a young couple who want to get married.

And then the children were allowed to tell their own stories. Angelo, Benedetto and Carlo were fascinated by the Middle Ages and told adventure tales of warriors and dragons. Gabriella and Daniella liked to make up stories of chaste women and handsome knights. The smallest children usually made up stories about their cats, Bacio and Zitto.

Except for one, all the children were healthy. Pietro's left leg was shorter than his right, which caused him to limp. He frequently caught colds and Maria made him stay in bed with hot compresses. And he stuttered. Because of all this he was terribly shy, and while the others became boisterous after dinner, he sat in his chair and laughed and applauded.

"What's going to happen to Pietro?" Maria often asked Antonio when everyone had been put to bed.

"I'm worried, too," Antonio said. "He's so kind, so worried about the others. I don't know what kind of work he could do, but it would have to be something where he could help other people."

By 1911, Angelo and Benedetto had joined their father at the Ondulato cardboard factory in Monsagrati. Unlike their father, who tolerated the hard work just like he tolerated everything else, they hated it. Especially Angelo. The work was too hard. The hours too long. The pay too little.

His complaints upset the others in the household, and Maria tried to change the subject.

Then something worse happened. Angelo was jilted by Angelica, his girlfriend of two years and four months. Just like that. With no reason. He was angry, heart-broken, revengeful, embarrassed. Worse, everyone in San Martino in Freddana knew about it and he quickly became tired of old ladies giving him pitiful looks and old men shaking their heads.

"*Cagna!*" he kept muttering. "Bitch!"

Angelo suddenly became more interested in the stories told by his friend Ezio. Two of Ezio's friends had recently gone to America and wrote back about their adventures, the beauty of the new country and, most important, the good pay they were getting. Ezio was planning to join them and invited Angelo and Benedetto to come along.

"What?" Antonio said when Angelo broached the idea. "You'd go to America? You'd leave us? Where would you go? What would you do there?"

As Maria began to sob in the background, Angelo said that Ezio's friends had found work in the northern part of a state called Michigan and that the country was as beautiful as Tuscany.

"No place is as beautiful as Tuscany," his father said. "What kind of work?"

"They go into a mine and dig out copper."

"What? Angelo, that's really dangerous! People get killed in mines."

"Well, the Ondulato factory isn't so safe. Remember Signor Fachetti? He had his hand cut off by the cutter. And Signor Lucchini? He wrenched his back so bad he had to quit work."

"But you don't even know English!"

"We'll learn," Benedetto said.

The conversation went on through the night. And the next night. And the night after. Maria couldn't stop crying, although the other children had different reactions. The boys thought going to America would be a wonderful adventure.

Finally, on October 5, 1911, Angelo and Benedetto joined Ezio and they went to Genoa and boarded a ship for the United States.

At home, even with eight children left, the house seemed empty.

In the next years, Angelo and Benedetto wrote about once a month. They didn't say much about their work—in fact, they ignored their parents' questions about it—but talked instead of good times and that they had met two girls, Suuvi and Tuula.

"Suuvi? What kind of a name is that?" Antonio wondered. "Tuula?"

"They're Finnish," Daniella said. "Remember how they wrote that there were a lot of Finns there?"

"I hope there are a lot of Italians," Antonio said.

Nevertheless, both expatriates sent a bundle of *lire* with every letter.

In 1915, Carlo was now 20 and carefully read all of his brothers' letters. He pleaded with his parents to let him join them.

"But you're so young!" his mother said.

"I'm 20. I can take care of myself. And Angelo and Benedetto are there."

His parents agreed that he could go only after they learned that a well-respected man from the village, Narciso Pini, was also planning to go.

"Narciso can look after him on the ship," Antonio said.

"I've always thought Narciso was a nice man, quiet, but very nice," Maria said.

The house now had seven children, and in the next years there were more empty beds. In 1916, at the age of 19, Gabriella married her longtime boyfriend, moved to Lucca and seven months later gave birth to the first of six children. She never returned to San Martino in Freddana.

In 1917, Daniella, who was always the most devout of the children, announced that she wanted to become a nun. She said she wanted to enter the Cenacolo di Montauto in Anghiari.

"But that's a cloistered sisterhood," Maria exclaimed. "We'll never see you again!"

"It's God's will," Daniella said. "We'll see each other again in Heaven."

One night the following year, Pietro waited until it was late so that he could talk to his parents.

"Papa, Mama, I've thought about this a lot, and I've prayed a lot, and I've decided I want to become a priest."

His parents were overjoyed, kissing and hugging him, but they were not surprised. Because of his sickly nature, Pietro had not been able to work, even part time while in school, and spent his days reading *La Sacra Bibbia,* praying in church, walking along the stream and, especially, talking to the pastor, Don Sergio.

"But, Pietro," Maria said, "aren't you too young?"

"I'm 17. That's when boys enter the seminary at Lucca. I know I'll be fine."

"Son," Antonio said, "we are so proud of you. We know you will be a great priest."

Through happy tears, Maria said she hoped that Pietro would be assigned to a parish near San Martino in Freddana.

"I'll go where they send me," he said.

In only six years, six of the children had left the happy home on Via Camaiore. Only Filippo, Giacomo, Francesca and Isabella were left.

Then in October 1918, there were reports that a new kind of "flu" was going around. Giacomo, 13, was the first to be affected.

"Mama," he cried after waking up one morning, "look at these spots on my face."

Two very dark spots had formed over the boy's cheekbones. And he couldn't stop coughing.

"Oh, Giacomo, Giacomo!"

"I ache, Mama. And I'm cold."

"Let's get you back to bed."

In just a short time, the darkness had spread over all of Giacomo's body and Maria tried to relieve his suffering by placing a cold wet sheet from his neck to his toes. Giacomo shivered and lost consciousness.

Meanwhile, Filippo and Isabella were crying that their chests were about to burst. Antonio and Maria ran back and forth between the bedrooms. Distraught, they tried everything they could think of. Francesca, who had shown no signs, mainly stood in the hall, sobbing.

Giacomo died during one agonizing night. The next days were a blur. The funeral home, burdened by dozens of other deaths in the village, came with the casket. A poster announcing the death joined dozens of others on the big village bulletin board outside the *mercato*. The body was placed in the living room and people came to mourn, kissing the boy on the cheek. The funeral Mass had to be scheduled between three others the next day. Francesca stayed home with Isabella and Filippo so that her parents could attend.

And then Isabella, only 11, died. The same rituals.

And then Filippo.

Three children gone.

Maria, also stricken and suffering in terrible pain, collapsed on the kitchen floor after Filippo's funeral and Antonio carried her to bed. He could do nothing. She died two days later.

Now Antonio's wife was gone, too. Only Francesca was left.

Over the next months, San Martino in Freddana lost dozens of people, all because of what they called *influenza delle stelle*. Some people called it the Spanish flu—not because it originated in Spain but because newspapers in Madrid were the first to report it. Eventually, it infected an estimated 500 million people worldwide, about a third of the planet's population. The pandemic had claimed 20 million to 50 million lives. In Italy alone, more than 400,000 people died.

Angelo, Benedetto and Carlo were somehow spared in America and Gabriella in Lucca. Daniella was safe in the convent and Pietro in the seminary.

In the next years, Antonio was not the man he used to be. He yelled at people who tried to help or he ignored them entirely. Once he became so angry he punched a hole in the wall. He went to the cemetery every day and collapsed at the graves of his wife and children.

But Antonio was Antonio. He knew he had to take care of Francesca, who was so traumatized that she mostly just sat in her room and stroked the cat on her lap. In 1930, she simply gave up and died. Don Pietro, a priest now for 14 years, asked the bishop if he could transfer to the church at San Martino so he could be near his father. The bishop granted his request.

Even though his house was small, it was too big for Antonio and it held too many memories. When Italy entered World War II in 1940, he sold it and bought a tiny home next to his friends Maria Assunta Pini and her son Narciso. It was near the rectory and Don Pietro visited his father every day.

NARCISO PINI

The pamphlet for the dedication of the plaque says only that Narciso Pini was born in San Martino in Freddana on May 14, 1870, to an "ancient family of farmers," that he went to America in search of work but returned a few years later. He became a dedicated sacristan at the church after the parish priest suffered from a slight paralysis. He especially enjoyed organizing celebrations for holy days. That was about it, but official documents provided other information.

Narciso Pini was the great uncle of the author's third cousins.

WITH SO MUCH work to be done, Angelo and Maria Assunta Pini needed to rely on their children for the never-ending chores on their farm just outside San Martino in Freddana. The boys, Eugenio, Narciso and Luigi, learned to brush the horses, prepare the pigs for slaughter, repair outbuildings and do other outside activities. The girls, Maria Eufemia and Maria Santina, were given instructions on how to cook, bake and clean by their mother. Everyone was taught how to gather eggs, milk the cows, plant and weed the vegetables.

It was a large farm, in the family for generations, and for one of the boys it became too much work. In 1893, Eugenio told his parents he wanted to go to America.

"You're not leaving us!" his father said. "You're too young."

"I'm 23."

"Right. That's too young."

"Papa, I can make good money there and I'll send it back to you. Then maybe you won't have to work so hard."

"You don't even know how to comb your hair right," his mother said. She was sobbing.

Everyone in the village knew that young men from Tuscany and other parts of northern Italy were leaving for America around the turn of the century. All of them were partly influenced by the *lire* that the immigrants sent back to their families.

Narciso was 19 when Eugenio left in 1998, and his father added his brother's duties to his chores. He didn't tell his parents, but Narciso secretly hoped he could go to America someday, too.

But then his father had a heart attack and couldn't do much around the farm. Narciso's younger brother Luigi and his sisters weren't much help, so it was up to him to be in charge. His dreams of going to America seemed out of the question.

Gentle and kind, Narciso took it all in stride. When Eugenio's letters arrived, with *lire* enclosed, he read them carefully and his parents noticed that he stayed quiet for a long time afterwards. His work didn't allow him to go to the parties at church, but once, when he saw a girl he thought he might ask out, his mother wondered aloud how the farm would run if he moved away. He didn't ask the girl.

In the years that followed, Luigi and Maria Eufemia and Maria Santina married and moved away, and in 1914, Angelo died of a heart attack. Maria Assunta decided she had enough of farm life and sold the farm to a younger man, Ulisse Viani. She and Narciso moved to a small house next to the church.

He was 34 years old and suddenly free.

Knowing that his mother had good neighbors, Narciso told her that he wanted to join Eugenio in America. He said he had talked to Carlo Poli, who wanted to join his brothers Angelo and Benedetto. He pointed out that the brothers were still sending *lire* home.

Maria Assunta eventually approved, and on May 10, 1915, Narciso Pini, age 35, and Carlo Poli, 20, took a train to Genoa and boarded the SS Stampalia, a passenger steamer built in La Spezia six years earlier. The ship could hold 40 passengers in first class, 220 in second and 2,400 in third.

Narciso and Carlo were in third, of course, somehow surviving the crowded conditions, the turbulence of the North Sea and the squalls off New York harbor. They were greeted at Ellis Island by Eugenio and Carlo's brother Angelo.

"Come with us," they said. "We're going to the Copper Country."

On the train to Chicago, and then to the far northern reaches of the Upper Peninsula of Michigan, Narciso and Carlo tried to get Eugenio and Angelo to talk about their jobs.

"Well," Angelo reluctantly said, "it's been pretty rough since the strike."

"What strike?" Carlo asked.

Angelo sighed and began a long story. He and his brother Benedetto and Eugenio Pini worked for a company called Calumet and Hecla and they went deep in the mines to drill out copper.

"When I first got there," Eugenio said, "we could tell something was wrong. The men were angry. They were working ten or twelve hours a day with only one day off a week."

Angelo interrupted. "Then the company brought in drills that only took one man to operate. There had been two-man drills. Me and

Benedetto were working together and now we were separated. We hardly knew English and everyone else was talking Finnish."

"There are a lot of Finns up there," Eugenio said. "It's hard to understand them. I suppose they don't understand us either."

"And," Eugenio said, "the work was dangerous. One guy was killed in a cave-in and nobody even knew he was missing for days."

There were, they said, many other issues. Then a union, the Western Federation of Miners, came in to try to organize the workers. The miners went on strike in July 1913.

"You should have seen us!" Angelo said. "Hundreds of us. We blocked all the mines and they were forced to shut down."

"The company," Eugenio said, "wouldn't budge. But then some guys relented and went back to work. There were a lot of fights. The president of the union was shot."

"So anyway," Angelo said, "the strike ended in April last year. We're still working and we found jobs for you, but don't be surprised if you're called scabs."

When they got to the Copper Country, Narciso learned that he would not go down in a mine but his job would probably be worse. He would work in a smelter, shoveling ore that was drilled from the bowels of the earth into a gigantic furnace where the temperatures reached into the hundreds. The blast furnaces worked day and night.

He wrote home to his mother every month, not saying much about the job but enclosing whatever *lire* he could afford.

He wondered whether he should have stayed in San Martino in Freddana. But now that the farm was sold what would he have done there?

In 1919, Maria Assunta wrote that the parish priest, Don Pietro Poli, was suffering from a paralysis that prevented him from doing anything other than saying Mass and visiting his father. He wanted to hire a sacristan. That was all Narciso needed to say goodbye to Eugenio and the Poli brothers and return to San Martino in Freddana.

The work at the church was not difficult. He climbed the bell tower at 6 in the morning, at noon and at 6 in the evening to pull the heavy bell for the Angelus. He put out the hosts, wine, chalice and cloths for the 9 o'clock mass and cleaned up afterwards. Sometimes he helped Don Pietro along when he visited his father and they had lunch together. He liked talking to Antonio Poli. Since both were the same age they remembered the "old days" of San Martino in Freddana but he knew that Antonio had suffered many terrible things in his life.

Narciso's favorite duty was organizing three festivals the church sponsored. In spring, there was the *Festa di San Giuseppe* honoring St. Joseph. After a procession carrying a statue of the saint through the village, everyone gathered at long tables on the street leading to the church for *Maccu di San Giuseppe,* a traditional bean soup, *Pasta di San Giuseppe,* pasta with breadcrumbs that symbolize sawdust because Joseph was a carpenter, and *Sfinci di San Giuseppe,* balls of dough fried in cinnamon sugar.

After the meals, Narciso guided three children dressed as the Holy Family to various houses where they knocked on doors asking for shelter, in memory of the Holy Family's seeking shelter before Christ was born. The re-enactment was called *Tupa Tupa,* meaning Knock Knock, and the children of course were given treats.

After that, and before the music and the drinking and the dancing, children gave their fathers presents they had made in honor of St. Joseph. This was one of many times that Narciso wished he had children.

"Well," he thought, "I can enjoy the others."

Each September 8, Narciso enjoyed the Feast of the Nativity of the Virgin Mary because it only involved children. Little girls would wear white dresses with blue ribbons and little boys would wear white shirts with blue bow ties. They would enter the church and sing two songs a cappella. First, the traditional "Ave Maria" and then the ancient and far more difficult hymn by Saint Alphonsus Ligouri, *"Sei Pura, Sei Pia."*

Still singing, they followed the statue of Mary out of the church and around the village. Parents weren't allowed in the procession but they lined the streets taking photographs.

When the children returned to the church Narciso would read a story describing how much Saint Anne and Saint Joachim loved their daughter Mary. He had found a script in which the story was told in rhyme and his deep voice could be heard even outside the church. There was, of course, another bountiful feast.

The major festival of the year celebrated the village's and the church's namesake, St. Martin de Tours, on his feast day, November 12. His statue led the procession, and there was also a special tribute to the saint. Legend had it that when Martin was in the military he cut his cloak and gave half to a beggar. That night, he saw Jesus in a dream wearing the cloak, but it had been restored in full. Martin was baptized and devoted his life to the poor.

In San Martino in Freddana, Narciso led the procession wearing a long red cloak.

Despite the war, the feast days were still celebrated, although in a reduced fashion. Narciso looked forward to the Feast of the Nativity of the Virgin Mary on September 8.

ULISSE VIANI

The memorial pamphlet tells us that Ulisse Viani was born December 26, 1881, in San Martino in Freddana to a long line of farmers, that he went to America as a young man and worked in a copper mine, that he returned to Italy, that he and his wife bought a farm and that they adopted an orphan girl. This is how we imagine his life.

WHEN HE WAS a boy, Ulisse Viani loved to listen to his grandfather tell stories of his ancestors. He'd sit on the floor near the fireplace while his grandfather sat in his big rocking chair smoking his pipe. His father would be cleaning up after being in the fields and his mother might be washing the dishes.

There were so many stories because his grandfather had heard them from his grandfather who had heard them from his grandfather, and on and on.

The farm where Ulisse lived, just outside of San Martino in Freddana, had been in the Viani family for generations, even centuries. His grandfather thought that the Vianis were there even in the Middle Ages, although they didn't own the land then but were serfs to the Duke of Lucca. Centuries later, they gradually gained possession of the property. Historians called them peasants, or *rustici*.

Ulisse liked to hear how the earliest members of his family dug rocks with makeshift shovels and cut down trees with big knives to form a space where they could plant potatoes, onions, cabbages, corn and grain. How they didn't have machinery but used horses to help dig and plant. How they had to get water from a cistern shared with other *rustici*.

"Tell me about the cows that lived in the house," Ulisse frequently asked Nonno. It was one of his favorite stories.

"Well," his grandfather said, "it wasn't a house like the one we're in now. It was made of stones, even the roof. There was a big chimney and at the base was an open fire where the women would cook. The family slept in a room next to this space.

"And the cattle?" Ulisse asked.

"There was another room on the opposite side and that's where the cows and sheep stayed at night."

"Yuk! Didn't they smell?"

"Of course. But people lived with it. Where else would they put them? The hayloft was upstairs along with a couple of spaces where the older kids slept."

"They had lots of kids, right?"

"Yes, but not all survived. If they had ten or twelve kids, maybe four or five would survive. The priest always listed the causes of death, and so we know about that from the records in the church here. Tuberculosis, typhoid, pneumonia, dysentery. With so little sanitation, it was very hard to keep all the germs away and to keep the diseases from spreading."

Nonno remembered that his grandfather Giancarlo Viani had nine children, but only four survived.

"He used to tell me so many stories," he said. "How the men and boys plowed, sowed, reaped and threshed the grain. How they chopped the wood for fire for the kitchen. How they pruned the vines in the spring and picked the grapes in the fall. How they tended the sheep and sheared the wool and slaughtered the pigs and salted the meat. Oh, so much more.

"And the women and girls cooked over the open fire in the kitchen and spun the wool and made the clothes and made the soap and stitched sandals from rags. You wouldn't want to live back then, Ulisse."

"I don't think I want to be a farmer when I grow up," the boy said.

"And what would you do then? The Viani family has always been farmers. What else is there?"

"I don't know. Maybe I'll go someplace else."

Although the industrial revolution had improved conditions, Ulisse began to hate farm work during his teenage years. He objected when people called him a farmer, or *contadini*. Then he heard about other young men in San Martino in Freddana who had gone to America, and he decided to go, too.

"You're going to hate it," his father said.

"No, I won't. It will be better than here. I won't have to work in the hot sun all the time and I'll make lots of money. And I'll be able to send you some."

In 1910, when he was only 19 years old, he left his parents and two brothers and sailed to America.

After a month working in a copper mine in the Upper Peninsula of Michigan, he wished he had never left home.

He had a partner, Paavo, a young Finnish man whose last name he couldn't pronounce and whose language he didn't understand. Every day they would climb into an iron man-car and descend deep into the dark and damp shaft where they had worked the day before and the day before that and the weeks before that. They operated two-man drills, pulling ore from the sides of the shaft.

It was dangerous. There were cave-ins and miners were injured and even killed. They could hardly see what they were doing. Although their helmets contained little candles, the boss told them not to light them because the candles consumed precious oxygen in the shafts.

They stayed there all day, taking a break to eat the lunch their landlady had made. It was something called pasties, meat, potatoes and vegetables wrapped in dough. Paavo said miners from Cornwall had eaten them.

Ulisse hated them. He was used to his mother's pasta, not pasties.

He worked six days a week, making forty-eight cents an hour.

He didn't go out at night, and stayed in bed most of Sunday. He rarely went to Mass at the local Catholic church. His only friends were Angelo and Benedetto Poli, two brothers from San Martino in Freddana who had arrived in 1911 and worked in another copper mine. They hated the work, too, but they liked the money and they had found two Finnish girls to take out.

In 1913, three years after Ulisse had arrived, Angelo and Benedetto told him about rumors that were rapidly spreading among the miners. Many men were fed up and they were talking about going out on a strike.

"What does that mean?" Ulisse asked.

"It means that if the company agrees, we'll get more money and we'll work less hours," Angelo said.

"It also means," Benedetto said, "that we may be without work for a long time."

"And we won't get paid?" Ulisse asked.

"Nope."

"Well," Ulisse said, "I'm getting the hell out of here."

The next day, he emptied the glass jar that contained all the money he had earned, took the train to New York and sailed back to Italy.

His parents and brothers were overjoyed.

"The Prodigal son returns!" his father said.

After the harrowing experience as a miner, Ulisse found that he actually didn't mind farm work. In fact, some days he enjoyed milking the cows or picking the potatoes. He thought of the stories his grandfather had told him and realized that some parts of farming were the same as during his ancestors' time. Maybe there were machines to help, but fields still had to be planted, cows and pigs still had to be fed, grapes and olives and cherries still had to be picked.

On Saturday nights he and his brothers, Ugo and Franco, went to a dance hall to drink some wine, tell jokes and meet a few farm girls.

One of them was Rosanna, just eighteen, who helped her parents on their nearby farm. She had twinkling eyes, freckles and a frequent smile.

Ulisse asked her out, and then again and again. They were married the following year and bought a farm from Maria Assunta Pini and her son Narciso.

Ulisse and Rosanna were so happy in the first years of their marriage that other people in the village commented when they saw them walking down the street hand in hand. The couple worked together in the fields, and, unlike other husbands in the village, Ulisse helped Rosanna when she cooked and baked.

Ulisse always remembered Rosanna's birthday with a bouquet of flowers from the *mercato,* and Rosanna made his favorite torte on Ulisse's birthday.

There was one thing that bothered them both, however. No matter how hard they tried, they could not conceive a child. Rosanna talked to her mother who never liked to discuss these thing and wasn't much help.

"Just wait," she said. "Be patient. And pray. Why don't you and Ulisse talk to the priest. He's very kind."

The priest may have been kind, but this was a subject he didn't know much about and certainly didn't want to talk about. He gave them a holy card with a saint's picture and told them to pray to Saint Gerard.

Months went by and they could only conclude that Saint Gerard was busy elsewhere.

Ulisse was now 30 and Rosanna was 31. All of their friends, even younger ones, had children, often more than one or two. The friends tried to avoid showing off the kids in front of them, but Ulisse would look away and Rosanna would wipe away tears whenever they saw a child holding its mother's hand or playing on the swings in the playground.

"I guess it's not going to happen," Ulisse said one night as they lay in bed.

"It's probably for the best," Rosanna said. "Maybe we wouldn't be good parents."

"Don't say that! You'd be a wonderful mother and me…well, I would try."

Reluctantly, they went to a doctor in Lucca. He examined them both, but since information about fertility was minimal in those days and the doctor didn't seem interested in their problem, they went home without a solution.

After a while, it didn't seem to matter so much and they made many friends in the village. They especially enjoyed meeting one young couple and played *briscola* with them every week. Since neither Leonardo and Stefania had any close relatives, they considered Ulisse and Rosanna their foster parents.

And then the couple had a baby, a curly-haired little girl they named Rosabella, after Rosanna. They often left the baby on the farm, and Ulisse pulled her in a wagon and Rosana made little dresses and bonnets.

Only months later, a terrible sickness spread over the village, indeed all of Italy and the world. When Leonardo and Stefania couldn't get out of bed, Ulisse and Rosanna moved in and took care of them, being careful not to let little Rosabella near her parents.

One autumn day, the young couple died minutes apart, holding hands. After the funeral, Ullisse and Rosanna brought Rosabella home. There was no question that they would adopt her. Though Italian laws were complicated and the process long, they eventually received the final papers.

They watched as the little girl grew. The new priest at the parish, Don Pietro Poli, taught her prayers, and his father, Antonio Poli, who missed seeing own grandchildren, gave her candy. The sacristan at the church, Narciso Pini, always saw that she had a prominent role in the parish celebration of the *Festa di San Giuseppe*.

Before they knew it, Rosabella had grown from a cute little girl to a stunning beauty and had numerous boys wanting to take her out.

In 1944, Ulisse and Rosanna looked forward to having a grandchild.

AMADEO GHIVIZZANI

We have only sketchy, but intriguing, information about Amadeo Ghivizzani. He was born in Lucca on November 14, 1904, and so, at 39, he was the youngest of the four victims. The pamphlet says he studied the violin under Professor Dante Nuti at the Pacini Musical Institute (now Boccherini) next to the Chiesa del Suffragio in Lucca, and played with an orchestra for ten years. During this time, he studied dental prosthetics under Professor Filippo Lucchesi, and passed an exam for dental technician in Pisa in 1923. He was married and had a family. It does not say why he changed careers or why he was in San Martino in Freddana on that fateful day.

WHEN AMADEO GHIVIZZANI was ten years old and in his first year at the music school, an older boy, Rocco, came up to him as they were leaving classes for the day.

"Come with me," he said. Rocco put his arm around Amadeo's shoulders.

Amadeo shrugged him off. "Where?"

"C'mon. It'll just take a minute."

Rocco pushed Amadeo across the piazza to the *Chiesa del Suffragio*. They entered the ancient church, built in 1675 and decorated with delicate stuccoes, and walked down the long aisle to the elaborate altar. Since it was late afternoon, the place was very dark, and the only light came from a stand of vigil lights at a side altar.

"So?" Amadeo asked. "I go here all the time. What's there to see?"

"You don't know what's under this church?"

"No."

"Bodies," Rocco whispered. "Thousands of dead bodies. Millions maybe."

"Come on."

"Really. But they don't want to be there. They hate it down there. So they come out at this time every day."

Amadeo shuddered. "They do not."

"Be quiet. Let's see if we can hear them."

Amadeo wondered why Rocco was slowly moving toward the altar, going in and out among the pillars.

"And sometimes," Rocco's voice could hardly be heard now, "you might even be able to see them."

Amadeo clutched the back of a pew. He couldn't see Rocco anymore. "Rocco? Are you there?"

Silence. Amadeo decided he'd better leave. Turning around, he tripped and fell on his face. Then he heard a noise, something like chains rattling.

"Who's there?"

From somewhere up above, perhaps in the choir loft, came a rumbling, and then a stomping, and then moaning.

"Who's there!" Amadeo repeated, louder this time.

The sounds continued, and the moaning got louder.

"Stop it!"

The sounds increased. Amadeo put his hands over his ears. He struggled to his feet, groped his way down the aisle and ran out the door. On the piazza, students in their blue jackets and short pants were milling about.

"Amadeo!" one called. "What's wrong? You look like you've seen a ghost."

Amadeo ran home as fast as he could. At dinner that night in the Ghivizzanis' Eighteenth century Palazzo Gelante, Amadeo dawdled over his soup and pasta, ate only a little of the chicken and even declined the dessert.

"Amadeo why aren't you eating?" his father asked. "Did something happen at school today?"

His voice in a whisper, Amadeo told of his experience with Rocco. His mother reached over and held his hand.

"It's all right, Amadeo. Giuseppe, tell Amadeo the story of the bodies under the church."

"It's true, Amadeo," his father said. "But not the way this Rocco told you. Remember how I told you once about the Black Death, the plague that killed thousands and thousands of people in the 1300s?"

"Sort of."

"Well, Lucca was especially hard hit. So many people died. It got to the point where they didn't have room in the cemeteries. And it was so contagious they couldn't keep bodies at home, so the people in charge found this empty space and they buried hundreds of bodies there. People wanted to keep the place sacred, and so they built the *Chiesa del Suffragio* over the graves. Now when we go there we should pray for all the souls who died in the plague."

"Rocco said there were millions down there."

"No, no, no. Not even thousands. Maybe a few hundred. And they don't come out, no matter what Rocco said. Never! Their souls are with God now. So just forget about it. Matilda, could you please call the maid so Amadeo can have his ice cream?"

Giuseppe Ghivizzani could trace his family back for centuries, to the town called Ghivizzano in the Garfagnana area north of Lucca. In fact, there are records showing its existence in Roman times and its very name was eventually derived from the Latin word *"clavis,"* meaning "key" because of its strategic position between other towns. "Clavis" became "Clavidianu" and then "Clavezzano" and finally "Ghivizzano." People from the town were, of course, called Ghivizzani.

Giuseppe had records showing that when a castle was built in Ghivizzano in 1316 an architect by the name of Ferdinano Ghivizzani designed the three-story guard tower. He also had drawings of a church named San Martino inside the castle that was expanded in 1777 with the name changed to honor Saints Peter and Paul.

Once, Giuseppe and his wife took their son to visit Ghivizzano. They found a village of red-tile roofs and a few markets but mostly he wanted

Amadeo to see the tower. Starting at *Chiesa dei Pietro e Paolo,* they climbed what Amadeo thought was a million steps to the first floor that was once a warehouse and then to the upper floors where the royal families lived. They saw the little museum with medieval costumes and family banners and crests.

"Wouldn't you have liked to have lived in the Middle Ages?" Giuseppe asked.

Amadeo eyed the steps they had to climb down. "No."

Although Giuseppe bore a proud royal name, the fortunes of the family had long been dwindling in Lucca. The Palazzo Galante needed new plumbing and roof repairs, and cracks were spreading in the stone walls. Only three maids, down from ten, were in attendance.

Giuseppe and Matilda doted on their only child, and when Amadeo showed signs of being proficient in music, he was enrolled in the prestigious Pacini Musical Institute, one of the oldest musical schools in Italy. Amadeo learned to love the violin, and soon became Professor Dante Nuti's favorite pupil. It was through Professor Nuti's recommendation that Amadeo was able to join the prestigious *Stabile Orchestrale Fiorentina* in Florence after he completed his studies.

He enjoyed being with the orchestra, but it played only two or three days a week. He also thought Florence was too big for him, and he missed Lucca very much. He talked about career options with his father but there didn't seem to be many. He was too shy to become a teacher, not bold enough to be a lawyer and knew too little about finances to become a banker like his father. They spent hours trying to think of alternatives.

"Well," his father finally said, "your uncle is a dental technician and he has a good practice here and makes good money. And he tells me he enjoys it very much and would like an assistant. Why don't you consider becoming a dental technician? You could even live at home."

Amadeo's mother liked the idea very much. She missed Amadeo even when he was in Florence for only a few days.

Amadeo thought about it. Making dentures was certainly far different from playing the violin, and yet there were some similarities. He'd be working with his hands. He could be a little creative. And he'd be in Lucca, which had taken on new meaning now that he had met Simonetta Massina, still a student at the Pacini Institute.

This meant going to Pisa to study under Professor Filippo Lucchesi but at least Pisa was closer than Florence.

Amadeo completed his studies in 1923 and joined his uncle's dental office in Lucca as a technician. He had always been a quiet, private person, so it was good to sit alone at his table making and repairing dentures, inlays, bridges and crowns. He enjoyed working with plastics, ceramics and metals, and rarely was one of his creations returned because of an ill fit.

The regular hours allowed him to spend more evenings with Simonetta. They walked hand in hand along the famous walls surrounding Lucca and enjoyed late night *vin santo* in the Piazza dell'Anfiteatro. Amadeo was in his thirties by now and had given up hope of finding a true love. Now he had.

Simonetta was the youngest of eleven children and all of her siblings had married, had children and moved to villages close to Lucca. She had two brothers in Santo Stefano, three sisters in Fibialla, a brother in Ponte San Pietro, two sisters in Sant'Alessio and a sister in San Macario in Monte.

She was especially close to her sister Alicia, only a year older, who had married, had a son and daughter and lived in San Martino in Freddana.

Amadeo Ghivizzani and Simonetta Massina were married in 1938. They found an apartment near the dental office and a year later welcomed a son, Roberto, and a year after that, a daughter, Lucinda.

Because he was an only child, Amadeo quickly learned about the fun and warmth large families could bring. He roughhoused with Simonetta's nephews and read stories to her nieces. Twice a month he and Simonetta traveled to San Martino in Freddana because little Roberto and Lucinda were so close in age to Alicia's children. Alicia Massina and her family lived next to the sacristan at the church, Narciso Pini, and he delighted taking them up many steps to the bell tower. There the little village stretched all around them.

"Doesn't San Martino in Freddana look peaceful from here?" Amadeo asked as he held both of his children in March 1944 so they could see out the belfry window. "The war seems far away from here, doesn't it?"

BEFORE THE DAY

WORD OF NAZI ATROCITIES spread through Tuscany during the summer of 1944 and villagers in San Martino in Freddana feared that they could be next. They had been on edge ever since June 14 when the body of a German soldier was found in the woods, and everyone knew there would be reprisals.

During that summer, the village was tormented by the sounds of bombs and reports of killings nearby. Shops closed and villagers were afraid to venture outside. Painful day after painful day, June turned to July and July to August.

The stories only got worse in August.

In Fiano di Pescaglia north of Lucca, Don Aldo Mei was part of a network of priests and nuns that sheltered Jews who would otherwise be rounded up and sent to a concentration camp in Germany. On August 2, fifteen SS officers stormed into his church shouting: *"Sie sind verhaftet! Kommen!"* With thirty other men, the young priest was taken to Lucca where he was beaten, handed a shovel and told to dig his own grave. He was shot twenty-eight times and the other men were then executed and buried.

On August 17 troops arrived in the hamlet of Bardine in the Fivizzano district in the Garfagnana to take revenge for the killing of sixteen German soldiers by partisans. They rounded up women, children and the elderly, killing159 civilians.

The first victim was a priest, Michele Rabino. He was accused of helping partisans and sheltering a Jewish girl. As he was shot he cried, *"Sia lodato Gesù Cristo!* May Jesus Christ be Praised."

Early in the morning of August 23, soldiers of the 16th SS Panzergrenadier Division invaded the mountaintop village of Sant'Anna de Stazzema. There, Elisa Benotti had been in labor for three hours and the contractions were increasing. Suddenly, four soldiers burst into the house. A soldier raised his rifle and shot her. Another took his bayonet, sliced the baby from the womb and shot it in the head.

In another part of the village the soldiers forced more than a hundred women and children from their homes.

"Raus! Raus!" the Nazis shouted.

Prodding the screaming victims with their guns, the soldiers shut them up in three stables, then threw bombs into the dilapidated buildings.

The soldiers were in a frenzy, yelling to each other as they ran from house to house killing and setting everything on fire. Many people crawled, coughing and screaming, into the square in front of the tiny church.

When all the villagers were there, twenty soldiers went into the church and dragged pews into the square, surrounding the villagers. Then the soldiers raised their rifles and killed them all.

Exhausted, the soldiers took out their canteens and ate their lunch. One of them had a harmonica and they began to sing.

The massacre at Sant'Anna di Stazzema was over in three hours, with 560 people killed. It was the second worst massacre by the Nazis in Italy in World War II.

Early in the morning of August 23 in the Fucecchio area east of Lucca soldiers of the 16th SS Panzergrenadier Division took gruesome revenge for the wounding of two German soldiers by partisans. The soldiers fired artillery into many homes and set some homes on fire. Only a few residents managed to flee.

The oldest victim was Maria Faustina Arinci, 92. Deaf and blind, she was killed when a hand grenade exploded near her. A total of 174 people, 84 men, 63 women and 27 children were slaughtered.

That evening, the Nazis celebrated in a castle singing, "Victory! The partisans are all *kaput!*"

North of Lucca, the Charterhouse of Farneta, built in the Fourteenth century, was intended to be a place where Carthusian monks could pray, work and meditate in complete isolation.

When the Nazis' 16th SS Panzergrenadier Division approached, dozens of fearful Lucchesi sought refuge there. On September 1, more than twenty German soldiers burst in with automatic machine guns. They stormed the chapel and took over the rest of the charterhouse. Only a few refugees were able to escape and the monks were tortured and killed.

Regrouping, the commander of the German forces told his men to look at a map. They determined where partisans were gathering now.

"Here," a soldier said. "Near San Martino in Freddana."

THE DAY

This is how the pamphlet begins its description of the fatal day: This "Valley of Terror and Death ended its Calvary with the unjust and cruel massacre at San Martino in Freddana in September 1944. Four men, among the most pious and harmless, responsible only for fulfilling their religious and social duty, were killed without justification. Their blood still soaks the earth, but their spirits live today and we want to honor it."

A WEEK BEFORE the feast of the Nativity of the Blessed Virgin Mary on September 8, the dauntless and defiant villagers met to decide if and how they could celebrate the feast under these dangerous circumstances. Don Pietro Poli sat at the head of the table in the church hall with his father nearby.

No one at the meeting wanted to cancel the observance entirely.

"Can we eliminate the feast afterwards?" Don Pietro asked. "I don't think we should be out in the open. "Once some men start drinking," he said, looking around, "they might start yelling."

Antonio Poli agreed. "My son is right, but we won't mention names."

Ulisse and Rosanna Viani, always concerned about the welfare of children, said that the procession with little girls and boys should also be canceled.

"They look so cute in their white shirts and blue ties and ribbons," Rosanna said, "but we need to protect them."

"They can still sing 'Ave Maria' and *'Sei Pura, Sei Pia'* in the church," Ulisse said.

"What," Narciso asked, "should I do about my little story about Mary and Anne and Joachim? Should I still do it?"

"Of course, of course," everyone said. "You always do that so well."

Narciso smiled and sat down.

"All right then," Don Pietro said. "We're agreed. The Mass will start at 10 o'clock. You should all be in your pews beforehand. I'll say the Mass and then Narciso will read the story about Mary and her parents and then the children will sing. Maybe I can come up with some treats before we go home."

AS HE DID EVERY DAY, Antonio Poli rose before dawn on the Feast of the Nativity of the Virgin Mary and went to the cemetery. Kneeling before Maria's white tomb, he dug out his wooden rosary and, because it was Friday, recited the Sorrowful Mysteries. "The Agony of Jesus in the Garden..." Then, wiping tears on the sleeve of his woolen jacket, he moved to the graves of his children. Giacomo. Filippo, Isabella. Francesca.

At home, he fed his cat, Nino, his only comfort for so many years, fried an egg, cut off a piece of crusty bread and made coffee.

It was only 5:30. Mass wouldn't start until 10. He sat in his old rocking chair, pulled Nino onto his lap and looked out the window.

Across the way, he saw Narciso Pini at his kitchen stove, also preparing an egg, toast and coffee. Narcisco always got up early to ring the bell for the morning Angelus, but today he also wanted to prepare for the Virgin Mary's feast day. Some of those little children always forgot to bring their blue ribbons or ties.

After eating, he put on a tie, a dark blue one that he only wore on feast days, and went to the church. It was now 6 o'clock and he climbed the stairs and rang the first bell of the Angelus for the day.

Then he went down to the sacristy and pulled out the items Don Pietro would need on the altar for Mass. The chalice, the paten, the ciborium, a communion cup, the pall. He went to the closet and lined up the vestments. The long white alb that was tied with a cincture, then the stole and the chasuble. He also brushed off cassocks and surplices for the two altar boys who would serve Mass. He hoped Fredo and Franco, twin brothers, would not giggle so much today.

Then he put the book with Mary's story on the lectern so it was there when it was time for him to read.

Satisfied that everything was in order, Narciso returned home. He waved at Antonio Poli next door, sat in his rocking chair and looked out the window. He could hear the Massina children on the opposite side. It was now 7 o'clock.

Alicia Massina was also up early because her sister Simonetta Ghivizzani was coming with her family from Pisa for the feast day. Amadeo Ghivizzani had taken the day off from his dental practice so that little Roberto and Lucinda could watch their cousins take part in the Mass and then play games the rest of the day.

Alicia tried to calm her children, who were practically bouncing off the walls.

"Francesco! Natalia! Settle down! They'll be here soon."

The children went to a window to look for their cousin's dark blue Maserati. Sometimes, Alicia became jealous of her sister's family, not only because they could afford a nice house and car but also because Amadeo had not joined the partisans. Alicia's husband had joined a band in May and she had heard from him only twice since.

At 7:30 the Ghivizzanis pulled up to the Massina's door and Alica and the kids ran out to meet them. Simonetta carried a plate of vegetables in one hand and a torte in the other. Amadeo lugged a bag of toys, and Roberto, Lucinda, Francesco and Natalia soon had Alicia's house in a mess.

"Children," Alicia said, "why don't you go outside and play."

"I'll go with them," Amadeo said.

Hearing all the joyful noise in the neighbors' yard, the two old men who were their neighbors, Antonio Poli and Narciso Pini, came over to watch. It was now 8 o'clock.

On their farm just outside of San Martino in Freddana, Ulisse and Rosanna Viani were up early because they wanted to work on secret projects before Rosabella got up. Since it was a feast day, Rosabella's high school was closed and she was still sleeping.

After breakfast, and with the dishes cleaned, Ulisse opened a can of paint for the baby crib he had finally finished making.

"Pink or blue?" Rosanna asked.

"I thought a nice light yellow."

Rosana opened a drawer and pulled out the baby blanket she was knitting. It was also yellow.

"Sometimes I wonder why we're doing this," she said. "Rosebella's still in school and not going to get married for years. Much less have a baby."

"She'd better hurry or we won't be alive to see it," Ulisse said.

"You never know," Rosanna said. "Things happen fast."

It was now 8:30.

"Looks like we're not going to make Mass," Ulisse said. "Rosabella's still sleeping."

"Let her sleep."

High in the hills, thirteen partisans had arrived from a campground four miles east. One had been shot and had his arm in a sling. Another was on crutches. All were tired but ready for another encounter.

"OK," the partisan named Verde said, "look at this map. Our source says the 16th SS Panzergrenadier Division will probably arrive at this town this morning. But they're tired and going crazy and killing right and left. Anything could set them off. We need to be ready."

"What's the town?" another asked.

"Something called San Martino in Freddana."

At the same time, the bedraggled soldiers of the 16th SS Panzergrenadier Division traveled in tanks and on foot out of Lucca and neared San Martino in Freddana.

"How many people do they want us to kill?" one asked.

"As many as we can," another answered.

"I want to go home," a third said.

They trudged on.

At 9:30, the residents of San Martino in Freddana began their way to their domed church in the center of the village. The church, once small, was rebuilt in 1904 with a large Romanesque section in front of the plain original one. Since the war, the statues had gotten dusty and the floor needed a good scrubbing. Because it was warm and very humid, the windows were open, but there was little breeze.

Elderly women, dressed in black, found their pews first and immediately began saying the rosary. A few old men found seats in the back. Children in white darted around until their mothers ordered them to be quiet, kneel and pray.

Alicia Massina and her two kids sat next to her sister Simonetta Ghivizzani and her two kids. Behind them, Amadeo Ghivizzani sat next to Antonio Poli. Narciso Pini was in the front pew, waiting for Don Pietro to give him the signal that it was time for Mass.

At 9:55, Don Pietro, seated at the right of the altar, nodded to Narciso, and the old man slowly climbed the stairs. He rang the bell once. Twice. Three times, Four. Five and Six.

Don Pietro went to the altar and prepared to begin Mass. He had opened the Roman Missal and began the first prayer when the doors were flung open and fifteen Nazi troops stormed in waving their rifles.

"*Raus! Raus!*" they shouted.

"No!" Don Pietro answered, trying to be calm. "We are just starting Mass. Please leave. It's a feast day."

"You are signaling to the partisans!" one Nazi yelled.

"Die partisanen! Die partisanen!" they chanted.

"No!" Amadeo Ghivizzani shouted. "We have nothing to do with the partisans! Leave us alone!"

Women and children screamed. One elderly woman fainted. An old man in the back hit his head when he fell.

Four soldiers forced their way into the bell tower, grabbed Narciso Pini by the neck and threw him down the stairs. Then they pushed him out into the courtyard.

You signaled to the partisans, they yelled.

No! he cried. No! It's not a signal! It's not a signal! We are only calling the faithful for Mass!

Antonio Poli and Amadeo Ghivizzani rushed to Narciso's side. Crouched in front of the church, they were surrounded by a half dozen soldiers. The soldiers pointed their guns.

"Schießen!" their leader ordered.

The three men were killed instantly. Don Pietro, hindered by his paralysis, hobbled from the church and tried to get to his father.

"Papa! Papa!"

The Germans kicked him away.

"Let me give them the Last Rites!"

"Nein!"

They forced the priest from Antonio Poli's body.

Sweating, confused and terrified, the Nazis fled the scene just as Ulisse Viani came running from his farm. They shot him instantly.

In the hills, the partisans heard the bell ring and the tanks rumble. They rushed down the rocky paths and arrived at the church just as German soldiers tripped and fell over each other in a desperate attempt to escape.

"Get them!" Verde shouted.

Although outnumbered, the partisans chased the Nazis to the center of the village, formed a circle around them and took them captive. Then, using the division's own tanks, the partisans marched the prisoners back on to the highway and to Camaiore, where they would be locked up in a makeshift prison.

Screaming and sobbing, the women, men and children filed quickly out of the church. Most did not dare to look at the bodies. At home, they locked the doors and pulled the window shades. Cries and moans echoed in the hills.

The next day, Simonetta Ghivizzani found an undertaker to take her husband's body back to Pisa and she followed with Roberto and Lucinda. The bodies of Antonio Poli, Narciso Pini and Ulisse Viani were placed in caskets in front of the altar at the church. The caskets were left open so everyone could see what the Nazis had done. The following morning, two days after the Feast of the Nativity of the Virgin Mary, Don Pietro said the funeral mass for his father and the two other victims from San Martino in Freddana.

In the afternoon, villagers were surprised to see members of the United States' 92nd Infantry Division enter the village. It was a segregated unit and they were called the Buffalo Soldiers.

The people of San Martino in Freddana had never seen a Black man before, but they approached slowly when the soldiers handed out candy and cigarettes.

A year later to the day, a brief ceremony was held and a plaque was placed on the cemetery wall honoring Antonio Poli, 74, Narciso Pini, 74, Ulisse Viani, 62, and Amadeo Ghivizzani, 39.

And in the church, a vast mural was painted above the altar so that the faithful would never forget September 8, 1944. At the center is the Virgin Mary, surrounded by Saint Martino and peasants. In the background, a devastated village. And in a prominent position, a military tank.

ANNA AND THE
TELEVISION PRIEST

When I was young I used to watch Bishop Sheen's popular "Live Is Worth Living" television show, um, religiously, and I wondered if there had ever been an Italian version.

IN ROME, no one climbed the Spanish Steps and traffic became so light that cars could drive around the Colosseum without stopping. In Milan, Piazza del Duomo was virtually empty except for the pigeons. In Venice, waiters ceased serving in the restaurants in Saint Mark's Square. Even in Naples, peddlers stopped shouting and you could hear underwear flapping on the clothes lines outside upstairs windows.

Every Tuesday night at 8 o'clock, in cities and villages, hamlets and farms, Italians would slow down for a half hour to watch the man universally known as "*il sacerdote dolce,*" The Gentle Priest. They switched their television sets to RAI Uno and waited for the announcer to say, "Welcome to 'Living Life Day by Day' with Father Giancarlo Moretti."

The priest, handsome and silver-haired but still youthful looking in his 50s, walked onto the modest set in Florence, smiled into the camera and started to speak. His voice was soft and comforting, and when he smiled he showed an expanse of white teeth. He sat in a comfortable chair and talked for a half hour. Then he stopped and said good night. That was it.

Sometimes he read from a Gospel and then talked about it. Sometimes he read parables and explained their meaning. Sometimes he told personal stories. Sometimes he used props. Once a month he had a guest.

No one could quite explain the program's popularity, but it had become a sensation, a *sensazione,* as the Italians liked to call it, or a phenomenon, a *fenomeno,* as the newspapers preferred. Father Giancarlo—everyone called him by his first name—was featured in adoring articles in newspapers and magazines, and more than a few women expressed sorrow that he had entered the seminary.

"*Il sacerdote dolce*" was, in effect, a religious rock star.

The program was unabashedly modeled after "Life Is Worth Living," an enormously popular television show in America in the 1950s that starred Bishop Fulton J. Sheen. In fact, not the least reason Father Giancarlo was selected for the Italian version was because he bore a striking resemblance to the bishop.

Even the day and time were similar. The American program put Bishop Sheen in competition with Milton Berle and Frank Sinatra, but people watched the bishop anyway. In Italy, the station reported that the show had almost as many viewers as when Gli Azzurri was playing a soccer match, and it widely advertised videotape copies of his program.

The station—and the church—couldn't have been more pleased.

Nowhere was the program more popular than in the cramped living room shared by two former nuns in an old palazzo near the Basilica of Santa Croce in Florence. Every Tuesday night, Anna Rossetti and Leonora Acara brought in bowls of Tuscan bean soup and took a break from managing Casa di Maria, the home for unmarried girls who were about to have babies.

"I live for this all week," Leonora always said as she turned on the small black-and-white television set. "I don't know what I would do without Father Giancarlo. He makes everything we do worthwhile, doesn't he?"

Anna had to agree. "He's a blessing," she often said.

Leonora was surprised, then, when Anna was not sitting next to her ten minutes before Father Giancarlo's program was about to begin on the second Tuesday of April in 1990.

"Anna," she called. "It's almost time."

Leonora helped herself to more soup and called again. "Anna, the soup's getting cold and Father Giancarlo is almost on."

Leonora had finished her dinner and still Anna had not appeared. Except for the times when Leonora was called to her father's funeral and Anna went to a reunion of former nuns who had left the Abbey of

Sant'Agata d'Assisi, neither had missed one of Father Giancarlo's programs for more than seven years, almost since the very beginning.

"Anna," she called again. "The game show is ending."

On the screen, women with long hair and short dresses held up the winning numbers of whatever game was being played. Anna and Leonora could never figure out what the game was and didn't care.

"Anna must be with Anastasia," Leonora thought. "There must be some emergency."

Still, three volunteers had been on hand with the young woman when Leonora had left fifteen minutes ago.

"It's starting!"

The screen went dark and then the words: "Living Life Day by Day with Father Giancarlo Moretti."

Anna suddenly appeared, sank into the armchair and picked up the bowl of soup. "Thank goodness, I made it. Anastasia was having problems. She's all right now."

The screen focused on the set, an upholstered couch and chair, a small table with a statue of the Virgin Mary and a crucifix on the wall. Father Giancarlo entered from the right and strode to the camera.

"Good evening. I'm Father Giancarlo Moretti and I want to thank you again for inviting me into your homes."

"We want to have you here!" Leonora said.

"Shhhh."

"Hasn't this been a wonderful day!"

"Yes!" Leonora answered.

"Yes, April in Italy. What could be better than that? Except maybe May, June, July—well, you know what I mean. But let's celebrate, and what better way to celebrate than with this quote from Saint Paul: "We are fools for Christ's sake, but ye are wise in Christ; we are weak, but ye are strong; ye are honorable, but we are despised."

"Fools for Christ? I've never heard that," Leonora said.

"Leonora…"

"Now," the priest said, "what does it mean to be a fool? Let's translate that as being a clown."

He took a red crayon from his pocket and drew two red circles on his cheeks and chin. He pulled out a red clown's nose and pushed it onto his own. Finally, he folded a red napkin into a clown's hat and put it on his head. Anna and Leonora laughed so hard they could hardly hear the priest say, "Perhaps we can all be fools for Christ?"

Still wearing his clown nose, Father Giancarlo said that we might appear to be fools because of our commitment to Christ. It isn't always popular to believe in Jesus, and we who do believe might appear to be fools. He went on to illustrate that with other examples, and soon the half hour was up.

"Thank you again for joining me in this conversation. Let's talk again next week. God bless you!"

He smiled and exited, and closing credits appeared. Anna turned off the television set.

"Well, that will give us something to think about in the next week."

"Isn't he amazing?" Leonora said. "I wonder what he's really like, I mean apart from the television programs."

"He doesn't seem to reveal much in all those newspaper interviews."

"I wish I could meet him," Leonora said.

"Really? Why? He's just a priest with a television program, isn't he?"

"Oh, Anna, you know you'd love to meet him and talk to him. Maybe someday you will."

"I doubt it. Well, I'd better get back to Anastasia."

ONE OF ANNA ROSSETTI'S earliest memories was the doll she carried around from morning to night. It had a porcelain head and a soft body. Its hair was tangled and its cheeks were stained. Her mother had made an outfit for the doll that was supposed to represent a girl in a dancing troupe—white blouse, red skirt with red suspenders. It didn't have any shoes.

Anna called her doll Michelina. It was one of the few nice memories she had of her childhood. The war was going on, but, except for occasional planes overhead or bombs exploding in the distance, it didn't seem to affect the Rossetti family. They had enough battles on their own.

Her twin brothers were always fighting. Her older sister ran off into the woods with her boyfriend and cowered in a corner when their mother yelled at her when she returned. For hours, it seemed. Her younger sister cried all the time. Their mother made Anna take care of her and both of them hated that.

Then when the war ended Anna's father returned, badly wounded in mind and in body. Her mother spent most of her time at his side, changing bandages but more often trying to calm him. He seemed to be still fighting on the side of the partisans.

Then her mother became pregnant and then, worse, had another girl. Anna was furious. She threw tantrums. She wailed on her bed. She refused to come to dinner.

Anna remembered the terribly hot August day when she decided to leave. It was four years after the war and she was fourteen years old. Almost everyone in her village remained inside, hiding from the relentless sun. Upstairs, Anna's mother and father were in their stifling bedroom, and her mother was attempting to calm her husband. Pietro kept yelling and screaming.

"They're coming! They're coming! Get down!" he kept shouting. He pushed his wife to the floor.

"No, no, Pietro. No one's here. It's all right." She took him by the arm and led him to the bed.

"Nonononononono…"

"It's all right, Pietro. It's all right."

Anna covered her ears.

Downstairs, Anna's brothers were engaged in one of their frequent loud wrestling matches, one of them pounding the other before the other got on top.

"Be quiet!" her mother kept shouting from upstairs. "Your father needs his rest!"

"We're being quiet," one or the other yelled back. "We're just playing."

The brothers continued to wrestle.

Her older sister came home singing loudly, her dress covered with grass stains. Her younger sister was tearing her dress and the baby was screaming.

Every day, the same thing. Her father's screams, her brothers' fights, one sister carrying on with that boy, the other two screaming, her mother torn apart. It was driving her crazy. She had to get away, find some quiet.

Anna clutched her doll. "It's all right, Michelina. It's all right." She kissed the top of its frizzy hair.

It was then that she thought about what a priest had said in his sermon last Sunday. It was the feast of Saint Clare of Assisi and, in between warnings about missing Mass and failing to contribute to the church, the priest described this wonderful woman who left her family and became one of the most important saints in heaven.

Anna made up her mind right then. She didn't want to be an important saint in heaven. She only wanted to get away, to find some peace and quiet. After all, she didn't mind going to church. She rather liked looking at all the paintings and statues and listening to the organ music. She even liked to say the rosary sometimes. She would become a nun. One of those nuns who never left the convent.

The cloistered routine of life for Sister Anna della Croce in the Abbey of Sant'Agata d'Assisi was comforting at first. Rising at 4 o'clock and going to the chapel for Lauds, then private adoration of the Holy Eucharist, followed by Mass.

The rest of the day was scheduled to the minute, something she always liked, even as a young postulant. Prayer, work, meals, more work, more prayer. Even the work was enjoyable, with the nuns lined up in the huge kitchen to make Communion wafers that were sold to churches throughout the region.

At night, the nuns had an hour of "recreation," and indeed a few of the younger ones played table tennis, but most knit or sewed. Anna liked to read books from the selection the governing sisters had reviewed. There was no television set, but a radio could be turned to classical music.

At 7:30 p.m., the nuns gathered in the chapel again for nightly prayers and the rosary, and at 8:30, everyone went to the long dormitory on the top floor of the abbey. By 9 o'clock everyone was asleep.

Then Vatican II changed so many things in the church. Many of the nuns who had gone into the convent to escape from something, just as Anna had, now found that they wanted something more. They wanted to contribute, to help people. So, after three decades in the convent, Anna left.

In Florence, she met a priest who was running a nursery in connection with a soup kitchen. *Figli di dio*, it was called. "God's Babies."

Volunteers helped with the staffing, but Anna was eternally grateful when another former nun, Leonora Acara, knocked on the door one day and asked, "May I help?" It soon became clear that there was another need. Pregnant young girls needed a place to stay before, during and after they had their babies. With the priest's help, an old palazzo in the back of Santa Croce was purchased and they called it Casa di Maria. Soon, pregnant girls arrived, had their babies and were guided to new lives, sometimes with their babies, sometimes not.

Occasionally, Anna missed the convent life, but it was easy at Casa di Maria to keep busy. She could forget that even with all the people around her, she often got very lonely. She still had her doll Michelina in a drawer.

IF ANNA ROSSETTI REMEMBERED the doll from her childhood, Giancarlo Moretti remembered his dog. A brown fluffy ball of fur, Primo had been found at the side of the road with his left leg broken and his left eye badly damaged. Giancarlo's father brought him home and laid him in a makeshift bed in front of the fireplace. The boy brought him milk and bits of wild boar or chicken twice a day.

Eventually, the leg healed, though there was always a slight limp, and his left eye looked in the opposite direction from the right.

Primo followed Giancarlo everywhere, sat under his chair at the table waiting for scraps, and slept on the corner of his bed. He answered the boy's roughhousing with friendly licks and a tail that wouldn't stop wagging.

Until he was old enough to go to school, Giancarlo and Primo ran through the hills near their home in the rugged Garfagnana region north of Lucca. Without any brothers or sisters, and with no other children in the tiny village, Primo was his only friend.

When he was fifteen, Bianca came into Giancarlo's life. Her family had moved to Montagna Sole and of course someone had to help her get acquainted. They went on bike rides. He showed her the little river that ran through the outskirts of town and the lake where they could swim. When she took off her dress to reveal her bathing suit, he looked away. And then he looked back.

Afterwards, the ravine was a good place where they could get to know each other even better. Giancarlo always remembered that summer as the time he became a man.

After Bianca drifted off with Ferdinando, Giancarlo found solace with Antoinetta and then Victoria and then Rosetta.

He had no plans after high school, but one night his mother brought the parish priest home. Giancarlo should have had an inkling of what was going to happen. His mother had been devastated ever since her husband had died in the war and except for going to church and shopping, she rarely went out and spent most of her time praying in her darkened bedroom. Giancarlo didn't know how to help her.

After the priest left, his mother sat down with her son at the kitchen table. Her eyes were filled with tears.

"Gianni, I have such wonderful news. Father Federico has arranged for you to enter the seminary. Gianni, you can become a priest! Oh, thank you, God. I have been praying for this ever since…since your father…"

"But…"

"I know you're surprised, Gianni. Maybe I should have talked about this with you before. But I wasn't sure if Father Federico could manage to get you in. Not every boy gets in, you know. This has been very special."

"But, Mother…"

"I'm so proud of you, Gianni."

As he had feared, Giancarlo found the seminary extremely difficult. He had never been away from home before. He had a hard time making friends and he missed his mother. And Primo. And Bianca and Antoinetta and Victoria and Rosetta.

Although he had never been an exceptional student, he managed to get through the history and theology and philosophy classes, but his favorite turned out to be homiletics. While other students considered sermons as "preaching," he thought of them more like conversations. He would get up in front of the class and talk about the stories in the life of Christ and try to apply them to daily living. His professor was impressed.

"Giancarlo," Father Antonio told him one day, "this is what people in your parish will want to hear. Not so much talk about hell and fire and brimstone. Giancarlo, you will bring humility to the priesthood, something that is so badly needed. I think you're going to have a very bright future, maybe even a famous one."

The seminarians were required to make a retreat before ordination. Aware of the warnings about developing "particular friendships," he worried that the priesthood would be a lonely place. He didn't know if he was ready. How could he help people who were so much older, so much more experienced, than he was? Especially, he didn't know if he could stand a life without a Bianca or an Antoinetta or...

The new Father Giancarlo Moretti found his first parish, as an assistant pastor in a remote Tuscan village, in disarray. The pastor was a serious alcoholic and sometimes couldn't even say the Mass on Sundays, let alone weekdays. Unable to cope with this, the housekeeper had quit. The first thing Father Giancarlo did was call home.

"Mother, I need your help. Can you come and be my housekeeper?"

In the first weeks, the new priest took charge. He talked to the diocesan people and found a rehabilitation home for the pastor, who went off surprisingly willingly. Although he was technically still an assistant pastor of the church, Father Giancarlo set up a schedule for Masses, baptisms, confirmations and weddings. He went to the school and arranged to teach Catechism to each of the seven grades. He rejuvenated the long-dormant Altar Society, the Christian Mothers Society, the Catholic Youth Club and the Men's First Friday Club. He organized a boys soccer team and served as referee.

Parishioners couldn't get over him. He was invited to homes for dinner. Father Gianni—for that was the name he wanted to be called—enjoyed this at first. Then something strange happened. When he returned to the rectory after one visit, he felt more alone than he had before.

"Did you enjoy yourself?" his mother would ask.

"It was all right."

"They're such a nice family, aren't they?"

"Yes."

"They have a lot of children, don't they?"

"Yes."

"Was it fun to watch them play?"

"Mother, I'm tired. I think I'll go to bed."

Father Gianni learned to pour himself into his work. Masses, parish organizations, the school.

"Why do you have to keep so busy?" his mother would ask.

"I need to, Mother. I need to."

As Father Giancarlo's reputation as a kind and gentle pastor, not to mention a great administrator, grew, he was transferred to a bigger parish. Then another one even larger. And then a third in the heart of Florence.

He found that the parishioners there, especially the women, wanted to have a more active role in the church than he'd been used to. In his second week, Signora Maria Brunetto asked to come to see him since she was the treasurer of the Christian Mothers Society.

Father Giancarlo expected an elderly, or at least middle-aged, woman. Signora Brunetto was no more than thirty-five, with short blond hair. She wore no makeup, and her face glowed.

"Welcome, Father! We are so pleased that you have joined us."

Her hand seemed to remain on his for an extraordinarily long time. He noted that her eyes were green. Antoinetta had green eyes. So did Rosetta.

He invited her into the parlor, where his mother brought them tea and looked disapprovingly at the visitor.

They talked about the Christian Mothers Society and the parish and the neighborhood.

"And your family?" he asked.

"My son, Franco, is twelve and my daughter, Lucia, is ten. My mother lives with us and she takes care of them."

"And your husband?"

"He's away a lot."

He didn't understand why she didn't say more and why she looked straight into his eyes.

He could smell a light sweet fragrance that he didn't recognize, and when she leaned down over his desk he could see a gentle cleavage. He lost track of what they were talking about and knew he had to end it.

"Well," he said, "I'm sure we'll see each other again."

"Yes, of course," she said.

"Yes…yes," he said.

"No…no," he thought.

That night, he couldn't figure out why he kept thinking about her. He had certainly worked with other beautiful women before. Perhaps he'd been attracted to one or two, but there was nothing beyond simple conversations.

"I'm forty-four," he thought. "What's going on?"

He needed air.

"Mother," he called. "I'm going for a run."

In the past year, he found that running helped to clear his mind and keep his waist trim. With his cap down and in his running shirt and shorts, no one recognized the priest as he ran through the tourists on Ponte Vecchio, up to Fort Belvedere, across on via San Leonardo, left at Viale Galileo, over to the Church of San Minato and back to Ponte Vecchio. He was back home in a half hour, too tired to think.

A week later, he was late for a meeting of the Christian Mothers Society and found that the only seat at the front table was next to Signora Brunetto.

"Nice to see you again, Father," she said, reaching for his hand.

"Yes." He pulled his hand away.

"I really need to talk to you about our finances."

"I'll have my secretary call."

Father Giancarlo had his secretary tell Signora Brunetto that she really had to talk to the church administrator.

"I can't get involved. I can't get involved."

Yet he did. He found that he had to go over the finances even after the administrator had looked at them. That required lunch at a nearby trattoria. He wore his Roman collar and easily greeted parishioners who stopped by their table. That was followed by dinner at a popular restaurant where he didn't wear his Roman collar. Followed by four dinners in increasingly secluded restaurants.

Followed by nights in even more secluded villas.

When he thought back on those three months, he realized how incredibly stupid he had been. He could have been seen and reported to the bishop at any time. There was, after all, a self-appointed watchdog group called Florentines for Morality that was on the lookout for such wayward priests.

Fortunately, both Father Giancarlo Moretti and Signora Maria Brunetto realized that they had little in common and no future together. The little fling was just that. Anyway, Signora Brunetto and her family moved to Milan.

There were three other near-relationships over the years, but none as intimate. Father Giancarlo increased his run from three miles to five to ten to twenty, and he ran four or five times a week.

"It clears my head," he told people who asked.

It also stopped him from thinking, he realized.

He got a dog, Secondo, to replace the long departed but never forgotten Primo. He spent more time on his homilies, and soon even people beyond his parish came to his Masses just to hear him.

One Sunday after he had been at the church for five years, he noticed that a man he had never seen before was in the back taking notes. The man returned the next Sunday with a tape recorder.

"Mother," he said after Mass, "did you think there was anything objectionable in what I said? I think I'm in trouble."

"Trouble?"

"Mother, I've heard that the bishop is clamping down on priests who say things that aren't quite what the church teaches. I know of one priest who dared to talk about the ordination of women and they transferred him to a retirement home."

"Gianni, you didn't say anything anywhere like that at all. I'm sure this is nothing to worry about."

The following week, the man was back again and Father Giancarlo was called in to see the bishop, who pointed to a chair across from his desk.

"I'll come right to the point," the bishop said. "You know, Giancarlo, there are so many terrible things happening in this world. Divorces, children not obeying their parents, teenagers taking dangerous drugs. Abortions! Priests and nuns leaving their holy orders!"

Father Giancarlo felt sweat developing on his forehead but was afraid to take out a handkerchief to wipe it off.

"It's terrible," the bishop continued. "People don't come to church anymore. Our churches are half empty, and those who do come are mostly old women."

"Excellency," Father Giancarlo said, "I have really tried to be faithful to the church's teachings in what I say. I go over and over my sermons. Every word. If you think there is something offensive..."

"Offensive! No, on the contrary, Giancarlo, your sermons are a breath of fresh air in this diocese. I've heard from so many people, and my communications director confirmed that. And when I listened to the tape recorder, I was convinced, too."

This time Father Giancarlo did pull out his handkerchief to wipe his forehead. "Well, thank you. Thank you, your Excellency."

"And so, Giancarlo, I want you to take on a new assignment. We want to reach out to every person under our jurisdiction and even beyond. Men, women, children. We have tried to do that, but always in the traditional ways. Church bulletins, announcements from the pulpit, our weekly newspaper. Now we want to use a method that everyone else has found so useful. Television!"

"Television?"

"Yes, television. Giancarlo, we would like you to have a weekly television program in which you would simply give the kind of sermons you have been used to giving at your parish. We would like this to be very informal. We would create a simple set somewhere in this palazzo, but instead of standing in the pulpit, which would be too formal, you would walk around or sit in a chair and just talk."

"Just talk?"

"Exactly. Just say what you say in your sermons, because they are from your heart, and we think people will listen."

"Excellency, I hesitate to ask this, but do you think people will actually sit in their living rooms and listen to a priest talk? Especially since there are so many other programs on television, game shows, movies, westerns?"

The bishop then recounted the story of how Bishop Sheen's program had been so popular in America.

"I'm not a bishop, Excellency."

"Giancarlo, I'll be frank. We want a personable, good-looking priest to be the face of the diocese, not some old fogy like...well, we won't mention names. You are just the man to do this."

Seven years later, "Living Your Life Day by Day" was one of the most popular programs on Italian television, and Father Giancarlo had something else to occupy his mind.

ANNA HAD MARKED THE DATE on her calendar, the third Saturday in April, but every time she looked at it she had mixed feelings. The woman she had known as Sister Fabiola had written to suggest that she and another former nun at the Abbey of Sant'Agata d'Assisi have lunch together. "Wouldn't it be great to see each other again?" Fabiola had written.

Anna wasn't quite sure. While it would be nice to see the two women again, she knew that after fourteen years, their lives had changed so much that they would have little in common. Anna knew that Fabiola had married a former priest three years after leaving the convent. As for Maddelena, she had been in the convent for only a year so Anna didn't know her well. Maddelena had also married and, she'd heard, had children.

"Should I go?" she asked Leonora.

"Of course! Why wouldn't you?"

"It's just…well, I don't know."

"You're afraid you're going to hear them talk about being married and having kids and wonder what your life might have been like?"

"Yes."

On Friday, Anna finally decided. She was going. It was her Saturday off anyway, and Leonora was perfectly capable of handling the various problems of the young women at Casa di Maria.

The trattoria was near Santa Maria Novella and Anna enjoyed the walk on the sunny day. She recognized Fabiola immediately.

"You haven't changed a bit," they both cried after a long hug.

"Oh, I have," Fabiola said.

"Well, I know I have," Anna said. "I've gained weight, my hair is entirely gray now, I have to wear glasses all the time."

"Well, your work must keep you young."

"It does. It does. Is Maddelena coming?"

"She called. She'll be a little late."

Anna described working at Casa di Maria. She said she often worked twelve hours or more a day and was grateful for Leonora and an army of volunteers to help.

"Oh, Anna. That sounds so hard. How can you do it? In the convent, we only had to worry about making Communion wafers."

"And you?" Anna asked.

"Oh, Anna," Fabiola said, "I am so happy. You don't know how happy I am. Anna, Franco and I were made for each other. After ten years, we are still so much in love. We like all the same things, even food! We like going to plays and the opera here. Last year we went on a cruise to the Greek islands. He's just wonderful, Anna. I hope you'll meet him soon."

"I'm glad, Fabiola."

"I know how people talked when we got married. I know they said that Franco left the priesthood because of me, but he didn't. He really didn't. He was thinking about it long before we met."

Maddelena arrived then, not looking a day, well, a year, older than when she left the convent. Her hair was now in a ponytail and she had gained just a little weight.

Hugs and kisses all around.

"Sorry I'm late. Matteo was late coming back from soccer practice with Filippo, Silvia had to go to her dance class, Tonio couldn't be found and Pero had to be changed. Oh, there's always something going on in our house."

"Oh, Maddelena, that's sounds so wonderful," Fabiola said.

"Yes," Anna said.

She wondered how anyone could handle four children, but she was distracted by the young family at the next table. Even though it was Saturday, the father wore a sport coat and tie, the mother a pretty pink dress. Their son, about eight, also wore a tie and his sister a frilly white dress. They were all laughing and talking and then a waiter brought a cupcake with a candle in it and put it in front of the girl. They all joined hands and sang "Happy Birthday."

Anna thought it was the most beautiful thing she'd ever seen.

Their own waiter, who had been hovering, took their orders, and for the rest of the meal Fabiola and Maddelena talked about their husbands and their lives and how happy and content they were now. Anna's mind wandered.

Fabiola interrupted her daydream. "Aren't you happier now, too, Anna?"

"Yes. Yes, of course." She fiddled with her knife, then her fork, then her napkin.

"Anna," Maddelena said, "if you met the right man, do you think you'd get married?"

"Married? Me? Good lord, I'm 54 years old!"

"Well, I'm 58," Fabiola said. "But I don't feel 58. Franco makes me feel, well, OK, 50!"

No one wanted dessert, and when Fabiola suggested they meet again, they all agreed, knowing full well that it would never happen.

When Anna returned home, Leonora wanted to know all about it.

"Did you enjoy yourself?"

"It was all right."

"It must have been nice to see them again."

"Yes."

"And one of them has children?"

"Yes. Four."

"Four! How wonderful! Well, you have a lot of babies to take care of here."

"Leonora, I'm tired. I think I'll take a nap."

In her fitful sleep, Anna dreamed of four children at a birthday party, holding hands and singing.

FATHER GIANCARLO had long wanted to have his old friend Father Lorenzo from the Basilica of Santa Croce as one of the monthly guests on his program. They'd run across each other many times over the years and Father Giancarlo had even been a member of a men's cooking class with him. By the time everything could be arranged, Father Lorenzo was working at the soup kitchen only part time and was involved in other parish activities.

Still, the priest had founded the *cucina popolare* and was actually a legend around Florence, especially after his work at the soup kitchen during the devastating flood of the Arno in 1966.

Father Lorenzo reluctantly agreed to appear on the program in May, "but only to talk about the other people and the volunteers."

Anna and Leonora were excited that their friend would be on television.

"I think you should get a haircut," Anna said when they stopped at the soup kitchen. "It's getting long in the back."

"As opposed to the bald spot on the top of my head," Father Lorenzo said.

"That's just your tonsure showing."

"And," Leonora said, "couldn't you ask for a new robe? That one is getting so shabby. The elbows are almost worn through."

"I'll keep my arms down. Nobody is going to notice me with the handsome Father Giancarlo on the screen."

The interview went fine, of course. Father Giancarlo spent a lot of time asking about the soup kitchen's work, and Father Lorenzo said that not only did people die during the flood and that many valuable pieces of art were ruined, but also that many Florentines lost their homes and their jobs. And there were still problems.

"There seems to be a perception that everyone here is wealthy," he said. "That's the face that Florence likes to present to tourists. But there is still a great need for volunteers to help the poor, and for donations."

A telephone number flashed on the screen.

Leaving the set, Father Giancarlo thought that the least he could do for Father Lorenzo was to offer him a drink. They sank back in the leather armchairs in Father Giancarlo's office off the makeshift studio in the palazzo.

"Thank you for coming, Lorenzo. That was great." He opened a bottle of grappa and a box of Toscana cigars.

"My pleasure. It's nice to have some exposure for what we've been doing. And you, Gianni? How have you been? You look a little tired."

"Well, I still have all the parish stuff besides this television gig. You know, meetings, meetings, meetings. Plus the school. Plus the kids' soccer team."

"Ever get away?"

"Hmmm. I went to Rome three years ago. For a conference on television ministry."

"That sounds really great."

"Well, I didn't go to some of the sessions."

"Good for you."

Father Giancarlo got up to take off his Roman collar. "Lorenzo, how old are you now?"

"Well, I'm 52. That's my actual age. Don't ask me how old I feel."

"And I'm 56."

"We should be up for old-age benefits pretty soon, right?"

"Such as they are."

Noisy Vespas rattled on the street outside as the two old friends contemplated getting old.

"Lorenzo, can I ask you something?"

"Of course."

"Have you—you don't have to answer this if you don't want to—have you ever, well, strayed?"

Father Lorenzo laughed. "Oh, my, you're asking me that? Hmmm. Well, Gianni, as a matter of fact..."

"You did? You really did? Lorenzo, I'm shocked. Shocked. Shocked."

"Oh, I know it's hard to believe. Holy priest that I am. Model of virtue. But let me tell you about something that happened to me, well, about sixteen years ago. I met this beautiful woman at a party in Siena in honor of my mother."

"Your mother the feminist leader."

"Yes. Well, this woman, Victoria, sat at my table and we got to talking. Gianni, she was gorgeous! American. Red hair, upturned nose, eyes that crinkled when she smiled, and she smiled a lot. She owned a jewelry shop in Rimini. Well, she was so interested in me. I mean, she kept asking me all kinds of questions about my life."

"And you, of course, told her all about your work in the soup kitchen."

"No! That's the thing. I couldn't—well, I didn't anyway—even tell her I was a priest. I didn't have my collar on, so she wouldn't have known."

"And she didn't guess? Lorenzo, come on."

"Well, if she did, she didn't let on. Anyway, I was so infatuated with her that I made up a lame excuse to go to see her in Rimini."

"Rimini! The hot sun. The golden sands. A beautiful woman. A handsome man. Oh, wait, the handsome man's a priest."

"I'm ignoring you. Well, I was there for three days. We spent time on the beach, walked a lot, had dinner, went to a movie. Gianni, I even danced."

"Now I know you're making this up."

"I did! Well, at the end of the three days, I told her the truth. She said she suspected all along. I came back to Florence. I had a very long confession with my superior, a great guy, and I've never seen Victoria again."

"OK, let's get this straight. You didn't actually...you didn't..."

"No, Gianni, we didn't. Almost! But we didn't."

"Wow. What a story. Have another cigar."

The smoke in the room was getting thicker, the noise in the street was getting quieter.

"Lorenzo, do you ever think about her, Victoria?"

"Oh, I suppose once in a while. But I'm sure I'll never see her again. I don't even know where she is. She's probably not in Rimini anymore."

"See! You have thought about her!"

"Well, OK, maybe once or twice."

"But that was the only time?"

"A few other possibilities, but nothing like that, no. All right, Gianni, I've made my confession. What about you?"

Father Giancarlo told his fellow priest about his brief affair with Signora Maria Brunetto, "but that was the only time for me, really."

"And that was years ago?"

"Yes."

"Other opportunities?"

"A few, I guess. But, no, I haven't. But lately, it's just…"

"Just?"

"Just that I've been feeling so lonely lately. I know, I know, the loneliness of the priesthood. How many books have been written about that? I could write one myself. I guess that's why I keep so busy, so that I don't have to think about it."

"Have any priest friends?"

"Oh, a few. But the older I get, the less I want to be with them. There were four of us. We got together to play poker, sometimes we went to a soccer game. But two of them started to drink. I mean really drink. And they all groused so much. Complain, complain, complain. It was painful to be around them. So I don't see them much anymore."

"We Franciscans have each other, I guess."

"You're lucky. Sometimes, Lorenzo, I just wish I had a friend, yes, a woman friend, that I could sit down and talk to. Maybe not anything more than that."

"But maybe more?"

"I'd have to see."

299

"You know, Gianni, I bet every priest in the world has felt the same way we do. And there's not much we can do about it."

"I guess not."

Father Lorenzo got up and stretched.

"It's getting late. Way, way past my bedtime, Gianni. Thanks for having me on the program, and let's talk more sometime, OK? Sometime soon."

They shook hands at the doorway.

"Good to see you, Lorenzo."

"Take good care, Gianni."

"Thanks for listening, Lorenzo."

"Oh, by the way, Gianni, if you want another guest on your program. There's a woman who does fantastic work for us at Casa di Maria. That's the place for pregnant teenage girls."

"I've heard of it."

"She's a former nun, actually. Her name is Anna. Anna Rossetti. Give her a call."

BOTH THE DIOCESE and the television station kept transcripts of all of "Living Life Day by Day," and the following excerpt was available for June 19, 1990:

ANNOUNCER: Good evening and welcome to another visit with Father Giancarlo Moretti and "Living Life Day by Day."

(Father Giancarlo and Anna Rossetti are seated in armchairs under the crucifix.)

FATHER GIANCARLO MORETTI: Good evening, viewers, and welcome to another of our weekly conversations. I hope you've had a good day. I did. And one of the reasons was because I was looking forward to talking to tonight's special guest. For many years, Anna Rossetti was a cloistered nun, but now she manages a wonderful place for up to twenty teenage girls who are expecting babies. It's called Casa di Maria, and it is near the Basilica of Santa Croce. She helps the girls before, during and after the babies' births, and we must be grateful for everything she does. Thank you for all your good work, Anna. May I call you Anna?

ANNA ROSSETTI: Of course.

FGM: Can you tell us how you became involved in all of this? Was Casa di Maria always this big?

AR: No, no. It wasn't.

FGM: So you started off slow.

AR: Yes.

FGM: And gradually welcomed more girls.

AR: Yes.

FGM: Anna, I know the bright lights here make people nervous, but don't be. Please?

AR: All right.

FGM: Instead of giving all this history, maybe you can just tell us about a typical day.

AR: Well, there really isn't a typical day. They're all different.

FGM: Well, maybe you could explain Casa di Maria.

AR: We established the Casa to take care of young women who were about to have babies and had nowhere else to go. Often, their parents have thrown them out of the house and their boyfriends have abandoned them.

FGM: I don't know if this is relevant, but I've read recently that the number of teenage pregnancies has been increasing in Florence.

AR: We've seen that. Girls as young as fifteen. Father, it would break your heart to see these girls. There really needs to be more education about how to prevent these pregnancies.

FGM: Yes, there certainly are ways.

AR: These girls want their babies so much, but there is no place for them to stay until the babies are born. No one seems to care. No one but us.

(A number flashes on the screen.)

FGM: Perhaps you could give us an example, not by name, of course.

AR: Well, last year, there was a girl, only sixteen years old. She became pregnant and her parents were furious. They kept yelling and yelling at her. The poor girl dropped out of school and stayed in her room all the time. She was afraid to go out of her room! She wouldn't eat and of course that wasn't good for the baby. Somehow, a friend told her about Casa di Maria and she came to us. A few months later she had a healthy baby boy. Her parents were so excited that they welcomed her back home. Now they're happy grandparents.

FGM: That's a wonderful story, Anna. Now before we go into another subject, I want to open this conversation up to our viewers. As you know, we accept calls on our telephone here and...

(The studio number flashes on the screen again and the phone rings.)

FGM: Well, here's one already. You're on the air, Caller. Would you identify yourself?

CALLER: Yes. This is Cosmo and I live over near San Maria Novella. I just want to make sure I understand what this is all about. Here's this woman who abandoned her vows as a sister and now she helps young women who have committed sins and she wants us to believe she's doing a good thing?

FGM: Cosmo, I'm afraid you're not understanding this right. Anna is helping many young women who have nowhere else to go when they are about to have babies. Is that right, Anna?

AR: Yes, that's exactly right.

CALLER: But what I said is true, isn't it, whatever your name is? Isn't it?

AR: My name is Anna Rossetti. Anna, as in the mother of Mary. I wonder if I could ask you a question, sir. What do you think the alternatives for these women would be? Would you rather that these women have their babies aborted? Well, would you? I'm waiting.

CALLER: Well...

AR: Since these women have nowhere else to go, would you rather that they live on the street? Become beggars? Have their little babies in alleyways? Well, would you? I'm waiting.

CALLER: Well...

AR: I'm so glad that you have all the answers, sir. That you are able to see things in black and white. That you have no mercy for poor unfortunate human beings. That you don't realize that one of these young women could be living next door to you, or maybe she is the daughter of your brother or sister or maybe, sir, just maybe she could be your own daughter. You, of course, wouldn't throw your daughter out because she was going to have a baby. No, of course you wouldn't. I just want to say...

FGM: Anna...

AR: Let me be, Father. I am so tired of people making judgments. I wish that people would come down off their pedestals...

FGM: Anna…

AR: …and have some sympathy and understanding for those less fortunate than they are and…

FGM: Anna…

AR: Well, Caller, how do you answer this? Would you answer me, Caller? Caller? Well, I guess you don't have any answers after all.

FGM: Well, I see that our time is up for tonight. Thank you, Anna Rossetti, for being such a powerful guest tonight, and thank you viewers for joining us again tonight. I hope you'll join us again next week.

(The closing credits.)

ANNA WAS STILL SHAKING when Father Giancarlo guided her into his office off the studio and into one of the leather armchairs.

"Are you OK, Anna?"

"I will be. Just let me sit for a while."

"OK. I'll be right back." The priest went into the adjoining room, took off his Roman collar and pulled on a light blue sweater.

"Grappa?" he asked when he returned. He brought out a bottle from the cabinet behind his desk.

"No, too strong for me, but thanks."

"Mind if I have one? I think I need it. How about some port?"

"That would be lovely."

He brought out another bottle and poured Anna a glass. There was no sound except for the Vespas on the street outside.

"Father, I'm sorry I caused that scene," Anna finally said. "I don't know what came over me."

"Anna, first, call me Gianni. Everyone does. Second, good Lord, there's no need to apologize. You were quite wonderful."

"I must have sounded like some crazy lady."

"Anna, Anna. No. Nothing like that. I'm sorry now that I didn't come to your defense and shout at that guy, too. The blasted bigot. Shithead."

"Father! Gianni!"

"Sorry. That just came out. I don't usually talk like that, especially in front of a woman I respect so much. Forgive me."

"Nothing to forgive."

"You know, I guess I didn't say anything because I was just so awed and inspired by your passion. You really love these women, don't you?"

"If you saw these women—girls, actually—every day, you'd be passionate about defending them, too. I get so angry when someone attacks them. Well, you saw that."

"You were wonderful. I'm sure the viewers were convinced."

"I hope so. Except for Signor Caller, of course."

"Shithead."

They both laughed. And smiled at each other.

"I wish I could be passionate about something," the priest said quietly.

"Gianni, aren't you? Surely in your work in the parish, in your television programs…there must be so many things for you to get excited about."

"Anna, I've been a priest for thirty-two years. I've had the television program for more than seven years. Anna, I feel like I've seen it all, I've done it all."

"You're not bored, are you?"

"No, not bored. Well, as I was telling Lorenzo—your friend Father Lorenzo—I get lonely. At night, in the rectory. My mother is there, she's my housekeeper, but as you can imagine my mother isn't exactly the best company."

Anna put down her glass. "There's lots of work to keep you occupied, but then you realize you're pretty alone?"

"Yes."

"Really? You feel that way, too? At night, after the girls are sleeping and the place is quiet, I have the same feeling. My friend Leonora isn't exactly the best company either."

The priest got up to pour another grappa for himself and more port for Anna. They sat in silence for a long time, not even listening to the sounds outside.

"You know," Father Giancarlo said. "This is really rather ludicrous. Here we are, in our fifties—if I may be so bold to guess that?"

"I'm 54."

"And I'm 56. Anyway, here we are in our fifties, we have successful lives, we do good work, people admire us…"

"Admire! Gianni, you're a huge television star! People adore you!"

"Yeah, sure. And here we are complaining about being lonely. It's laughable."

"You're right. Other people would give anything to have what we have."

"We should be grateful."

"Yes.

They looked at each other a long time, as if daring the other to blink. Then Anna picked up her pocketbook. "Well, it's late, and I need to get home."

"Where's your car?"

"Car? I don't own a car. I walked. It was such a beautiful night."

"Well, you're not going to walk home alone. I'll walk you."

Anna's protests were ignored, and they walked down from the center of Florence to the Arno. A cool breeze drifted over the river as it shimmered in the moonlight, and the only people around were young lovers holding hands.

"Beautiful night," Father Giancarlo said.

"Yes."

"Cold?"

"Just a little." She hadn't brought a sweater along and had borrowed Leonora's best linen dress for the television appearance.

"Here, let me." He took off his jacket and put it on her shoulders. Then, unexpectedly, he put his arm around her waist.

"We'll keep each other warm," he said.

By the time they reached the National Central Library, the breeze had gotten stronger and they had to walk faster. By the time they reached the palazzo that housed Casa di Maria, they were almost running. And laughing.

"I'm almost out of breath," Anna said as they stood at the doorway.

"Take a minute."

He kept his arm around her and she wondered why she didn't resist.

"I've enjoyed tonight, Anna. You have no idea. Thank you for being on my program, but thank you even more for listening to me."

"I am grateful that you told me these things, Gianni. I really am. And thanks for listening to me."

"Let's talk again soon, OK?"

"Yes."

He took his jacket from her shoulders and put it on. In the awkward moments that followed, both felt as if they were teenagers on a first date. Anna finally resolved the question.

"Good night, Gianni." She kissed him on both cheeks and he suddenly hugged her close. He kissed her gently on the lips. She kissed him back harder. They could both feel how excited he had become.

"Anna," he whispered.

"Gianni."

They kissed again, long.

"No, we can't," she said.

"You're right."

Reluctantly, he ended the embrace and turned and went down the steps. When he looked back to wave she was still standing there. Suddenly, he bounded back up the stairs and they kissed again.

"Good night, Anna. I'll call you."

TWO DAYS LATER, Anna was surprised to receive a call from the Office of Social Justice for the diocese. She wasn't home, but there was a message on her machine. "We saw you on the program the other night. Can you come to our office on Friday at 2 o'clock?"

"Oh, God. Now I'm in trouble."

"Anna," Leonora said, "what kind of trouble could you be in? You didn't say anything wrong. You just said things you believe in. OK, maybe a little too strongly, but nothing the church would object to."

"I don't know. There might have been something."

"Anna, Casa di Maria is under the Franciscans. It's not under the diocese so even if they did object to something, they couldn't do anything about it."

"Leonora, the church would always find a way."

She called Father Giancarlo. "Gianni, I just got a call from the diocese and..."

"I did, too. Meeting Friday at 2."

"Am I—are we—in trouble?"

"No, no. Well, I don't think so. Let's see."

The Office of Social Justice was in yet another palazzo of the diocese.

Since it was one of the smaller departments, it occupied three cramped rooms on the third floor. Anna and Father Giancarlo were surprised to be greeted by a young woman not even thirty who introduced herself as Viola Petrini.

"Yes," she said, opening a notebook. "I know it's hard to believe, but I'm the director of this office. Well, I'm also the secretary and social worker and…I'm the staff, in other words. Thank you for coming."

They sat on folding chairs across from Signorina Petrini's desk.

"I called you both because I saw your program the other night, Father. Nobody misses it, as you know."

"Thanks."

"And, Anna, I want to thank you for what you said."

Anna and Father Giancarlo exchanged looks of relief.

"Here's why I called you here today. My superiors and I have been talking about how we can help women, young and old, like those at Casa di Maria who are about to have babies and have nowhere to go. We've been mulling this over for many months, and frankly, we are at a loss for ideas. We just have no experience in these matters. So it was such a relief to learn more about such a successful place here in Florence, and we'd like to use it as a model for what we would want to do."

"That's wonderful," Father Giancarlo said.

"Yes," Anna said. "Is there any way we can help?"

"As a matter of fact, there is. That's why I asked you to come here today. I wonder if we can ask you two to spend some time and suggest to us how the diocese could establish such a place. We would provide you with the information for four areas to study: possible facilities, finances, resources and the problems of liabilities. If you could put your heads together and come up with some sort of master plan, we'd be most grateful."

"You're asking both of us to do this?" Anna asked.

"Yes. I know you, Anna, have had the experiences with the young women, but you, Father, have the experiences or running a parish. I think you'd complement each other."

Anna and the priest looked at each other.

"I think it's great that you're considering this," Father Giancarlo said. "Yes, of course, I'd be happy to get together with Anna and think this out."

"I'd be willing, too," Anna said. "It would be good to have another

307

place in Florence. Casa can't handle any more. I think we could develop a plan, right, Father?"

"Anna," Father Giancarlo said, "we could meet in my office maybe a couple of times a week. Would that be all right?"

"I could arrange that."

Signorina Petrini raised her hand. "Actually, we were thinking of something a little more intense than that. We've found that if people get together for two or three days, maybe even a week, and spend the entire day on a project, the results are much better than if they work on something sporadically, piecemeal, as it were."

"Well, I guess, we could spend a few days in my office, Anna?"

"That would be fine."

Signorina Petrini raised her hand again. "I have an even better plan. We have a retreat house about eight miles north of here. It's an old monastery that we've converted, Villa San Martino. It's very quiet and secluded. Next week, the place is empty except for the cook, so you'd have the place to yourself. Perhaps for four or five days. The spaces are nice to work in, and all the meals will be provided, of course. You'd have your own rooms, which are simple but very nice. We would pay you each a stipend, of course, and I think it will be generous."

Anna gripped her handbag. She felt her head spinning. "Stay there? Just the two of us?"

"Well, the cook will be there if there is an emergency."

"Down in the kitchen?"

"Yes, of course. You'd be working, so you would need the peace and quiet, wouldn't you?"

"I suppose so."

"But, well," Father Giancarlo said, "there's my television program."

"Right," Signorina Petrini said, "I thought about that. But aren't they taped? Couldn't you show an old one just for one week? I think you've done that before."

"I guess so, but..."

"Also," Anna said, "I don't know if I could get away for that long."

"It would just be for a few days," Signorina Petrini said. "Aren't there are others who could run things at the Casa?"

"Well, I guess so."

"The stipend, as I said, would be very generous. I'm sure the Casa could use the money?"

"It can always use money. Desperately. It's just that…well, I just don't think I can."

"Oh," Signorina Petrini said, "that's so sad. I had been so certain you would be able to help us to assist all those poor women and girls who have no place else to go. Just as you said the other night, Signorina. You were so passionate about wanting to help them."

Father Giancarlo felt perspiration forming on his forehead and he unconsciously began to twist a handkerchief. Anna opened her handbag for her own handkerchief.

"Well," Signorina Petrini said, closing her notebook. "I guess we don't have to establish a place like this for all those poor girls and women. After all, we've never had one before and somehow all these poor girls and women have managed to have their little babies."

"It's just that…" Anna said.

"Yes, it's just…" Father Giancarlo said.

"Is there a problem with the stipend? I can certainly ask that it be increased."

"No, no," Anna said. "We aren't thinking about the money."

"Oh, I know," Signorina Petrini said. "You're worried about what people might think, a handsome priest and an attractive woman spending a week together in a secluded villa. Is that the problem?"

"No!"

"No! Nothing like that."

"Good, because I know you are two honest and sincere people and, well, you're not exactly teenagers anymore, are you?"

"No, we're not!" Anna said.

"No, hardly!" Father Giancarlo said.

"Well, then, would you agree to do this?"

Anna and Father Giancarlo were afraid to look at each other.

"OK, I guess we'll do it," she said.

"Yes," he said.

IF ANNA HAD MOVED any farther away from Father Giancarlo as he was driving, she would have fallen out of the Fiat Tipo. He had picked her up at 8 o'clock on Monday morning and except for a "*buongiorno*" they had not spoken a word during the drive through the outskirts of Florence and into the verdant hills to the north.

Anna looked out the window, not seeing anything, while the priest stared straight ahead as he concentrated on his driving. The backseat was filled with boxes containing scores of file folders, their work for the next several days.

Neither could forget what happened on the steps of the Casa di Maria, and neither wanted to talk about it. What would happen when they were alone for days?

At Villa San Martino, they were greeted by a stone-faced woman in a green housedress who identified herself as Signora Valenti.

"I am the cook and the housekeeper. In other words, I am the entire staff this week. Follow me."

She led them to the second floor, which in its previous life must have been the monks' dormitory.

"Take these two rooms," she said. "The bathroom's down the hall. Lunch is at 1 o'clock. Dinner is at 7. I don't do laundry."

"Nice to be greeted so warmly," Father Giancarlo whispered when Signora Valenti had departed. It was his first real sentence of the day.

Anna smiled but did not reply.

The rooms were adjoining and identical: a bed, a desk, a chair.

Without asking, Anna picked the one on the left and Father Giancarlo took his suitcase into the one on the right.

"Well, let's see what the place looks like," he said.

They found a maze of rooms on the first floor, some with expansive views of the countryside, others without windows and only a little larger than closets. The chapel, preserved from the building's Eighteenth-century beginnings, was at one end. The dining room was in the middle, with a wood-paneled library on one side and an airy solarium on the other. Both had long tables equipped with typewriters.

They lugged in the boxes from the car and decided that they would split duties. Anna would go over the reports about facilities and resources; Father Giancarlo would focus on finances and liabilities. She would work in the solarium, he in the library.

After a lunch of soup, crusty bread and apples, with a conversation that was at best awkward, they went to their two workplaces and opened their files.

And so the task began. Work in the afternoon, have dinner, more work at night, bedtime.

Tuesday, the same routine.

Wednesday, the same routine.

Their silence didn't lessen the tension and, in fact, it only increased.

By Thursday afternoon, both Anna and Father Giancarlo had completed their work. Now they had to combine their efforts and, obviously, had to work together. The library was chosen. Anna brought in her stacks of papers and they sat across from each other at the table.

As if giving a report to a group of bankers, she proceeded to read out loud her proposal to convert an old palazzo near the Church of San Marco as the best alternative to those suggested by the diocese. She gave seven reasons in detail. Discussing resources, she proposed that a separate board be established apart from the diocese so that management would be independent. She outlined the benefits.

Father Giancarlo then discussed finances and presented a budget that called for a private foundation to supplement diocesan contributions. The budget would adequately take care of both staffing and maintenance. Aware of the liabilities that might threaten such an institution, he had researched Italian laws and outlined preventive measures.

All they needed to do now was put their typewritten reports together in a binder.

"If you stand next to me, it will be easier," Father Giancarlo said.

Anna was more than three feet away at the start but gradually moved closer. Occasionally, their arms touched, and both jumped back. At one point, Anna reached for a page at the same time as he did, and she scratched the back of his hand.

"I'm sorry!"

"It's all right."

"It's bleeding!"

He wrapped his handkerchief around it. "There. It stopped. It's fine."

Then he dropped a paper clip and they both bent down to fetch it and their foreheads clashed.

"Ouch!"

"Ouch!"

Father Giancarlo laughed. Anna did something she hadn't done since she was a child. She giggled.

When they had put all three hundred and twenty-two pages into the three-ring binder, they congratulated themselves with smiles and a very small hug.

"Let's look at it one more time," Father Giancarlo said.

They went through it page by page.

"Oh my goodness," Anna said, "where is page one hundred and eighty?"

They looked.

"Here it is," he said, "behind two hundred and forty-four. And two hundred and sixty is behind two hundred and eighty-five."

For some reason, this seemed hilarious.

Laughing uproariously, they put the pages where they belonged and collapsed on the leather sofa opposite the table.

"Well, that's that," Anna said.

"Yes."

"And we can go home tomorrow."

"Yes."

"And go back to our lives."

"Yes."

Anna suddenly started to weep, slow tears going down her cheeks. "Gianni, I just wish things were different."

He put his arm around her and held her close.

"Anna, can I tell you something? After I left you on the doorstep that night, I couldn't stop thinking about you. I couldn't sleep nights. I went on long runs, but that didn't help. I was supposed to referee a football game Saturday morning and I made terrible calls. I couldn't concentrate hearing confessions Saturday afternoon. I suppose Signora Pocatelli wondered why she was supposed to say ten rosaries when she usually gets only one. I barely made it through Mass on Sunday. Thank God I don't have to do the television show this week. Anna, I couldn't wait to see you again after we got the call to go to the diocesan office."

"Gianni, it was the same with me. Only when I'm upset, I get nasty. I'm sure Leonora wondered why I yelled at poor Anastasia when she wouldn't hurry, or when the deliveryman put the packages in the wrong place. I even got upset with Father Lorenzo, and you know what a saint he is. I was on edge all weekend after that call because I was thinking about you."

"So where does that leave us?"

"I don't know, Gianni."

"I don't either."

"You know, a few weeks ago we didn't even know each other. It's all Father Lorenzo's fault."

"Thank God for Father Lorenzo."

"I suppose," Anna said, "we could go back to our rooms and continue what we started the other night."

"Are you serious?" Father Giancarlo asked.

"No! I was just talking like a teenager. But then, as Signorina Petrini so delicately reminded us, we're not teenagers anymore."

"No, I'm afraid we're not."

"You know, that was the first time I was kissed by a man. And you know something else? I liked it."

"But you don't want more?"

"Gianni, I have a way of life that would be hard to change. This is who I am. I don't think I could be anyone else. But let me tell you one thing. If I were able to love someone, truly love someone and commit myself to that person for the rest of my life, it would be you. You are so kind and generous and thoughtful. I'll always be grateful for the time we've had together. Yes, and for those minutes on the steps of Casa di Maria. I'll never forget that. I'm going to return to my life knowing that someone could care for me, even want me. I never thought anyone would."

"Anna, for the first time in my life, I feel the same. I'm grateful that you came into my life, especially when I most needed someone like you. You are quite wonderful, you know. And I too will go back to try to be a good priest, but I'll know that someone could love me as I am. And, you know, I'll remember that kiss always, too. But let's not end it, all right? Can we still be friends? I need a friend, Anna. I badly need a friend to talk to."

"Gianni, I need a friend, too."

"I need you, Anna."

"And I need you, Gianni."

They hugged and, yes, they kissed.

Driving home the next day, they told stories about their childhoods and their friends. He talked about life in the seminary and she about life in the convent. He told funny stories about his parishioners and she described the joy she felt holding babies. They laughed. They cried a little. They even told jokes. And when he said good-bye at the door of the Casa di Maria, they embraced and made plans to see each other very soon.

ABOUT THE AUTHOR

As a journalist, Paul Salsini worked at *The Milwaukee Journal* for thirty-seven years as a reporter, editor and staff development director. He was the Wisconsin correspondent for *The New York Times* for fifteen years and his travel essays have appeared in *The Times* and elsewhere. He taught journalism courses for many years at his alma mater, Marquette University in Milwaukee, and is now the writing coach for the Milwaukee Neighborhood News Service.

As someone knowledgeable about musical theater, he founded and was the first editor of *The Sondheim Review*, a quarterly magazine devoted to the works of Stephen Sondheim. He taught the History of Musical Theater course at Marquette for a fifteen years and donated his extensive Sondheim collection to the university library. He now presents programs about the musical theater at retirement homes.

As a late-blooming author, he wrote the six-volume "A Tuscan Series" (*The Cielo, Sparrow's Revenge, Dino's Story, The Temptation of Father Lorenzo, A Piazza for Sant'Antonio* and *The Fearless Flag Thrower of Lucca*). The series follows a group of villagers from World War II to the year 2000. *The Cielo* won first place from the Council for Wisconsin Writers and the Midwest Independent Publishers Association; *Father Lorenzo* won first place from the association and third place from the council. He is also the author of *The Ghosts of the Garfagnana* and two children's books. He received the 2011 Sons of Italy Leonardo da Vinci Award for Excellence in Literature.

He and his wife, Barbara, have three children and four grandchildren and live in Milwaukee with their cat, Rosie.

A CONVERSATION WITH
THE AUTHOR

What prompts your love for Tuscany?

My father was born in the small village of San Martino in Freddana near Lucca in Tuscany. He came to the U.S. at 20, went to the Upper Peninsula of Michigan and became a copper miner. Other people from San Martino had arrived there earlier, and he boarded with a family that had five sons and a daughter. Yes, he and the daughter fell in love and married—my father and mother. So both sides of my family are from that same village in Tuscany and when I go to the cemetery there I see the Salsinis and the Consanis all together.

I made my fist trip to Italy in 1985 and have visited there thirteen times. The best part of every trip was visiting my cousin Fosca, my father's niece, who lived in the house where she was born in the village. She was just wonderful. Sadly, she died last May at the age of 96.

Your first novel, *The Cielo: A Novel of Wartime Tuscany,* was inspired by actual experiences.

On one visit, Fosca told us about living through World War II. She said she and neighbors from San Martino in Fredanna fled to the hills, literally, when the Nazis occupied the village. Some people stayed in barns, some in the woods and some in old farmhouses. She and her friends stayed in an abandoned farmhouse high in the hills. It was called the Celli and had been in the family for centuries. They remained there for three months, sometimes hearing nearby fighting between the Nazis and the partisans, until Allied forces liberated the area. The horrific massacre in nearby Sant'Anna di Stazzema also plays a major part of the story.

Those events became the basis for my first novel, *The Cielo: A Novel of Wartime Tuscany*. Surprisingly, it won several awards, and then something unexpected happened. The characters would not leave my head. I'd wake up thinking about them. They demanded to be heard again. So I wrote a sequel, *Sparrow's Revenge*, and then another and another until finally there were six books in all. I called them "A Tuscan Series." All of the stories are set in the fictional Sant'Antonio, not unlike San Martino in Fredanna, and in Florence. The original characters age (some die) and some new ones arrive.

Your career was at a journalist. How was the transition to writing fiction?

There are actually some similarities. Straight-forward writing. Attention to details. Much research. Use of quotes. I'll have to admit that the first time I changed a character's quote I thought, "I can't change a quote" because it's at least a mortal sin for a journalist to change a source's quote. Well, since I had made it up in the first place of course I could change it.

I've always felt that, for me at least, the research was the best part of both journalistic and fiction writing. All of my stories required reading books, consulting online sources and even conducting personal interviews. I find it so exciting to discover information I never knew before. For example, I had little knowledge about the Albanians seeking to move to Italy, or about the women who helped the partisans in World War II, or the anti-femicide movement, or the massacre at San Martino in Freddana, or almost anything about World War I. Writing becomes an education in itself.

How did you learn about the *staffette*?

I knew women played an important role in the Resistance but it wasn't until I did considerable reading that I understood their great significance. Or that they even had a name. Their story is so inspiring because they faced incredible challenges and met them so selflessly. I wanted to tell the story through the experiences of just one *staffeta*, and having a documentary made of her life seemed a good way to do that. I wish someone would make an actual documentary about the *staffette* because their story is so fascinating. I've also read that they didn't receive the honors and acknowledgements they deserved—that sometimes they were excluded from victory parades or they found themselves walking last and many times jeered at. Women apparently just weren't recognized as "fighters."

Why did you write the World War I story in epistolary form?

Our daughter Laura, a professor of Italian at the University of Delaware, has made Italian women writers a focus of her research, and in fact wrote the well-received "Addressing the Letter: Italian Women Writers' Epistolary Fiction" (University of Toronto Press, 2010).

That inspired me to write this story in epistolary form. I thought having a soldier at the front in World War I writing letters home, and getting responses, was a good way to show the contrast between the terrible life at the front and the clueless life of his girlfriend and mother in Florence.

The "white war," as it was called because it was fought in the Alps, had a devastating effect on Italy. Besides the 650,000 soldiers who were killed, more than a half-million civilians died, most of them as a consequence of food shortages and poor harvests in 1918.

Why did you write "Roberto and Giuliana" as a play?

It was just so irresistible and obvious. To this day, the feuding *contrade* in Siena hold so many similarities to the House of Capulet and the House of Montague. I used a little of the language in the play but obviously, because this was set in the 1930s, much had to change. Also, since I wanted a happy ending, the plot developments were different. I enjoyed writing the balcony scene even though Roberto thought the original was "a little sappy." Father Lorenzo, of course, is modeled after Friar Laurence and Pasqualina after The Nurse.

How did you come to write the story about the Albanians who commandeered a ship to get to Italy?

I somehow stumbled on Daniele Vicari's amazing documentary "*La nave dolce*/The Human Cargo" and was shocked by its heart-breaking scenes. The ship was so overloaded with men, women and children seeking new lives in Italy that it looked like a floating anthill. The estimate was

17,000 people but there may well have been many more. And then to see all those people spread out on the dock with almost no food, water or medical services. Italy refused to let the Albanians stay and sent them back home. This was in 1991 and refugees, now mostly from Africa and nearby countries, are still trying to get to Italy, creating a huge humanitarian and political crisis.

The story about the massacres in front of the church must have been a challenge.

I had visited the cemetery at San Martino in Freddana many times but it was only in recent years that I studied the plaque at the entrance and discovered that one of the victims, Narciso Pini, was a distant relative. With the help of cousins, also named Pini, and a genealogy search, I was able to put together a family tree and wrote an article, "Looking for Narciso," that was published. Actually, I'm still looking. I feel bad that we don't know more about the life of this interesting man and, in fact, about all of the victims.

The pandemic that you describe in "Nonna's Story" had so many effects, in Italy and all over the world.

When Italy became one of the first countries hit by the virus we worried about our relatives in Tuscany. They would tell us about the quarantines but they didn't talk about how this was affecting their lives. We could only imagine what it would be like to be cooped up, especially with little children, for weeks and months. It must have been maddening and frustrating. Italy is opening up now but who knows what will happen if this, or some variant, comes back?

What will happen between Anna and Father Giancarlo?

I don't know. They haven't told me.

Made in the USA
Las Vegas, NV
26 October 2021

33105814R00184